The Necessary Evil

André Couvreur

The Necessary Evil

translated, annotated and introduced by
Brian Stableford

A Black Coat Press Book

ISBN 978-1-61227-253-5. First Printing. April 2014. Published by Black Coat Press, an imprint of Hollywood Comics.com, LLC, P.O. Box 17270, Encino, CA 91416. All rights reserved. Except for review purposes, no part of this book may be reproduced or transmitted in any form or by any means, electronic or mechanical, including photocopying, recording, or by any information storage and retrieval system, without permission in writing from the publisher. The stories and characters depicted in this novel are entirely fictional. Printed in the United States of America.

Introduction

Le Mal nécessaire by André Couvreur, here translated as *The Necessary Evil*, was originally published by Plon, Nourrit & Cie. in 1899. It was the author's first novel, and provided the foundation stone on which his future literary career was built. It was advertized as the first volume of a trilogy collectively entitled *Les Dangers sociaux* [Social Dangers], and was soon followed by two sequels, *Les Mancenilles* [a noun improvised from the specific name of *Hippomane mancenilla*, a highly toxic shrub] (1900) and *La Source fatale* [The Fatal Source] (1901), the former dealing with the threat posed by syphilis and the nexus of infection maintained by the prostitutes of Paris, and the second with the perils of alcohol abuse.

After completing his first trilogy, Couvreur began a second, collectively entitled *La Famille* [The Family], with *La Force du sang* [The Strength of the Blood] (1902) and *La Graine* [The Seed] (1903),which he was due to complete with *Le Fruit* [The Fruit] (1906). Before finishing the third volume, however, he digressed into fiction of a very different sort by producing another, very different, sequel to *La Mal nécessaire*, featuring the same protagonist: *Caresco, surhomme, ou le voyage en Eucrasie: Conte humain* (1904; tr. as as *Caresco, Superman; or, A Voyage to Eucrasia*)—a rare example of a boldly fantastic sequel to a grimly naturalistic work, all the more exceptional because of the existence of the two thematic sequels that already existed.

Couvreur might have considered that unusual move necessary because, unlike *Les Mancenilles* and *La Source fatale*, in which it is very obvious what the "social dangers" featured therein are, *Le Mal nécessaire* does not make it entirely clear exactly what its featured social danger is. By comparison with syphilis and alcoholism, the ineffectuality of institutional control of medical practice seems a minor issue, even if one considers that it permits the occasional dangerous individual to wreak havoc. In *Caresco, surhomme*, the social danger ostensibly posed by the kind of thinking and ambition that Armand Caresco represents is made luridly and hyperbolically clear, in a fashion at which its Naturalistic predecessor could only hint obliquely.

As things turned out, the supplementation of *Le Mal nécessaire* by *Caresco, surhomme* was a sign of things to come. Although Couvreur did go on to complete his second trilogy with *Le Fruit*, the core of his subsequent literary work consisted of a series of speculative novellas dealing with potential developments in biotechnology, credited to one Professor Tornada. Tornada began his career as a markedly different character, but soon assumed Caresco's extraordinary surgical skills and various other aspects of his paradoxical character, eventually deciding to term himself "the Superman," just as Caresco had, and embarking on a large scale project of social engineering analogous to, but very different in ambition from, the one adopted by Caresco in Eucrasia.

The present volume is the first of five, and will be followed by *Caresco, Superman* and three volumes collecting the entire Professor Tornada series, collectively entitled *The Exploits of Professor Tornada*. Within that context *Le Mal nécessaire* is something of a generic anomaly, but it also the essential seed from which the entire complex and bizarre literary edifice germinated, and is vital to a proper understanding of the growth and metamorphosis of a remarkable sequence of works. In the course of that sequence, Couvreur returned again and again to the idea of "necessary evil" first sketched out in the present novel, treating it both as a curious phenomenon to be studied and as an acute problem to be elaborately explored in various thought-experiments, with a view to a deeper understanding of the assumed necessity.

"André Couvreur" was born in 1863 at Seclin in the Nord; his baptismal name was actually Achille-Émile-Henri Couvreur, but he signed his early literary works, all of which were intended for the theater, "A. Chils," adapting his Christian name. The first production that was staged, in Lille in 1885, appears to have been a farce entitled *Ipéca et Cuana*. It is now difficult to determine whether any others were produced prior to *Le Secret de Polichinelle* [The Secret of Polichinelle, that being the French equivalent of the English puppet character Punch], a satirical play in verse staged in 1893, which appeared in print in the same year under the extended pseudonym of "André Chils." No further theatrical endeavors achieved print publication, but at least one other was produced thereafter: *La Consultation* [The Consultation] (1914, credited to A. Chils). The author retained the André, however, when he began to use his own surname instead of the improvisation

By the time *Le Secret de Polichinelle* was produced, Couvreur had qualified as a physician, receiving his degree in 1892, slightly belatedly, perhaps because he had been pursuing his literary ambitions in parallel with his studies. His doctoral thesis explored the relationship between pulmonary tuberculosis and tubercular tracheobronchial adenopathy. His father and older brother were both doctors, and he had doubtless been encouraged to follow in their footsteps, perhaps a trifle reluctantly, but it must have been obvious by 1892 that medicine offered him better opportunities to make a living than literature, and he doubtless made a firm commitment to make a decent living when he married in 1893. Obviously, however, he never surrendered his literary ambitions, and when his novels began to appear he was quick to become an active member of the Societé des Gens de Lettres as well as maintaining his medical endeavors.

The 1890s must have seemed a good time to begin writing novels set in the world of medical practice, which was becoming a fashionable literary topic, aided by the abundant publicity given to the medical advances it was hoped that intensive scientific research—like that carried out at the Institut Pasteur, founded in 1887—might soon produce. Michel Corday, with whom Couvreur was later to collaborate on the speculative novel *Le Lynx* (1911; tr. in 1913 as *The Inner Man*), had caused something of a sensation in 1894 with his novel *Le Cancer* [Cancer], which had broken new ground in its consideration of the psychological and social effects experienced by its protagonist after receiving the diagnosis of his condition.

Léon Daudet had caused a sensation of a different kind in the same year with his scathing satire on the medical profession in general and surgeons in particular, *Les Morticoles* [a slang term for doctors, approximately decodable as "death-sowers" by analogy with *agricoles* (agricultural workers)]. Daudet was prompted to write the latter novel by his resentment at failing the internship

8

that would have completed his medical qualifications; although Couvreur was writing defensively from inside the medical establishment rather than attacking it from outside, and his novels are therefore essentially antithetical to Daudet's, *Le Mal nécessaire* does have concerns that overlap those of *Les Morticoles*, being similarly suspicious of the tendency to arrogance exhibited by avant-gardist surgeons, and is certainly not devoid of scathing sarcasm.

There had, of course, been numerous other novels featuring adventurous surgeons prior to *Le Mal nécessaire*, some of which had even dared to broach such potentially-shocking topics as the methodology and occasional necessity of hysterectomies, but none had ever offered such an explicit—not to say flamboyant—depiction of an operation of that sort as the one in *Le Mal nécessaire*, and none had ever imagined a situation akin to the moral dilemma in which Caresco's assistant eventually finds himself, as a result of the surgeon's rather original perception of such a necessity. When one considers the immense diplomatic care exercised in the handling of gynecological topics in *Faiseur d'hommes* [Maker of Humans] (1884) by the dutifully pseudonymous "Yveling RamBaud and Dubut de Laforest," one can easily appreciate the contemporary shock value of the brutal frankness of Couvreur's novel.

Couvreur's depiction of Caresco's surgical exploits, with particular reference to young women, was by no means without precedent, but much of the relevant precedent had been contained in a literary tradition that extended back through the *contes cruels* and *romans frénétiques* of the Romantic Movement to foundation stones laid by the Marquis de Sade. Couvreur was not a pornographer—although he probably attracted a few accusations to that effect when he wrote *Caresco surhomme* and the second and third Tornada novellas— but there are subtle literary affinities between *Le Mal nécessaire* and Sade's most notorious works, which help to make it a discomfiting book, even though its narrative voice adopts a conscientiously horrified attitude to the nasty things it describes, and the sympathetic characters featured in the novel are dutifully extreme in their moral conservatism.

Caresco's most evident literary precursor is Dr. Gael in Louis Michel's *Les Microbes humains* (1886) and *Le Monde nouveau* (1888),[1] who is introduced as a conscienceless researcher casually carrying out experiments in human vivisection and surgical modification, but is ultimately recast as a physical and intellectual superman whose discoveries might enable humankind to take a great evolutionary leap forward after the cataclysm that is scheduled to destroy the corrupt capitalist world order. Couvreur was at the opposite end of the political spectrum to the anarchist Michel—although not as far to the right as the position Léon Daudet eventually took up—and it is possible to read the two Caresco novels as a critical counterblast to the idea that a surgeon like Gael could possibly be regarded as a hero, especially if he could change the world in conformity with his utopian ideals. Caresco, however, certainly adopts that view of himself.

In spite of his flagrant disapproval of Caresco's morality and alleged madness, Couvreur remains willing to give his views serious consideration, and to explore their

---

[1] translated respectively as *The Human Microbes* and *The New World* and available in Black Coat Press editions, ISBNs 978-1-61227-116-3 and 978-1-61227-117-0.

potential in a manner that refuses simply to write them off *a priori* merely because they are tainted with megalomaniac delusion. Indeed, the remainder of Couvreur's writing career continued that exploration, always exercising a mind that, if not fully open, was at least ajar. Professor Tornada made his literary debut as a raving mad mass murderer, but by the end of his frankly paradoxical "career," he was being affectionately addressed by his hapless friends as "Old Nada" and doing his sardonic best to make a world that he judged to be utterly corrupt and essentially irredeemable a slightly better place.

The ultimate balance of the initial assessment of Caresco's maneuvers featured in the plot of *Le Mal nécessaire* undoubtedly surprised many of the novel's contemporary readers and might well have shocked some, and that is one of the things that makes the novel exceptional and interesting. It would be inappropriate to say more about the plot here because it would work as a spoiler, but I shall add an afterword offering some further comment on the highly unusual nature of the story's conclusion, and its relationship to the further development of Couvreur's extended *contes philosophiques*, as featured in the other four volumes of this series of translations

This translation was made from a copy of the Plon, Nourrit edition, identified on the cover as the third edition but presumably identical otherwise to the first.

Brian Stableford

THE NECESSARY EVIL

Preface

Certain malign minds are bound to try to put a name to the physiognomy of the protagonist of this book. The author wishes to declare, right away, that he has not written a *roman à clef* and has not depicted any real individual.

However, although the character traced in the following pages does not exist, he could exist. The beneficent power that the law accords to the scientific elite could, in other hands, become a veritable danger, and it would only require a disequilibrated brain to render real a fictitious case, to animate an improbable story.

The interest of this study thus resides in the critique of power without control with which our society invests certain individuals. The author would declare himself to be perfectly satisfied if a philosophical idea were to emerge from his work.

A.C.

CHAPTER I

On a warm morning in the month of July, Madame Bise, the owner of the Château des Bolois, near Gaillon in the Eure, was installed in the small chalet that her late husband, Monsieur Bise, a section president of the Conseil d'Etat, had built on the edge of the lake. By her side, her sister-in-law, Madame de Jancy, sitting in a large wicker armchair, was busy with some trivial needlework.

There was a fundamental contrast between the two women. While Madame de Jancy, simple and gentle in appearance, with a bountiful expression engraved on her features, conserved a moderate, patient and tranquil demeanor in all circumstances, a noble reserve of gesture and movement attributable as much to her prefect distinction as to the dread of overstressing a weak heart, Madame Bise, on the contrary, manifested an exuberant, nervous and domineering character that penetrated her slightest attitudes.

Madame Bise was a small woman of about fifty, originally from the Midi, whose accent she was unable to lose, with a figure that was still slim and a face as dry and wrinkled as a rennet apple, in which the gray-green eyes had an extraordinary mobility. Originally Henriette de Jancy, she had married late and had not been able, in spite of legitimate efforts, to have children. Thus, she had an authoritarian attachment to her two nieces, her heirs, Madeleine de Jancy, the daughter of her late brother, and Aline Romé, who lived with her parents in a château in Les Andelys, not far away.

Every year, in summer, Madame Bise invited Madame de Jancy and Madeleine to come and spend a few months at Les Bolois. In truth, that holiday was not entirely enjoyable for her relatives, but the prospect of an inheritance imposed such a sacrifice. Madame de Jancy submitted to it in the interests of her daughter, to reestablish a fortune that her husband's follies had diminished.

While the two ladies occupied themselves variously in the cool tranquility of the lakeside dwelling, nature completed her awakening outside. The whinnying of horses, the calls of gardeners, the chirping of birds in the large trees, the squeaking of a wheelbarrow and the leap of a carp in the water—distant and vague noises, muffled echoes—manifested external life.

Through the broad doorway of the summer-house, opening on the same level as the silvery expanse of water, a clump of trees was perceptible in the distance, in a gap in the landscape, beyond which golden fields extended. Three hundred meters away, the château loomed up, with its slate-roofed turrets shining in the sun.

It was only nine o'clock in the morning, but the implacable sun, without a caress of wind, was already filling the air with heavy warmth, stupefying the great trees in the park, and eating into the grass of the lawn, which had almost disappeared in places, dead for want of water. A gray mist, the last alms of freshness that the morning gave to the heat of the day, was completing its evaporation, still tinting the woody horizon with a veil ripped by broad golden sunbeams.

Madame de Jancy raised her head, put down her work and asked her sister-in-law: "Do you know where Madeleine is?"

"Probably at the gardener's cottage," Madame Bise replied. "She must have gone to see Mahu's child. Can you understand why she's always hiding with those people?"

"Madeleine loves children," said Madame de Jancy. "Her dream is to get married, in order to have children, to care for them, to coddle them..."

"What! You're not thinking of marrying her off already! She's very young, the little darling. And then, don't you think, my dear, that she's not been very well for some time."

"Yes...perhaps. I'm not anxious, though."

"It's necessary to look after her, the poor thing."

Madame de Jancy responded with a vague but reassuring gesture. However, and although she was familiar with the range of the illnesses that tormented her daughter, she was saddened, deep down, to see the stigmata of a nervous disorder that the child had inherited from her father reappearing, after two years of perfect health. A wrinkle of anxious reflection furrowed her brow.

She remembered Madeleine's agitated childhood, the convulsions of her infancy, the threats of meningitis, and, above all, the attacks of nerves that had arrived as soon as the woman had revealed herself within the girl, on the day of Monsieur de Jancy's death. What pain and fear she had experienced when, running in response to the fearful appeal of a chambermaid, she had found her daughter prey to contortions. She had thought her doomed, poisoned, and had wondered if she could survive a double mourning.

Fortunately, Dr. Cartaux, an old family friend, who had witnessed the end of the crisis, had hastened to reassure the poor mother, by telling her that the malady, so terrible in its appearance, was not really very dangerous, and that it was curable by a course of treatment. Indeed, careful hygiene, prolonged hydrotherapy and a calm life, exempt from worldly excitations, seemed to have reckoned with the alarming phenomena, and for two years, Madeleine had been showing all the signs of radiant health.

However, a certain nervousness of character persisted: abrupt mood changes, a sensory hyperesthesia, and sometime also an inexplicable depression that lasted for entire days. In those symptoms Dr. Cartaux recognized the latent continuation of the malady. The nervous disorder was brooding beneath the ashes, and a counter-offensive was to be feared one day or another. He had even observed abrupt attacks of catalepsy in similar patients among his clientele, whose general health had not deteriorated.

Madame de Jancy wondered what new provocative element could be stirring her daughter's soul, to cause the reappearance of those alarming symptoms, precursors of more serious disorders. She watched over her child with a vigilant tenderness, extended beneath her footsteps a carpet woven from calm and kindness, and sheltered her from exciting reading matter. She had not noticed anything in the simple routine of her family life that could have had a harmful influence on Madeleine's health.

"Yes, it's necessary to look after her," Madame Bise continued."

"I've taken her to see Dr. Cartaux again," Madame de Jancy replied. "His examination was reassuring, though."

"Bah! Dr. Cartaux is an old physician who knows nothing about it. You need a young one—a scientist, like

Dr. Caresco. What do you think about her going to see Dr. Caresco?"

"I confess, Henriette, that I don't like the idea at all. I've heard so many bad things said about the surgeon in question."

"First of all, the surgeon is my friend. Then again, you're too late. I've just asked him to come and spend a few days at Les Bolois. He'll be arriving any minute. The carriage has gone to pick him up at the station."

Having made this declaration, Madame Bise fell silent, to give her sister-in-law time to digest it. She understood that she would not approve, that conflict might result from the difference of opinion. She wanted to avoid that, at a moment when, out of an obscure zeal for her niece and an enthusiasm for her doctor's science, she was about to submit Madeleine to an unwelcome investigation.

Madame de Jancy, knowing how imprudent it was to engage in a debate, held back the observations suggested to her by the personality of the young surgeon, thirty-six years old and already famous, on whose count so many various rumors were going around. She experienced a muted discontentment with Madame Bise, who had so deliberately made a decision of which she disapproved. Faithful to her system of prudence, however, she suppressed her resentment.

In any case, the noise of a carriage announced the arrival of the physician. Blossoming, Madame Bise set off in the direction of the château to meet him.

"My friend! Are you well?"

Armand Caresco leapt down from the carriage with a lithe agility. Clad in an elegant pale gray traveling costume, he bowed to the chatelaine, took her hand and kissed it. Madame Bise, radiant at that gallantry, introduced the surgeon to her sister-in-law, who arrived out of breath.

"My dear, this is the greatest surgeon in the world!"

Madame de Jancy replied by a slight nod of the head to the man's exaggerated reverence. She considered him with a slightly haughty expression. His guileful appearance made an unfavorable expression on her. There was something feline about him.

His face was handsome, but undermined by a curved nose and, above all, by a stereotypical smile, displaying two rows of perfect teeth. His eyes were dark, profound an illuminated by avid gleams; they had an ungraspable expression, not looking one in the face, seeming to retreat before investigation, as if to hide the reflection of the desires that were fermenting in a perpetually-seething brain.

All of the individual's coquetry seemed to reside in his neatly-groomed brown hair, abundant and curly, and in his evenly-distributed beard. His body was of medium height, harmonious in form and vigorous, the arms and hands very muscular. He held his thumb enclosed by the other fingers, a sign of his ancestry. The ensemble was suggestive of something powerful and shady, authoritative and fugitive, which was gripping and revolting—all fleeting impressions, which could only be concentrated in an observant mind.

Madame de Jancy thought: *That's a handsome man*, but immediately added: *I don't like him.*

The manservant brought the doctor's trunk and deposited it in the hall.

"Good, you've brought your luggage. You can stay with us for a few days?"

"With your permission, my dear Madame, I shall be very happy to stay in your château. I've been working very hard recently; I've just finished a book on liver surgery and I feel weary." His gaze became positive again, and he continued, speaking in a low voice into Madame Bise's ear: "And do we not have a young invalid to observe? It is primarily to manifest my gratitude to you by caring for her that I've come, as you know."

"Shh! Shh!" replied Madame Bise, with a suspicious glance at her sister-in-law. "Let that remain between us. Anyway, here's the child now."

A delightful creature appeared on the fine gravel path. She advanced meditatively, her head bowed and her bands behind her back, her body swaying harmoniously, in an infinitely graceful manner. She drew nearer.

Caresco, who was seeing her for the first time, could not retain an exclamation of admiration. The simple pink surah blouse enclosed the frail bosom of a young woman of eighteen, which marriage would surely bring out. The slightly short skirt, lifted up by her stride, allowed a glimpse of the stocking of a delicate and solid leg, terminating in a finely-chiseled ankle, surmounting a small foot shod in red leather.

Most impressive of all, the most dazzling aspect of that marvelous ensemble, surmounting a slender neck, was the infinitely graceful head, with the pale complexion of a Parisienne, a delicately curved mouth, small translucent ears standing out slightly from the cranium, partly buried beneath a landslide of gilded hair, cleverly pinned up, and bright blue eyes full of an azure mirage, sometimes veiled by a blink characteristic of the myopic.

Before that triumph of nature, the skeptical surgeon, accustomed by a stout mistress to the worst caresses, allowed himself to be seized by a charm. He cherished overflowing flesh, vast surfaces proportionate to his gluttonous appetites, baths of soft and flaccid matter, and yet, the young woman's delicate vigor and fine silhouette impressed him.

"How are you this morning, darling?" asked Madame Bise. "Have the vapors passed?" She turned toward Caresco. "Doctor, may I introduce my niece, Madeleine de Jancy. She'll have need of your care, alas."

Madeleine, who had not yet perceived the doctor, who was in the shadow of the vestibule, inclined her meditative head toward him. Immediately, though, a shudder ran through her. She had just been traversed by an inexplicable flash of hostility.

She had encountered the cutting edge of a sharp, cold, cruel, avid and masterful gaze. It was like something that attracted her and which she wanted to flee: an unknown force, an obscure turbulence that drew her in, and from which she would have been glad to detach herself. That powerful and fugitive gaze plowed her, and left her for a few seconds in a state of unconsciousness and moral atony.

When she pulled herself together, astonished and troubled, the strange influence of the man had quit her, and fixed on something else, but she retained a vague alarm, an imprecise suspicion that gripped her again every time she resumed contact with the surgeon.

In addition, a few minutes later, while she was studying Armand Caresco, engaged in a conversation with her aunt, she recognized the extent to which the unfavorable expression had been prepared by Madame Bise's laudatory verbiage, and the whispered confidences of her cousin, Aline Romé. The latter, the same age as her but more knowing, more expansive by nature, raised by parents less scrupulous in the choice of their relations, had often reported remarks she had overheard regarding the surgeon to Madeleine.

She knew that he was the son of a homeopathic charlatan, an Austrian Jew, who, having arrived in the country with a diploma that the Faculté, by virtue of a customary aberration, had simply converted into a French diploma, had set up a practice in Paris, exploiting the sick with neither shame nor conscience. Armand had carried out his studies in Paris; he had also passed his internship in Paris, and as soon as his education was complete, he had thrown himself into the battle of life, setting up a house of operations at his own expense in the Avenue Hoche, where he performed surgery often and brilliantly, under the protection of Madame Bise and several other patronesses glad to pilot a famous man. Nor was a prudent and intelligent hunt for game uncon-nected with the surgeon's success.

Aline had also told her cousin that, in order to ob-tain credit with his protectresses, and to dissipate their scruples, Armand Caresco had denied the God of Israel and had loudly converted to Christianity. All means were good for his glory and his profit; to flatter the chauvinism of his clients he had had himself naturalized French, once the law no longer permitted him to be called up for military service. In that fashion, the uproot-ed individual had benefited from all the advantages that France offers her children, without being subject to their duties. That was a routine trick, familiar to the mind of his race, which contented the versatility of opinion and almost won him the decoration of the national Order.

What had revolted Madeleine more than anything else, however, was another confidence, more serious in her view. Did not the doctor, beneath the austere exterior of religion and work, lead a disorderly life in company with a mature mistress who was popularly known as "the beautiful Tripe-merchant"?[2] Aline, as a person who knew about and excused such things, had obligingly gone into extensive details regarding the courtesan in question, the luxury of her house, her carriage and her clothes.

Madeleine's puerile imagination could not conceive of anything more abominable than such a dissipated existence, and the memory of Aline's gossip confirmed the strange repulsion that she had just experienced, the sudden recoil before the disquieting, irresolute and ambiguous aspects of the gaze that had alarmed her.

Again, the shrill voice of Madame Bise rose in pitch; she was responding to further apologies on the part of her guest.

"At least we shall try to amuse you. First, tomorrow, we're having the people from Les Andelys to lunch: Monsieur Romé, my brother-in-law, his wife, and Aline, their daughter. On the following days, we'll organize excursions. Won't we, Madeleine?"

Madeleine did not reply. Her eyes directed toward the park, she was lending all her attention to the approach of a countrywoman, followed by a blond infant paled by a recent illness. It was the wife of Mahu, the gardener, who was watching her child's hesitant steps. During her sojourn at Les Bolois, Madeleine, vaguely moved by maternal instinct, had spent her idle hours in the company of the infant, who had such astonishingly bright eyes and such a charmingly innocent smile.

"There's little Mahu!" she exclaimed.

---

[2] The author capitalizes *Tripière* [tripe-merchant] to emphasize that what the person in question is famous for selling is access to her own entrails. The wordplay is idiosyncratic, not borrowed from commonplace argot.

Without worrying about the puerility of her impulse, she ran to seize the child in her arms, covering him with caresses, sowing kisses on his thin cheeks and his golden head.

Madeleine's voice, her protective gestures, her teasing laughter and the entire atmosphere of love and attention with which she surrounded someone else's child astonished the surgeon's passionate soul. What a bizarre impulse toward progeniture, when so many women went out of their way to suppress their ovaries in order not to procreate!

A rapid vision of an abdomen opened by his scalpel, of a body lying on his operating table, with the face paled by chloroform and the entrails bloody, passed through his mind. That scene summarized his life, his glory and his profit.

He smiled.

An incident plunged him back into reality. Madeleine had put the infant down on the ground. Liberated from her tutelage, he tried to run toward Madame Mahu, who was keeping a respectful distance, but stumbled and fell. His head had hit a pebble, and a thin trickle of blood emerged from his forehead, descended in a red rill over the right eye, ran down the side of the nose and extended to the chin. It was an innocent injury, around which others hastened. The mother took her child in her arms, trying to soothe him with kisses. Madame Bise's exuberant clamors mingled with the infant's plaints.

All Caresco's attention, however, was focused on Madeleine. He saw her come running toward the vestibule, where he was standing, and then suddenly stop, immobilized by anguish, a strangulation that caused her to put her hand to her throat, as if to extract something that was choking her. At the same time, cries of revolt, inarticulate appeals, emerged from her mouth, like a violent protest against an imminent evil. Her eyes blinked; her face contracted, losing the grace of its harmonious symmetry. She had time to collapse on a chair, defending herself against a loss of consciousness.

"I'm choking! I'm choking!" she said, all the muscles of her neck striving for the air that was no longer entering into her lungs.

Madame Bise and her sister-in-law, distracted by the accident to little Mahu, came back into the vestibule hurriedly.

"Oh dear! She's ill!" cried the chatelaine, exaggerated the gravity of an attack that was hardly manifest. Turning to Madame de Jancy, who was looking sadly at her daughter without raising a finger, she said: "What! You're not going to do anything?"

"Monsieur Cartaux has instructed me not to oppose her crises, not to touch her. The fit will dissipate in a minute or two. The poor child was distressed by that injury..."

Madame Bise, however, could not reconcile herself to tranquility. Her exuberance inflated things, demanding movement and alarm. She turned despairingly to Caresco, and implored him: "Save her! Save her!"

The surgeon repressed an irony. "Don't worry," he said, "it's nothing. A slight nervous accident. Loosen her clothing and dab a little fresh water on her face, if you want to do something..."

While Madame Bise expended her vitality by running to the kitchen shouting: "Water! Water!" as if she wanted to put out a fire, the man of science contented himself with studying the various phases of the pathological manifestation.

He recognized that the crisis was dying down. The limbs tensed slightly, the upper body stiffened with the effort of respiration; then the energy of the struggle eased; the features relaxed and became animated. The eyes moved beneath the eyelids. Faint sighs vanquished the obstacle in the gullet.

Finally, Madeleine started to weep.

"Look! She's crying now!" proclaimed Madame Bise, coming back with a steaming glass of hot water.

"It's the end of the malaise," said the surgeon, restoring a smile to his guileful and hypocritical face.

Madame de Jancy knelt down, and took her daughter's head, bathed in scattered blonde hair, in her arms. She drank the poor tears that seemed to have been shed over the annihilation of the fearful moment.

CHAPTER II

Abruptly, the carriage stopped. A gate opened, pushed by the gardener. At the end of a straight pathway bordered by sun-burned chestnut-trees, the château appeared, a rectangle of white stones pierced by two rows of windows, and flanked with turrets with shiny slates. Monsieur and Madame Romé and their daughter Aline, extracting themselves from their torpor, patted their dusty clothing and struck more alert poses. While the brake set off again at a rapid trot Aline directed her eyes toward the house, in order to catch sight of her cousin— her best friend and confidante—as soon as possible. A voice emerging from a lateral pathway, however, revealed her dear presence.

"Stop!" shouted the pretty young woman.

Before the coachman had even had time to bring his team to a halt, Mademoiselle Romé had opened the carriage door and fallen into her cousin's arms. There was a charming effusion of kisses and rapid words, which astonished the dry soul of Caresco, who was accompanying Madeleine, and caused him to search for motives independent of pure friendship.

"Go on," said Madeleine to the coachman. "We'll come on foot."

The doctor bowed profoundly to the young woman, and then continued his stroll alone following the carriage.

The two young women, one as blonde as sunlight, the other as dark as shadow, with their arms around one another's waists, harmonized the undulating rhythm of their stride, and started up a joyous and tender chatter as

28

they went along the avenue of chestnuts. The sun, filtering through the branches, attached an occasional gleam to Madeleine's gilded hair; in her impatience, scornful of sunburn, she had come out without a hat.

"How good of you to come," said Madeleine, squeezing Aline's arm again. I feared that the heat might make you stay behind in Les Andelys."

"I came for you, my dear."

"Thank you, little cousin," Madeleine went on. "I have things to confide in you—but what makes your presence at Les Bolois even more precious is the desire not to have to suffer the perpetual presence of the gentleman who was with me. Did you notice him?"

"He looked like a jolly fellow to me. Who is he? Is that *him*?"

Madeleine laughed in an exaggerated fashion. "Him! Oh no... you can't possibly think so!"

The "him" in question had been the subject of a confidence made to Aline a week before by Madeleine. The "him" was the personification of all the dreams and utopias that young female brains can nurse, the realization of the latent desires and unconscious pressures of sex, which give rise to such forceful and lengthy thought, which trouble, delight and panic, which bring rushes of blood to the pallor of the cheeks, and which make laughter pearl on lips and tears in eyes. "He" was the tangible object of the fatal evolution of an instinct; he was Georges Ponviane, a tall fellow who had only had to appear one evening to Madeleine's dazzled eyes and show her the softness of his own eyes, and the dazzle of his smile beneath his brown moustache, effortlessly to collect the heart of a young woman, which delivers itself entirely.

"Oh no, you can't possibly think so," Madeleine, repeated. "Didn't you look at him?"

"I confess that I was paying more attention to you than him. Who is he?"

"That's the young Doctor Caresco, about whom you've told me so many things..."

"The lover of the beautiful Tripe-merchant, Mathilde de Guinac...impossible!" Aline's face was masked by astonishment. She had formed an entirely different idea of the person in question, whom she knew only by hearsay. She added: "He looks like such a pleasant fellow!"

Madeleine became impatient. "Don't judge him. You can weigh him up later." Already, other ideas were singing in her head, other words burning her lips—but she waited for her cousin's invitation.

"And what's new?" Aline finally said. "Have you dreamed about him?"

Madeleine nodded her head affirmatively, and her eyes were a blue smile.

"Have you spoken to him?" Aline asked.

"No."

"What, then?"

"What divine poet has said that people need to speak to understand one another? Hasn't Baudelaire celebrated the mute canticle of the eyes?"[3]

"You've sung that canticle?" said Aline. "Where?"

"Last Sunday, in church, while the curé of Les Bolois was singing mass."

---

[3] Yes he did, in a fervently erotic poem in *Les Fleurs du mal* entitled "Femmes damnées" [Doomed Women]—a title whose ominous quality Madeleine evidently does not appreciate.

"Little minx! Is it to that that you devote the hours destined for the good Lord?"

"I believe that it's the best means of praying to Him."

"You're right."

"So," Madeleine continued, "he had learned that I go to the eleven o'clock mass every Sunday. Just between us, I don't think he's very pious—and then again, it was the opening day of the season, and I knew that he's very fond of hunting, so I scarcely expected to see him. Well, he was there anyway. I've been so happy, so happy, my dear!"

"And did he speak to you?"

"He didn't dare. It's also necessary to tell you that I wasn't with Maman—you know that she still has heart trouble, which flares up from time to time. So she was suffering, and had entrusted me to the chambermaid. That's probably why he didn't dare come over. He's very discreet. But he had a bouquet of violets, which never quit his lips throughout the service."

"How do you know?"

"I know because, although I appeared to be very absorbed in my meditations, I never took my eyes off him."

"You'll tell that to your confessor?"

"I'll tell him...later. So, I followed him with my eyes and I saw him with that bouquet—which he'd evidently picked himself, because the flowers were very badly tied—always raised to his lips, and that caused me a delightful emotion. Anyway, you know what it's like, since you..."

"Oh, me," said Aline, in a tone that implied: *I'm already blasé about such matters.* "And then?" she continued, with a little sigh.

31

"And then, when the mass was finished, as if by chance he left the bouquet on his seat, which was one of those on the edge of the middle aisle, in such a way that, as I passed by on the way out, behind my maid, I only had to bend down slightly to pick it up. If you'd seen his joy, when he saw me come out of the church in possession of his violets!"

"How did he manifest his joy?"

"With a flourish of his hat—but if you'd seen that flourish!"

Aline uttered a giggle, which she quickly suppressed in response to Madeleine's alarm.

"You don't believe that he loves me?" said the latter. "Oh, if you knew the splendor of my dream! To marry that handsome fellow, to live in profound, absolute happiness...to have children that resemble him!"

Aline shrugged her shoulders. But the young women's conversation was interrupted. They had arrived at the house. In the vestibule the greetings were still going on. Madame Bise was introducing her doctor to Monsieur and Madame Romé.

Monsieur Romé looked at Caresco attentively, faithful to the inquisitorial habit of magistrates. He noticed the fleeting gaze and his first impression was unfavorable to the surgeon. He held out his hand, but was surprised to find a hand that also fled, which abandoned itself weakly, indifferently, almost limply, reflecting a profoundly egotistical heart. The man of the world and the professional were able to get the upper hand, however, and conceal the traces of astonishment and suspicion. In a level voice he expressed his delight in making the acquaintance of such a celebrated scientist.

Then there was the lunch, banal and heavy, with all the heaviness of the weather. Conversations died as soon as they were begun, stifled by the heat. Madame Bise drank a great deal. Three times a domestic replaced the carafe of wine in front of her.

Caresco, by contrast, hardly drank anything. At a certain moment, he was able to extract his neighbors from their torpor by telling them about one of his operations. He was very interesting as soon as he broached such a subject, knowing how to accommodate himself to the scope of ignorant minds. His eyes then implanted themselves with an extraordinary persistence on the person to whom he was talking and whom he wanted to convince.

In the present instance, it was for Aline that he deployed the elegance of his talk, and Madeleine found herself relieved of the malaise of finding the man's attention weigh upon her. By contrast, Aline did not take her eyes off him, seemingly riveted by him.

As he spoke, clearly and eloquently, even Monsieur Romé sensed the repulsion that he had felt at first evaporating. Evidently, he was in the presence of a superior man. The surgeon was giving details regarding the organization of his clinic, the service of his nurses—the good sisters, whom he never tried of praising—and the mortality figures consecutive to his interventions.

"I have no more than a three per cent mortality rate," he said, "and yet I carry out improbable operations, notably all the operations on the liver of which I'm the pioneer."

Three per cent! Madeleine had heard, however, that there were many deaths at his sanitarium, that there had once been several interments at the same time, which had filled the little street into which the dead were brought out with an unaccustomed animation. Aline had told her that—the same Aline who was now listening to the surgeon with an interest that she was not accustomed to show.

"Three per cent is very low," said Monsieur Romé. "I thought the statistic was generally much higher."

Caresco protested. It was indeed higher among the other surgeons of Paris, the Official ones, who operated badly, without neatness, without surety, and with desperate slowness.

"But the surgeon Monant," said Monsieur Romé, "is reputed to be a skillful man. He operated on the wife of one of my friends, on an abdominal tumor, and the operation was a perfect success."

"That was luck," proclaimed Caresco, "for Monant is one of the sorriest operators the French school possesses. He takes an hour and more to do what I do in five minutes. He's maladroit."

That was his method: extravagant, continual denigration of everyone and everything. The sown seed always gave birth to something. Enough of those bad seeds had been thrown to the wind in his own direction!

Madame Bise approved with a nod of her head, seeming to comprehend. She was waiting for an opportune moment to throw into the conversation a remark that she always put in when she brought her protégé to talk to people who did not know him.

"Tell Monsieur and Madame Romé about the little girl from Étampes."

Caresco narrated the story, told a hundred times before, about a peasant girl from Étampes who, having climbed a tree one day to pick cherries, lost her balance and unfortunately fell into a hedge. That hedge was maintained at intervals by stakes, solidly-planted in the ground and pointed, with the result that the child, falling on to one of them, was literally impaled. The wooden stake had entered her buttock and penetrated all the way to the middle of the back, so profoundly that the girl was suspended in mid-air and it was necessary to saw through the stake to get her down from that painful situation. In that state she had been brought to his operating theater, and you can imagine the great dilapidation of the flesh that was necessary to rid it of that unfortunate foreign body.

"And she was healed, Doctor?" asked Aline, decidedly very interested.

"She was healed...naturally. But the most amusing part of the story is that, a few months later, she brought me her piece of the stake in a superb velvet case, asking me to keep it in memory of her. I exhibit it in my display-case, in the midst of my anatomical specimens."

There was laughter, and Madame Bise laughed more loudly than the rest. It was cheerful, like the intervention of the comedian in a drama. Armand Caresco, when he was in society, possessed to a supreme degree the art of modifying the horror of his surgical exploits by means of an innocent wit. He extended over them a veil of humor, like a tailored crepe in the mantle of a mourning-costume. He knew that it rendered them less terrible, dispelling from their atmosphere of cutting anxiety the apprehension that brewers of blood involuntarily provoke.

And while the anodynely macabre jokes followed the evolution he had indicated, he resumed his observation of the guests. How rarely was he able to take his place at a family dining-table in this manner! Intimacy only existed for him in the home of his plump mistress, and was then often troubled by the comings and goings of strangers, the guests brought by Mathilde's caprice or his own professional propaganda. However, he sometimes experienced, in the desert of his life, a need for intimate peace, an oasis of consanguinity. These people seemed united; they tasted tranquil enjoyments of which he was ignorant. Why should he not strive to create a hearth like theirs for himself, to attach himself to life other than by the vain fibers of his love for a courtesan or his immeasurable ambition?

Facing him, two type-specimens of young women were offered to the covetousness of his dream: one, Madeleine, whom he had already analyzed yesterday, pretty, who would become powerful, as he liked women to be, when her delicacy had ripened; the other, Aline, drier, more vibrant, brunette, with the attitudes of a she-wolf, also pretty, in her ardent fashion, with her haughty hooked nose and the violent incarnadine of her red lips against her mat skin.

The former, whom he sensed, in any case, to be hostile, offered him, in spite of an unhealthy nervousness that would disappear as a result of marriage, a passive submission, an internal gravity and calm joys, like those of which he dreamed. The latter was a harpsichord from which he could drawn shrill harmonies, sensual and tempestuous chords; the tremulous fashion in which she had been looking at him since the start of the meal, the undulations with which she shivered at the words that emerged from his lips, the unconscious offer that she made of her being by her gestures and the intonation of her voice, all proved it.

And yet, Madeleine seemed preferable to him, in spite of her coldness, by reason of the glorious promise of her body

The effort of his imagination was, however, cut off by the imperious memory of his mistress. In the wellbe-ing of digestion, he relived burning minutes.

The meal concluded. Faces became more serious again, ceremoniously frozen. Madame Romé folded her napkin in order to go into the drawing room. There was a noise of moving chairs, a rustle of skirts, the clinking of a few rapidly-emptied glasses, and Madame Romé took Caresco's arm.

In the drawing room, Madeleine and Aline poured the coffee with a light grace.

Aline said to Caresco: "A glass of liqueur, Doctor? A cigar?"

"Thank you, Mademoiselle, neither liqueurs not tobacco..."

"You're a phenomenon, then? At table you didn't drink, and now you're not smoking..."

"Alcohol and tobacco can make the fingers tremble, and I need a great surety of hand."

"For your operations?"

"For my operations, and my exercises in pistol-shooting."

"You fire a pistol?"

"Very frequently." He was, in fact, a remarkable shot. Every day, he went to shoot a few targets at a fashionable range, and was cited as one of the most skillful exponents. That did no harm to his reputation as a surgeon, and in the special milieu of sportsmen he had created useful connections, which opened the doors of the aristocratic drawing-rooms from which he drew his clientele.

Aline allowed herself to be enveloped by a strange attraction emanating from the man she was seeing for the first time, and who seemed to be putting himself to the expense of flirting with her. She judged him to be different from the people she knew: stronger, with something about him that was indefinable and terrible and—in spite of that—attractive. She was also glad to observe that the hard-working and tenacious scientist was varnished with worldliness, and that he was evidently a sportsman.

Before these appreciations, the malevolent reportage with which the surgeon's character had been soiled melted away, and was annihilated, giving way to a confused admiration. The reaction was all the sharper for being unexpected, under the imperious influence of surprise. Less impressionable than Madeleine, Aline did not run into instinctive repulsions, abandoning herself entirely to the seductions of external qualities, of that which does not emanate from the darkness of the self.

So, when her cousin, having drawn her to one side, asked her: "Well, what do you think of him?" she replied: "Quite remarkable. One divines great intelligence in him, and I can't explain the antipathy that he inspires in you. I can assure you that I'll be very happy to see him again in Les Andelys."

CHAPTER III

The carriage that was taking the chatelaine of Les Bolois and her guests to Les Andelys had been traversing a large plain for ten minutes, with white, chalky roads, which were well-maintained but whose reverberation further augmented the overwhelming influence of the stifling heat. The thermometer marked thirty-two degrees in the shade.

Armand Caresco had titled his straw hat in such a way as to protect his face from the sun's rays and to be better able to gaze at the delightful young woman with the eyes full of light. He was astonished to see her so valiant after the week in which he had been living in proximity with her and watching her. No repetition of her nervous fit; a charming evenness of mood. Her nights, he had been told, were peaceful; Madeleine was sleeping calmly. However, he followed certain contractions of her physiognomy that still indicated a malaise, albeit explicable by the fierce heat.

He evoked the night that he had just spent, far from his mistress, in the narrow bed of the château. If Madeleine's sleep had been reparative, his had been shaken by dreams. An evolution had taken place in his brain. Madeleine had been its object.

In the tension of a forced continence, he had dreamed about the splendid young woman, no longer suffering calmly, but agitated by passionate attitudes similar to those he had so often observed in the hysterics of the Salpêtrière. The unfathomable mystery of urges had poured sensuality into that mold of chastity. Morbid contortions had been transformed into appeals of sensuality.

The throat, tranquil and pure after the tempest, the firm roundness of the erect breasts glimpsed during the crisis through the opening of the loosened corsage, the gracious curve of the legs, and the movements of the loins themselves, the broad hips so admirably formed for maternity—all those harmonious manifestations sanctified by nature had aspired the gross desires fermenting within him, and deflected scientific observation toward lasciviousness. The hours of darkness had flowed by in seizures of the flesh, violent and impetuous.

Now that he had the young woman facing him, in the jolting of the carriage, his knee brushing hers, his blood heated up, his flesh harassed by the Saharan heat, he allowed himself to be increasingly carried away by the wings of his desire. To vary the contention of her attitude, and also to flee Caresco's knee, she had crossed one leg over the other, displaying the beginning of a soft calf.

The surgeon's imagination became enthusiastic at that sight; he undressed the rest of her body, seeing the cleavage burst forth like a flower from its bud. Even the corset fell away, and Madeleine was radiant in the apotheosis of the splendid contours and delicate fires of her flesh.

He sighed loudly.

Embarrassed by the burning persistence of the gaze that repelled her, and by which she felt possessed, without being able to defend herself, Madeleine turned away, almost fearfully, to gaze at the landscape.

The brake had just passed over the level crossing at Gaillon railway station, and had arrived at the Seine, which ran not far away. The horses, already sweating, had slowed down. The vicinity of the water spread a slight freshness in the increasingly fiery atmosphere.

Madame Bise stopped the carriage and they all had the leisure to contemplate the panorama that extended into the distance, in great green bands cut by the ribbon of the Seine and the chalky patches of cliffs. In that land of ancient knights, populated by historic châteaux, convents and towers, on the left, before arriving at the Seine, there was the ancient wall of a Charterhouse, and then the peninsula of Tosny, a sprightly green hill beneath which the Roule tunnel had just been dug. To the right there was the little village of Courchelles, and, standing on the cliff, an isolated tower of medium dimensions, which Madame Bise named as the signal tower of Portmors. The bizarre sonority of the name caused Armand's head to turn away; he was already weary of the landscape.

The horses resumed a trot, going through lamentable villages—Bouafles, Vezillon—and past a narrow gorge at the end of which Château Gaillard was visible. Peasants went slowly by, carrying tools over shoulders stooped by heavy years of toil and poverty, saluting the carriage with a finger negligently raised to the rim of their straw hat. Madame de Jancy and Madeleine responded with nods of the head; Caresco looked at them disdainfully, from the full height of his strength of a man tailored in Herculean fashion for the battle of life.

Oh, the existence of those poor fellows: an animal existence, devoid of desire, of conflict, of enjoyment eternally concerned with tomorrow's morsel of bread; an existence of brute labor, days commenced too soon and ended late, to gain a few francs; the existence of the imbecilic and dogged toiler—how he despised it, and how he despised those who were its victims!

"This region doesn't seem to be rich!" he said to Madame Bise.

"Ha! Not rich! They don't work!"

To corroborate what she said, the brake went past a gang of twenty laborers.

"This," Madame Bise continued, "is the richest soil one can imagine, but they don't know how to take advantage of it. They remain in the rut of their primitive manual labor. For instance, look at all those apple trees and cherry trees, and the extraordinary quantity of fruit they produce! They don't know how to exploit their wealth. Can you guess, my dear doctor, how much those beautiful greengages are sold for in certain establishments in England? As much as a shilling. And do you know how much they're content to sell a five-kilo basket for here? Between one franc fifty and two francs!"

Caresco's mercantile soul, his atavistic soul, caused his eyes to gleam. Oh, if he were a landowner in this region, how he would be able to make his exploitation pay! He would have an outlet in London to convert those beautiful products of Norman soil into a rain of gold! And how truly stupid these people were to remain enmired in their trivial role as producers, not having any business sense, not understanding the eternal conclusion of La Fontaine's fable, that when one takes the chestnuts from the fire, it's necessary to eat them…not to know, in sum, what had been the strength of his own race, the intermediary role so obstinately played throughout the ages and in all circumstances by those of his blood.

He arrived at Monsieur Romé's home with his heart exultant with a new audacity, swelled by flamboyant energies. He was already reproaching himself for the unproductive inactivity of his week, the somnolent hours spent observing a young woman who was not ill, whose hereditary flaw, so little manifest, was not provoked by her habitual practices. He would leave, having reassured Madame Bise, telling her that his operations were recalling him to Paris. A week of contention, a week of suppressing the impetuous ferment of action and movement that was seething within him, was the full measure of the devotion that he accorded to his protectress. Tomorrow, he would throw himself back into the violent current of his life, to struggle in the intoxication of the conflict, in the determination to triumph. Tomorrow, Paris, his operating theater, and Mathilde, imperiously desired!

With that prospect, his acerbic humor became obsequious and charming again. He accepted the proposal of going, after lunch, to visit the ruins of Château Gaillard. He would find vestiges there of battles and of domination in conformity with the ardor of his sentiments. He scarcely accorded any condescendence to the anticipations and the solicitude of Aline, who never took her eyes off him and deployed all her femininity to awaken his sympathy. Madeleine, by contrast, seemed to be retreating ever further into a cold reserve.

Madame Romé prescribed the departure for the visit to the ruins. It would be necessary to hurry if they did not want to be caught in the storm. In fact, black clouds were already massing on the horizon, giving the sky a leaden hue. Madeleine could feel her nerves tensing.

Madame de Jancy protested in vain that they would not have time to take the excursion, that they would surely get wet. Madame Romé made the remark, however, that storms in the region always took some time to prepare, and that visiting the château would take half an hour at the most. They departed on foot, in separate groups, under the threat of a stifling atmosphere.

CHAPTER IV

The path that led to the ruins sloped upwards tortu-
ously. Foreheads were covered in sweat, legs became
heavy, lungs oppressed. Madame de Jancy, fearing to
overtax her bad heart, soon declared that she was giving
up the ascent, and to keep her company, Madame Romé
returned to the château.

The intrepid continued to advance in two groups:
Monsieur Romé, Armand Caresco and Aline in the lead;
Madame Bise and Madeleine at the rear. At a bend in the
rocky path, the ancient mass loomed up. About thirty
meters still remained to climb, via paths that were
scarcely traced, overgrown by scorched grass. Then the
enormous vestige of a tower rose up sheerly, to which
one gained access by a narrow stairway hewn in the
rock, with majestic sections of wall in uneasy equilibri-
um, leaning toward the precipice, lamentable fragments
with openings that were like squinting eyes staring out
over all that desolation: glorious debris that had conserved through the centuries the threat of heroic battles.
Behind, two hundred meters further on, isolated from the
principal mass, further ruins recalled the memory of de-
pendencies.

Madame Bise had presumed too much of her
strength. At the sight of the arduous route that remained
to be traveled, frightened by the peril of the passages,
and thirsty after the libations of lunch, she renounced the
ascent. Madeleine, who felt a kind of dull anguish, and
excitement of her entire nervous system, at the approach
of the storm that was continuing to mass in the depths of
the sky, had to run to catch up with the other walkers,

who were already scaling the slope. Monsieur Romé, playing the showman and narrating the topography of the old feudal castle, was talking about an original enclosure that had disappeared behind what had been the round-path, of which traces could still be seen.

"You can imagine," he said, "that this citadel overlooking the Seine was impregnable, organized for battle and capable of resisting monstrous assaults. Even in our time, with our engines of modern warfare, it would be difficult to make a breach in these walls, four meters thick. From the battlements, out of harm's way, the defenders launched their projectiles down on the enemy. Look—here are the remains of machicolations, those chimneys through which the combatants poured molten lead on to the assailants. What a defensive organization, and how far it is from our improved rifles, giving free rein to personal initiative and courage!"

He recounted the souvenirs of his reading, legends full of drama and fear. By means of a stairway excavated in the rock, whose safety was guaranteed by an iron railing, they penetrated into the main tower.

"This," said Monsieur Romé, pointing to a hole that had been filled in, "is the remains of an oubliette. Prisoners were thrown in there, or people in whose disappearance the lord had an interest. The unfortunates died there of hunger and cold when they were not killed instantly. Over there you can see, at the foot of that staircase, the commencement of the subterranean workings, which have collapsed. It's possible to get into them; they provide a shelter in which vagabonds come to sleep on summer nights. But let's go up into the principal room, the lord's private apartment."

They went into an immense circular stone hall, open to the sky. A colossal fireplace could still be seen there, in which entire tree-trunks must have blazed, warming the weary limbs of hunters, cheering up the long vespers of the chatelaine, beneath the crush of the massive walls, with the crackling of sparks. A gaping hole, the memory of a window, overlooked the Seine, whose waters, dirtied by the blackness of the sky, were flowing eighty meters below. Directly beneath, a smoking factory seemed singularly shrunken. To the right, the agglomeration of Les Andelys extended along the arc of a circle formed by the river valley.

Madeleine, on leaning over the edge of the precipice, felt attracted toward it. A desolation emerging from those somber and heavy walls penetrated her soul. She listened, terrified, to what her uncle was saying, recounting that from the window where she was standing, a queen had been suspended, alive, by her hair. History claimed that the daughter of knights had been put to death there and left as fodder for the crows.

Monsieur Romé narrated other terrible tales, and the horror of those crimes rose up within the young woman, blossoming within her, and her eyes stared desperately into the void. When the others had gone, continuing their tour, she stayed there, retained by the legend, at the precipice, before the immensity overcharged with vapors.

Sustained by the power of that ride through history, Monsieur Romé, Caresco and Aline continued their stroll, forgetting Madeleine. They followed a round-path, went down a little slope in order to go another few hundred meters to cast an eye over other vestiges, isolated from the principal mass.

Aline no longer left the surgeon's side. Monsieur Romé, carried away by the impetuosity of his memories, did not notice the behavior of his daughter—who, under the influence of a violent attraction, was yielding herself, by her voice and by her eyes, to that unknown man. Many times, she called upon the support to the dominator, under the pretext of needing help for a perilous step. Then, she stuck the palm of her hand to the formidable hand that had sown so many disasters and so many joys by means of the knife—and the violation of that contact troubled her with unknown frissons of a delightful asperity.

Stirred by the appeals of that passion, and also by his unaccustomed continence, Caresco responded secretly to the young woman's appeals, but prudence and, above all, the minimal attraction of Aline's person, counseled him to an absolute reserve. Ah, if he had been solicited by Madeleine, instead of Aline...

Suddenly, large warm raindrops began to fall. The tense atmosphere melted, becoming a deluge. The heavens rumbled.

The strollers ran to the ruins in search of shelter. They backed up against the segments of the desolated walls. In the disarray, they were all thinking of themselves. Then, suddenly, Monsieur Romé exclaimed "Madeleine! Where's Madeleine?"

"She must have stayed in the big tower," Aline replied.

"How imprudent it is to leave her alone!"

"I'll go look for her," said the surgeon.

A flash of jealousy passed through Aline's eyes. In an abrupt tone, she said: "I'll go with you." But Monsieur Romé retained her with an anxious glance, and she remained angrily in place while Caresco retracted the path they had just traveled, running through the rain.

How long had Madeleine been plunged in the anguish of her reflections? Later, she remembered that she was still at the gaping opening when the first clap of thunder had given the signal for the unleashing of the furious atmosphere. Large drops of water fell vertically, causing centuries-old dust to spring up under their impact and lashing the stone, which rendered a cry, accumulating to form rapid rills that became cataracts. Lighting zigzagged, streaking the sky magnificently with bolt after bolt, the enormous voice of the thunder responding to its appeal, prolonging its rumbling all the way to the foundations of the ancient mass, which seemed to be trembling at the memory of the cyclopean assaults to which it had been subjected in the distant past.

In spite of the fear and the nervous tension that had gripped her throat, as at the approach of the much-redoubted crises, and in spite of the danger, Madeleine remained standing, upright beneath the downpour, indifferent to the wrath of the elements, overwhelmed by horror and admiration in the contemplation of the most sublime of spectacles.

Eighty meters below her, the Seine, Petit Andely and the peninsula of Tosny had almost disappeared behind a liquid curtain; beneath her feet and all around her, the downpour of stones, the steep slopes, the round paths, the walls, the stairways, the battlements and machicolations were shining, filling up with noisy puddles, ferrying torrents, mingling their voices with those of the heavens.

It was a concert of devastation, a revolt against calm. Clamors emerged from everything, the dormant echo of lamentations uttered long ago, reawakened by the storm; they were the plaints of violated women, the groans of those walled up, the gasps of the dying. All the infamy of long-gone crimes, all the terror of the martyrized, was exhaled by the monstrous debris.

Now, Madeleine was no longer gazing; she closed her eyes, and yet she could see...

She saw passing before her a horde of ironclad warriors howling at her and brandishing their reddened weapons. They eyes were ablaze; they had the debris of human flesh on their fingernails. She saw a procession of lamentable prisoners, lacerated and harassed, laden with chains, so thin that, in places, the bones were erupting through the skin. There were women sobbing, children dying, old men weeping blood.

Further away, there was a stag being ripped apart by dogs, its entrails emerging from a gash in its belly. Closer, within arm's reach, was a long, pale, spectral form suspended by her hair from the bars of the window; agony filling her gaze, her lips blue-tinted by death, she was frightful and soft.

Finally, someone was behind her, whom she could not see, but whose presence she divined. She guessed that it was the terrible lord of the manor, the bloodthirsty man who persisted through the generations, the hero of all appetites and all lusts. It seemed to her that a fluid was flowing from him toward her, that it was making the nape or her neck prickle and injecting fear into her flesh. Then that fluid became more focused, settling on her epigastrium like a claw, like a crawling hand that was rising toward her throat and compressing it to stifle her.

She moved, as if to draw away from the anguish in her chest, and shook her golden hair. It had no effect. Then she turned her head.

Caresco was already beside her.

He was looking at her, smiling avidly. His eyes were avid too. He said something to her that she did not understand, because vertigo was blurring her hearing as well as her sight. A closer flesh of lightning zigzagged in front of the gap.

Madeleine uttered a scream, and took a step toward the abyss, making a gesture to protect her wandering eyes. But her gesture stopped half way, and she stood there rigid, her mouth open, with the purple of her pale lips, her eyes almost closed, her brows furrowed, her body slightly inclined forward, sculpturally.

"Catalepsy," murmured the surgeon. "One more step and she was over the edge."

He did not hurry to abstract her from the danger. His science, his studies of catalepsy at the Salpêtrière, reassured him as to the young woman's stability. Firstly, as a scientist, he studied the subject's pathological stance. He noticed that the muscles of the limbs and the body were not contractured, but conserved the delicate grace of their form. He moved closer, observed the insensible slumber of the nerves by touching the hardness of the pulp with his fingertip, and pinched the arm, without obtaining any reaction. It was death in life.

He modified his observation then, emerging from the medical domain in order simply to admire the splendid harmony of form. What a loss it would have been for the pleasure and joy of a fortunate possessor if Madeleine had advanced a few centimeters more! She would have fallen into the abyss, and the fictitious annihilation would have become a veritable annihilation.

Then, in order to withdraw himself from the obsession of that threat, he wanted to draw the radiant creature of amour away from peril, to shelter her from the downpour in the refuge formed by the entrance to the subterranean workings. There were a few paces to travel, a few steps to descend with a burden that seemed all the lighter because his muscular strength was exasperated by a week's continence, and by the fire that Aline had been feeding since the morning.

He seized the young woman in his arms, as if for an abduction and carried her down the glistening stairway—but on feeling that glorious flesh against him, which the wet fabric rendered to him as if naked, and the erect splendor of her breasts, and the triumphant curve of her lips, he was heated up by a surge of brutal folly, desiring a more absolute contact.

When he reached the dark covert, he lay the stiffened body down on the dirty ground, the gilded hair scattering. A tamer of all resistance, he parted her legs abruptly.

Outside, the storm was raging; the isolation and the unconsciousness of his crime were accomplices. Madeleine retained her automaton attitude, the pallor of her cheeks, the virginal wandering of her eyes and the furrowing of her brows...

A few hours later, in a room on Monsieur Romé's château, to which she had been transported, unconscious, Madeleine woke up, her head heavy and her limbs aching. Her first thought was the astonishment of finding herself lying in a bed with exceedingly white sheets in a strange room. Slowly, she turned her head, divining someone nearby.

Sitting in a armchair next to be bed, Madame de Jancy was waiting for her to wake up; a smile welcomed her gaze; then the smile became a kiss, long, affectionate and comforting, mingled with the soft and innocent words that mothers can say to their children.

"Madelon, my Madelon! You've been ill again. Pour dear, it's that villainous storm that took you by surprise. But it's nothing. The doctor has recommended rest. Be good; I love you."

Now, Madeleine understood. A shadow passed over her face. What! Another crisis! She thought that she had been freed from that frightful malady! How had it happened?

She racked her brains, but from the moment when the lightning had blinded her, everything had been effaced from her mind; there was a lacuna in her memory. And yet, it seemed to her that something had happened: that an event that was not a dream had occurred.

But what?

She made a weary gesture, and uttered a sigh; her head fell back on to the pillow, and thought seemed to quit her brain for a few seconds more. A fresh breeze came to reanimate her, however; Madame de Jancy had opened the window over a sumptuous view of the valley.

It was six o'clock in the evening; the storm had washed the sky; the sun was completing its triumphant course, seemingly enlarging as it fled, setting the entire horizon ablaze. High up, in the distance, little clouds were catching fire, like errant flames escaped from an immense crater of fire. In the plain, windows caught by the reverberation of the light also lit up, responding to the red fire. The heart of the heavens was bleeding; it was a magnificent outburst, an enchantment of the eyes such as the most skillful painters could never achieve.

Then it changed; the fire became golden; an immense Pactolus flowed through the azure. The spectacle stimulated Madeleine's artistic soul, reactivating her nerves, and before her mother could move, she was at the window, her eyes madly extended toward the horizon, her bosom swelling in order to be more amply penetrated by the refreshing oxygen.

Gently, Madame Jancy, worried by that unhealthy agitation, drew her back toward the bed and tried to make her lie down again, but she resisted that excess of tenderness. In a trice, she had dressed, thrust a tortoise-shell comb through the scatter of her opulent golden hair, and, well buttoned-up, went down to the lawn to play her part in the game of tennis that had been arranged before dinner.

For a long time she deployed a vigor and a skill in that game that reassured the audience, bounding with the ball and uttering joyful exclamations at each successful shot.

Equally adroit, Caresco, on the opposing team, contested with her, riposting with a dexterity that would have enabled him to pass for a practitioner of that mundane tourney, if he had not been known to be a man of science.

Not for a moment did his lips abandon the amiable and false smile that masked his thoughts, and would have dissimulated his remorse—except that he had no remorse.

CHAPTER V

At the beginning of September, Armand Caresco, on returning to Parris, went to the clinic where his father, the director of the Institut Homeopathique de Passy, gave free consultations. The institute, whose benefits were advertised on all the public urinals of the capital, consisted of a miserable little apartment in one of the dirtiest houses in the Rue Scheffer.

What distinguished that dwelling from other similar ones situated on the same landing was a vast copper plaque fixed to the door, on which the following inscription was engraved in black letters:

Institut Homeopathique de Passy
founded in 1863
for the cure of all diseases
by Dr. Caresco's system.

Some time ago, the doctor's name had been scratched out, and was almost no longer legible.

Once through the door, one penetrated into a somber little room, scarcely illuminated by a window looking out into a gloomy courtyard. The furniture was of the utmost simplicity; it consisted of a few vulgar benches, dirty and greasy, disposed in parallel lines. Along the walls, frames enclosed attestations of cures.

Pale-faced wretches sat limply on the benches, arranged in order of their arrival, clutching a piece of cardboard bearing the order number given to them on entry by a grave domestic in a formal jacket. They waited meekly for their turn to come to penetrate into Dr.

Caresco's consulting-room. To pass the time, some of them read the pinned-up letters, commenting on the signatures, comparing the lists of symptoms with their own; other chatted about the method—thirty years of success!—employed by the physician they were going to see, a method whose result had been cures so miraculous that the newspapers had reported them.

In one corner, apart, having not found anywhere to sit down, stood a poor old grandmother preciously cradling in her arms the burden of a child who was dying of tubercular meningitis. She had summoned a physician to her home; alas, he had immediately diagnosed the malady and offered an estimate of the days of life remaining. There was nothing to be done in such a case, the doctor had said. However, as she had read in the newspapers about the cures obtained by Dr. Caresco's new method, maddened by the fear of that crushing inevitability, determined to make the ultimate sacrifices, she had made the resolution to bring her child to the Savior.

It was her whole life, that little parcel of flesh on its way to extinction, the daughter of her daughter, who had died at twenty-three of tuberculosis, the hereditary disease of the family, which she had escaped herself by a fluke of chance. She surrounded the infant with a thousand attentive cares, rocking her amorously, feeling a stab in her heart every time that a faint, plaintive, distant cry emerged from the baby's dry throat, or a convulsion, revealing the whites of the eyes, passed like an escape of death from the body in which life was no longer reflected.

Wearied by that cherished burden, which she could not put down, leaning against the wall, humble and pitiful, how anxious the wait was for her! How desperate were the glances she darted toward the door of that consulting-room, too slow to open again, behind which an imbecile faith told her that she would recover health for the creature dearest to her in all the world!

Armand Caresco went through that room rapidly. The domestic bowed to the authority of his attire; a few of the wretches stood up as he passed by. He paid no attention to them and went into his father's consulting-room without knocking.

The latter was in the process of writing a long prescription for an old man who had just submitted to him the horror of a paralysis immobilizing half the body. He looked up and, without interrupting his task, said: "It's you." Then, turning to the old man, he said: "Here, my friend, this is what it's necessary to do. Friction every morning; two granules at midday, two in the evenings, before meals. All that is written down. Go to get these medicaments from the pharmacist along the street, to the right as you go out. He's the only one who can supply them. You can go."

The man made a vague gesture with the arm that he could still move, and, his heavy tongue making it difficult to get the words out of his lop-sided mouth, asked: "Will it cost much? I'm not rich..."

"Does it cost much?" the old practitioner replied, irritably. "I don't know"

He knew perfectly well that the prescription would cost the poor devil eight francs, of which the pharmacist would give him fifty per cent—which is to say, four francs. The consultations were free, and that loudly-trumpeted gratuity brought people flocking to his clinic, but the payment of the account at the pharmacy—the only one who could supply the remedies he prescribed—was colossal. That was the arrangement the two scoundrels had made to rob the unfortunates, safe from any criminal sanction, their system being based on the most wretched thing in the world: the exploitation of the maladies of the poor.

To be sure, a law exists that forbids these infamous and fortunately infrequent associations, but how can the abomination be proven? How can anyone be present in the wings to catch the bandits at the moment when they are sharing out the fruits of their theft?

The man left, dragging his hemiplegia painfully. The father and son remained alone, looking at one another. The old physician had a benevolent, happy smile for the young surgeon, the pride of his old age. As Armand's physiognomy remained grave, however, he became anxious.

"What's the matter, son," he asked.

The son did not reply, but, taking a newspaper out of his overcoat, he placed it before his father's eyes. The homeopath immediately understood that it was a matter of an advertisement that had appeared that morning in a sensational form in the rag that Armand was holding out to him.

"Well," he said, "do you think there's something wrong with it?"

"Not that it's badly-written; evidently, the audience for this sort of newspaper will be interested in the story of this little child condemned by everyone else and saved by you"—he had a slightly ironic smile—"but truly, Papa, you're abusing publicity. You know that it harms me—why continue?"

"But I haven't put my name on it!"

"That makes no difference; the sign of your clinic is sufficiently well-known and everyone can put the signature at the end of the article that isn't to be found there. Thus, this morning, at the Hôpital de la Charité, I went into Professor Maral's department and found a group of students in the process of reading the very article that I've brought. Oh, I promise you that they were paying, in venom, while listening to your prose being read out, and if you'd heard the reflections that those imbeciles were making...as unflattering for me as for you!

"You must understand that it causes me a great deal of prejudice. I'm already very badly judged by the Faculté, whose qualified surgeons, the mandarins, are jealous of my skill and my success; if you get mixed up in it too, and cause trouble for me by providing fodder for their calumnies..."

He did not finish what he had set out to say. Fundamentally, he was scornful of his father, not because of the commerce to which his homeopathy obliged him, but because the old man industrialized his art so miserably, on such restricted lines. However, a kind of restraint persisted in his relationship with the old physician, which did not derive from respect, but depended on the submission to elders and the family spirit appropriate to Jews— the sacred traditions and authority of the legendary high priests of the Talmud. Then again, did he not owe to the aid of that stunted mercantilism the first steps in his career, the lessons so well-learned, not in matters of science—the old man being incapable of giving any, having only made the vaguest studies with a view of obtaining the conversion of his own nation's diploma into the diploma of a officer of health—but practical lessons concerning the commercial side of the profession: an apprenticeship in business, as the atavistic soul understands it.

Now, the head leaning on the back of his armchair, while Caresco senior reflected on his own account, Armand thought with a certain pleasure about his initial difficulties. He recalled, as he darted a glance around that somber room, now dilapidated, how he had begun the edification of his surgical reputation after four years of internship in the hospitals of Paris.

Yes, it was in this obscure hovel that he had carried out his first operations, before possessing the sumptuous town house that he had made into his clinic, before even having a little house of his own on the Boulevard Péreire. What memories were revived within his brain by those narrow walls and dirty parquet—veritable breeding-grounds of microbes—and, most of all, the narrow, badly-ventilated room behind his father's consulting room, in which he had abandoned to the care of a part-time nurse the creatures—always poor disinherited pauperesses who offered no more interest for him once the operation was terminated—whose flesh his scalpel had just violated, in which he had trained his hand *in anima vili*.

It was his father, the old homeopath, who had chosen from his clientele the victims of those scientific sacrifices, the price being not very high and paid in advance. The operations always succeeded, but death often followed. There had once been a sequence of seven deaths…but how well, in the wake of that massacre, the young surgeon had known how to carry out further resections of the ileocecal appendix! After the complaint of a husband, however, on whose wife he had operated without authorization, the people at the Prefecture of Police had become strangely excited by such a hecatomb; a discreet investigation had been ordered by a judge.

That was also one of the rare occasions when Armand had experienced an emotion; he generally floated with a monstrous indifference above all human sentiment, and had rarely felt such an anguish stirring in his heart as on the day when he had seen a grave black-glad man go into his father's study: the Commissaire of Police, come to inspect the registers in which every clinic had to record operations and their nature.

Very courteously, the man in black had explained that it was a simple formality, and that he was convinced that the affair would have no further consequences. The registers were there, in the desk drawer; the surgeon could have handed them over—but they were incomplete; their surrender would have provoked further investigations, perhaps leading to his conviction.

By virtue of a stroke of fortunate audacity, Armand had told the Commissaire that the books were at his private house, and that he would send them as soon as he got home—and with what fervor, as soon as the magistrate had gone, the key having been turned in the lock, the father and son, gripped by an atrocious fear, had set about correcting the register! They destroyed the pages that bore the observations of fatal operations, and added others in which they created wholesale accounts of magnificent results in the cases of people since vanished.

And in that haste, in that panic, of what presence of mind they had nevertheless given proof—he smiled at the memory—when they had nixed a certain quantity of cigar-ash with the ink, to give the writing an appearance of age! The law had been deceived, and the file had been closed.

Armand also remembered the profound joy he had experienced on the day when, his initial savings having been liquidated, he had finally been able to get his fortunate career off the ground, rent a small house on the Boulevard Péreire, install an operating theater there, still modest, in reality, but already permitting him to invite

Parisian, provincial and foreign colleagues to the manifestations of his talent. Thus, he had exalted his mastery, satisfied his pride and allowed himself to be led to celebrity by the accomplishment of the work of life and death.

Thus, with the contentment of the peril effaced, he thought about those old tribulations. Now, things were marching triumphantly, the past eclipsed by the joy of present success.

To be sure, he still did operations that, for the great majority of other surgeons, would have been veritable crimes; certainly, the thousand-franc bills that he needed to appease the gluttony of his aging mistress led him to apply himself, knife in hand, even when the result of his interventions was almost certain to be death; certainly, he acted in such a way that the desperate rich came to him to finish their calvary in the tomb, and that one of the most honest surgeons in Paris said in speaking of some inoperable case: "Only a madman like Caresco would operate here"—but he had a sturdy back with which to support such unsuccessful endeavors and such appreciations. How well-known to everyone the near-genius of his skill was! He had the most beautiful and cleanest of surgical installation in Paris!

What is more, he operated in broad daylight, surrounded by a host of colleagues, who marveled at his manual skill and rapidity. Foreign scientists in Paris never failed to pay him a visit; his books were discussed; his ideas had taken on weight; and he had published so many cases thought incurable by others and cured by him that he did not care at all about the quantity of cadavers that still disappeared through the back door of his house of operations.

He abandoned his incursion into the past and turned to his father, who was meekly respecting his silence.

"So, Papa, it's understood, isn't it? No more advertising."

The old Semite adopted a lachrymose tone that strangely exaggerated the accent particular to exotic Israelites—a stigma that he corrected in ordinary circumstances, but reappeared, an indelible trace, when he was excited.

"But I won't be able to earn a living!"

"A living! Get away!" Armand growled. "A living! As if you didn't have enough to live on—don't tell me that. Anyway, I'll compensate you. From now on, I'll let you keep all the money for the operations on the patients that you send me. Is that agreed?"

The father acquiesced. To tell the truth, those sums were mostly derisory, but there is no profit small enough to neglect. Then again, he would make it up in the quantity. The agreement straightened his face.

"Let's see," said Armand. "What do you have to offer me today?" He was talking about patients on which to operate. "You know that the surgical conference opened yesterday. I'm making two reports on my operations on the liver; they'll generate a lot of talk! I have a dozen cases of resection of the gall bladder. You can see the faces of our dear colleagues now, can't you? Can you imagine that in one case I unblocked the bile duct...?"

Having started to describe an extraordinary case, however, his enthusiasm was cut short by the indifferent physiognomy of his father. What had prompted him to take science to that old businessman? Gall bladder...bile duct...did he even know where they were? Why try to scrape the rust from that superb ignorance?

"It would take too long to explain," he continued. "I'll tell you about it another time. So, the congress has opened and the foreigners are coming to watch me operate tomorrow morning. The members of the Faculté aren't budging, of course. Oh, they'll be able to make a comparison, the foreigners! I have at their service in the same morning two livers, a kidney, one abdominal hysterectomy, another vaginal, a tubercular tumor on the foot, and a resection of the shoulder. A lot of surgery, eh!"

He laughed loudly, allowing he ardent gleam of his teeth to pass through his lips. "I'm only lacking a skull," he continued. "Do you have a skull to offer me? What's wrong with the child in the arms of an old woman waiting out there? It reeked of meningitis at fifteen paces when I went past. If it's meningitis, I'll operate. Have the old woman come in."

Before his father could reply, he pressed the button of an electric bell, which was on the table between the papers.

The domestic appeared.

"Send in the old woman with the child," said Armand.

The old woman was introduced. Timid and anxious, she took her place on the seat indicated to her by the domestic. The grave faces of the two physicians, the manservant's uniforms and the imminent moment of the verdict weighed down upon her. She had prepared words that she could not pronounce, and contented herself with rocking the inert parcel of flesh.

Solemnly, the father began to question her. How long was it since the illness began? What were the antecedents? Armand shrugged his shoulders at the futility of the information. Rapidly, he had the child undressed, and when the old woman's anxious hands could not find the pins he finished the task himself, without repulsion at the dirtiness of the linen.

The little invalid, drawn out of her torpor, opened her eyes momentarily, deflected by a squint, but closed them again to plunge back into unconsciousness. The body was slightly folded upon itself, the fact red and pale by turns, the hollow belly emphasizing the projecting ribs and hips. Two thin arms, in which the blue furrows of the veins were visible, formed a cross over the breast; she seemed to have adopted the pose of immolation. The amplified respiration sometimes became precipitate, only to stop suddenly, as if death had already accomplished its work—but it began again, at a precipitate rhythm: an anxious breath that had difficulty getting out through contractions of the jaw which made the teeth grate.

The tableau was typical of tubercular meningitis in its second phase. Armand, studying the symptoms scientifically, took note of the irregularity of the pulse, felt the dry heat of the skin and, by means of repeated pinches along the limbs, established anesthesia. Absorbed by his study, oblivious to the grandmother's suffering, he nodded his head in satisfaction; he had found a skull to open. The spectators of the following day's operations would be astonished. It was now only a matter of persuading the old woman of the necessity of an operation—but that was child's play, for him.

As his father tacitly interrogated him, he said: "Tubercular meningitis, second phase, of course. There's no doubt about it. The child is doomed, unless an operation..."

He looked at the grandmother. Tears were swelling her eyelids; dolorous wrinkles were plowing her shriveled features.

"An operation?" she said. "There's an operation for meningitis, then? My God! An operation!"

"Understand, Madame," the surgeon went on, "that the operation is to release the water that is in the head. She has water in her head, your child, and that fluid is compressing the brain. The operation consists of making a little hole, as one empties a cask of wine. You've taken wine from a cask, haven't you? Well, it's the same thing."

It was an explanation of the sort he adapted, with skillful composure, to the assimilation of restricted intelligence. The old woman did not take it aboard immediately. She knew that one can have water in the belly, in the joints and in the lungs, but the rudimentary gossip of common folk had never told her that one could have anything but the brain inside the skull. If she had been told that her granddaughter had a sprained nerve or crumpled flesh, she would have understood that elementary explanation more easily. She had, however, heard mention of trepanning. Her newspaper, the *Petit Journal*, had related curious operations carried out by means of that instrument; she was even following a *feuilleton* in which the operation of a trepan had been described at length. But that was very serious; could one even survive it? Tearfully, she asked that question.

"Can one survive it!" Caresco exclaimed. "But of course—as certainly as two and two make four. It's an operation I've been doing every day for years without ever having had a mishap. The worst that can happen is that the cure will only happen slowly. In any case, the attempt is necessary, if you value your child..."

If she valued her! The invocation of her eyes to Heaven proved that eloquently. But to decide so rapidly! She had a further moment's hesitation, moved by obscure impulses in her exhausted brain, and in order to put on a brave face she took a multicolored check handkerchief out of her pocket, with which he mopped her brow. Then, finally making up her mind, she said: "Take her."

It was submission, abandonment without revolt. Armand smiled triumphantly. He got up and clapped the old woman on the shoulder. Right! Her little child would be cured. He congratulated her for having understood that it was the only chance of getting out of it. And how happy the child would be on the day when she could return to the aged relative and hold out her arms to her again! It was necessary to operate without delay, the following morning for example, before the malady got any worse. The child had to be brought to his private clinic, where she would be admirably received by Sisters of Charity.

As for the conditions, it would be sufficient to arrange those with his father; Armand was generous toward the poor and would even operate, if necessary, for nothing; the grandmother would only have to settle the account for the accommodation, medicaments and the maintenance of the surgical equipment.

The old woman was now looking at him with gratitude. After the doubt, confidence widened her heavy eyelids and a gleam of admiration departed from her eyes to envelop her benefactor. Armand knew that gaze, which he had so often provoked; he was sure that no power on earth could prevent the grandmother from entrusting her child to him; she came to him like a night-flying moth to a light-source, stupidly and blindly.

No longer having anything to retain him, he stood up and picked up his hat.

"It's agreed," he said. "Arranged for the morning. I start at eight o'clock, You'll be there, won't you?"

He left without saying anything more, without a tender glance at his father's white hair. He was a stranger to effusion, the warm family embraces that charm the heart so much. He had never experienced the emotion of hugging the old paternal breast to his own, of pressing his lips upon that forehead faded by work, by the cares of existence, and perhaps the education of his son.

The old physician, it is true, scarcely attracted tenderness; his past of imprecise honor, his lack of altruism, and his soul on sale to all were not made to solicit effusion and left the field free for the abandonment of affection, but even if things had been different, Armand would not have felt his secret fibers stirring. He did not vibrate; his heart was only tickled by the satisfactions of self-esteem or cupidity. Outside of those sentiments, setting aside his aging mistress—but that was another complex sentiment, also formed by vanity, and carnal satisfaction—nothing moved him. His soul was refractory to any surge or impulse.

Caresco senior, left in the presence of the old woman, took a piece of paper and a pen and absorbed himself in calculations while watching his prey out of the corner of his eye. She was re-swaddling her treasure.

When she had finished, he said: "That will cost you two hundred francs."

Two hundred francs! The old woman shivered n fear.

"But Monsieur le docteur," she moaned, "I don't have two hundred francs! Oh, if I had them I'd gladly give them to you…and the rest too…but I don't have them, my poor Monsieur. Oh, how unhappy I am!"

She sobbed, resuming the regular rocking of her child. Caresco senior's nose moved toward to toothless mouth.

"One can't, however, always work for nothing," he said. "The other day, I lost two hundred francs at that game..." He resumed his original accent: "How much do you earn?"

"I earn three francs a day for doing housework, and I have eighty francs saved. I don't have another sou. I'm telling you the truth, my poor Monsieur."

Right! All was not lost. The Semite remade his calculations. By adjusting his figures, he estimated that the transaction might yet bring him a hundred francs. His heart was soothed.

"There!" he said. "You're going to give me your eighty francs and sign four promissory notes of twenty-five francs each payable over four months. Can things be arranged that way? I'm losing out, personally."

The old woman acquiesced. She could have been asked for twelve months hard labor and she would have agreed to it. The physician scribbled on pieces of paper, which the old woman signed awkwardly.

"Good! You can see that everything is arranged. We have good hearts, my son and I. Take your little girl at three o'clock tomorrow to the operating house in the Avenue Hoche. In the meantime, you can give her this.

He handed over a prescription, again recommending the neighboring pharmacist, and then let the old woman out through the door to the corridor. He rang for the uniformed domestic and told him to introduce another patient.

The waiting room was full. He continued his abominable work.

For his part, Armand, as soon as he left his father's house, had leapt into his victoria, shouting to the coachman: "Avenue Hoche, and quickly!"

His consultation period at the Avenue Hoche was from one o'clock until three, and—contrary to habit—he did not intend to be late. Usually, he left the care of the tedious work of consultation to his assistant, Dr. Bordier, and only arrived shortly before three o'clock, at the last minute, to examine a few patients that his aide had reserved for him, either because the diagnosis remained dubious or because his astonishing influence and persuasive talk was required to persuade those who were still hesitant to attempt the throw of the dice of the operation. Today, however, he had a meeting with Vicomtesse de Mesma, an old woman very well connected in society, on whom he had once operated to remove an ovarian cyst, and who was one of his best publicists.

The weather was radiant. A warm caress was descending from the trees in the Avenue Henri-Martin, refreshed by the water-jets of the municipal water-sprinklers.

Carriages went past Armand's victoria; he saluted them with a cheerful gesture and a pearly smile. He was well-known in the Passy quarter. He had a kind of local glory that the passers-by demonstrated.

After crossing the Place du Trocadéro and the Avenue Kléber, the carriage stopped at one of the houses in the Avenue Hoche, a large building of sumptuous appearance, displaying the luxury of six large windows on the outside. Here again Armand felt content on seeing the file of carriages stationed at his door. One of them bore the Vicomtesse de Mesma's coat of arms.

Nimbly, Armand leapt from the footstep before the vehicle had stopped and pulled the sculpted handle of the bell-rope. He was expected, for the massive door opened immediately; the powerful frame of a footman appeared in the gap, and then stood aside to let his master pass.

He went in quickly, without saying a word, glanced complacently at the large entrance that gave access to carriages, and then escaped briskly to the garden, at the back of which stood the elegant construction of the common.

Mentally, he compared the entrance to his clinic with his father's. Back there in the Rue Scheffer all was poverty and petty profits. However, he thought, the logic of the commerce was the same here as it was there, deriving from the driving force of disease—only the exploitation differed. Turning left, he climbed five white marble steps to the vestibule. A second footman did not leave him the trouble of opening the door.

The vestibule, the light of which was filtered by stained-glass windows, was sumptuously decorated with suits of armor and marble statues, outlined against ebony colonnettes. He went through it without bothering with the kindness of attention, only liking beautiful objects for the appearance of wealth that they gave to his house.

He was about to go into his consulting room, a large room on the first floor overlooking the Avenue Hoche, when the door opened from inside. His aide, Dr. Jean Bordier, appeared, letting out an old gentleman of military bearing, severely dressed in a black coat, on which a large rosette formed a red patch.

Caresco recognized the visitor; it was General de Rion, one of his former detractors, who had now become an enthusiastic defender since he had treated him.

"Bonjour, General," he said "Are you feeling better?"

The general pulled a face, muttering explanations. Still that damned prostate tormenting him, and swollen legs too.

In his turn, Dr. Bordier explained: "I've examined him. The prostate is still hard and hypertrophic; the general is suffering; medical means are not succeeding."

The surgeon leaned against the door-jamb. He seemed to reflect momentarily. The general awaited the master's words anxiously, seeking his gaze, which fled, annoyed by the smile creasing his lips.

Caresco understood the old man's nervousness, seeing him twisting the tip of his white moustache. "You see, General," he said. "You didn't want to believe me— it's necessary to resort to the scalpel."

"The scalpel doesn't frighten me. I've already been skewered several times after being wounded, notably in the Crimea—damn it, what a storm that was! What I fear is the after-effects of the scalpel. I've been told that the operation you're proposing—the section…what do you call it?"

"The resection of the *vas deferens*."[4]

"That's it—the resection of the vas difference..."

"Pardon me," Caresco interjected, "but it's *deferens…deferens*."

---

[4] It is not obvious that a vasectomy would have any effect on a hypertrophied prostate, but prior to 1899 prostate problems had sometimes been treated surgically by castration, albeit without any discernible benefit, and vasectomy—which was beginning to attract attention as a method of sterilization potentially applicable in eugenic programs that were then being ardently promoted—probably seemed to be a kinder option, especially to patients worried about the side-effects of castration.

"I accept correction…out of deference," the old warrior replied, with a smile. "Well, I've been told that that operation won't change my condition at all. So, you understand…"

The surgeon protested. The operation, carried out by experienced hands, was indeed quite harmful; but carried out by him, that was something else. In any case, he general had only to seek information from certain patients on which he had undertaken the same operation. Then again, there was nothing else to be done.

The general was decidedly impossible to convince; he had never encountered anyone who raised so many difficulties before allowing himself to be convinced.

"Then again," he said, "if the operation were serious, I'd understand your hesitation—but it's just a simple little cut here, in the vicinity of the groin." Sure of himself, he indicated the place with his index fingers, after dropping his trousers. "The consequences are always benign. You ought to understand that, being an intelligent man; you ought to have confidence in what I say, knowing as you do that I don't operate for the pleasure of operating. All your friends will tell you that…ask the Vicomtesse de Mesma."

At the name of the Vicomtesse, the general smiled. Already ill, he had only had a totally platonic intrigue with her, a septuagenarian flirtation, which had surprised him somewhat—but not overmuch—and which had led his making the young surgeon's acquaintance, when, in despair at seeing the futility of the treatments employed for the cure of his ailment, he had allowed his great friend to bring him to Caresco.

"Yes," he said, "the Vicomtesse de Mesma never stops saying good things about you. She confessed to me yesterday that you had carried out an extraordinary operation on her. She's there now, in your reception room."

Caresco held out his hand. "Then I must hurry, because she doesn't like to be kept hanging around. *Au revoir*, General."

The general left, as if regretfully. The surgeon went into his consulting room, followed by Bordier. It was a rectangular room with two large windows overlooking the avenue, furnished with a more sober taste than the vestibule, but nevertheless very luxurious. Gobelins tapestries representing mythological scenes covered the walls, causing two marvelously expensive and elegant bookshelves to stand out even more. Like the worktable, they were made of solid mahogany encrusted with copper. In a corner, near a window, was a chaise-longue covered with antique Oriental upholstery.

As soon as Bordier had closed the door, Caresco sat down at his desk. Mechanically, he riffled through a numerous accumulation of letters that Bordier had already unsealed: emotional letters of thanks; dry letters veiling anger, which contained the settlement of bills on behalf of individuals on who he had operated—and killed; and respectful letters from provincial colleagues asking for meetings or advertising patients, commencing with the words "*Cher maître…*" a phrase that always tickled the ambitious eyes of the surgeon agreeably. The letters had been summarized by Bordier in a couple of lines, sometimes with a single word.

"Nothing new, then," said Caresco, finally, having run through his assistant's blue-penciled notes.

"Nothing."

"How is the patient I operated on yesterday doing?"

"Which one? Three women had operations yesterday."

Armand shrugged his shoulders. Bordier knew perfectly well that when he referred to the person he had operated on the previous day he meant Baronne Spirs, on whom he had carried out a hysterectomy. The other two women did not count; only the Baronne had commercial value.

"Well," said Bordier, adjusting his gold-rimmed spectacles, yesterday evening she was doing well, but she had a bad night, and at ten o'clock, she started shivering."

"Is she on her way out?"

"It's probable."

Caresco shook the table with a violent blow of his fist; his brow furrowed. In front of his assistant he did not suppress his gestures or his words.

"That's annoying, Bordier, you know—the Baronne! That's going to lose me several operations. Something's been the matter with the recovery rooms for some time. There was the twelve—you know, the suppurating kidney cyst. The five and the seven died of infection—infection, you hear, my dear chap!—and now the Baronne, a miserable hysterectomy, who's going to croak too. What's going on in there? I'll need to have the place disinfected, you know. The walls are putrid with microbes. It's annoying!"

He meditated for a moment, but without a hunt of concern. For some time, his scalpel appeared to have been subject to a streak of bad luck. He was going through one of those inexplicable black patches that, without any apparent reason, follow happier sequences—but never before had one been so prolonged.

He searched for a cause, in vain. It would have been comprehensible once, in his father's house, the wretched and insalubrious lodgings in the Rue Scheffer, but here, in the most sumptuous clinic in Paris, where all the rooms were well-ventilated, where the gleaming parquets could not conceal the slightest grain of dust without it being perceived, where everything was arranged according to the most absolute regime of antisepsis, and where everything, from the depths of the cellar to the eaves was swept, dusted, scrubbed and polished in a constant war against infectious germs—here, in this veritable palace, the mere sight of which excited the laudatory exclamations of visitors, in this purified environment—it was truly inexplicable.

Was it because, wanting to maintain his reputation as a brilliant operator, he went too quickly, doing too many operations at a time, and not taking, in that flesh race, the extremely scrupulous care and infinite precautions with which every surgeon had to surround himself? No—he carefully maintained his reputation as the most hygienic practitioner in Paris as well as the most skillful. Each of his operating sessions was monitored by too many eyes, often malevolent—the eyes of colleagues who would have been glad of an opportunity to criticize—for him not to observe himself rigorously.

It was necessary, then, to attribute these astonishing series of successes or failures down to chance, to the organization of hazard thanks to which bad operations presented themselves simultaneously, as did the good ones: the petty secondary circumstances that, in combination, could decide the fate of the operation being favorable at some times and unfavorable at others.

Yes, his judgment stopped at such an astonishing appreciation. He did not want to admit it; unlike many of his colleagues, who only cut into the flesh if success was evidently probable, he operated on all those who came to his scalpel.

Sitting at the desk, with his head supported in a hand to delicate to be that of a surgeon, his forehead intelligent and his eyes thoughtful and candid behind the mirror of his spectacles, Bordier, leaving the young master to his meditations, was reflecting on his own account. Yes, decidedly, too many people were dying in the clinic. In the three months since he had accepted the functions, envied by so many others, of being Armand Caresco's collaborator, the back door of the house had already opened to coffins on many occasions. Why had he come to take his place beside the celebrated surgeon? How had he let himself be convinced by the persuasive and enveloping speech of that skillful seducer?

He would, alas, have been able to make the same reply and give the same reason as others, his predecessors, notably the last of them, Dr. Savre: the urgent need to live. How, when the plethora of physicians and the exaggerated development of gratuitous care and mutual societies made money scarce, when he had no personal fortune and parents who had bled themselves dry in supplying a dowry for a rich marriage, when the landlord held out his hand, the butcher complained and the tailor refused to deliver for lack of money, could one not listen with a grateful ear to the propositions of a colleague who had arrived and become famous—and who would bring you, by the simple fact of collaboration, along with any easy life, a relative celebrity?

After serious studies at the Collège Stanislas, Bordier, whose father was then rich, moved by a need for labor and for science, had studied medicine. The first steps on that path had not been without a certain disgust offered to his delicate nature by the dissection of cadavers, but everything can be overcome, everything becomes habit. He had been able to penetrate the amphitheaters of dissection, attach his palpitating intelligence to the study of anatomy, to overcome the fragility of his nerves to the point of suffering, without falling inanimate, the emanations of the thirty or forty fragmented cadavers that lay on the stones, and, above all, to see without dying himself the horror of butchered limbs and open bellies, and the frightful grimaces of physiognomies denatured by death.

What will-power he had required, too, to support the contact of sick people in the hospitals, place his ear upon the wheezing thoracic cavities, palpate dirty limbs and bandage wounds bathed in fetid pus. Everything had offended the delicate education of his senses: touching sticky flesh, tumors that were deepening frightfully, and breathing in the presence of all that human putrescence, while thinking that the act of breathing   was introducing a little of it into oneself.

Alongside those horrors, which exasperated his physical sensibility, it had also been necessary to vanquish the sentiments they provoked, to support the display of moral lapses and the miseries that causes them. Rich then, cradled in the quietude of fortune and luxury, he had had to assimilate the comprehension of poverty, to get used to the repugnant idea of obscure hovels where numerous families huddled, where maladies and vices were transmitted from parents to children. He calculated those misfortunes; unlike his comrades, who passed them by indifferently, he soothed them with his advice and his purse.

Later, progressively, he had acquired the habit of those heart-rending contacts; his soul was less bruised by them, less wounded. Then he became as indifferent as his comrades, and isolated himself definitively in the passion of scientific research. With joy, clad in a white smock, he penetrated into the vast wards of patients, following his master's visits, content to listen at the foot of each bed to the scientific discourse. The sick person became a subject, before whom he made the abstraction of the moral individual.

Finally, there were the hard hours of the work of preparation in the concourse of the hospital internship, the prolonged period of sleeplessness, during which he accumulated in his active memory the summaries of the questions of examination, a stupid labor of recitation in which no preponderance was accorded to intelligence and personality, in which memory was the only intellectual capacity employed. On, those avid nights on which, alone in his room, in absolute concentration, he had isolated himself in that sterile task, reddening his eyes reading scribbled notes and waiting the first rays of dawn to throw himself, defeated and brutalized, upon his bed, and sometimes continuing his mental overwork in enervated slumber!

In the first year he had landed on his feet, after having succeeded in the ordeals of admissibility; in the second year he had won the right to wear the black velvet cap, the distinctive sign of interns, an emblem accorded to the conceit of those young scientists, a vestige of the pointed bonnet of old. Only then did he harvest the fruits of the seeds sown, profiting from the accumulation of the questions of internship.

Every morning for four years he spent hours at the hospital, in collaboration with famous masters. The first year, at the Lariboisière, he entered into the medical service of Professor Cartaux. He had acquired sage principles there under the direction of a master he loved to follow, for his studiousness, his intelligence and the thoughtful limpidity of the blue eyes behind his spectacles. The ward was neat and clean, marvelously maintained by nurses and a supervisor. The external students he had under his orders were serious and hard-working. He gave them lessons, teaching them what he knew himself; he was well-liked by them, and by his patients. In the afternoons he went to study bacteriology in the laboratories of the Faculté or the Institut Pasteur.

It was a peaceful and happy year—but medicine seemed to him to be fruitless; his delicate nature wanted to accord itself to brutal surgery, whose results appeared to him to be more reliable and more immediate. The other three years of his internship were therefore spent in surgical services. There, the work was more active, incessantly renewed. There was one at the Hôtel-Dieu with an honest and prudent surgeon; one at the Charité with a brilliant and carefree operator; finally, his fourth year was spent with a celebrated professor, much occupied by his clientele and his work, who left his interns an absolute initiative.

He carried out numerous operations during that final phase of his student life. Fearful at first, his hand became firmer and bolder. In rotation, the interns in a hospital work twenty-four hour shifts; avid for his day on duty, he often took the days of others. In that fashion he learned emergency surgery; his education was complete.

It was during that final year of internship that his father had died, completely ruined; it never became known how that death had occurred; he kept the secret of frightful death-throes in a wrecked room, on the carpet of which there was a small-caliber revolver in the middle of a sinister pool of blood. That catastrophe had rendered him poor. He was forced to make a trade out of what he had wanted to make an art.

He had nursed his hard work with the dream of competing for the hospitals, for a professorship, but once his internship was complete he was obliged to install himself in a poor quarter of Paris. The numerous poorly remunerated visits he made were insufficient to nourish him, and, too proud to go complaining of his poverty to his former masters, who would have helped him, he often wept over his foundered fortune, his collapsed illusions.

In Paris, physicians who want to remain honest need to have enough to live on while waiting for a clientele; he remained honest in spite of his lack of resources—which is to say that he had to struggle bitterly against miserable worries. He was the laborer who, for a problematic reward, climbed up to the sixth floor of houses, who, all day long, traveled the little streets with greasy cobblestones, going past obscure houses whose corridors and shops gave off the damp reek of poverty and alcohol. He was the humble individual who, by reason of his humility, is treated condescendingly and exploited, and whom one does not pay.

After three years he had competed for a job as a physician in a charitable organization and won. That was twelve hundred francs a year falling into his purse; he began to breathe. At the same time, his reputation for charity and science won him a few rich clients and better-rewarded visits. Success was finally commencing to smile on him when he met Armand Caresco.

The later was looking for an assistant, the one he had then, Dr. Savre, having notified him, without any plausible reason, that he was leaving. Bordier was seduced by the proposition of the young surgeon, who offered him twenty thousand francs a year, on condition that the occupied himself exclusively with his sanitarium. The surgeon's reputation was known to him, but he was ignorant of his moral value. He accepted, resigned from the charity, quit his clientele and his quarter, and came to take up residence in a small entresol in the Avenue Hoche, delighted to recover a little of his former luxury and also to devote himself once again to surgery, the science of his predilection.

And now, here he was, confronted by the sinister list of the operational results of the sanitarium, the so-oft-repeated mourning that darkened the joy of his studies, the operative fury for which, being naïve, simple and good, he had not yet understood the motive, even though he was beginning to divine it. Here he was, gripped by a kind of fear of this sanguinary collaboration, and glimpsing the possibility of an abrupt abandonment of his present situation, as Dr. Savre had done, and a return to his form life of obscure labor, in which, after difficult days in which physical exhaustion was compounded by cerebral fatigue, he was not sure of having earned enough to meet his needs.

Someone knocked. Caresco shouted an invitation to enter in a voice that still contained a residue of anger. The footman appeared, announcing that Madame de Mesma, in something of a hurry, was asking to be seen without delay. At a sign from the surgeon, the Vicomtesse was introduced. She entered with a smiling expression, her hands extended toward her young friend. Then, perceiving Bordier, she suspended her enthusiasm.

"Dr. Bordier, my new assistant," said Caresco. And, as the presence of that third party threatened to be unwelcome, he added: "Bordier, will you please leave us alone momentarily; I need to talk to Madame la Vicomtesse in private. Go and see Baronne Spirs; give

81

her an injection of serum, and above all, prevent her from receiving visitors."

Bordier left, slightly astonished to have been dismissed. Generally, he was present even during the non-medical conversations that took place in the consulting room.

Left alone with the surgeon, the Vicomtesse de Mesma offered him her hands again. "My dear friend…my savior…how are you?"

She sat down in a high-backed Cordovan leather armchair, facing the surgeon. She was aristocratic in her bearing, with lively and malicious eyes violently marked with crows'-feet, a pointed and malevolent nose and a jaundiced complexion whose withering clever make-up could not succeed in hiding. Her face gave the impression of a life filled with adventures and bruised by enjoyments. Formidable rumors had run around on her account, and she had been mixed up in the intrigues of the Boulangist movement. She was still received in certain salons, however, by reason of her great name, her marvelous urbanity and the fear she inspired in certain individuals whose secrets she possessed and who wanted her to keep them.

So, installed in her armchair, at ease, calm and gracious with the man who had cured her, she asked: "Well, how is that young Baronne doing? That's what I came to see you about."

"The Baronne is done for."

At that vulgar expression the Vicomtesse started, expressing her astonishment at such language with a significant moue. To repair the disaster, Caresco entered into explanations.

"You understand, Vicomtesse, that I'm very annoyed by that. The Baronne's case was particularly grave, and although the operation was carried out with the skill that you know I..."

"Oh, that's true—you're a genius," the lady thought it appropriate to interject, "and if you haven't succeeded, who could have?"

"There were such complications," Armand continued, "that I was astonished to be able to continue the operation...I've never had such a difficult hysterectomy."

He was lying shamelessly.

"Really?" said the Vicomtesse. But what did the complications of the Baronne's operation matter to her? She straightened the upper part of the body against the back of the armchair and followed the patterns in the carpet with the tip of her umbrella. Then, without looking at her interlocutor, she said: "And...have you been paid?"

"Yes, immediately after the operation."

"I said that that was the custom of the house. Four thousand francs, wasn't it?"

"That's right. By the way, my dear Vicomtesse, permit me to thank you for your obliging aid..."

He took a envelope out of his pocket containing a thousand-franc bill, which he handed to the tout. The dying woman's money did not seem unduly heavy in the spare fingers. The fingers in question swiftly buried the envelope in the mysterious depths of a handbag.

Every time she received similar remunerations for her secret services, Caresco admired the superb, entirely aristocratic ease with which she accepted them. Very observant, he thought that no one of his own race would have had such elegance in prehension, in grabbing something while maintaining the appearance of wanting to let it escape. His conversion to the Catholic religion had not varnished him with such an apparent disinterest in monetary matters. He stored the gesture in his memory.

"There's something else," the Vicomtesse went on. "I've brought you—and I mean that they're in the reception room—the wife and son of a rich farmer from the North. The son has had a coxalgia since birth.[5] I ought to tell you that it would be preferable not to talk about the operation immediately. These people are quite backward, you know." In a lower voice, still in a detached tone, just as she had taken the thousand-franc bill before, she added: "You can ask for two or three thousand, I think. They're miserly, but rich. He's their only child. Have them come in—I'll have to go soon; I have a charity sale at three o'clock."

The farmer's wife was introduced. She was pushing ahead of her a child whose gait was awkwardly contorted. She was red-faced and robust; grease was emerging from the pores of her nose, spreading out in a shiny glaze. Very confused, petrified by the grandiose appearance of the house, the livery of the servants, the luxury of the tapestries and the furniture, by the presence of the Vicomtesse and the cold expression of the surgeon, she became tangled up in explanations. Yes, there had been a fall...not a fall, but a disturbance during the pregnancy. She was lost in confusion.

---

[5] Coxalgia, as the word suggests, means a pain in the coccyx or general pelvic area, and is nowadays used in that conscientiously vague sense. At the time when the novel was written, however, it carried a heavier burden of implication, being linked by contemporary conviction with tuberculosis, as were many symptoms that can now be recognized as having various causes.

Caresco asked her to undress the child. When he was naked, he made him walk back and forth, then said: "Who told you that your child had a coxalgia?"

"Our local physician."

"Well, personally, I don't believe it is a coxalgia. It's what is called a congenital dislocation of the hip. It can be cured by...." He was about to say "an operation," but the Vicomtesse rolled her steely eyes. He understood and continued: "a method of my own. Would you care to leave your child here for a time under treatment?"

The rubicund face of the farmer's wife expanded. The frightening spectacle of the scalpel had not been raised before her eyes, and her child did not have a coxalgia, he only had a dislocation. Her local physician, an obscure officer of health, was mistaken. That news was well worth the trip to Paris and she did not regret having abandoned the cows' milk and the chickens' eggs.

She expressed a desire to remain with the patient. Nothing simpler; two rooms would be put at their disposal; it was just a matter of paying a double fee. The farmer's wife accepted, and then, at Armand's invitation, dressed the child again.

"I'll go now that my role is complete," said the Vicomtesse de Mesma. Turning to the weary rustic, she added: "You can see that you'll be well cared for here, and your son even better." Aristocratically ceremonious, she extended her hand to the surgeon, who got up to escort her to the door. Before going out, she said: "Look after my young friend Baronne Spirs, and send her back to me cured, won't you?"

The two accomplices parted with a glance of tacit understanding. Then, the child being dressed again, Caresco offered to give the farmer's wife a tour of the house. Ordinarily he left that to Soeur Cunégonde, the supervisor of the eight sisters he had in his service, but as he wanted to go to see the Baronne anyway, whose condition was worsening, he invited the countrywoman to follow him.

They went up the staircase, whose wrought-iron railings and white marble steps, cutting through an Oriental gallery, influenced the mind of the farmer's wife, alarming her economy. She would gladly have run back down that luxurious stairway to flee the sum would have to pay out, but the hopping gait of her son, who was climbing up painfully, incited her to continue, and she was torn between the fear of her eroded savings and the lameness of her offspring.

On the upper floor the luxury became more sober. Two corridors opened to the right and the left, with numbered doors.

"I have sixty beds," Caresco said. "Every room has a bathroom, and there are connecting rooms, in case relatives want, as you do, to remain with the patients. I'll show you one of the rooms; they're all constructed on the same model."

He asked a passing maidservant where there was a vacant room. She indicated number six. Followed by the farmer's wife and her limping boy, he turned into a corridor, stopped in front of the door in question, knocked, and, when there was no rely, went in. A frightful scene caused him to close the door again abruptly—but not quickly enough, for the farmer's wife had seen something horribly tragic, and she was gripped by terror.

Emerging from the curtains of a bed, a head had appeared to her, waxen in complexion, with hair that descended like a veil over the agony of the face, the prominent cheekbones and eyes veiled by the ashes of death. The mouth that was open to let out gasps and the hand, whose fingers were clutching at an imaginary object, still indicated the final struggle for life.

Kneeling next to the bed, two sisters were praying, and in the background, Bordier, in a white smock, in the transparency of the window, was gazing by daylight at the coloration of a liquid serum with which he had filled a large syringe, with which he was preparing to make a subcutaneous injection.

It was a spectacle that struck the farmer's wife with fear. Greatly embarrassed, the surgeon summoned the maidservant and said, harshly: "I asked you for an empty room—did you not understand?"

"I meant to say ten," the maidservant stammered.[6]

There was, indeed, no one in number ten. Caresco exhibited a bright, cheerful room overlooking the green foliage of the garden. That sight effaced the earlier scene. The farmer's wife smiled at the walnut-wood furniture and the onyx clock.

"And the fees?" she asked, becoming serious again.

"Oh, I don't occupy myself with that," Caresco replied. "Arrange it with Soeur Cunégonde. Here she is now."

Indeed, a sister with a white head-dress framing a fat acne-strewn face had slipped silently into the room.

Soeur Cunégonde was one of the pillars of the surgeon's sanitarium. Remarkable intelligent and acute, she had had been in Armand Caresco's service for six years, and possessed all the diplomacy and savoir-faire of her master, for whom she had had a kind of adoration since she had aided, or believed she had aided, his conversion

---

[6] It is easier, in French, to confuse *dix* and *six*, than a parallel mistake would be in English.

to the Catholic religion. Marvelously endowed with intellectual flexibility, she had quickly adapted to the practices of antiseptic surgery, and by virtue of her activity, her preparatory skills and her zeal during operations, had succeeded in acquiring an authority over Caresco's mind that was advantageous to both of them.

The surgeon appreciated her, because she was indispensable to him. They were like two accomplices, lending their courage and abilities to the same cause, which consisted for the one of serving his personal interests and for the other in serving the community to which she was attached. Of an unexaggerated piety, and a cool and constant activity, she was, with a different objective, as accurate in calculation and as interested as Caresco.

Armored by her profession, she remained indifferent to the suffering of the poor wretches that came into the homicidal house to serve as subjects for the young surgeon's experiments, but she had an astonishing compassion for the tribulations of the rich. He acne-ridden face did not pale at a death to which she had implicitly contributed; her pulse-rate did not increase and no anguish gripped her throat; but she had such a fashion of crying after an unfortunate result: "God has recalled her!" that the exclamation disarmed all hearts.

She had an intuition of the degree of grief that the families of the deceased were experiencing, and, basing her judgment on the verity or the fiction of that grief, always knew whether to say nothing or to offer her condolences—banal, to be sure, but those to which one always listens in moments of rude suffering. With an extreme skill, enveloping the temporary residents with seemingly irrelevant questions, she penetrated their intimate lives, their relations, their fortunes; she entered into their state of mind by means of a slow violation of their thoughts, and took possession of information that was often useful to her master.

She did not say much, but was very active, without ostentation, like a hand in the shadows. Nothing is the house remained unperceived by her, even things that she had never seen. Everything pivoted around her, and she gradually assumed the importance of an axle around which a machine turns.

In the depths of her soul, while sometimes suspecting that she was giving impetus to a frightful mechanism, she nevertheless devoted herself to the realization of a benevolent work—useful, at any rate, to the community of which she was the obscure and powerful servant. Under her orders, eight other sisters and the domestics were occupied in caring for the patients, maintaining vigils, cooking and cleaning. Caresco had understood the prestige that the presence of the sisters could offer him when a ferocious reaction had expelled them from the hospitals.

"Sister, would you be good enough to take care of this young patient, who is going to be staying with us for a while?"

Soeur Cunégonde had already embraced the young cripple. Caresco made a sign to her and drew her into the embrasure of a window.

"Well, the Baronne is a lost cause," he said. "Has the family been informed?"

"I've sent for the abbé to administer extreme unction, but the family hasn't been told."

"Do so quickly, Sister—it's time."

"A doctor came a little while ago; he's the Baronne's physician. He wanted to see her. I refused, on the pretext that it's not a custom of the house."

"You did well, Sister. Colleagues must never…that's all I need!"

As her master did not seem to be in a good mood, Soeur Cunégonde dared not tell him that the physician had gone away furious, proclaiming that he would tell the Baron everything.

Caresco left the farmer's wife in the grip of the pious servant. He went along the corridor, his footsteps muffled by the carpet. As he went past the Baronne's door, he could still hear the sound of groaning, disturbing the peace of the corridor. It was the Baronne uttering her last plaints.

He shrugged his shoulders. What did one more death matter to him? Had he not done everything he could to preserve the creature's life? In truth, perhaps one might have dispensed with an operation, but that would have meant no more of a life for the poor woman than spending day after day lying on a chaise-longue. Then again, it would also liberate her husband, whom the company of an ever-suffering spouse would have plunged into an abyss of constant desolation.

In sum, logically, he had done well in attempting the operation, since its success would have cured the invalid, and in failing, he was saving her from a world of bitterness and pain.

Taking his reflections further, he considered himself a useful force. The work of death accomplished, the cadaver would be returned to the humus and would disintegrate in obscure conflicts, becoming pasture for new animal evolutions, infinitely small, which would be annihilated in their turn, melting into the earth to permit the birth of new beings. Death, which he assisted, served prey to life, in a monstrous cycle that destroyed some in order to create others.

Thus it was that he, Armand Caresco, played his role in Creation.

He went back down to his consulting room to continue his beneficent work.

Up above, Soeur Cunégonde haggled over prices with the farmer's wife, while the lame boy hung on to his mother's skirts, in tears at having to inhabit that calm and empty room, sensing fear and the unknown stir round his tender soul.

An ultimate cry of anguish from number six reached their ears.

CHAPTER VI

Soeur Cunégonde, who monitored everything, came up from the basement where she had gone to inspect the boiler, which was only lit in that warm season in order to heat the operating theater. That morning, Armand Caresco was conducting an operating session to which he had invited a considerable number of foreign surgeons attracted to Paris by the surgical conference.

When she reached the vestibule, Soeur Cunégonde opened a door opposite that of the reception room and went into a simple, narrow room which, solely furnished with a bed on wheels, was used exclusively for putting patients to sleep. She went to interrogate a thermometer attaché to the wall, and, observing that the temperature was not elevated, went to put her hand over the heating vent that was emitting warm effluvia in a corner. The current bathed her hand; she lingered in that warm caress for a minute, pleasant at the beginning of September. Then she went into the operating theater next door, pausing on the threshold to gaze at the ensemble.

It was there that Armand Caresco had set out on display all the luxury, so costly in its simplicity, of the surgical apparatus. There were no more tapestries, no more curtains, no more gilt, and no more furniture ornamented with futile sculptures, and yet, the eye was immediately seduced by the clean white harmony that everything emitted.

The operating theater was a room between eight and ten meters long and as many wide. The walls, rounded at the corners in order not to give any purchase to the dust that contained gems of infection, were varnished with white paint, and on one side, a large window fitted with frosted glass let in considerable daylight, further augmented by that of a skylight in the ceiling.

Sunk into the wall, a chamber for the sterilization of instruments added the bright note of its nickel. Placed methodically, white marble tables were aligned, covered by sterilized sheets, preciously protected by an impermeable envelope, and other tables, on which metal boxes filled with sterilized compresses were disposed, with trays designed to receive the instruments emerging from the sterilizer when the operation began.

In one corner, there was an autoclave for the disinfection of linen, and two wheeled carts with fountains containing antiseptic liquids for the surgeon's hands. In an alcove next to the entrance door there was a bright white marble wash-basin, impeccably clean, with two taps for hot and cold water. Finally, in the middle, the adjustable operating table with its extended leg-guards and its system of nickeled handles and shiny gears.

In sum, there was nothing frightening in all that for the eye of someone in need of an operation. So Soeur Cunégonde gazed at the apparatus with interest, admiring above all the meticulous cleanliness of the remotest corners, the mosaic surfaces so easily washable, over which it was sufficient to pass a damp sponge after reach operation to remove the bloodstains and the human debris, and return them to their initial cleanliness.

She also inspected the operating table, which seemed so elegantly constructed, easily mobile in all directions, perfected in its slightest details and able to give the body of a patient the most various positions, in accordance with the necessities of the surgical intervention. She experienced a certain contentment at that spectacle, like a factory worker in love with his work considering with joy the mechanisms that power his tools, or a painter gazing with satisfaction at the palette and brushes that are to aid his art.

Pressed for time, however, she undertook her customary tasks, arranging the bowls and the cloths, methodically putting the tables in their customary places, turning the rack of the operating table to raise it up slightly. Then, remembering that she had forgotten the scalpel, which was only disinfected at the last moment in order not to wear away the blade, she ran to the consulting room and came back with a box full of metal scalpels. She picked out several, tried the blades lightly on the skin of her index finger and then, having chosen one, she went to plunge it is a saucepan full of phenol that was boiling on a gas burner beside the sterilizer.

At that moment, someone knocked on the door, which opened to allow the appearance of an opulent mass, corpulent and bearded, surmounted by vast gold-rimmed spectacles and a top hat. It was a professor from Vienna by the name of Stermann, a surgeon celebrated in his homeland; passing through Paris he had come to watch Caresco operate. He came forward, holding out a visiting card to Soeur Cunégonde, who did not seem surprised by his arrival.

Foreign physicians often introduced themselves, attracted by Caresco's renown—he was more famous abroad than in France, thanks to his discreet advertising, his publications in the journals of all nations, and his presence at international conferences at which French surgeons generally neglected to appear. No operation took place in his sanitarium without Caresco having a few exotic individuals around him.

He welcomed them in the most amiable fashion, showing himself full of concern and gratitude for them, showing them displays of curious anatomical specimens collected during his operations, knowing facts about each of his visitors, citing results analogous to theirs, always omitting to talk about his Parisian colleagues—the official scientists of the Faculté—or only mentioning them in order to take casual swipes at them, which brought an amiable smile to the lips of his listeners, for human nature is made in such a way that even distant glories always annoy local glories. Then, when they had been seduced by his charming attentions and dazzled by his operating skills, he often took them to dinner in some fashionable cabaret, continuing his work of fraternization with good food and wine.

When he was dealing with young people, future luminaries, he took them to Mathilde's house for lunch; the food was less succulent and less costly, but the beautiful Tripe-merchant compensated for that defect with her usual camaraderie, with equal attentions and sometimes also with furtive hours of amour in some furnished hotel—sacrifices to her lover's success, a devotion that swelled the savings she was squirreling away in secret. And all of them returned to their homelands with the name of Caresco on their lips, recommending their colleagues not to neglect, in their visits to the surgeons of Paris, the opportunity to watch the young French surgeon operate in his sanitarium.

That inflated his glory and augmented his fortune. Invalids from all nations were sent to him for consultations by the physicians he welcomed so graciously. Instead of simply giving his advice regarding the desirability of an operation, he surrounded these patients with cares, took possession of their will by virtue of the power of suggestion that radiated from his person and his speech, and, having sufficiently talked them round, operated on them. Sometimes, the foreign colleague was annoyed and wrote an indignant letter protesting against such methods, but Caresco always succeeded in excusing his conduct under the pretext of a complication that required an urgent intervention.

Meanwhile, the large individual with the vast gold-rimmed spectacles was having difficulty making Soeur Cunégonde understand. "Caresco...Caresco..." he jabbered. "Not French...not French..."

The sister beckoned to him to follow her. She took him into the reception room and left him there alone, gesturing toward an armchair in which he sat down heavily.

When the sister returned to the operating theater she found Bordier, who had just arrived, in the process of washing his hands at the basin. His jacket set aside, and his sleeves rolled up, he was scrubbing his arms and hands vigorously; soap foam was flying on to the parquet. The pallor of a bad night, entirely consecrated to the bitterness of the reflections suggested to him by the death of Baronne Spirs, further accentuated the thinness of his features. He watched the acne-ridden face of Soeur Cunégonde come in, scarcely responded to her *bonjour*, and no longer had the strength to address to her the few amiable words with which he usually gratified her.

An accomplice, that one, he said to himself, and it pained him to add: *like me*.

He applied a file to his fingernails, carefully, and then plunged his hands into a solution of sublimate, twice.[7]

At least, he though, as he exaggerated these antiseptic precautions, *if any harm is done, it won't be my fault.*

He turned to Soeur Cunégonde, his forearms held apart from his body, avoiding wiping them.

"Let's see, Sister, what have we to do this morning?"

"One kidney, two livers, a fibroma, a hysterectomy for a fibroma, a tubercular tumor on the foot, a resection of the shoulder and a skull," Soeur Cunégonde listed. "You know—the little girl who has meningitis? Her grandmother brought her yesterday evening, on behalf of Monsieur Caresco's father."

Bordier had counted eight operations. "That will be a lot for one morning. Anyway, we'll do what we can."

He went to the sterilizer and opened the nickeled doors. Long flames of gas maintained a microbicidal heat there. Instruments of various firms—pincers of all dimensions, straight and curved needles, long and short separators, large and small probes, valves, curettes, scissors, gouges, hammers and saws, trocars and rasps, bizarre steel rods contorted according to the necessities of their usage and the imagination of inventors—disposed on iron latticework trays were receiving the immunity of asepsis pell-mell. With the aid of forceps, which he employed in order not to infect the instruments and not to be burned by them, Bordier selected a certain quantity from the heap and submerged them in trays filled with

---

[7] "Corrosive sublimate" (mercuric chloride) was widely used at the time as an antiseptic, but its use was abandoned because of its excessive toxicity to humans.

boiling phenol, the vapors of which impregnated the room, gripping the throat.

He inspected the sterilized compresses, the padding in the large nickel boxes, the antiseptic liquids in the mobile carts, and then prepared the threads of catgut and silk for the ligature of vessels, and horsehair for stitches. Then, having nothing further to do, he put on a white smock whose sleeves only came down to the elbows and sat on a stool to await Armand Caresco.

His eyes fell upon a large ivory Christ set above the door, who seemed, by the lamentable gesture of his crucifixion, to be protecting that apparatus, as grim as a torture chamber in the times of the Inquisition. Derision! It was in his name, under his cover, that the surgeon carried out his hazardous work!

In the vestibule, people were arriving. Introduced by a footman, they went to wait in the reception room. The bell rang repeatedly. Soeur Cunégonde was gladdened by that influx; her face blossomed.

"There will be a large audience," she said. "That's good. But Monsieur Caresco is late. He must have called in at the church to pray to the Lord to accord him success."

And she began to tell her rosary beads.

Finally, Caresco appeared, apologizing for being late. His father, who was with him, had gone to join the crowd in the reception room, to ask them to be patient.

"Quickly, Sister, have the fibroma sent down. Bordier, be kind enough to begin the chloroform while I wash and change."

A woman of about forty, with a bulging abdomen, and a face thinned out by malady and fear, came down, supported by two sisters, her legs weak. She was undressed in the next room and hoisted on to the bed. Her enormous abdomen formed a bump under the chemise. Bordier applied the chloroform compress; a glimmer of infinite anguish passed through her eyes. She began to breathe noisily, struggled, rebelling with all the congested and vociferous tension of her being. Wisps of gray hair scattered, and she sank into an abysmal world from which she believed that she would never return.

After having lifted the patient's arm, which fell back inertly, in complete resolution, he palpated the insensitivity of the cornea. Then he abandoned the chloroform compress to a sister and pushed the temporary bed of slumber toward the operating theater. The woman, heavy with the entire weight of her inertia, was deposited on the bed of the operating table; her legs were attached to the sleeves of the table-legs, her arms knotted so that she could not struggle—and Caresco, finally scrubbed, clad in a huge apron of waxed cloth, like an abattoir-worker, judging that he could begin work, left the room to go and fetch the foreigners.

"Come in, come in, Messieurs," he cried, opening the door of the reception room, calming the impatience of the long wait with his presence.

The guests passed into the operating theater one by one. The surgeon, remaining close to the door to the vestibule, guided them with his voice and gestures…that way, and to the right...

To some, whom he knew, he extended the limpness of his hand; to others, unknown practitioners brought he knew not how, strangers who might not even be physicians—journalists, students or mere lovers of tragic spectacles—he accorded a slight inclination of the head, his eyes always fugitive.

That day, his famous reputation had attracted more than usual: about thirty. The frock-coats or black jackets, some bearing exotic decorations, group themselves in such a fashion as not to miss any of the young master's gestures. In the meantime, he went to the wash-basin, and, the sleeves of his shirt having been rolled up by Soeur Cunégonde and fixed by means of special pins, he completed a final scrubbing of his arms and hands by steeping them in a solution of sublimate. Then, without wiping them, in order not to reinfect himself and to keep himself impregnated by antisepsis, they went to the operating table, on which the patient was continuing her noisy sleep, with the cornet of chloroform surmounting her pale face, over her nose.

Bordier finished cleaning the abdomen, preparing the operational area. After having swept the abdomen and the vulva with a razor, he soaped the skin until it was red, bathed it in a solution of phenol, dried it with sterilized compresses that he took out of a nickel box as needed. Finally, he surrounded the region in which the operation was about to take place with aseptic cloths.

"Are you ready, Bordier?" asked Caresco. "Do you have everything you need to hand?" He palpated the abdomen, delimiting a region. "You see, Messieurs, that it's a large fibroma, rising well above the navel. Daylight, Messieurs, I beg you—move back a little."

He spoke authoritatively. The spectators stepped back. A frisson of expectation passed through them, as at the approach of an important event. From among the instruments drowned in the phenol solution that filed two trays on a movable table within arm's reach, the surgeon seized a scalpel, and without seeming to be in a hurry, while cleaving the skin from the navel to the pubis, continued speaking.

"I'm carrying out a total abdominal hysterectomy in accordance with my own method. Sponge, Bordier."

A large furrow was traced; blood filled it. When Bordier had sponged it with tampons of wadding steeped in a solution of sublimate, the sides of the furrow appeared, a granite of yellow fat, and at the bottom, a gleaming white nacreous tissue, the aponeurosis.

With a single stroke, the surgeon had brought his scalpel directly to the place he wanted to go. That magisterial cut immediately denoted the astonishing precision of gesture with which he was endowed.

He replaced the scalpel on the tray, seized a pair of scissors, and with a single stroke, like a seamstress cleaving fabric, he cut through the aponeurosis and the subjacent peritoneum, the envelopes of the viscera. A flood of entrails sprang forth, which he compressed with his hand, while Bordier fixed the peritoneum with two clamps. Beneath Caresco's hand, a monstrous block of flesh, rounded in form and violet in color, striped with red vessels, surged in its turn from the cage that imprisoned it, coming to float on the surface of the enormous gaping wound. It was the fibrous tumor.

During the impressive minute that the surgeon's maneuver had lasted, silence had reigned. The watchers had even held their breath, and the patient, in that grave moment, seemed to be doing likewise. Her respiration, having become calm, elevated the disgrace of her bare breasts regularly, while the sister administering the chloroform parted the eyelids in order to appreciate the insensibility of the cornea—red, congested and tearful—with her index finger. When the tumor appeared, however, a murmur of astonishment ran through the assembly. What! So rapidly! The young master had scarcely had time to pick up his instruments, and the fibroma was already uncovered! Only the Austrian professor and a

French physician conserved the placidity of their physiognomy

Armand Caresco turned to the audience. He saw the three rows of the thirty faces attentive and excited. A surge of pride brushed his heart, but he suppressed it, determined to be entirely modest today and not to say, as he usually did: "Well? I don't think there's another surgeon in Paris capable of opening a belly as rapidly!" He merely smiled.

"It's a very simple case, Messieurs. There are no adherences. I would have liked to show you something more difficult, but I think the operation will be swiftly terminated."

He was gripped again by the interest of his work. Bordier sponged; once the tampons were soiled with blood he threw them on the floor. The wound remain neat and clean. The intestines were pushed back, maintained by sterilized cloths that Soeur Cunégonde presented with forceps. The tumor, lifted as far as possible outside the abdominal cavity, was thrown toward the thighs, and Bordier arranged cloths around it, ornamenting it with a kind of coquetry

They paused momentarily to pass their hands through the sublimate again.

"Now, Messieurs," said Caresco, "I incise the vagina behind the neck, guiding myself with forceps introduced through the vulva."

His gesture followed his voice. While working with an astonishing presence of mind, Caresco gave his audience a veritable lesson, without departing from the minutiae of his precautions. He sensed the approbation and the astonishment behind him; he garnered it like an intoxication that ran through his veins, rose to his brain and multiplied the agility of his fingers tenfold.

A journalist asked: "My God, what is he doing? It's frightful!"

A physician in the entourage took responsibility for whispered explanations. "The operation known as total abdominal hysterectomy consists of removing, along with the fibrous body, the matrix on the flanks of which the fibroma is implanted, like a kind of monstrous parasite. The first condition of success is not to spread blood in the abdomen. The surgeon must, in order to succeed in that, make ligatures in the principal blood vessels nourishing the matrix before cutting them. Those vessels are located in special ligaments known as broad ligaments, which also serve to maintain the matrix; you can see that Caresco is occupied in searching for the ligaments—and with what mastery, Messieurs, with what genius! The rapidity, precision and audacity are marvelous!"

Indeed, his hands plunged into the abdomen whose walls Bordier was holding agape with the aid of broad-tipped separators, the ardent operator was palpating the sinuous contours of the tumor. He gazed. The light shed by the ceiling window only illuminated a dark opening where blood was coagulating.

"Sponge, Bordier!"

Bordier swept the abdomen with a compress imprisoned in the jaws of a forceps. Again the surgeon's hands plunged. His brows were furrowed. All of his will-power, and all of his attention, were absorbed in that obscure search. The tumor was in his way; with the back of his hand, he nudged it.

Around him, the people who could not follow the delicate work straightened their curved stances, abandoning a fatiguing pose. The Viennese professor put an end to all the whispered conversations with a gesture.

"There's the broad ligament on the left!" exclaimed Caresco. "The ugly brute—it wasn't easy to find. Bordier, a double silk thread!"

The aide took special threads from a tray and applied them to the needle that Caresco was holding out. The needle was plunged into the black void, pricked, brought back, and Bordier made a knot. The ligament was ligatured.

"You see how my needle functions, Messieurs. Is it not practical? And can you imagine that it isn't used by all the surgeons in Paris? But then, I'm not *in the Club* myself. It appears that I frighten them..."

He turned to the grave Viennese professor and continued in German: "Herr Stermann, it's truly regrettable that public education is not organized in France as it is in your homeland. I'd have all the students of the Faculté at my operations...whereas they dare not come..."

While speaking he had tied the second broad ligament. A few strokes of the scissors permitted the detachment of the uterine body. The surgeon's fingers plunged into the mass of tissues, lacerating and tearing adherences, twisting shreds, decorticating the perineum, accomplishing as much work as the instruments. An abrupt traction brought the tumor and the matrix out of the abdomen. Violently projected, the fibrous mass bounced on the floor, rolling to Soeur Cunégonde's feet; she kicked it to one side. Another sister picked it up and plunged it into a bucket. Approving murmurs ran through the audience. A pale journalist, with large drops of sweat on his face, was obliged to sit down.

Armand Caresco calculated the depth of the abdominal wound. At the bottom, a pool of blood was slowly expanding; a blood vessel must have been torn by the violence of his movements. He looked at the patient, whose lips were pale, but nevertheless allowing a regular breath to escape.

"Sponge, Bordier."

Compresses plunged into the viscera, bringing forth streams of blood.

"There's the vessel that's bleeding," said Bordier, imprisoning it with the jaws of a forceps.

Caresco took a piece of thread and tied it.

"You see, Messieurs, how simple it is," he went on. "I pass the threads of the ligature through the vagina, I complete the hemostasis of the broad ligaments with a few clamps, which I leave in the vagina, and which I shall retract tomorrow. I shall also leave a drain in place there that will permit liquids to flow away, and I shall stuff the vaginal cavity with iodoformic gauze. My method is elegant and rapid. It remains now for me to close the pelvic peritoneum by means of an oversown suture; then I stitch the abdominal wound, after having taken care to clean out the cavity completely."

Indeed, he swept the floor of the abdomen by plunging in compresses fixed to long forceps. To begin with, those compresses came back stained with blood, but were clean and dry thereafter.

As the patient seemed to be waking up, he ordered the sister to render chloroform, and by means of a long needle, into the eye of which Bordier passed threads, he brought together the walls of the abdomen, linking them with several rows of sutures.

"A little more chloroform, Sister, for the closure of the skin. That's always the most painful part.

The sister poured anesthetic on to the compress. The patient's breathing accelerated noisily, with inarticulate noises, vague and incoherent plaints that emerged from her throat. For greater surety, the sister gripped the tongue with special forceps, and pulled it out of the mouth. And the operation was concluded thus, without any further alert, with a general contentment at seeing that everything had gone well, without the abrupt asphyxias that throw alarm into hearts.

While Bordier surrounded the wound, now closed, with a pad of cotton wool and a tightly-secured body-bandage, in the relaxation that followed, the surgeon took off his waxed cloth apron and made the stains on his arms disappear under the hot water tap.

Colleagues pressed around him, indifferent to the cares consecutive to the operation, to the bustle of the sisters and male nurses, and to the hasty words of Soeur Cunégonde, who was supporting the swaying body of the patient in her arms, passing a decent chemise over it, and ordering: "Over the arms now. Quickly! Lift up the basin! Clean the thighs, over the undersheet..."

No, all of that counted for nothing compared with the interest of what the young master was saying—who, while soaping his muscular and powerful arms scrupulously, was affirming once again the value and rapidity of his method, citing statistics and offering the standard fare of denigrating the surgeons of Paris, his competitors, in ironic terms...

"Do you think that Monant and the rest would have operated as I have just done? Get away! An old fossil, Monant, who has never known how to hold a scalpel. For one thing, his statistics are false! What he tells the Societé de Chirurgie doesn't stand up, I can assure you!"

Then, his toilette concluded and his hands dry, in the triumph of his young and vigorous talent, he accompanied his guests to the reception room, desirous of sensing yet again the incense of congratulations, abandoning his patient to the care of the two sisters who replaced her on the wheeled bed that had already served to put her to sleep, and pushed her on that apparatus to the elevator. They took her out on the third floor in order to transport her, still asleep, her breathing agonized, to the room she occupied.

As for Bordier, he remained in the operating theater to supervise the cleaning that the sisters were carrying out on the parquet and the tables, and to prepare, with the same scrupulous precaution, the instruments utilizable in the trepanning operation that was to be carried out on the little girl dying of tubercular meningitis.

Upstairs, on the fourth floor, in an attic room, the old grandmother, sitting next to a child's cradle, was contemplating the atonal face of her granddaughter despairingly. She had arrived the previous evening, on foot, carrying her precious burden in her weary arms. As soon as she had crossed the threshold, an anguish had swollen her heart. The sisters had received her in an indifferent fashion. Pressed by the urgency of their work, and insouciant in regard to a poor client, they had not cast the benevolent dew of consolation over her, or soothed her with the pious words that calm simple natures.

After being taken through the luxury of the stairway, she had been shown to a stifling little mansard, scarcely ventilated by a narrow hinged panel, only furnished with a commonplace bed, a chair and a miserable wooden table. Very late, a domestic had come to shave the head of the dying girl, make up a crib without curtains, and, after having lit a night-light, had retired, indifferent and mute.

Terribly sad and worn out, she had not gone to bed, allowing the ashes of the cold and darkness to fall upon her shoulders, desolate and exhausted, without revolt, spending the night beside the crib, holding the hands of the dying child in her own withered hands, watching out for a glimmer of consciousness in the child's extinct gaze, frightened by the croaks emerging from the dry throat and the contractions that reawakened the numb limbs. Her poor, hollow aged eyes had no more tears to shed; her brain was devoid of thought; there was a dolorous annihilation, which only permitted her a heart-breaking contemplation, rendering her insensitive to hunger and the torpor of the shadows.

Then, the daylight had appeared, slowly, wan and gray at first—as gray as her soul—until the moment when the sun's rays, entering triumphantly through the window, had come to pose on the child's dear and pitiful head, bringing out the bumpy contours and inequalities of the lamentably shaven head. And that ray, the kiss of the dawn, as gentle as a heavenly caress, had finally reawakened the dried-up source of her tears, and brought large bitter drops to the furrowed wrinkles of her cheeks, subtly bringing the obsession of external joys, of the nature that was waking up, of the triumph of life.

"It will be early tomorrow morning," Soeur Cunégonde had said to her.

How long the hours were in passing, how slowly time marched in its course!

Now, a madness took hold of her, bidding her to flee, to take her treasure away, not to submit her to the frightful practices of surgeons. What if they were going to kill her? What if her darling might get better without the operation?

And yet she stayed, nailed down by the force of reason, of hope.

Down below, footsteps made the parquet creak. An agitation rose up. A ringing bell made her shiver. Others succeeded it, which were followed by the sound of male voices.

Someone came in, who spoke to her. It was a sister with blue eyes. What was she saying? She did not reply. More time went by, punctuated with muffled sounds, of footsteps on the stairway, of the banging of doors, of more ringing of the doorbell. The old woman did not let go of her darling's hand.

Finally, Soeur Cunégonde came in, followed by a domestic.

"It's your turn now," she said.

She was in a great hurry, out of breath from climbing the stairs. She went back down right away. The man took the child in his arms and followed her. The grandmother did not make a single gesture, did not pronounce a single word. Her head in her hands, she was frozen in stupid contemplation of the empty crib.

When the child was brought in, Bordier, instead of putting her to sleep on the chloroform bed, put her down on the operating table immediately. While the sisters attached her arms and legs with thongs, he soaped and passed sublimate over the swaying shaven head. He garnished the operating area with compresses, and then, very gently, began to provoke sleep.

At the same moment, Caresco came back from the reception room, followed by his cortege of admirers.

"Go gently with the chloroform, won't you, Bordier?" he said, as he went to scrub his arms again, while the spectators arranged themselves. Then, while continuing to soap himself, he went on: "Messieurs, this little girl is, as you can observe, in the final phase of tubercular meningitis. All the signs are there; in any case, the diagnosis has been made by my father, here present."

Old Caresco inclined his head, and then straightened up proudly. Gazes attached themselves to him, fixing on his multicolored rosette.

"This patient is irremediably lost. I shall therefore attempt to snatch her from death by means of the following operation: I shall trepan each side of the cranium, or, in preference to the trepan, carry out a veritable craniotomy and draw back two large bony flaps, which will uncover the encephalum.

"If I'm fortunate enough to happen upon a meningitis only affecting the convexity of the brain, I shall remove the fibrino-purulent exudate that covers it; I shall clean all that surface of the encephalum and destroy with fire the tubercular granulations seated on the lymphatic sheath of the vessels of the *pia mater*. I shall then fold back the bony flaps, being careful to leave drains in place for the outflow of liquids; the bones, at that age, will fuse together rapidly.

"Evidently, there is a chance to attempt. I believe that I'm the first to try such an intervention for meningitis. It goes without saying that in the incision of the scalp I shall avoid the region of the temporal artery. In any case, we are going to make a kind of preventative hemostasis by circling the base of the cranial hemisphere with a taut rubber band. Let's place the band, Bordier."

The inert head of the child was lifted up; an elastic band was placed around it, circling the forehead with a black strip passing above the ears. During that maneuver, Caresco, to while away the time for those surrounding him, continued his self-promotion.

"Remember today's date, Messieurs. I ask you for that favor because others, as soon as my intervention becomes known, will inevitably want to snatch the priority away from me. Those are present surgical mores, and every new step taken in the domain of the science is followed by a struggle to defend one's rights. Yes, I'm the first to open the skull for this reason. Has not one of our colleagues, who is not of the Faculté, had the idea of using a dentist's drill powered by an electric motor for uncovering the encephalum? Get away! The blind force of electricity will never replace the powerful intelligence of muscles. Muscles and reason! That's what I have at my service."

And he imposed on the spectators the violent irradiation of his force, of his wrestler's arms and his superb forehead rich in audacity and ideas. Emotion took hold of hearts, alarmed by the unexpectedness of the attempt; Bordier had a slight tremor in his fingers; but Caresco, impassively, put on his large waxed cloth apron. Soeur Cunégonde had taken the chloroform compress; with a slow and regular movement she approached it and drew it away from the child's nose.

"Take hold of the tongue, Sister," said Caresco. "We might have need of a few tractions. We'll begin. The right side first. Hold firm, Bordier."

He dipped his hands in the sublimate again, and then picked up a scalpel from the tray of instruments. An immense self-confidence ennobled him. His dark eyes gleamed with the flamboyance of boldness, of triumph in the struggle. How much stronger he was than the people surrounding him! Who, among those surgeons grouped behind his back—some of whom might be famous abroad—who, among those men whom his scalpel held breathless, would have dared to risk a similar exploration of the brain, and be as able as he was to accord no more credit to this living body than a cadaver extended on the autopsy table? Yes, he was the strongest, the one most organized for victory. Neither his heart not his hand would falter.

From the forehead to the occiput he flourished his audacity with a magisterial curve. The scalpel touched the bone; blood inundated the furrow.

"Sponge, Bordier!"

He widened the wound further with a rasp and detached the periosteum.

"The trepan!"

Bordier handed him the instrument, formed like a brace and bit. Caresco applied the point to the cranium, weighed upon it with all his strength, and began to turn, and turn.

The bone screeched, a bloody pulp carried away by the gyratory movement soiled Soeur Cunégonde's white habit and head-dress, and flew up to lodge in Bordier's eye; he did not flinch. Then there was a tearing sound like breaking wood; it was the roundel of bone giving way, which was about to permit the introduction of the gouge. The first stage was complete.

Caresco looked at the little girl. Her face had a waxy pallor beside the red cranium. A pair of tongs dangled from the mouth, with the tongue in its jaws, repeating like a crazed pendulum all the movements imparted to the head. But the respiration was calm and regular; the surgeon continued his work, excavating further holes in the skull with the energy of a wrestler.

"Messieurs, to open the skull I'm going to follow the furrow traced in the scalp, sectioning the bony bridges that I've just created by making these crowns with the trepan. You'll see that it will give us a nice flap. My only fear is that of falling upon a sinus of the *dura mater*, which would produce a lot of blood. But that would only be a minor misfortune. I have no fear of blood, you see.[8] I leave that anxiety to poor operators, those who go slowly. Bordier, pass me the gouge and the mallet."

Two graceful nickel-steel instruments were placed in the master's hand. In that powerful hand, they would do the work of destruction, enter victoriously into the bone of the cranium under the effort of repeated blows, as a sculptor's chisel carves stone. It was the same shrill sound that it rendered, and that sound echoed from the metallic framework of the operating table, becoming dull and deep.

Caresco struck with a ferocious intoxication, insensitive to the splinters of bone, to all the horror of that red disorder, and to the frisson that was shaking the watchers. One of them had fainted. Caresco did not hear him fall, continuing his terrible volley. Half of the furrow was hollowed out. A tide of blood surged forth.

"Sponge, Bordier!"

He had struck the sinus that he had dreaded attaining. Blood flowed, and flowed, invading the linen, designing a rill on the metallic bed and came to fall on the floor, splashing.

"It's bleeding heavily," Bordier breathed, fearfully.

"All the more reason to hurry. Hold firm."

Again he made the gouge groan. The danger multiplied the strength of his wrist tenfold. There was a minute of anguish. Suddenly, he let go of the mallet and, making us of the gouge as a lever, lifted up the bony flap

---

[8] In 1899 blood typing had not yet made transfusions feasible during operations, so blood-loss was often a critical factor in determining their success or failure, lending some plausibility to Caresco's claim that his operational speed is a great asset.

that he had just excavated. Through the larger opening blood passed more abundantly.

He slid his fingers between the cranium and the brain, tugged the resistant bone violently toward him, and with an effort that tensed his physiognomy as well as the muscles of his arm, with a traction beyond human strength, he finally folded back the jagged bony window that hung down over the ear, maintained by a hinge of scalp, laying the encephalum bare.

He applied a tampon to the gaping sinus, and then passed a cloth over his forehead, constellated with drops of sweat.

The circle tightened around him. Curious heads leaned over the hideously sanious, red, congested viscera, speckled with a purulent exudate. The Viennese with the gold-rimmed spectacles could not restrain his astonished exclamations. Journalists were taking notes.

Soeur Cunégonde, momentarily anxious, on seeing the respiration embarrassed, pulled the tongue; a few respiratory efforts were produced, lifting the meager breast, making the ribs stand out. Serenely, she added a few more drops of chloroform to the compress.

"Is the thermocautery ready?" demanded Caresco.

He picked up a curette to sweep away the exudates that were veiling the cerebral circumvolutions—but again blood came to saturate the tampon that he had placed over the sinus. A stain showed at the surface; it expanded and enveloped the entire compress.

"What!" he murmured. "It's still bleeding!"

Anxiety caused him to dart a glance at the little girl and interrogate the anxious physiognomy of Soeur Cunégonde, who pulled the tongue again. Then, alarmed, he exclaimed: "But Sister, the patient is no longer breathing!"

She was, indeed, no longer breathing. Her face abandoned by blood, the lips blanched, the eyes vitreous, extinguished by death, she was lying on the elevated bed in the midst of white sheets speckled with red, her lamentable, little body thin and lived, with her limbs tied, with the horrible tear of the wound giving her the attitude of a torture victim. The spectacle, exciting a moment ago, became frightfully tragic by virtue of the panic of the entourage, contending with the inertia of the cadaver.

"Artificial respiration, quickly!" cried Caresco.

With a thrust of the hand he replaced the bony flap over the brain and, taking hold of the two arms that the sisters had just freed from their bonds, with a regular and methodical movement, he extended them and then brought them back to the thorax. He repeated that maneuver for some time Bordier pulled on the forceps suspended from the tongue, producing a rhythmic traction, and leaned on the thorax to assist the artificial respiration.[9] Vain attempts! The throat rattled several times, but the beast did not rise of its own accord, conserving its mute inaction.

"Compresses of boiling water in the hollow of the stomach!" Caresco howled. "An injection of serum!"

The sisters hastened to obey. Bordier inserted the needle of a large syringe under the skin, injected the liquid, which formed a swelling, and massaged the swelling. The body maintained its rigid indifference.

---

[9] Movement of the arms and traction of the tongue were the standard methods of "artificial respiration" at the time, as futile as many other commonplace methods.

"Done for!" groaned Caresco. Then, wearied by his muscular efforts, already seeking an excuse, he turned toward the consternated watchers.

"Messieurs," he said, "be good enough to withdraw for a moment. As you see, we're in difficulties; you might hinder our movements. Go to the reception room, and don't worry—I've brought patients back from further away than this."

He smiled. Some tried to meet his gaze and failed. There was a general retreat toward the reception room. The most nauseated made for the exit door.

Bordier had resumed the artificial respiration, without conviction. His muscles were unaided by his will; he was deeply distressed by what had happened, and felt his legs weakening. Although accustomed to contact with cadavers, which he had been dissecting for a long time, the skin of the little corpse whose arms he was agitating caused him an impression of anguish that squeezed his throat frightfully. He would have been glad to see Caresco fall down dead in front of him. He judged himself a victim of that fatal endeavor, and tried to deny his share of the responsibility. A revolt filled his soul, a scorn for his collaborator's base smile. He was clawed by a crazed desire to hurl his resignation at the other's head, finally to let out all his disgust, all is abomination and to flee that murderous house.

"My poor Bordier, your efforts are futile," Caresco said to him. "Nothing to be done—she's been dead for ten minutes; it's necessary to accept it. Let's take advantage of the opportunity, since the cranium is open, to test the electrical reactions on the encephalum, and see how sensitive that organ is at the point of death. That might be the object of an interesting communication to the Societé de Biologie."

Such was the funeral oration that his base and ferociously egotistical soul dictated to him.

Upstairs, in the mansard, the old woman was waiting. Plunged in an abyss of sadness, still was still staring dazedly at the empty crib. Suddenly, a noise of footsteps made her shudder.

Soeur Cunégonde appeared before her.

"Madame, God is submitting you to a hard trial..."

She did not understand at first, and stammered a few words that tumbled with difficulty from her toothless mouth.

"Yes, the child's operation did not go well..."

She uttered a howl of distress. "She's dead?"

"She was very weak, the poor child. You brought her too late. In sum, everything possible as done to save her from death..."

"She's dead?" she demanded, again, sinking her fingernails into the wood of the crib.

"Pray for her...she's with the good Lord."

The old woman stood up, her eyes crazed. She twisted toward the heavens her arms, now useless, being no longer destined to support their cherished burden. Gray wisps escaped her bonnet, striping her face, even more withered by despair. Foam covered her lips.

"They've killed me! They've killed me!"

And before Soeur Cunégonde could stop her, she ran out on to the landing, stopped for a second to look down into the dark space of the stairwell, stepped over the railing, and hurled herself into the void.

Her body spun, rebounded from the second floor, and then crashed head first on to the marble flagstones of the vestibule.

Bordier, who was coming out of the operating theater at that moment, understood the whole drama. At a hectic run that cut short his respiration, he went to inform Caresco.

The latter, however, after having examined the body, still master of circumstances, coldly said: "Fracture of the skull; she's still breathing...no liquid from the nose, mouth or ears, so nothing fundamental. We'll trepan it. We might save her."

And the grandmother was carried into the operating theater as the cadaver of her granddaughter was being removed.

The surgeon went back into the reception room.

"Messieurs," he said, "I believe I can offer you an operation similar to the one I've just done. We've just been brought the body of an attempted suicide who threw herself from the fourth floor and fractured her skull. We're going to trepan her. If you'd care to go into the operating theater..."

CHAPTER VII

In an elegant house in the Rue du Bois de Boulogne, which Armand Caresco provided for his mistress, Mathilde de Guinac—still known as "the beautiful Tripe-merchant" to her good friends—a sumptuous dinner was in preparation. In the drawing room, Mathilde, clad in silk, was supervising a waiter who was lighting the long candles of a chandelier. A black dress, forcefully tightened at the waist, thinned the opulence of her flesh. From a neckline covered with golden embroidery the milky whiteness of her breasts emerged, as if from an over-filled vase, ready to overflow. At the back, the neckline plunged much further, almost to the waist, allowing a vertebral column masked by fat to be divined. That block of flesh was dominated by a small head, chubby and child-like, plastered with cream, the kohl of the eyes and the incarnadine of the lips accentuating the features corroded by adipose tissue.

As the candles lit up, the bad taste of the furniture stood out, more richly and more garishly. Bright gilt caught the light and reflected it toward the mirrors; the silk upholstery, red curtains were varnished by the gleam; expensive trinkets mingled with absurd futilities picked up in department stores or suburban fairgrounds. A Tanagra figurine was set shamefully beside a small golden clyster-pump.[10]

---

[10] A clyster-pump is more commonly known in English as an enema pump, prudishly ignoring the fact that it is equally useful for administering vaginal douches. Simpler variants of the mechanism use a funnel that has to be raised in order to take

There was a ridiculous and offensive clutter of disparate things scattered over the furniture, haphazard objects symbolizing the mistress of the house: souvenirs, to each of which Mathilde could have accorded a lover's name; the detritus of mercantile nights, kisses and spasms offered at variable prices, according to the current tariff. The occasional picture came from a painter who had screwed her and paid in kind, not being able to do so in cash. A little ivory phallus had been given to her by an old debauchee she had flagellated. An onyx vase was the offering of the keeper of a brothel to which she went in quest of a few louis when she ran short. Every object was sealed with the shame and infamy of her life as a merchant of amour.

When the waiter had finished lighting the chandelier, Mathilde sent him away. Alone, waiting for her guests, who were late, at first she sat down in an armchair, picked up a book that she immediately abandoned, yawned, then got up and went to pose before the mirror over the fireplace.

Her gaze fell upon a photograph of a child that depicted her at a young age, in a communion dress. How old had she been then? Twelve. How old was she now? She could no longer remember exactly, by dint of lying about it. She made the mental calculation, counting on her fingers. Then, meditatively, she leaned her elbows on the marble mantelpiece, facing the mirror, and contemplated the puerile image for some time.

---

advantage of hydrostatic pressure. One assumes that only Parisian prostitutes of a certain prestige possessed a gold-plated version equipped with a pump, which could be displayed in the drawing-room as a status symbol.

The slender form was naïve and stilted; the keen dark eyes made a black patch in the whiteness of the skin and the costume. How much she had changed since then! She glanced at herself again in the shiny mirror, deploring her stout stature. But what a road she had traveled—what intrigues, what parties, what celebrations, and what debacles too!—since the age of sixteen, when as a little errand-girl in a factory she had succumbed to the solicitations of an accounts clerk whose moustaches had such a conquering twist! She had loved him for three months, and had then abandoned him when she became infatuated with an actor, a star of the Théâtre de Belleville who lubricated his voice with absinthe that he did not water down.[11]

The Thespian had forced her to quit the factory in order to live with him full-time. Then, one day, the great leading actor having no more voice at all, the director of the Théâtre de Belleville had fired him. There was atrocious poverty; in order to live, the man tried to give lessons in declamation, but neither advertisements in newspapers nor leaflets handed out in the street brought pupils to his lodgings. It was Mathilde who brought in the money necessary to the household expenses; she went on to the streets every evening to obtain the price of shameful acts of kindness.

She knew the filthy furnished rooms in which, under sheets soiled by others, she submitted to the proximity of dirty men, greasy hands and lips reeking of alcohol, who left traces of caresses and kisses on her skin. Oh,

---

[11] The Théâtre de Belleville still exists and is nowadays perfectly respectable, but in 1899 it would have been regarded as a rather louche establishment, Belleville then being regarded as one of the most disreputable quarters of the city.

the hours of horror and disgust when, an octopus of amour, naked on the bed in accordance with male fantasy, shivering in fireless rooms in winter, she simulated the intoxicating joys of erotic excitement, biting the pillow in order not to yield her healthy mouth to the sanious mouth! What bitterness, what a calvary!

She had paid in those frightful times for everything she had obtained from men subsequently. One night, she was picked up in a police sweep. At Saint-Lazare, the doctor had recognized the first signs of a horrible disease; they had kept her there for four months.

When she came out of prison she had found that her lover was dead. The idea occurred to her of living decently, of putting on the modest dress of the factory again and resuming a calm existence of toil and virtue. The mirage of a peaceful home with an honest worker and children dazzled her heart. But could she, now that she had begun her fall into the abyss, escape it unaided, without a saving branch to which to cling? What employer would take on a girl without qualifications, with short-cropped hair, with garments that were not simple enough, although well-worn? What lover would offer marriage to a former inmate of Saint-Lazare, obliged to submit every three months to a special examination, and still at risk of seeing the stigmata of a shameful malady reappear from time to time?

She did not think of addressing herself to the societies that occupy themselves with the rescue of fallen women of her sort. Then too, vice kept her imprisoned in its harsh claws; in spite of her disgust, she was dominated by voluptuous memories, by miry habits. She recommenced streetwalking in the evenings; a few savings permitted her to get a place of her own; she triumphed over poverty.

Later, she could be seen traveling along the Allée des Acacias in a victoria harnessed to two horses. She knew Jewish bankers, snobs and foreign princes. A leader of the right in the Chambre became her lover; she made law. Improvident, she neglected to fill a stocking for the future. By the time she was forty, she had grown enormously fat. She was about to fall off her pedestal into the ultimate mire when, at a supper at Sylvain's, she had met Armand Caresco, whom the opulence of her flesh immediately inflamed, and who took her away in order to take a flesh-bath.

The following morning, on quitting Mathilde's bed, Armand had decided to keep her as a mistress. Independent of the real attraction that he experienced for her powerful, ever-practical body, he imagined the benefits he might obtain from a woman so well-known, who had connections in all levels of society. And for three years they had been living together, he retained by a violent sensual habit, she deploying all the science of voluptuousness that twenty-four years of practice had taught her, in order to retain the prey that an unexpected windfall had thrown into her claws.

His liaison with Mathilde de Guinac—a true *noblesse de jupons*[12]—had served the surgeon well. Mathilde had been able to bring a number of her former lovers to him and to entertain them with an amiable camaraderie at a savant table. A shady society frequented her drawing-room; demi-mondaines of her acquaintance

---

[12] A satirical literary pun on the phrase *noblesse de robe*, which referred to a particular section of the aristocracy in the days of Louis XIV, entirely dependent on his favor. The ennobling "de" in Mathilde's name is, of course, a blatant fiction.

brought their protectors. She always had an invitation to dinner on her lips.

Painters, sculptors, journalists and musicians came to sit down at weekly dinners; Jewish bankers fraternized there with politicians, defenders of Catholicism and the pope. Over glasses of champagne there was an affable meeting of the mandarins of farce and patented gamblers.

Among them, Armand Caresco, humble, insinuating, his hand limp, never meeting anyone's eye, insidiously inflated his reputation, imposing his personality. Newcomers were taken up by him; he slipped into conversations interesting accounts of the successes he obtained in his operating theater, his skill, his rapidity, his discoveries. Scorning the observation of the principles of professional secrecy, he cited the nature of his interventions carried out on important people; he made the slightest cuts into veritable surgical events.

Suddenly, his voice would rise up in the middle of the drawing-room: "Oh him! He had a lucky escape…can you imagine…?" And he would describe a frightful operation; one could hear the flesh cry out, see the blood flow. His gaze was no longer fleeting but imposing, fascinating is interlocutors. Usually, he finished his speeches with loud laughter. "He was lucky to fall into my hands—another wouldn't have been able to get him out of it. I believe I'm the only man in Paris capable of carrying out such an intervention."

People quit his presence hypnotized. His name passed from mouth to mouth; fame swelled its organ-pipes for him. His reputation spread like a pool of oil over the human wave. His murderous endeavors became exploits of fortunate daring. So it goes with the renowned: an abominable act, initially reputed as such, imposes itself subsequently as a heroic deed. History is filled with such examples, science even more so.

Mathilde interrupted her contemplation and turned her head. Caresco was in the room, correctly dressed in an elegantly-tailored suit.

"They're late," Mathilde said, pointing at a glass case in which a small clock was already indicating half past seven. "The roasts will be overcooked. Should I alert the chef?"

"No need—they'll be here," said the surgeon, going to sit down on a divan and draw her toward him by the waist.

She sat down beside him, meekly. A wisp of hair was forming an untidy curl over her lover's forehead; she replaced it with a dainty gesture; then, taking Armand's face in her plump hands, she kissed his forehead.

"You're very handsome, my wolf!"

Under the caress of that flattery, a smile curled the man's lips, causing his pearly teeth to appear. He was always sensitive to the compliments he was paid, which corroborated his own self-esteem. He wanted to be the most handsome, the strongest, the most intelligent of men; an immense conceit was corroding him.

"Israel's coming, you know," Mathilde continued, in a seductive voice. "Have you paid him?"

"Oh! Israel's coming..."

"Yes, my wolf."

Israel was the banker from whom Armand had borrowed a hundred thousand francs in order to satisfy one of Mathilde's whims, to buy her a pearl necklace she wanted. The surgeon, who possessed a hereditary prudence in the organization of his expenses, no longer counted costs where his mistress was concerned. Money flowed from his hands to the courtesan's as a stream goes from its source to the river; he was dominated by the sensual need for the beautiful Tripe-merchant to such a degree that all the other primordial considerations of life were effaced before the satisfaction of that lust; and, for fear of losing her, he abandoned madly to her what he cherished most in all the world: money.

If it sometimes happened, when he was away from her and less directly subject to the demands of his temperament, that he wanted to draw back, criticizing himself for an absurd generosity that he had formerly criticized in others, and felt, in his mercantile soul, the agony of his passing coins, all of that vanished as soon as he was close to her again, in contact with her skin, his sense of smell intoxicated by the fat woman's reek. Cupid with others, he became prodigal with her, opening his hands without calculation to let thousand-franc bills blow away in the wind of her desire.

Mathilde profited skillfully from his weakness; she had manipulated enough men to know that such generosity was only temporary, and that the day would come when the surgeon, disillusioned, would discard her like something filthy, all the more casually because it was in his egotistical nature to rid himself brutally of things that had become useless. When that day came, she would not find any more takers for her flaccid feminine charms. He was an unexpected, miraculous opportunity, manna in the desert. Her appetite was, in consequence never satisfied. In three years she had saved up more than six hundred thousand francs under the pretext of old debts to liquidate, and the pearl necklace that she had just had offered to her had not, in reality, been purchased; it had been hired from an obliging jeweler, on bail.

"Oh! Israel's coming," Armand repeated, anxiously.

"Yes, my great tomcat. You've paid him, haven't you?"

"No, not yet. The bill fell due a week ago, but there's plenty of time in hand. I'll settle up at the end of the month. I'll be doing a few fruitful operations this week..." He leaned back on the divan, looked at her anxiously, and added, between his teeth: "You cost me dear, you know..."

In a tone of perfect sincerity, Mathilde protested. "Oh, my wolf...if you think...it's the first time I've asked for something for myself...and then, I don't ask, you give...it's very kind of you, my big rat. You can't think that I love you for your money!"

She was almost speaking into his mouth; a kiss completed the sentence. A waiter appeared, introducing the guests; they pulled apart rapidly.

A sculptor and a celebrated painter came in. The sculptor was threadbare; his hair was full of dandruff. The painter was elegant; sapphires and rubies covered his fingers; the velvet collar of his jacket was immaculate.

Almost immediately, the drawing-room filled up; the carriages bringing the diners made the widows tremble. Two young men who were squandering fortunes amassed with difficulty by their ancestors came in with their mistresses, dancers at the Opéra, old friends of Mathilde's.

Then, at the same time, came a composer of operettas and a professor of the Faculté de Médecine, a member of the Académie, whose specialty was launching new pharmaceuticals. The handshake he gave Armand Caresco was vigorous; an understanding existed between the two men.

Then, others appeared: a député; a former singer from Montmartre; an actor in third-rate theaters, his face clean-shaven.

Then came Bordier, silent and reserved, his eyes calm behind the transparency of his spectacles. He had been invited for the first time, and had thought that he could not refuse. His entrance caused a sensation in the feminine clan; his delicate features went straight to women's hearts. He was followed by Dr. Savre, his predecessor in Caresco's employ. The two physicians, who had not previously met, engaged in conversation to one side. Savre had a physiognomy carved in abrupt angles, a direct eyes and a great sobriety of gesture; Bordier liked him.

At each arrival Mathilde stood up heavily, extended a plump hand and said: "How nice of you to come..."

She was pleased by that meeting of men, almost all of whom had plumbed the mystery of her body; she delighted in the flutter of costumes, the cleavages of her friends, all lanky, whom she had been careful to choose from those uglier or older than herself. The odor of the cuisine came through the double curtain that separated the dining room from the drawing-room, hollowing out stomachs.

Armand Caresco came to join his mistress.

"Shall we start?" he said.

"Israel hasn't arrived, my wolf."

"It's eight o'clock—too bad."

He was nursing the secret hope of not seeing his creditor—but Israel came in, apologizing for having been delayed by business matters He was accompanied by an actress much appreciated in the boulevard theaters, his mistress. He was short, fat and bald, and his nose plunged toward his lower jaw. The avid regards of the women saluted the appearance of the golden calf. He suffered them amiably, a great lover of women, very perverse, inclining the mirror of his occiput before each lady. At the appeal of the *maître d'hôtel*, the beautiful Tripe-merchant took the banker's arm and they went into the dining room.

The beginning of the meal was icy. The majority of the guests were unacquainted; the women, not yet under the influence of the generosity of the wines, adopted attitudes that they strove to render dignified. They observed one another, copying one another's gestures. Only the voices of the waiters announcing the dishes and the wines, and the sound of forks colliding with porcelain, broke the silence. The candle-flames fluttered, pouring a cheerful light over the harmony of colors, caressing the blue and pink tulles of necklines and bare shoulders, softening the contrast between whites and blacks among the men.

Mathilde was radiant in all the solidity of her flesh; to her right, Israel guzzled; opposite, Caresco, a hearty eater, a gourmand of nourishment as of everything else, filled his plate and his cheeks, but found time nevertheless to recount his operating achievements to his neighbors. One of them, the actress, listened with interest; the other, one of the two stars of the Opéra, remained indifferent to his eloquence, and had great difficulty suppressing the yawns occasioned by the sleeplessness of the previous night—and the ennui that she emitted seemed to pass along the table from one guest to the next. Conversations begun in loud voices became gradually quieter and then stopped, cut off by silence.

Bordier, relegated to a corner, as an individual of no importance, had the good fortune to be seated next to Dr. Savre. They were the only ones in the assembly exchanging ideas—the grave professor of the Académie de Médecine, the dear master, was only exchanging winks with the other dancer, who was sitting opposite.

A mute sympathy was established between the two young physicians, formed by a symmetry of ideas and an equal fundamental honesty.

"What do you think of Caresco, in sum?" asked Bordier. "I don't know him, and can't succeed in fathoming him."

"Shh! Let's not talk about that here," Savre replied, lowering his voice.

The champagne loosened tongue, however. Voices gradually rose up, cheeks colored, eyes became languid. The women let out volleys of laughter, abandoning their poses. A digestive well-being spread over physiognomies. As soon as the glasses were emptied they were filled with the heady dry wine. The waiters had instructions to pour copiously; their gestures rounded out, interrupted whispers; the glass filled, they gave the bottle a rapid twist that brought the drop about to escape back into the bottle, avoiding staining dresses. The women remarked that the service was impeccable.

The actress, now watched closely by Mathilde, who thought that the conversation with her lover as going on too long, said to Caresco: "Doctor, one of my friends, whom you know well, Stella, of the Opéra-Comique, has abdominal pains. She's suffering terribly. She went to consult Monant, the surgeon at the Lariboisière..."

"One doesn't go to see Monant," said Caresco, shrugging his shoulders. "He's old and soft in the head."

"Oh, I didn't know—I thought he had a good reputation," said Israel's mistress, surprised. "In any case, he said that there was nothing to be done surgically."

"Of course, if there was anything to be done, he wouldn't know about it. Send your friend to me; I'll tell you if she can be cured. No promises."

Now the voices were rising, and a certain communicative abandon initiated by the younger members of the party overtook the more serious. The two stars of the dance, animated by the alcohol, were babbling, with their elbows on the table. Their minds were going astray in a buoyant overflow.

One of them, avid to smoke long before the end of the meal, took a packet of Oriental tobacco from a golden case attached to her belt and showed it to Mathilde, who approved with a wink. Immediately, she rolled a cigarette with an expert hand, lit it and perfumed the air with a blue-tinted incense.

Others followed suit, and an intimacy was established, complete with lewd jokes and stupid puns. A sorbet was served; they waxed ecstatic over its pale pink color.

"The color of excited mucus," said the grave professor, dedicating the quip to the dancer that he coveted more among the two.

The color of excited mucus…the witticism passed from mouth to mouth, illuminating Israel's eye, causing Caresco and the artistes to laugh loudly, but only bringing a wan smile to Bordier's lips. It was stupid and hilarious. After having pretended to more reserve than in respectable houses, the formal pose dissolved. It only required a waltz tune to be tapped out by the composer to unchain delirium when they returned to the drawing room. A disheveled quadrille began.

Wild dances agitated arms and legs; there was a disorientation of gestures and faces, the epilepsy of the Moulin Rouge. One young man, in launching a high kick, knocked a tray out of the hands of a waiter. Cups broke; coffee stained white silk cushions and filled the professor's opera hat, which caused Mathilde's opulent bosom to heave with gargantuan laughter. Beside her, Israel, whom she had warmed up with secret pressures of her foot throughout the meal, was mentally calculating the price of her favors. The bargain was concluded in low voices. Thus, Mathilde avenged herself on the actress she believed to be guilty of wanting to attract Caresco's attention.

The atmosphere filled with cigar smoke and the powerful sonorities of the piano. The clean-shaven actor intoned the latest popular tune, the refrain of which was repeated in chorus.

Savre and Bordier, strangers to the unleashing of these follies, decided to leave. Caresco, who had noticed their retreat, came to catch up with them in the vestibule.

"You're going already?" he said, with a note of criticism in his voice.

"Yes, Bordier replied. "I have to be at the Avenue Hoche at seven o'clock in the morning to prepare for the operations."

"And I still have work to do this evening," said Savre.

"Will you come tomorrow?" Caresco asked him. "We have a jolly session—we're operating before all the foreign members of the surgical congress, aren't we, Bordier? Come—you'll see how our successor conducts himself. Then, if necessary, you can lend us a hand."

"I shall always take pleasure in admiring your work, but as for getting involved…no, that's over."

In those words and the tone in which they were spoken there was a hostility that surprised Caresco. As usual, he did not react to it.

The two men left. The night, sown with a dust of stars and gently caressed by a breeze charged with the perfumes of the Bois, solicited a stroll. Cigars in their teeth, they went along the Avenue du Bois de Boulogne toward the Arc de Triomphe. Their footfalls struck the dry ground methodically. A few rare carriages were bring entwined couples back to Paris, fleeing the bustle of the Café Chinois, whose bright lights delimited blocks of shadow, seeming to be as many eyes charged with keeping watch through the black hole of the Porte Dauphine on the mystery of the Bois.

Bordier was haunted by an obsession, a question that was burning him. The moment seemed propitious to him for amicable confidences.

"Were you with Caresco for a long time?" he asked.

"A year."

"You left him on good terms, it seems to me."

"Yes, on good terms."

"And why did you leave?"

Savre hesitated momentarily; then, gripping Bordier's arm and forcing him to stop, he said: "My dear chap, for anyone else but you I'd probably cite banal reasons. but I want to tell you the truth, because I trust you. Well, I was afraid of him."

Bordier started. In the semi-darkness of the night, he considered Savre's serious and rude face. The latter, however, with his energetic and hard forehead, his keen and straightforward eyes, did not seem to be a man prone to dread, to puerile fears.

As Savre spoke, a veil was ripped before Bordier's eyes; he heard the expression of disillusionment, distress, and fears that he had experienced subconsciously himself. In the brutal revelation that had been made to him he found the state of his own soul.

"Yes, old chap," said Savre, "I was afraid, not of what he was doing, but of what he was making me do. Look, it seems to me that I was living a dream during that year of collaboration, caught in the incessant struggle between my conscience and the interest that overflows from his scientific labors.

"You haven't yet been able to appreciate that; you've only recently been attached to him—but he's exciting...exciting and frightful. He's an evil genius. Some days, during his great operations, his marvelous dexterity, his coolness, his rapidity of decision wrung cries of admiration from me; then, when the session was over, when I was no longer under his diabolical influence, when I returned to my heart, fear seized me and I asked myself why. Why did he do all that? Why those great dilapidations of the flesh, those broken bones, those perforated organs? Why that bloodshed? And I rubbed my hands, like Lady Macbeth, to erase the stains.

"Gradually, I allowed myself to be penetrated by the frightful reasoning that the man's actions are guided by two equally culpable motives: firstly, his unfettered ambition, the ambition he has to be the foremost surgeon in the world, the one about whom people talk the most, to whom the most desperate cases can be confided; and secondly, I'm ashamed to say, his base cupidity, his avidity for gold, to satisfy his enormous needs and the caprices of that Mathilde, who eats him away, draining him through every pore.

"To arrive at those results, he doesn't recoil before any compromise, or any crime. He races through life head down, blindly, like a bull at a red rag. His red rag is blood, also red, the sight of which seems to procure him a kind of intoxication. Sometimes, I wondered whether he might be mad, or at least on the edge of madness, in that region that touches on both alienation and sublime reason, as for all types of genius. I searched for other signs, but once his moment of exaltation has passed, he gets a grip on himself, masters himself—he even has too much self-control.

"I owe it to the truth to say that he's attempted interventions that seemed impossible, which have yielded marvelous results. I've seen him successfully remove tumors twice the size of my head. In other hands, the patients would have been done for. Yes, he's saved some lives. But alongside that, how many deaths! How many unnecessary operations, under the appearance of good ideas?

"Look at his work on the liver: is it not extraordinary in its invention, its technique, even its reasoning? Well, the operations succeed, but the result has always been trivial. Ameliorations that have made him utter cries of victory, repeated, like the bleating of the sheep whose Panurge he is, by the echoes of a press in his pay...but the ameliorations are only temporary, followed more often than not by aggravations. Why operate, then, frightening families and risking death?

"Is not the role of the physician, when he understands that his science is vain, that his therapeutics have no influence to a fatal evolution, simply to palliate the death-throes, not to attempt a throw of the dice, a success as chancy as winning the jackpot in the lottery?

"Some have said to me: 'even so, you're doing useful and benevolent work, for in suppressing life you're suppressing bitterness and suffering.' But to what point am I the master of the existence of my peers? What right, what moral law, permits me to dispose of them?"

Savre stopped talking. People passing by turned to look at the two men in suits who seemed to be arguing.

The avenue was increasingly depopulated; the Café Chinois put out its lights. They resumed walking toward the Arc de Triomphe, which stood out clearly against the fluid dark blue of the firmament.

"Yes," Savre continued, "it's a frightful problem that tormented me from the first day. I wondered what my share was of the responsibility for those audacious attempts, with me assisting, as the only aide.

"Some nights, I couldn't sleep, and to put an end to my distress I ran away from my home, scarcely dressed, to go and see how the patients were doing. I had a key and went in silently. Generally, I found the sisters asleep and the patients who had undergone operations brutalized by morphine—for the good sisters stuff them with morphine, as you must have seen...

"Well, I only found one means to solve the problem that haunted my nights, which pursued me even into my dreams: I fled."

Bordier felt that his companions had opened the utmost corners of his heart to him. He thought the same; like him, he sensed that he was going to flee that guilty collaboration. He was almost confused by not having already done so. Having the lack of decision of the weak, however, the uncertainty of a dreamer, would he have the courage to impart his decision to Caresco without invoking an appreciable motive?

"Yes," he said, faintly, as if replying to an intimate question, "the man is culpable, very culpable."

"Culpable, but necessary," Savre continued, "as evil is necessary to good. Don't shake your head my friend— let me explain my thinking. It's a frightful thing to say, which truly makes one doubt at times a superior intelligence and bounty, but whichever way you turn your head, in the history of things as well as peoples, you see

136

that those things and peoples only arrive at a definitive harmony after frightful destructions, ruins, revolutions, the slaking of hatreds and prolonged battles.

"Good doesn't install itself straight away, of its own accord. Peace wouldn't exist if war hadn't existed. Look among the inferior animals, and further still, among the creatures of which one can't say whether they're vegetables or whether they mark the first phase of animal life: what incessant strife! Remount the scale of beings: everywhere it's the same.

"Arrive at humans, in the end, and tell me whether or not it has required bloody epochs, suffering, heroism and death to arrive at the constitution of empires! Calculate what our Revolution cost, and look what frightful threats there still are on the horizon of socialism? Everywhere, always, conflict and evil—and progress accomplished as a result.

"Well, it's the same in the particular case of surgery. More, perhaps, in that science than others there's a need for men like Caresco, devoid of moral sense, swollen by ambition and sometimes by cupidity, whose shoulders are solid enough to support the weight of sin. They destroy, they gaze upon destruction—but then others rebuild on those ruins, taking advantage of what they have seen. It's horrible, but that's the way it is, always the same old formula: good has its source in evil; evil is necessary to good."

They had arrived at the Arc de Triomphe. On the pillars, the stone carvings stood out, causing heroic gestures to project, sublime epics in the peace of the night. Savre indicated them with a broad sweep of his hand, as a consecration of his speech. Then, lifting his finger toward the infinity of the sky, he went on:

"But all that, the sky, the stars, all the magnificence of the forces that dominate us, our fellows have never been able to admire. They're riveted to their miserable earthly passions, and don't understand the heavens. Let's pity them, and remain as we are, shall we, Bordier? That's preferable."

They shook hands and separated.

Bordier went home, his heart disturbed by what he had just heard. He went into his bedroom, glad to be back in his little intimate corner, the only place where he was truly at home. He cast a satisfied glance over the familiar objects: the table covered with newspapers, the books piled up in a small bookcase beside the bed, within arm's reach.

The lamp set on the mantelpiece brightly illuminated a portrait of a woman that he went to pick up and considered for a long time. It was the photograph of a young woman of about eighteen, pretty, with thin features, further attenuated by the incomparable gleam of two large shining eyes. The photograph had been ineptly taken by a photographer of mediocre ability, and yet it was all that remained of a love story, his only love story, as modest and passionate as everything that involved him.

Yes, the thoughtful Bordier, that apostle of god, that scientist for the humble, that saint in whom humor often veiled immense pity, that utterly materialistic man, had also had his moment of poetry—but how brief and heartbreaking!

One evening, while he was still a neighborhood physician, a poor devil of a seamstress, attracted by his reputation for humanity, had come in search of him to visit one of her friends, a seamstress like her, a twenty-year-old orphan whom pulmonary tuberculosis was killing slowly.

In a dark house, he had followed the woman through the corridors of misery. In a sadly furnished room, on a soiled camp bed, lay a pale invalid, as pale as candle-wax, and so thin that it seemed that the bones were about to burst through the skin.

Between two suffocations, in a child-like voice, she had explained her lamentable odyssey to him, the eternal story heard a thousand times: childhood bronchitis, spitting blood, endless transpirations, emaciation, projecting ribs—the entire heart-rending cortege of consumption—and also her struggle to make a living, her disappointments when rich dressmaking establishments closed their doors on her because she was too weak to work, because the spectacle of her decline frightened her companions in labor; then the trips to the hospitals, her attempts in consulting rooms in which, having finally reached the doctors, she had been sent away because her illness was chronic, because there were no beds available, and because her case was not sufficiently interesting to invite the research of scientists, which would at least have admitted to her to a charity bed.

And Bordier, whose time was ordinarily too precious for him to listen to such stories, so banal in their atrocity, had lent a sympathetic ear to that one, responding to it with brusque and kind words, the yelps of a licking dog, had gently ausculated that skeleton covered with skin, which he feared to break by moving it. Then, when the consumptive, taking a dirty purse from beneath her pillow, had tried to pay him the fee for his visit with her last sous, Bordier had been seized by a burst of laughter emerging from the heart, in which there were sobs, and had forced her to put away her poor money, and promise to pay him later, when she was better.

The next day, he had returned of his own accord, bringing a cluster of grapes and a little champagne—all that she could drink. He was not, however, under any illusion regarding the efficacy of his visits, and the power of his medicine, knowing that he was incapable doing anything against the malady, even delaying it in its course; but he was able to soothe, to calm the crises, and above all—above all!—to give the abominable debris that was on the way to extinction some hope, benevolent hope, to throw into that sinking heart the mist of illusion, to which consumptives cling so willingly.

Beneficent and merciful work, which is also the finest recompense of the medical apostolate, as the young physician understood. For he was one of those, fortunately still numerous, who make their consulting room into something more than the antechamber of the pharmacist's counter. Wearied by the sickening work of *savoir faire*, rendered desperate by the insufficiency of the remedies that he administered sagely, to aid nature and not to cure, he had faith in the moral medicament. The majority of maladies, especially in women, being the result of nervous decline, the ensemble of a few vague symptoms exasperated by the sensibility of the entourage, he treated them with suggestive remedies.

Like Charcot, he understood Lourdes; he regretted that Gruby[13] had not had a chair at the Faculté, and that

---

[13] The Hungarian physician David Gruby (1810-1898), who worked in Paris, nowadays remembered for his pioneering work in microbiology and his early adoption of anaesthesia by means of chloroform. During his lifetime he was more celebrated for "curing" famous patients, including Alphonse de

the illegality of the methods of a certain charlatan[14] did not permit him to send his own patients to seek a cure in a famous wooden tub. Not that he doubted science, which he considered as the sole regenerator of society, but he envisaged it from a superior point of view, indemnified of all the ignominies of professionalism, the base work of commerce. For him, a great discovery became an abominable thing when it began to be exploited; he felt a disgust for it, similar to what a composer feels when he hears his music massacred by be quavering of a barrel-organ. And yet, his role was neither to discover not to compose; he was a popularizer, an interpreter—so he often suffered, in his mercy and his honesty, in being reduced, by the harsh requirements of life, to the exercise of a profession rather than an art.

Beside the poor consumptive he had felt flowing in his soul all those initial aspirations that hard daily labor, the fatigue of running around and human ingratitude tended to annihilate. Next to her, he had become once again the apostle ready for sacrifice, the lay priest in the purest sense of the term. To the tears in his patient's eyes the tears of his own heart responded; the plaints of that ripped breast gave impetus to the words that calmed, that put fear to sleep.

He went to see her every morning at first; he came back in the evening. Later, he acquired the habit of going up to see her several times a day, when the hazard of his work took her past her door. Every time, there was some

---

Lamartine, Alexandre Dumas, Frédéric Chopin, George Sand and Franz Lizst, by means of suggestive methods applied to what would now be considered psychosomatic ills.

[14] Anton Mesmer, who notoriously employed a curative *baquet* [wooden tub] in his "magnetic" treatments.

further alms that he made her accept discreetly: one day, a comfortable bed, which, he claimed, was cluttering up his apartment; the next day, after frightful coughing fits that had held her suffocating, folded in two all night long, he installed a nurse permanently at her bedside.

Surprised at first by so much devotion, she had acquired the habit of receiving the man she called her savior. Her savior! She really believed that. Under the effect of sage medication and the relative comfort with which the young physician surrounded her, her coughing fits became more spaced out. Her transpirations, already so abundant that the friend who lived in a neighboring room had to get up twice a night to change the sheets on her bed, diminished in consequence. But what she still did not have was an appetite. She experienced an increasing horror of all kinds of nourishment, and it required Bordier's influence to make her absorb a little specially-prepared meat broth.

And as the consumption accomplished its inevitable work, she believed that she was coming back to life, interpreted as a good sign every new symptom, the telling of a fatal chaplet. She even found the strength to make herself up when she knew that her physician was going to come; she kept a mirror on the bed, before which she rearranged her hair, sticky with sweat. One day, she curled it, and had a joyful rush of blood to her cheeks when she perceived that Bordier had noticed her coquetry.

He put caresses into his voice when he spoke to her, lingered in lowering his head on her fleshless back when he ausculated her, maintained in the solidity of his hands the poor thinness of hers, as if he wanted to pass some of his vital fluid and his energy into that dying flame. Those touches were exclusively platonic; what could he have desired, in any case, of that lamentable carcass, those poor frail limbs, that torso where the ribs outlined their arcs and where the vanished breasts no longer indicated anything but the nipples—from all of that ruin, so miserable in sum, so shrunken and so thin, that she only occupied the space of a child in that big bed?

What persisted, however, was the eloquence of the large dark eyes; in them, the life was intense and ardent; whereas the rest of the body was dissolving into sputum and sweat, they conserved such a gleam that Bordier could not help admiring them. Oh, how infamous Fatality was to have thrown the escheat of malady over that creature, so splendidly created to love and be loved, and what credit could it accord to the superior Force to destroy its work so wretchedly in suffering? It was a monstrous perversion of nature, the frightful aberration of a sculptor destroying a statue with small blows of a hammer after having made it perfect!

And the more he got to know her, the more he came to appreciate the woman that she might have been, the more tender his feelings for her became. The consumptive responded to that with an unconscious affection, an ever-increasing emotion that almost made her forget her illness, removing her from the egotism typical of the chronically ill, especially those with diseases of the lungs.

The young physician did not take long to divine the nature of the influence that he was having on his patience; he thus conceived an act of supreme pity, which he put into execution.

One evening, not long before she died, the day had been better and they were chatting. Sitting beside her bed he was holding her feverish hands.

"My friend," she said, "How will I repay you for all that you've done for me when I'm better/"

"Don't talk about repaying me," he replied. "I'm the one who is glad to have encountered you. Don't play the innocent; you know very well that you've given birth to a sentiment in me..."

"A sentiment?" she said, astonished.

"Yes, a genuine sentiment, in sum. My dear friend, how it warms the heart to know that one has sown joy and will harvest gratitude!"

"An infinite gratitude!"

"And to think," Bordier continued, "that the person to whom one has done good might perhaps consent one day, when she has recovered her health, to march through life by her benefactor's side..."

"What do you mean?" she said, raising herself up from her pillow with unaccustomed force, so violently had the surprise shocked her.

"I mean, Jeanne," Bordier replied, calling her by her forename for the first time, at which she shivered, "that you are a heavenly angel, and that I love you to the point of making you my wife, if that does not displease you."

"Your wife! We'll be married!"

"Yes, we'll be married."

She lay there, her throat constricted by emotion, only able to utter a few delighted stammers. But the young man was paid for his generous act of pity by the illumination of her wide eyes. Thus, she was perfectly sure of being cured, since Bordier wanted to make her his wife. What a happy life she would have with that man, and what a folly of devotion and abnegation she felt in regard to the person who, after having snatched her from death, was offering her love, and a home!

"How happy I am, my friend, how happy I am!"

Large tears followed the meager furrows of her cheeks. Bordier sponged them away gently with his handkerchief, calming her overexcitement with a few soothing words, under whose influence she went to sleep, exhausted by so much happiness.

A few days later she passed away, in all the joy of the illusion, her large dark eyes fixed until the last moment on the man she adored, on the savior of her soul, if not her body, carrying into the afterlife the radiant purity of a soul given birth in death.

CHAPTER VIII

On the insistence of Madame Bise, Madame de Jancy and her daughter Madeleine had consented to prolong their stay at the Château des Bolois. The month of September came to an end. After the heavy rains that had lasted for a fortnight, the weather had become fine again, and that afternoon, the warm rays of a sun that was concluding its orbit too soon were offering a joyous expansion to the château's guests, who, by habit and by inclination, where sitting outside beneath the shade of the lakeside chalet, on the edge of the lawn.

Madame Bise, comfortably installed in a hammock, was lending all the effort of her futile brain to reading a report of a feminist congress in which she had taken part. She had been taken there by a friend, Miss Pisword, an old English spinster who wanted to claim the prerogatives of a sex that her ugliness had prevented her from utilizing in commerce with men. At times, that overly arid study, combined with the work of a slightly laborious digestion, misted her cerebral cells; the report escaped her hands and a discreet and regular purr, inflating her mossy lips, caused Madame de Jancy and Madeleine—who were working beside her—to raise their heads. They looked at one another, smiling maliciously, and then resumed their occupations, quietly, in order not to interrupt their relative's happy torpor

Madeleine, her back curved over the embroidery of an altar-cloth, straightened up and stretched her limbs, abandoning herself to the back of her chair. She looked at the calm silvery water. The leaping of carp occasionally troubled the silent harmony, and concentric ripples spread out, grew and died on the bank. She looked at the green carpet of the shore, which dead leaves enriched with patches of gold. She looked through a gap in the trees at the dull vista of the countryside denuded by the harvest, the horizon magisterially delimited by a distant row of poplars, and the blue immensity of a sky purified by a sun that she could not see.

Everything was clear and precise in the atmosphere, as in her soul; there was an equal bliss on high, on earth and within her. She could not see her sun any longer, but it was present; she could feel its benevolent effluvia passing, and it bathed her in its calm warm light. Her sun was her love for Georges Ponviane—a love that had now received an official consecration, since the engagement of the two young people had been declared.

Oh, the dear affection of the tall young man! How that sweet and powerful sentiment filled her with an intimate peace, an absolute quietude, and put an end to the surprises of the hereditary nervousness that had tormented her youth to such an extent! Now, Madeleine no longer felt the desire to laugh or cry at everything, as before. A great joy had put her nerves to sleep.

Her last emotion—violent, of course—dated from the day when Georges Ponviane's father had come to make Madame de Jancy party to his son's proposal. The manufacturer had not had recourse to the preliminaries generally employed by prudent bourgeois who have the terrain explored by a third person. He had come directly to the point, as in business. He had hitched up his victoria and had presented himself at the Château des Bolois.

Madame de Jancy and her daughter had been in the drawing room, the coolness of rainy weather not permitting them to take up their favorite location that day. They were alone, for Madame Bise, always in a fever of agitation, had gone to Paris in order to squander the energy of her southern temperament at the feminist conference. Madeleine and her mother, absorbed by reading, had raised their heads on hearing the sound of carriage wheels screeching on the gravel of the driveway. Who could it be? It was not a day for reception. The valet had come to say that it was a gentleman asking to see Madame de Jancy. At the same time he held out a card that Madeleine was unable to read, in spite of her keen curiosity.

"I'll go," she had said to her mother, who had not tried to retain her. As she went out, however, she almost bumped into an elegant individual about sixty years old, very distinguished in appearance, the sight of whom had made her shiver.

There was no doubt that the gentleman was Georges Ponviane's father. There was, on a larger scale, the same silhouette, the same carriage of the head, the same slightly hooked nose and above all, she had recognized the same dimple in the cheeks when he smiled—for he had smiled, the elegant old gentleman, as he moved aside to let her pass, bowing graciously. My God, what had he come to do at the Château des Bolois?

Having gone up to her bedroom she had fallen tremulously into a chair, torturing her brain with a thousand imaginations, each more baroque than the last. Might the gentleman have come to tell Madame de Jancy that he knew everything, and that he could not permit a young woman to court his son in that way? Had he brought back the bouquet of violets negligently abandoned by her on a seat in the church? Or—for the two families had acquaintances in common—had he come to ask for Madeleine's hand in marriage for someone other than Georges?

She did not suppose, although it was the only really plausible possibility, that the father had come to plead his own cause—and, mad with anxiety, compressing her breast, raised up by the beating of her heart, she had persuaded herself that the interview could not fail to end in disaster. However, the gentleman had not given the impression of being ill-intentioned; she had even thought that there had been something affable, good and protective in his greeting and his dimple.

At the window, she had watched for the visitor. He had come out of the drawing-room, escorted back to his carriage by Madame de Jancy. They seemed to be on good terms with one another. Before climbing into his victoria, Georges' father had lingered for a moment, chatting. His gestures indicated that the view they had before them was the subject of their conversation. Nothing terrible in that! Then, when Monsieur Ponviane had installed himself in his carriage to depart, a handshake had terminated the meeting.

Right! Madeleine's heart had settled down. Quickly, she had gone back down to the drawing room to resume her reading, quite astonished by the silence of her mother, who did not say a word to her about the visit. Strangely enough, though, all afternoon and all evening, Madame de Jancy's gaze, which had weighed upon her, seemed to be charged with a tender fluid, and her goodnight kiss had been longer than usual,

O charm of tender, simple hearts, how Madeleine had been cradled in the days that followed, how she had been enveloped by the instinctive atmosphere of love with which mothers surround their children in hours of separation or illness!

Time had passed thus; Madame de Jancy still said nothing. One morning, on the table in the vestibule where the valet placed the post before distributing it to its addressees, Madeleine, having come down early, had perceived, among other letters, one sealed with red wax, bearing on the envelope the monogram of their notary in Paris. The sight of that letter, which would have left her indifferent at any other time, excited her.

That's the information arriving, she had thought.

She picked up the letter in her delicate fingers, turned it over and over again, held it up to the light to search for the opacity of the writing through the translucency of the paper. She could not see anything; the envelope was too thick. Then she had slid the missive back among the others and, criticizing herself for a culpable curiosity, had fled into the grounds.

That day, Madame de Jancy still remained mute. Madeleine kept anxious watch on her mother's gaze. Was the news bad, then, to occasion such obstinate silence? At table she did not eat and submitted sadly to the disapproval of her entourage. Someone was hunting in the vicinity; gunshots made the valley rumble—perhaps it was Georges! She shivered at the sound of the rifles.

The next day, Madame Bise being absent, she and her mother had been working by the waterside, as they were today. Madame de Jancy began: "My child, I have something to tell you..."

What a furious emotion had sounded the charge for her heart! One might have heard it hammering against the walls of her thorax. But the anguish soon turned to delight. She scarcely heard the Madame de Jancy's affectionately moderated words, as she eulogized Monsieur Ponviane and his son.

"In any case," her mother concluded, with a hint of malice, "you know Monsieur Georges better than I do, and you like him!"

"I know him?" she said.

She judged her conduct stupid and burst into sobs. Her mother wept too, and those combined tears calmed Madeleine's nerves as a brief shower refreshes a tense stormy atmosphere.

The most difficult one to convince was Madame Bise. She almost had an apoplectic fit that evening, when she returned from the feminist congress, her brain overheated by oratory conflict, and heard Madame de Jancy submit her intentions and those of her daughter. What! She had other plans, the dear aunt! They should have spoken to her sooner! Things were done differently in the Midi. One went about them with less Tartuffery. She did not mince her words, and the jet of her speech offended Madame de Jancy, who was ordinarily very reserved before the aunt with the inheritance.

"Georges Ponviane! What is he? A manufacturer? That's nice! Different, in the Midi! That's not a marriage! Talk to me about Armand Caresco…that's a marriage…but Ponviane! Ponviane!"

Deep down she had allowed the idea to flourish of a union with the surgeon. It was really for that reason that she had invited the surgeon to come and to return to Les Bolois.

As she was a good woman, however, whose resentments flew away as rapidly as her ideas, the next day, she invited the Ponvianes to dinner. That was the delightful and charming consecration in which, since then, Madeleine had allowed herself to bask, as she was this afternoon, while gazing at the calm, silvery lake, the golden leaves and the blue infinity of the firmament.

"*Bonjour*," said a deep and musical voice.

Georges Ponviane appeared at the entrance to the summer-house. He was wearing an elegant hunting costume in pale gray velvet, slightly faded in the trousers. The absence of gaiters revealed the gracious line of a vigorous leg. For the moment, large straw hat was hiding his dark eyes and shading his pink, lightly sun-tanned cheeks. He had a cavalier bearing and an altogether gentlemanly appearance. He was groomed without exaggeration, sufficiently masculine. His brown moustache was sufficiently turned up to allow healthy teeth to gleam. The ensemble spoke of strength, grace and simplicity. His astonishingly soft gaze immediately went to offer a caress of welcome to Madeleine, who blushed.

Then, perfectly elegant, he lifted a game-bag off his shoulder, through the mesh of which feathers and fur projected, set it down with his rifle in a corner, took off his hat and came to kiss Madame de Jancy's hand.

Madame Bise, extracted from her doze, quite dazed and not wanting anyone to suppose for a moment that she could have been distracted from the powerful interest offered by the reading of her report, tumbled out of her hammock, contracting her features, masked with puffiness in order to make herself seem wide awake.

"Pardon me, I was just reading something interesting," she said to Georges, as he bowed to her.

Georges took the report and read the title.

"Oho! The feminist congress! A serious question, my dear Madame, well worthy of interesting a serious mind like yours."

Madame Bise became radiant. Georges thought that she was even more stupid than she seemed.

"And you, Madeleine," he added, turning to the young woman, "Are you a feminist?"

She leaned toward him and replied in a whisper: "I'm content to be a wife…a wife for you."

Madame Bise did not hide a disapproving moue. The amorous abandonment of Georges and Madeleine irritated her, like a fine dish that others are eating and which one cannot touch oneself. Those mute or manifest caresses revealed the ashes of her sixth sense, reminding her of the valor of the late Bise, causing the down on her upper lip to quiver and the congested nostrils of her amorous nose to flutter.

She suppressed the reawakening of an appetite, manifested an enthusiastic gaiety, and while Madame de Jancy was considering the young couple's joy with a placid and benevolent smile, she said: "What! They're whispering in one another's ears now; they have confidences to make. Go for a walk in the park, you'll be more tranquil there." She winked at Georges, and added: "And above all, no hanky-panky, eh?"

They went out. The wood offered itself to their footsteps; they went into it. The dying rays of sunlight were passing obliquely through the yellowed vault of the trees, already half-denuded. Their feet trod on a bed of golden leaves. Odors of cut hay brought from the fields by a fresh breeze intoxicated their young heads, but not as much as their love intoxicated them.

There was the harmony of calm that emerges from the splendor of things. Immediately, Georges put his arm round Madeleine's waist, and she let her adorable head sink on to his robust shoulder.

They were supple, delighted, infinitely happy, allowing themselves to wander at random. They did not say anything at first. What had they to say, anyway? Nature spoke for them; they allowed themselves to be lulled by the song of her voice.

The excursion extended, and they went with an equal intoxication. Rabbits and a hair fled at their approach. Madeleine turned the mischief of her luminous gaze to Georges. He shook his head, smiling. Neither the hare nor the rabbits tempted his destructive inclinations. Then she rested her head on his shoulder again, and he took her wrist with his free hand, raising it chastely to his lips.

He had never kissed her in any other way, fearful of bruising her innocence—but that day, under the empire of the intoxicating evening, the odor of the cut hay and the inebriation caused by an already over-extended anticipation of the young body, ardently desired, the pure form that he felt, at that moment, so united with his own, so tenderly enlaced that in understanding its harmonious contours, a desire came to him to kiss those cherry-colored lips, a divine mirror of health and life, flowers blooming for the folly of kisses.

He stopped—and she did not resist, vanquished long before, chastely surrendering her chastity. They responded to the appeal of their lips. Their mouths united; Madeleine swooned under the kiss.

"Madeleine! Madeleine!"" he said, his voice so tenderly soft and deep that it seemed to be a music that made her quiver with pleasure.

He gripped her hands again and contemplated her desperately. A tear ran down the young woman's cheek; he breathed it in with his lips. He drank the joy and the love in it.

"Madeleine," he went on, "we've just exchanged a kiss that seals our love definitively. Tell me, oh, tell me that you love me!"

"No, I don't just love you; I love you utterly, I'm yours, utterly. I make that solemn oath, and I shall die on the day you disappear, Georges, dear Georges."

Yes, he sensed that she was truly his. Their hearts and their senses were vibrating in unison; they were at the apogee of passion. They were no longer seeing, they were no longer thinking. The splendor of the ambient nature, the great trees with golden leaves, the caressant evening air, the azure infinity, all the powerful seduction of that declining day, about to vanish into the torpor of dusk, no longer existed for them. They were isolated from the world, transported into a paradise of felicity.

Again, he took long possession of her lips; again, Madeleine shivered with intoxication.

But while he held her in that embrace, he saw her suddenly go pale, stiffening herself against an interior pang.

"Madeleine, my beloved, what's wrong?" he said, frightened. "You seem to be ill…"

"I don't know…a slight malaise; it's nothing…nothing at all."

And immediately, doing his best to support her, he became alarmed. He thought he was dealing with one of those nervous crises about which he had been told, which he attributed to the emotion she had felt under his kisses.

Gently, he led her to a bench on to which she almost collapsed, still very pale. And while he cradled her in his arms, striving, by pressing her against his male breast, to pass a little of the life that was beating in him into her, Madeleine apologized for that absurd malaise, which bore no resemblance to her crises of old. It was a very different sensation, never sensed before, comprised primarily of nausea and a strange respiratory hindrance. And scarcely recovered, confused and desolate, she asked Georges to forgive her for that untimely malaise, with words that explained and implored, her gaze charged with regret and love.

"As you see," she said, with a forced smile, "I'm weak by nature. You'll find me difficult when I'm your wife..."

"I'll be so glad to prove my devotion..."

"Georges, my Georges, what must you think of me? Leave me anyone for a moment, I beg you. In a few minutes, it will be completely dissipated. Go fetch me a little sugared water—and above all, don't say anything to Maman."

The young man disappeared at a run, still anxious. When he came back a few minutes later carrying a glass into which he had poured a few drops of a vulnerary, Madeleine seemed less distressed; however, her forehead, bathed in cold sweat, testified to the heroic efforts she had been obliged to make to vanquish the crisis. Amorously, Georges wiped his fiancée's temples with his handkerchief, smoothed her stray hairs, and presented her with the ardent beverage, which cheered her up.

"Oh," she said, getting to her feet, "what a poor little woman I am beneath my robust appearance, and how brave you are, Georges, to want me for a lifetime...it's a long time, you know, a lifetime...have you thought of that?"

They had resumed walking. Drawing Madeleine's head toward him, he kissed the pale brown ornament of her hair. "Yes, my dear, dear angel, I've thought of that, and I must say that it hasn't weighed in the balance for an instant. In any case, I can assure you now of the future state of our health; I have the approval of the Faculté, do you understand?"

"Of the Faculté?"

"Yes, Dr. Cartaux has assured me that marriage will dissipate these fits of malaise that you've experienced during your childhood..."

"Dr. Cartaux?" she said, surprised. "You know him, then?"

"He's my father's doctor, and mine. He's also our friend."

"And ours. How glad I am! He's so devoted, so knowledgeable, so gentle; he's a veritable saint. I love him."

"You're going to make me hate him, then?"

She put her hand over his mouth. "Not like you. You, that's something else, something that I can't describe, something that makes me weep and laugh at the same time, something soft, profound and powerful, as soft as the evening air, as powerful as the heavens and as profound as the sea...you...I can't see anything beyond...after you, I die. No, I can't tell you all that I experience, here."

She put her hand on her heart. He was listening, surprised and delighted by such a speech. She went on: "Him, I love with veneration, religiously. I'd have liked that man to be my father."

Her simple nature, devoid of preparations, devoid of conventions, revealed itself completely in that last statement. Others would have conserved in their words the conventional hypocrisy that attaches love even to unknown parents; she, whose father had died when she was still very young, and who had only ever heard him described in imprecise terms, hiding the disapproval of a riotous life, admitted naively that she would have liked to have been Dr. Cartaux's daughter. And that chimera, in the intoxication of the moment, seemed entirely natural to Georges, who did not believe what she said.

"Yes, I like him a great deal too," he said. "He's brought my poor Maman through several serious illnesses, and it was during one of her voyages that the poor woman died. Then again, I've heard so many good things about him from my close friend Dr. Jean Bordier, who was his pupil. You'll meet him, Bordier, and you'll see what a charming fellow he is…and what a saint, too! He's presently the assistant of Dr. Caresco, the surgeon."

Madeleine's face filled with astonishment. "Your friend is with Dr. Caresco?"

"Yes. Do you know him?"

"I've met Monsieur Caresco; he spent several days here. Oh, I didn't like him at all!"

"Really?" said Georges. "I don't know him. Bordier tells me that he's very skillful, and that he performs very interesting surgeries. That's all I know about him."

"I don't know any more than you, Georges, but that man doesn't seem to me to be good."

She became sad, under the influence of an intimate anguish. She could not explain it, and did not remember anything, but something passed through her mind like an unconscious return to a frightful scene that had once unfolded—and it was a strange thing that the surgeon's name fell into that conversation of peace and love like a funeral cortege through the midst of a celebration, at the very moment when Madeleine was experiencing the first symptoms of a physiological distress that had been occasioned by an abominable crime.

At any rate, Georges quickly effaced that obscure melancholy with tender kisses; in the woodland pathway, the somber drapery of the dusk turned the ocher of the dead leaves gray.

"It's six o'clock, my beloved Madeleine," Georges said. "I'll leave you in order to go change my clothes, and come back to dine with you. I have just enough time.

Madeleine retained him with her lips. The new kiss was absolute. Madeleine put into it all her love, all her joy and all her glorious confidence. They were marching toward ardent felicities, she innocent and chaste, agitated by a strange awakening of the senses combined with the cerebral exaltation to which superb love gives rise, he already acquainted with women but not blasé, moved like her by a noble, troubling, imperious folly bathed in mystery and force, such as he had never experienced.

They parted at the edge of the wood. She went back slowly along the path, still quivering at her fiancé's kisses, and also astonished by the strange malaise she had felt.

CHAPTER IX

In the hall of the surgical conference, which was being held in the great amphitheater of the Faculté de Médecine, Armand Caresco was speaking, standing at the small podium garnished with red velvet fringed with gold, from which orators delivered their endeavors to the appreciation of their colleagues.

Beneath the flamboyant gaslight and the glory of the allegorical frontispieces with gilt inscriptions that overhung the stage, the young master finished his lecture, taken from notes that he had scribbled in haste a few hours previously. He turned toward the members of the committee installed in the copious armchairs reserved for them on the stage, at the table covered in green baize, who were listening with interest to the surgeon's communication. Then, addressing himself specifically to the chairman, an old man whose clean-shaven face was aureoled by abundant white hair, he concluded:

"Evidently, the last word has not been pronounced on this surgery of the liver of which I am the initiator. I believe, however, in the light of the results obtained—results revealed to you in my statistics, and also, thanks to my methods and the instrumentation that I have the honor of submitting to the conference, that it will be possible henceforth, with regarding to the infections of the liver to which I have referred, to set aside the dire expectation, so prejudicial to the life of sufferers, and have recourse to a surgical intervention that is all the more efficacious for having been so rapid."

He bowed briefly to the chairman, who replied with a similar salute, while the other members of the committee, abstaining from any manifestation, remained impassive. He observed the attitude of Monant, the surgeon at the Lariboisière, who, alone among the scientists seated on the stage, was leaning toward one of his neighbors and speaking to him in a low voice, with slow gestures charges with disapproval. He divined in him the most convinced adversary of a candidature for the following year's committee. Perhaps someone had repeated to Monant the appreciations that he never ceased to offer publicly on his account.

However, enthusiastic applause burst forth, coming from the crowded floor, and compensating for that muted hostility. While picking up his sheets of paper, his eyes made a tour of the amphitheater. He recognized confusedly certain friendly faces, and also, disseminated among the swarm of applauding hands, the faces of the professors of the Faculté, imprinted with animosity and ill-concealed scorn. He preferred not to pay them any heed, and descended slowly from the podium, sustained by the bravos that the foreign delegates showed upon him and the numerous students who had come running from their lectures to listen to the audacious words of the innovator.

His bold endeavors seduced young intelligences avid for progress. In vain the professors and the hospital surgeons, some by virtue of reason and some out fear of the nascent glory, attempted to stifle the enthusiasm of their pupils beneath the discredit of sane evaluation. It was all the more difficult for them to succeed because Caresco drew in his wake an entire cortege of the obscure, the spoiled and those whose lack of worth, jealousy and disappointed ambitions embittered them against officialdom and colleagues who had achieved important positions by chance, stubborn hard work and

161

protection. He was their man, the triumphant, dazzling exception, thrown in the face of all those who supported the Faculté.

Caresco, with the practicality that dominated him, had quickly understood the benefits that he could extract from the support of unindocrinated colleagues, who were legion. He had been seen speaking at banquets of dosimetrists, homeopaths and other unorthodox societies, lauding the benefits of a medicine in which he did not believe, of whose practices he was scornful, in spite of being so worthy of scorn himself.

That is why, in order not to abandon the line of conduct he had adopted, he never neglected conferences, at which, before numerous assemblies he imposed his personality. Access to the podium at such scientific meetings is open to any physician; a modest fee giving the title of member, anyone can come to them to propound his theories, recount successful operations that are impossible to verify and display statistics that are easy to falsify. The proceedings of the sessions are published by the medical press, and even reproduced in some political or literary periodicals avid for sensational news—and renown is thus extended to the entire world.

Caresco always presented statistics in which mortality was considerable less than those of other conference-members. Those who did not know him marveled; those who had seen him operate, who had observed the surety of his hand, his rapidity, his impetuosity and his brio, without being informed of the consequences of the operations, similarly applauded without hesitation; only colleagues who were too directly in rivalry remained skeptical: the hospital surgeons interested in doubt, or those like Savre and Bordier, who had followed him closely enough to know that deception marched side by side in their man with audacity.

When he had retired from the hemicycle by the special door reserved for members of the congress, he had to submit once again to the ovations of people who were watching out for him in the corridors, and shake hands that were sometimes unknown to him. To all of them he offered the importunity of his pearly smile, the abandonment of his limp hand.

His father, who had swelled the applause from a corner of the amphitheater, ran toward him, but, being in haste to catch up with Professor Stermann of Vienna, who was addressing laudatory gestures to him from a distance, he did not respond to his affectionate advances.

Finally, traversing the courtyard of the Faculté, filled with the carriages of masters and a bustling crowd of curiosity-seekers who got out of his way, while naming him, he reached his own carriage, in order to go to meet Israel. The banker had summoned him. Now, away from the conflict, seized by the indifference of the street, he felt that he had fallen from the height of his pedestal to recommence another battle, with financial embarrassment.

As he climbed up into his coupé he spotted Bordier. He called to him: "Hey! I've had a success. Have you see the faces the Parisians are pulling? They're drooling—take it from me, they're drooling. Are you coming with me? I'll drop you off on the way."

"Thanks," Bordier replied, "but I'm waiting for one of my friends, who's coming to pick me up: Monsieur Ponviane, Mademoiselle de Jancy's fiancé. We're going to dine together and then go on to the engagement party, at Madame de Jancy's. house."

"I know; I've been invited."

"Will you be coming?"

"No, I don't think so; I have a lot to do. I want to publish the new edition of my treatise of liver surgery without delay. I'll be working this evening."

"Look, here's Ponviane now."

Bordier pointed to an elegant victoria, from which his friend, having seen him from a distance, was waving to him. The young man was in evening dress, beneath an elegant winter overcoat belted at the waist.

Instead of drawing away, Caresco remained on the sidewalk, retained by an unhealthy curiosity to make the acquaintance of the man to whom he had caused the most cowardly and infamous damage.

"Well, Bordier, introduce me."

The spontaneous nature of Georges Ponviane went out to the man, already famous, whom his friend Bordier had praised. He extended his hand forthrightly and, like others, was surprised by the limpness of the hand he gripped.

"I'm very glad to meet you, Doctor. People I know speak highly of you, and..."

He suspended the sentence; he had been about to add that everyone thought well of him, but he remembered his fiancée's aversion.

In any case, Caresco replied: "I'm equally glad, Monsieur, to offer you my congratulations. I've had the honor of being close to Mademoiselle de Jancy and I retain the fondest memory of her."

*I've had the honor of being close...*the phrase emerged by chance from his lips seemed to him to be full of a diabolical implication. He found a very particular savor in the cold irony with which, in his inner tribunal, he accompanied his sins. Superior to others by virtue of his lack of scruples, his dead or stillborn con-

164

science, he experienced a kind of keen satisfaction in spicing his wickedness with an atrocious joke.

Did Georges Ponviane have a prescience of the danger that the frequentation of that man would offer? Was he alerted by the indefinable interior voice aroused by the proximity or the abandonment? Was it, as in so many others, simply the physical repulsion of a gaze that turned away, a hand that did not exert pressure? Or was he subject to the after-influence of the woman he loved, who was like his good angel? At any rate, he suddenly felt the impulse of his heart die away.

"*Au revoir*, Doctor, we're pressed for time!"

And, followed by Bordier, he climbed into his carriage, while Caresco, surprised by that retreat, climbed into his own.

The evening being sufficiently mild to permit the victoria to travel with its awning down, under a splendid sky, the two friends experienced a visual blossoming. Georges put his arm around Bordier's shoulder; a fraternal embrace united them, enabling them to admire, without saying a word, the animation of the Boulevard Saint-Germain, along which the carriage was taking them, and the joyous animation of the student quarter in the early dusk.

Lamplighters, with their long lances over their shoulders, were setting the streets ablaze. Twenty-year-old madcaps, were filling the sidewalks with their cries, their merriment and their pursuits. Other students, more serious, with briefcases under their arms, were hastening to their lodgings. Couples passed by, offering heartwarming little collages. In the roadway, private carriages, fiacres and trams crossed paths, coachmen cursing, in a rumbling ride that was always rising and never ebbed. Cyclists of both sexes were like birds gliding gracefully at ground level through the multiple encumbrances of the intense life of the great artery.

The victoria sped on, causing the marvels of the autumnal panorama, of the Parisian evening, which is a second day within the day, to fly past the eyes of the friends in rapid succession. And all of that society, that swell of carriages and omnibuses, denuded trees and sidewalks cluttered with multicolored kiosks—and the gas-jets ignited in the reflectors, and the violent flamboyance of the shop-fronts and posters, and, further on, higher up, the sovereign perspective of the sky overtaken by the dark blue twilight, already pierced by the scintillation of stars, with the ironic bloom of the moon looking down on the houses—threw a veil woven of melancholy over their souls, as if they were admiring the décor of a dream. And they did not speak, both thinking the same things, their artistic sentiments whipped by the same astonishment.

At Bordier's home, two places had been set for the cold dinner served by the domestic. The conversation was banal and general; the presence of the maidservant was not conducive to confidences. In the young physician's bedroom, however, where cigarettes were lit, while Bordier changed his clothes in his friend's presence, Georges said to him: "You seem a trifle sad this evening, my friends. Is something worrying you?"

"Worrying…no, not exactly—but I'm profoundly disgusted with the life I'm leading."

"Come on! Your black ideas are getting a grip on you again!"

"No. Three months ago, before I was employed by Caresco, when I complained about my profession, the difficulties of the life, the back-breaking stages, night visits, the improper methods of certain colleagues, I

166

thought it was the truth—but after a good night's sleep, the wheels greased by ardor, I set off again with a certain pride in honest labor and services rendered to suffering humanity, as one says in funeral orations. But now...!

"Now, my work is less onerous, more rewarding, more regular; a certain consideration reflects on me from my collaboration with the famous surgeon; imbeciles even envy me; nothing would be easier for me than to make useful contacts among the people who frequent the house in the Avenue Hoche; in sum, in Caresco's wake I might go on to wealth and honors...and yet...

"And yet I detest the role that the man is making me play. My dear Georges, I'm the accomplice of atrocities...veritable crimes. This morning, again, a child died during an operation. Yesterday, two women died out of six who underwent operations. The day before yesterday, and the day before that...what do I know? I can no longer tell you how many. And I assist in these deaths, I collaborate with these cadavers. There! I disgust myself!"

Ponviane burst out laughing. He knew the nervous susceptibility of Bordier's character. He believed that he was under the impression of one of the periods of demoralization to which he had seen him subject before, probably caused by that morning's accident—a straw fire all the more lively because it is so brief. Had he not often witnessed the exhalation of those atonal moments, and had to combat the depressions of that child-like heart with humorous philosophy? This time, once again, he adopted the strategy of steering that easily-manageable skiff toward badinage.

"Come on, you big baby! It's sheer chance, those fatalities. Any industry..."

"My profession isn't an industry."

"I agree. Let's say practice. Any practice is fatally exposed to produce hitches. How many times, in our cotton-mills, do we have to eject whole batches of unsuccessful thread? There are profits and losses. Do you think you can never fail? That would be too good. Then again, viewing things from the most elevated viewpoint, it isn't desirable."

Bordier was knotting a cravat in front of the mirror. He turned to Georges, bewildered.

"Why is that?" he asked.

Although it was not in Georges' mild and reserved sentimental complexion to have recourse to macabre jokes, and the dark humor of medical students did not suit his refined character at all—especially in the period of amorous tenderness that the melancholy grace of his fiancée had brought out in him, inundating him with an incomparable delicacy and giving him a veritable nobility of ideas and speech—he nevertheless directed his wit toward a brutal theory often expressed in the wards of large hospitals, in order to change his friend's mood.

"It's obvious," he went on. "You know full well that your work as a destroyer is useful to society. Don't you think that when you, a Charles IX of cripples, have made a Saint-Bartholomew's Day Massacre of all these wretches, instead of patching them up sufficiently to allow them to reproduce creatures condemned in advance, and to disseminate the seeds of their maladies in agglomerations of people, that you've protected Society against a danger all the more terrible because nothing can be done to combat it? No, my friend, continue your liberating work: kill! Kill!—or, at least, is you let them live, suppress their genital organs. They'd have the resource of singing in the Sixtine Chapel."

Bordier straightened his face and shrugged his shoulders before his friend's puerile humor. He put on an elegant dinner-jacket.

"And then," Georges concluded, throwing his cigarette butt into the fireplace, "you won't bore us this evening with your black ideas. This evening ought to be an hour of enlightenment for you, a reflection of my intoxication, for this evening I'm introducing you to my fiancée. Come on, you great fool. Put on a good winter coat. You won't be back before eight o'clock in the morning. Are you coming?"

And he dragged him to Madame de Jancy's house, having almost recomforted him, turned him like a glove with a few facile jokes, by reason of the influence he exercised over that accessible soul, that weak and disabled character, like a rudderless ship drifting with every current.

Madame de Jancy lived with her daughter in a luxurious house in the Rue Pierre-Charron, the aristocratic artery that extends from the Champs-Élysées to the Trocadéro. That evening, a festival animation filled the vicinity of the house, extending to the threshold of the dwelling. The coaching entrance, wide open and bathed in electric light, gave access to private carriages. Muffled couples and diamond-decked ladies emerged from them to climb the steps to the vestibule, decked with foliage. The brightly colored ball-gowns made a violent contrast with the somber furs of their cavaliers. In the street, idlers and passers-by, servants and belated delivery-boys, formed groups, commenting and watching the shuttered façade, whose windows allowed a little of the joy of the interior to filter through.

In the first-floor drawing rooms, as soon as Madeleine saw her fiancé appear, she detached herself from several ladies of the feminist congress, in whose midst Madame Bise was enthroned, and ran toward him.

"Madeleine, my dear beloved," said the young man, "I reproach myself for not having been here with you already for a long time. That fault lies with the best of my friends, to whom I now introduce you, Dr. Jean Bordier.

Madeleine extended an elegantly hand to Bordier, gloved in pink suede that extended to the elbow, leaving the firm white roundness of the upper arm bare to the short sleeve of the low-cut dress in pink surah.

How delightful and dazzling Bordier found her, with her impeccably milky shoulders emerging from the tender corsage, with slender, vigorous and supple line of the throat, and a bosom over which the little blue threads of the veins ran timidly, and, above all, with that marvelously graceful blonde head and blue eyes with a dark gaze—the whole dominated by the overwhelming gilded mass of the hair, which, that evening, in the combined light of candles and electricity, appeared more golden than ever.

Yes, truly, she was an adorable creature, gentle and strong, tender and passionate, aristocratic from the tips of her little feet, imprisoned in black satin, to the last vaporous wisp of her hair, and well worthy of determining the life of his friend.

"No, you're not too late. Maman hasn't come down yet; she's taking her time getting dressed. You can't imagine how coquettish Maman has become, since I've been engaged!"

Georges interrogated his friend's physiognomy. Bordier could not repress a sign of admiring approval. Madeleine perceived it.

"You'll make me blush," she said. "I'm so glad to have made myself beautiful for you."

People were coming in: plump or stiff mothers with tall or short daughters, flat-chested beneath the tulle of their low necklines; a polytechnician with a pimply forehead; dandies in jackets with flowers in the buttonholes and monocles in their eyes, dragging their sickening futility through the salons. Madeleine had taken her fiancé's arm, exchanging handshakes and kisses, happy and proud, triumphant in all her splendor and joy.

Madame Bise, self-important and noisy, as if she were giving the party, was accepting greetings, making introductions, entirely at home, waving an immense fan that, with every flip of the wrist, caused the power with which she had thought it appropriate to ornament her apple-cheeks to fly away, attracting attention with exclamations in a southern accent: "There you are! What! Go on! What a shame!"

Nearby, draped in a bright green costume, was a tall, stiff, bony individual of masculine appearance coiffed with a torsade of dark gray hair, with a mouth garnished with prominent, widely-spaced incisors: Miss Pisword, the president of the feminist congress, also harvesting a part of the honors and attentions of the worthy aunt, infatuated with her. With her British arrogance, imprinted with a Puritan reserve, like a mainmast swaying from side to side, she subjected to introductions, greeting them with comical replies, grotesque in her violent costume, her fleeting profile, her fleshless bosom and the yellow mossy smile that she sometimes sketched in reply to compliments.

And everyone twittered and fluttered, back and forth and around and und, bowing, sitting down on the velvet benches, issuing or accepting invitations to dance, which they inscribed on their cards.

"I don't know what Maman is doing to be so late! I must go tell her that there are a lot of people here already."

Georges did not retain her. She flew off as birds do, in a flutter of wings.

People were still arriving and, disorientated at not being received by the mistress of the house, were spreading out randomly through the salons. An orchestra of strings and woodwinds came to gather around the piano, disposing music-stands and scores.

The Vicomtesse de Mesma, sprightly and precious, appeared with her round raptorial eyes. She embraced Madame Bise, and then had herself introduced by her to a lady whose thin and bilious daughter seem to be suffering.

Then Monsieur and Madame Romé made their entrance, Madame Bise welcomed them with an exclamation. "There you are! How are you? *Bonjour*, Aline. Are you well, darling?"

No, Aline was not in good health, and complained of it to her aunt. For some time, she had felt pains in her liver. The family physician, Dr. Cartaux, had said that he could not find anything wrong. Deep down, she was convinced that Monsieur Cartaux was behind the times, that he did not understand her malady. And she added, in a whisper to Madame Bise: "I'd have liked a consultation with Dr. Caresco."

"Which? The father or the son?"

"The son, Armand Caresco, naturally—the one who's much occupied with diseases of the liver, I'm told. So, I wanted a consultation, but my parents didn't want to take me. They say all sorts of things, and don't want to admit that I'm suffering. Yes, I'm suffering a great deal. Is he coming this evening, Monsieur Caresco?"

"No, my darling. He has too much work to do."

"How annoying that is! I would have been so glad to see him." A cloud of sadness veiled her pretty face—but when Madame Bise had promised her in a whisper to take her to see Armand Caresco in secret from her parents, she became immeasurably joyful.

"He's astonishing, that young surgeon," Madame Bise continued, out loud, in a fashion to be heard. "He worked another miracle not long ago—all the newspapers are talking about it. Look—there's his assistant, who can tell us about it. Hey! You over there!"

It was Bordier, who was passing by, to whom she called out in that irreverent fashion, waving her fan. He did not understand the signal to begin with; then, when he had understood, he turned his back and drew away—but Madame Bise sent Aline after him, who graciously requested his arm.

"Well, young man, it appears that you've worked another miracle, over there in the Avenue Hoche?"

Bordier, vexed by that patronizing tone, felt a surge of anger, He wanted to reply with ridicule.

"Miracles? We work them every day…we're opening a branch at Lourdes."

Madame Bise swelled up with pride.

Accentuating the thinness of his smile, he continued: "And if I can't say that you're their Holy Virgin, at least I'm intimately convinced that you're no stranger to the birth of these miracles."

He had spoken as malevolently as his timid nature permitted, with a sudden reversion toward the hateful ideas with regard to Armand Caresco that had still been filing his soul a little while ago—but Madame Bise had not understood the sarcastically exaggerated allusion that the young man had made, for, in sum, if she extolled the surgeon so much, it was purely out of enthusiasm, southern ebullience, a need for expansion, in the same way that she was presently occupied with feminism. So, not understanding, she said: "You're right"—which caused Bordier a certain amazement.

After a moment's silence, she added: "And is she doing well, at least?"

"Who?"

"The mother."

"What mother?"

"The grandmother of the little girl who threw herself off the fourth floor."

Bordier did not understand. "What, there's a little girl who threw herself off the fourth floor?"

"No, silly, it was her grandmother. Come on, don't play the innocent—anyway, it's in all the evening papers."

And she took out of her pocket an article clipped from a newspaper, which she held out to Bordier. In the form of a brief article relating the accident and the operation that followed, a skillful advertisement lauded the surgeon. Bordier was revolted to see his own name similarly made public, attached to that of Caresco.

That he falsifies a claim for himself, he thought, *that he takes advantage of a suicide—of which he is, in sum, the cause, since the suicide derived from a cadaver—to sound the mercenary trumpet of renown, is one thing...but to mingle my name, previously obscurely honorable, with his atrocities, I absolutely refuse to tolerate!*

And he stood there, frowning, in contrast with the exuberance of Madame Bise, who, surrounded by the fluttering and rusting circle of ladies, read the printed article aloud.

The Vicomtesse de Mesma had drawn the bilious young woman and her mother into the group; she uttered enthusiastic exclamations at every sentence the reader inflated with her southern dissonance. She underlined the reading with: "He's astonishing, you see!... Admirable!... Marvelous!..."

Standing to one side, but following the conversation, Monsieur Ponviane, who had just arrived, was surprised by that enthusiasm and the importance that the newspapers were according to the publicity of a simple incident.

"You see," Madame Bise said to Bordier, when she had finished her dithyrambic peroration, "that I was right to say that you work miracles."

Bordier shrugged his shoulders politely.

"You're truly too modest," said the Vicomtesse de Mesma, who had noticed the gesture. "I absolutely owe my life to Dr. Caresco. He operated on me when I as condemned by all the other physicians." And with a gesture of ecstasy, looking heavenwards, she added: "Ah, without him! Without him! For me, you see, there are two things in the world: God and Caresco!"

The bilious young woman was prodigiously interested by the conversation. Blood flowed to her face, chasing the stigmata of chlorosis from her cheeks. She said a few words to her mother, who then approached Madame Bise.

"You see, Madame, the state that my poor daughter is in. She no longer obtains any benefit from the various treatments that he physicians have prescribed for her. It's her liver that's causing her to suffer. Tell me, since Dr. Caresco is one of your friends, will you introduce us to him?"

The Vicomtesse de Mesma, comprehending that she would lose the profit of her touting if it were Madame Bise who introduced the invalid into the house in the Avenue Hoche, rose to the challenge. Her eyes shone, her nose, like a hawk's beak, accentuated its curve. With an avalanche of words, like a shopkeeper talking up his wares, she threw herself on the prey that as getting away from her,

"But I'll take you there myself, to Dr. Caresco. He has a great affection for me, as he loves all of those whose lives he's saved. You'll see, he's a charming man. It seems that it's him who owes you all the gratitude for the good he's done you. And one is so well surrounded in his operating theater! It's so clean, so comfortable! The sisters are so gentle with the patients! Oh, don't talk to me about other nurses; there's no one like the good sisters for showing devotion, is there, Madame? And if you knew how many of my friends he's rescued from distress, how many I've taken to him who, like you, Mademoiselle, felt desperate, and whom he got back on their feet in a week!"

The discussion continued. Rendezvous were arranged.

At that moment, a chambermaid irrupted into the salons and, slipping through the groups that were beginning to dance, reached Georges Ponviane.

"Monsieur, come quickly…Madame and Mademoiselle have been taken ill."

"Bring Monsieur Bordier immediately," said Georges, running to the stairway.

He went into the bedroom, of which another fearful domestic dared not cross the threshold, where the door stood ajar.

By the dubious light of the single candle that, the lamp having been knocked over, was feebly illuminating the intimate luxury of the objects, blurring the embroidered flowers of the silk curtains, magnifying the shadows of the alcove, where garments were strewn pell-mell on the bed, in the silky precipitation of a hasty toilette, George was terror-stricken by the sight of two bodies lying on the parquet in fixed, stiff attitudes: the ornamented bodies of the mother and the daughter, their bare shoulders emerging from their dresses. Around them was the disorder of things knocked over in the fall, including an overturned chair.

"Oh, my God! My God, what's happened?"

He ran to Madeleine first, knelt down, felt her cold hand, and raised her read, which was resting on the pillow of her golden hair. Her expression was calm, her eyes closed, her features pure.

"Madeleine!" he moaned, "What's wrong...? One might think that she were dead! Madeleine, my beloved Madeleine, speak to me, answer me!"

And with despair, overwhelmed by the suddenness of the drama, unconscious of his ideas as of his movements, he stood up, looking for something or someone—he did not know.

Fortunately, Bordier appeared. Georges felt his anguish diminishing.

"Oh, my friend, what a horrible thing! Look at Madeleine! It's frightful!" His respiration was halting. In his amorous egotism, he forgot Madame de Jancy, seemingly ignoring the fact that she was lying inanimate alongside her daughter. He squeezed the physician's arm vigorously. "Save her, my friend. Save her!"

Bordier disengaged himself from the fearful grip, leaned over Madeleine, measured her pulse with his fingertips, lifted her eyelids and interrogated the eyes.

"Fainted!" he said, briefly. "Unlace her corset and dab her face with a damp cloth. It's nothing."

Georges sighed loudly, steeped a napkin with water from a carafe, and returned to kneel beside his fiancée while Bordier, now leading over Madame de Jancy, observed that she was nothing more than a cadaver, already cold.

"Georges," he said, standing up, "you need to get Madeleine out of here, urgently, before she comes round. Her mother is dead."

Georges started trembling again, while Bordier conserved all his composure and authority. Aided by a chambermaid, he carried Madeleine's limp body into the next room, which was her own.

It was the first time that the fiancé had crossed his beloved's threshold—and in what terror, what catastrophe! Instead of entering that sacred refuge with the harmonious figure of the young woman on his arm, with laughter in the eyes and lips full of love, it was an inanimate body that he was sustaining with difficulty, which he helped to place heavily on the blue satin coverlet. Instead of the luminous radiance that would have greeted him in any other circumstances, it was a room scarcely lit by urgent flickerings, in a funeral disorder! Instead of amorous words and joyful exclamations prompted by the ingenuities and the thousand trivia that decorated the room, there were Bordier's bleak instructions, the futile haste of the maidservant, the slap of the damp napkin on the young woman's cheeks: all the disarray of the drama, with the irony of the muffled rhythm of the orchestra downstairs, violating the drama up above.

On the landing, Georges' father and Madame Bise, alerted to what was happening, dared not penetrate into the room where Madame de Jancy was still lying on the floor, and stood there in confusion, letting the catastrophe drift. The aunt, however, unable to suppress the religion of science, called out to Bordier as he went past.

"Well, what a story! She's dead! Are you perfectly sure? Perhaps it's only a attack...people have been known to be buried alive! Are you sure that she's dead? And of what? Tell me, of what?"

"I don't know," Bordier replied, irritatedly. "Probably a ruptured aneurism—but I don't know."

"I know," said Madame Bise. "It's something in her chest that will have burst. My sister-in-law must have had a malady of the chest. She often had difficulty breathing. I wanted to take her to see Dr. Caresco—the father, the homeopath—who would surely have cured her, but she refused. My God, what a calamity! Are you perfectly sure that she's dead? What if someone were to fetch Dr. Caresco? For you're very young..."

Bordier looked at her blue eyes, anguished by distress, behind her lorgnon. Always Caresco! Caresco: a fatal name, which seemed to sound like a knell, accompanying the deaths to which he was a witness. Even when he had nothing to do with the event, a bizarre destiny brought that name to the ears, imposed it strangely, along with the funeral cortege, the shroud, the bier...

CHAPTER X

In his mistress' house, Armand Caresco had reserved a room for himself on the first floor, where he had installed a kind of study. A vast table in blackened wood, contrasting, in its vulgarity, with the rest of the furniture, was covered in pamphlets, scientific papers, notes, newspapers, and all the elements of a book that he was revising, on the surgery of the liver.

These papers, methodically classified, arranged in various piles, symbolized by their neatness the practical mind of the man who was utilizing them. Within arm's reach there was a portable telephone, putting him in communication with his sanitarium and the rest of Paris, a marvelous apparatus that transported his thought in a second to wherever he wanted it to go, a worthy complement of his activity and feverish affairs.

The remainder of the furniture consisted of miscellaneous items, the detritus of the beautiful Tripe-merchant's former habitations: a chaise-longue, once very useful in a professional context, now abandoned; a Chinese cabinet, the gift of one of the sons of the Sun, an ambassador in Paris; low chairs originating from a room she had furnished in secret from a lover with whom she was cohabiting. On the walls there were gross imitations of tapestry, and, surrounded by a bright gilt frame, a sickening color print, representing an Emperor of Russia and a President of the French Republic giving one another the accolade. At the back of the room, on an iron tripod, there was a target.

It was here that Caresco, indifferent to the ambience, utterly engrossed in his work—and, in any case, not very artistic—spent hours hard at work. Here, there was nothing of the surgeon, everything of the man of science. The long late nights were his best work, when Mathilde did not drag him to her stupid demi-mondaine gatherings, went to bed early, or, under the pretext of going to the theater with friends, went to consummate an illegitimate adultery in some Montmartre cabaret.

In the calm and peace of that solitude, the surgeon, after the physical expenditures of the day, the fatigues of operations, consultations, trips to the establishments of manufacturers of surgical instruments, bookshops and publishers, still found sufficient energy for cerebral function. He needed that obstinate labor in that quiet corner, in order to produce so much, to astonish the medical world with the quantity of the works conceived by his powerful brain.

On the other hand, that physical and cerebral hyperactivity was welcomed by the surgeon's adversaries as a weapon that they turned against him. One doesn't burn the candle at both ends, said some. Overwork leads to folly when it doesn't lead astray, others thought.

That afternoon, however, Armand Caresco, sitting at the blackened wood table, was not working. Before his eyes he had numerous letters from the morning's mail, brought by one of the footmen from the Avenue Hoche—for, confident in Bordier's punctuality, he had not yet made the daily visits to the patients on whom he had operated the previous day. A depressed lassitude overwhelmed him; his indifferent hand rummaged through the letters without deciding to open one.

Nothing connected with his clinic had given rise to his depression, however; his latest series of operations, apart from one female pauper who had died on the table—a trivial concern, a pauperess!—had been successful. No patient had manifested disquieting convulsions, and the telephone call he had received a few minutes ago from Soeur Cunégonde had announced the departure of the old grandmother he had trepanned, also recovered.

What intimate contrariety, then, rendered his hand limp and veiled his thoughts vaguely with the mists of discouragement? He took a small notebook from his jacket pocket and opened it. Figures were aligned there which he added up. That notebook never left him; he inscribed his expenditure and receipts therein, without details, in round numbers. Every week he established the balance; every month and every year he added up the totals.

Armand Caresco leaned his elbows on the table, interrogating the pages of the notebook from the beginning, turning the pages slowly. Thus he reviewed the history of his income during the twelve years he had been practicing, from his father's wretched clinic to the superb establishment in the Avenue Hoche. What a road traveled!

The takings of the first years were very modest, in truth; his receipts barely covered his expenditure. Then, suddenly, from fifteen thousand the sum jumped to fifty thousand, during the fifth year. It was a giant step that had been further amplified in the years that followed. And last year, had he not taken in four hundred and fifty thousand francs? Almost a fortune. At first, the expenses had not followed the pace of the receipts; he had had savings; a little longer, and he would soon have been rich. But the installation in the Avenue Hoche, and, above all, Mathilde's rapacity, had swallowed up his savings.

Desperately, he went over the figures again, as if searching for an arithmetical error, a fortunate slip that would chase away the anguish of observing his vanished wealth. Besides, why linger over his calculations? Was his wallet not empty? Did he not have, for the fifteenth of December, that absurd debt of a hundred thousand francs borrowed from Israel—a debt that he finally had to repay, for the banker had told him firmly the day before yesterday that he would no longer renew it and that he would leave the bailiff the care of acting in favor of his interests if the money was not forthcoming. Israel, a former fellow in religion, a man he had invited to his home so frequently, whom he had treated as a friend! Caresco recognized the traditional rapacity of the race of which he regretted being a member. The Jew was threatening him with the bailiff, and he would do as he said.

For a moment, the surgeon thought about taking out a further loan, of finding some lender confident in his future and his success—but where could he turn? Of friends, he had none; usurers would only advance him a hundred thousand francs at enormous rates of interest and in the short term—at the end of which he would find himself in the same situation, doubtless aggravated. It would be climbing higher in order to fall further.

Ask Mathilde? Mathilde, who was the reason for the difficulty—for it was for her, to satisfy her stupid caprice for that necklace that he had got into debt? His mistress would put her hand in the fire to pull him out of the abyss, he was sure, but could she do it? She was as poor as him. All the money he had given her had only gone to fill in her own gulf. She had often told him that, and Mathilde did not lie.

Sell the necklace? Perhaps—he would talk to her about it. The sum they would get back would be far from sufficient, but might it not persuade Israel to be patient? Then again, in the month between now and the settlement date, he could anticipate a few fruitful operations. He had a few in prospect, which he could hurry along: General de Rion, the farmer's wife, and Stella, the member of the company at the Opéra-Comique, who would be brought by the dancer with whom he had dined a few days before, and two others already announced by the Vicomtesse de Mesma would help to fill the hole.

Already, he had established a scaffolding of certainty on those probabilities, losing—as the desperate do—a precise sense of things, his clarity of vision, the sage coordination of affairs that had always characterized him before he had been caught in this labyrinth of worries. Yes, truly, he had not anticipated, when he had gone a few months before to hold his hand out to the banker, that he might end up in such an impasse, drowning so piteously in the bankruptcy of his common sense! What a disaster! Was it worth the trouble of being so organized, so strong, of having worked so hard, to have done so many operations, to find himself, in the final analysis, dragged by the claws of bad luck to the base of the rock, where the howling pack of creditors would tighten its semicircle to tear him apart, without his being able to escape, to sink into the rock that opposed his flight!

Oh, money worries! The worst of all, after Mathilde!

He replaced the notebook in his jacket pocket on the left side, the side of the heart, devotedly, as if he were placing the portrait of a lover. Then, determined to chase away the shadows of his anxiety with the light of work, he picked up the abandoned penholder, consulted his notes, and exerted his mental strength upon the lines he was writing.

But his mind could not follow his will; his thoughts flew away toward the image of a strong-box filled with gold and thousand-franc bills that he could extract as he wished, making gold coins spill from torn sacks. Then there was the raptorial face of Israel, which surged forth between himself and his abstraction.

Generally unimaginative, very much the master of his intellectual distributions, he was momentarily astonished by these obsessions. And, definitively unable to apply himself, he pushed away the books and pens, and abandoned the work.

Then he opened a drawer, took out a case that contained a superb pair of dueling pistols, chose one and, without moving from his seat, extended his arm and took aim at the target. Shot after shot rang out, and every one hit the bull's-eye. The black cardboard circle was eaten away by the bullets; soon, nothing was left of it.

Satisfied with his skill, he went to detach the target, and considered it at length.

"Here you are, with your toy!"

It was Mathilde coming in, returning from the Bois. Her plaited black skirt rustled. Her rounded doll-like face, whipped by the keen cold air of the excursion, had rediscovered the pink colors of its cheeks; her opulent bosom filled the room.

Armand put down his weapon, stood up, and put his arms around his mistress' study waist.

"There you are my dear; did you have a pleasant excursion? I'm glad you're here; I need to talk to you seriously. You need to help me alleviate serious concerns..."

"Poor rat! There are serious concerns!"

She covered his face with little cold kisses, pressing the pulp of her lips upon his tanned skin, going to search his neck for the favorite place. Those caresses usually sufficed to avert the threat of serious conversations, but this time, Armand seemed to remain insensible to their advances. Mathilde, sensing the question of money approaching, abandoned the embrace and went to sit in an armchair, seriously.

"What is it, then?"

"Israel doesn't want to know any longer."

"You've seen him?"

"The day before yesterday. After renewing the loan for a month and a half at ten per cent—which is nearly a hundred per cent per annum—that if I'm not in a position to reimburse him by the fifteenth of December, which is in forty-five days, he'll send the bailiffs in and have my sanitarium seized. Not the instruments—he doesn't have the right—but all the furniture, the tapestries, the pictures, the works of art. You can imagine the scandal, can't you?"

"The old Shylock!" exclaimed Mathilde, feigning indignation. "What do you owe him?"

"The price of the necklace—a hundred thousand. A hundred and ten with the interest."

"Well, between now and then..."

"Between now and then, my dear, I can't earn a hundred thousand francs. Operations on which I was counting have fallen through; others haven't been paid for and never will be. No, I can't see how I can get out of it."

"Ask your father."

"My father! My father, part with money! It's obvious that you don't know him. Then again, he hasn't a sou."

She did not raise any more objections, but contented herself with a little sigh, smoothing the pleats of her skirt. The feathers in her black velvet hat stirred silently along with her body. She avoided her lover's gaze as he fixed her with his black gaze, a burning demand on his lips.

Now that the anguish of money was suggesting the shrinkage of reality to him, he was wondering by what chain of events, by what aberration, he had arrived at a passionate attachment to that woman. Doubt regarding his strength and his habit of victory were mingling within him, since he, always the master of others and sometimes of destiny, lowering the flag before the omnipotence of the beautiful Tripe-merchant, had reached this point for her, for a caprice of coquetry, of getting into debt, into the impasse at the end of which is ruination.

That necklace! In giving it to his mistress he had committed a lapse of judgment for which he reproached himself dolorously, and a certain rancor took hold in his heart against the fat woman. His eyes, in coveting her, distilled the voluptuousness of his sentiments, but brief gleams were also passing here, charged with anger against the person who dominated him with her imbecile power. He tasted a poison that was simultaneously bitter and sickly.

"Yes, he went on, "it's the necklace that has sunk me. Without the necklace..."

The beautiful Tripe-merchant continued her refusal to understand. Her coated mask conserved the same cheerful placidity, of a contented woman with a good digestion. But she divined that a recourse to her delicacy was about to be attempted, and internally, she was preparing the eventual story.

"Yes, my cat," she said, "it's that accursed necklace..."

Then, even though there was no desolation in her tone, nothing in hr physiognomy, her gesture or her voice that could give rise to the supposition of a regret for that unfortunate purchase, a generous impulse of her heart that might drive her to restore the ruinous pearls, to throw them at the feet of the unfortunate lover who had given them to her, Armand, as a skillful duelist, took advantage of the sentence to bring up his proposal.

"Oh, my dear Mathilde, don't reproach yourself. No, I gave you those pearls with great heart, without foreseeing the embarrassment in which the gift would place me, so I certainly wouldn't want to dispossess you of them, to accept the sacrifice that I sense that you're disposed to make."

Mathilde could not master a certain amazement. He continued: "However, perhaps there's a middle course to which I could easily reconcile myself. It would consist of borrowing on the necklace, from the same jeweler who sold it, a sum..."

He did not finish. Mathilde, behind the fine batiste handkerchief that hid her eyes, was playing the comedy of tears.

"My wolf...forgive me, my big wolf...it's already done!"

"What! It's already done! Oh, my Tithilde, how generous you are!"

He had completely misunderstood. Mathilde sensed how unfavorable the reaction would be to her, and the difficulty she would have in completing her lie. She was burning her boats. Too bad! Did she not have enough to live on? She would never be naïve enough to give up property acquired. Such follies were all very well for inexperienced youth, but it had cost her too much to be generous in those times for man who had no gratitude for her sacrifices.

"You don't understand. How annoyed I am by that! You know that I still had thirty thousand francs in debts..."

"You told me ten thousand..."

"I told you ten thousand? You're mistaken, my rat. It was thirty thousand. So I went to find Jacob, the jeweler who sold me the necklace, and asked him to advance me that sum, leaving him the necklace in pawn. He accepted, and just now, I paid off my debt. Hold on—I have the receipts in my pocket...would you like to see them? No, you don't want to, my poor cabbage! I'm utterly, utterly desolate!"

With her infantile gaze, she studied her lover's distressed expression. Implausible as that retreat was, it seemed nevertheless to be accepted by the surgeon, who fell into an armchair in despair, his head in his hands, sunk in an obscure melancholy.

Mathilde, in order to distract him from his obsession and not to give him time to appreciate futility of her lie, resolved to fall back on heroic means. Rapidly, with a sure and habitual gesture, she removed her hat, caused her bodice and skirt to disappear and, clad in her open-necked chemise gripped in her corset and her pink silk bloomers descending over her black stockings, she went to stand in front of him.

Generally, he could not resist the sight of that overflowing flesh and the sight of Mathilde in that costume, the contrast of colors, the transparency of fabrics and the provocation of the silk having the gift of animating his desires, of striking the spark that ignited the beast, of making him forget his cares of his occupations, and the lassitude of toil, in order to plunge into the ardent satisfaction of the senses.

This time, however, he pushed her away, almost brutally, refusing the flesh-bath that she was offering him.

"No, not today. I'm tired."

"Your fatigue never stops you, my wolf. Why do you no longer want the woman who loves you?" She pressed herself upon him, soliciting him with her bare arms, her globular breasts, the heady atmosphere that emanated from her.

Again, however, he pushed her away.

"No, no, no. Go away. Leave me alone."

Offended by that disdain, she rapidly picked up her clothes and took refuge in her bedroom.

He picked up his hat, went out, leapt into the carriage that Mathilde had just quit, and had himself taken to the Avenue Hoche. On the way, he opened his mail, of mediocre interest: emotional letters of thanks, demands for money—he shrugged his shoulders at those!—clippings from newspapers concerning him, marked with red pencil, sent to him by an agency. With a rapid glance he scanned the pieces of paper, and then tore them into little pieces which he scattered in the wind through the lowered window of the coupé. Nothing inspired attention, nothing promised an operation.

In his consulting room, Soeur Cunégonde came to join him.

"Well, Sister, what's new?" He was thinking about the condition of his patients.

She replied: "Number six—you know, the little seamstress with the ovariotomy—has left without paying."

"Again! But you shouldn't have let her go!"

"She didn't have a sou, Doctor. Her uncle, who was supposed to pay the bill, thought the sum too high and didn't want to settle it. She said that she'd pay it off in installments. I got her to sign bills. Here they are."

She took four pieces of paper from her money-clip, which Caresco took angrily. Everything definitely seemed to be turning against him, even the humble, who were generally the most punctual payers, were also proving unwilling to hand over cash at the very moment when Israel was threatening him.

"Has Monsieur Bordier come this afternoon?" he went on.

"He's still upstairs, Doctor."

Followed by the sister, who hastened her steps to keep up with him, he went up the stairs at a run. No urgent necessity solicited such haste, but he was in his active mood, needing to expend energy, and anger was causing his soul to seethe, urging him to throw himself into his work, to enter more energetically into the fecund struggle of life, the struggle of endeavor and productivity.

He opened a door. On the bed in the room, a man on whose liver he had operated two days before was moaning.

"What's the matter? Are you in pain?"

"Yes, a great deal."

"An injection of morphine, Sister."

He lifted up bedclothes and removed the pins securing the body-stocking fitted over the dressing. Then he brought forward a wheeled apparatus containing a fountain for washing and disinfecting hands, and a ray with a few instruments of primary utility, bathed in a solution of phenol: scalpels, forceps, scissors, probes and drains. While he made the soap-foam fly, Soeur Cunégonde filled a small Pravaz syringe with a morphine solution taken from a wide-necked bottle.

"Not now, Sister."

He opened a tap, dipped his fingers in sublimate, returned to the patient and removed the wadding of the dressing. The odor of the iodoform with which the wound had been coated was released. The scarring was proceeding normally; the suture-points in the skin were not even reddened by inflammation. The patient considered the wound unemotionally.

"The wound is perfectly fine, Monsieur. Why are you complaining?"

"Doctor, I'm suffering horribly."

"Give him the injection, then, Sister."

In reality, the man was not in pain. He was complaining in order to obtain the morphine, for which he had already acquired a habit, which plunged him into a benevolent bliss. It was his second injection of the day.

The surgeon was not deceived. What did it matter to him if the patients contracted fatal addictions during their sojourn in his sanitarium? Was it not the surest way of obtaining the immobility necessary to the closure of the wounds, and also of shutting up the groans of pain, the cries of distress? By that means, people were healed without suffering or died without complaint. But the majority of those who were cured took away an indelible vice, the seeds of another death even more frightful, a disastrous passion that organized the simultaneous decay of the body and the soul, to end at Sainte-Anne.

It was the second injection of the day. Soeur Cunégonde, unalarmed by the man's sex, pinched the skin of the thigh, plunged the needle in horizontally, and injected the clear liquid. What compunction there was in that gesture, what generous commiseration in her expression!

Every evening, the good sister injected the patients. It was so pleasant for her to think about the calm night that the poor sufferers would have, without the persecution of the blade, without the anguish that causes sudden awakening, gripping the throat and squeezing the heart, and brings forth the incoherent babble of fear. And then, did not that insomnia also entrain that of the sister, the nurse, who would be constrained to quite the soft warmth of the bedclothes to address reassuring words that would send the patient back to sleep?

Yes, along with the injection, the good Soeur Cunégonde passed on a little of her devotion, convinced that the clear solution was truly a blessing of heaven, which, by means of those few droplets slipped beneath the skin, plunged the entire being into a profound forgetfulness, a blissful annihilation, a holy intoxication, a lacuna in life...limbo on earth, she often repeated to herself.

They went into other rooms. Visits had already been carried out by Bordier; the dressings did not need disturbed again. The surgeon contented himself with taking pulses and looking at temperature charts. He also made a few banal comments, calmed anxieties with a smile. Some patients were accompanied by relatives, mothers or spouses, who stood up as he entered, serious, attentive and respectful. He bowed humbly, looking away, and then, before leaving, distributed reassuring words, the manna of hope. It was Faith that entered with him; his soul experienced a constant pride in that.

In a room on the second floor he was struck by the insipid odor particular to suppurating wounds. The man in the room, who was poor, had undergone an operation a month before to remove a strange abdominal cyst, of an unknown nature, a large incision having been made in the abdomen without any attempt being made to seek the origin of the cyst. The man had been laid low as much by fever as by morphine. His skin burning, his cheeks red and prominent, collapsed on the bed facing the wall, he did not even turn round when Caresco came in. The latter took off the dressing. From a gaping hole circled by vinous flesh, a black and fetid pus was escaping through a rubber drain. Above the hole, the ribs displayed their arches, with which the skin seemed to have fused, so much was the poor devil eaten away by the malady.

"The cavity is always washed thoroughly, Sister?"

"Twice a day make boric injections. A great deal of pus comes out, and also a kind of black pulp. Monsieur Bordier thinks that he's going to die."

"It's necessary to make a counter-opening. The cavity never drains on that side."

He looked at the man, who still seemed lost in the mirages of his fever. Momentarily, he thought about giving him chloroform, to suppress the sharp pain of the new wound he was about to inflict, but was it really worth the trouble of disturbing so many people—the sisters, and Bordier—and wasting so much time for a simple stroke of the scalpel? He also reflected that the man was poor, hat he had carried out the operation gratuitously, that he would even have difficulty recovering the expenses of a stay in the sanitarium.

"Bring the apparatus nearer, Sister."

The wheeled tale was pushed by the sister. He selected a scalpel from the tray and swiftly, profoundly, plunged it into the side. The man uttered an atrocious cry of surprise and pain.

"Don't move—it's over."

He searched the depths of the flesh with long forceps, through the opening he had just made, shoved, and caused the apparatus to reappear through the first orifice. Between the jaws of the forcers he fixed a rubber drain, and pulled again, drawing the tube through the path he had just created. The man groaned dully; a tear ran through the gray hair on his hirsute face.

Soeur Cunégonde took his hands and patted them. "Come on, Monsieur, calm down. Remember that Our Lord Jesus Christ also had his side pierced, and did not complain. And in his case, it was to save humankind, while in yours, it's only to save you."

Oh! Our Lord Jesus Christ! The poor fellow was impressed by that! Already he had been reclaimed by his burning inertia; his limp head fell back on the pillow, his cheeks, paled momentarily by the unexpected pain, were covered in scarlet again. He sank into the empty gulf of his misery, insensitive to the cold jet that the surgeon caused to pass through his agonized and bloody flesh.

"We'll get him out of this, Sister," Caresco said. "He did well to come and find us. He'd already be dead if he'd remained in the hands of the hospital surgeons."

In the moral as well as the physical sense, he washed his hands. He added: "The old woman's gone, then?"

"Yes, Doctor. She no longer had a temperature, but she was half-mad. She was talking about killing you."

He shrugged his shoulders. He felt uneasy, however. Although his conscience was anesthetized in remembering the dead, he feared the imprecations and reproaches of the living, only responding to them by abstention and flight. He went out on to the landing. From a door that stood ajar opposite, muttered prayers emerged, which caused him to suspend his march and held him there, hesitating.

With Soeur Cunégonde behind him, he went into the chapel, a spacious room at the far end of which was an altar, with rows of simple benches in front of it. On the walls were naïve decorations, the work of the sisters, and the ex-votos of patients. Two sisters were kneeling down, praying aloud. One was old and let the act of faith fall indifferently from her lips; the other, whom he did not recognize, was young and pretty, pale beneath her head-dress. Caresco went to kneel down beside her, pretended to pray, and violated her purity with his desire.

The son of Israel that he still was coveted the handmaiden of the Christian God momentarily. He judged her to be thin beneath her habit, however; he evoked his adipose mistress, and forgot the white head-dress. Then, five minutes having gone by, he crossed himself and left, followed by Soeur Cunégonde, radiant at the fervor of her new convert.

He went downstairs, darted a glance into his study and the reception room, and then went back across the vestibule and into the operating theater. Dusk was beginning to extend its ashes over things. He switched on the electric light, and a bright sheet of light bathed the room. Under the blaze, the nickeled plaque of the sterilizer, the linen autoclave and the metal boxes lit up with white reflections. In a closed glass display case the shining instruments were lined up, their multivarious forms confused.

A skillful scene-setter for the edification of colleagues, Caresco demanded that all those objects should always be scrupulously maintained and exposed to universal appraisal. No surgical establishment in Paris could offer such an assembly and such a variety of rare implements, the majority of which bore the seal of his inventive and practical imagination, and facilitated surgical interventions by means of ingenious modifications, appropriate curvatures and clever mechanisms, ornamented for all eventualities.

He opened the display case, and picked up forceps, curettes and a probe at random, inspected them minutely. Not a single speck of dirt or stain of rust; everything was clean and correct.

He replaced the objects in the glass cage, satisfied. "That's very good," he said to Soeur Cunégonde, who was expecting praise.

At that moment Bordier came in, attracted by the unusual flamboyance of the room. He was still clad in his white smock, his arms bare and his hands reddened by caustic solutions.

Caresco held out his hand. "Well, is everything going smoothly?"

"Yes, apart from the man with the suppurating cyst. I thought of making a second opening; I've had chloroform prepared..."

"No need. It's been done without chloroform. He bawled a little...but that's of no importance."

The wretch, who could have soothed the pain and had not wanted to! Bordier shuddered in revulsion. Should he, at that moment, hurl his resignation in his face?

No, he would wait. He had changed his mind. He had seen the seven patients who had undergone operations a few days before showing very mild post-operational consequences. There had, however, been two interventions of an unexpected difficulty, two relatively desperate cases, and those patients were doing well, seemingly on their way to recovery. Caresco would have saved two lost lives. He did not think that anyone else, among surgeons of renown, was capable of having acted as brilliantly—with the result that, given his slightly impulsive character, lacking active resolution, afflicted with a versatility due to his pampered education, he had put off the moment of decision, wanting to conserve the hope of having served a useful and beneficent man.

He forgot what Savre had said, believing that the skeptic in question had exaggerated the dark side of the situation, perhaps speaking under the influence of rancor, and resumed an unqualified admiration for the man touched by the wing of genius, of conceptions so vast, with such an organized brain and scintillating hand. He sought and found excuses for the faults that were the underside of his qualities; he forgot the treason of his gaze, the slackness of his handshake.

He went into the next room to put on his city clothes, and then came back to Caresco.

"By the way, did you know that Madame de Jancy is dead?"

"Madame de Jancy?"

"Yes, Madame Bise's sister-in-law. The funeral is tomorrow. Are you coming to the ceremony?"

"I don't know…I don't think so."

Madame de Jancy…the fulgurance of a memory caused him to see Madeleine again, fixed in her catalepsy, in the midst of lightning-flashes thunder and rain. What dominated that reappearance was the medical attitude of the young woman, the purity and vagueness of her blue eyes, the stiffness of her limbs, and their insensibility—not the abomination of the criminal act that he had committed. To his infamy, he accorded no concern; he no longer thought about it, as a vagabond forgets the chicken whose throat he has cut in a corner of a wood.

Was he not, in fact, a vagabond too, a pariah on the earth, in the midst of all his scientific glory, devoid of friends, devoid of love, devoid of children, with no hearth other than one hired too cheaply for a mistress, pursued, ever unfulfilled, like his ancestor the Wandering Jew, across the inevitable stony ground of life, by the insatiable demands of his egotistical and ferocious heart?

CHAPTER XI

Aline Romé, Madeleine's cousin, sitting at the table where she was eating lunch with her parents, seemed more impatient than ever that day to finish the meal. Distractedly, she listened to the conversation that had been pivoting for three days around the same subject: the death and funeral of Madame de Jancy.

When the initial surprise had passed and the first tears had been dried, the family had gradually grown accustomed to the sad shock, and the concert of monotonous reflections was now attenuating, with lowered voices and weary, moderated gestures. It was like a remembrance, a prolongation of attitudes struck in the mortuary chamber before the pale and cold cadaver and behind the pomp of the coffin.

Yes, the funeral had gone well, without a single discordant note. Madeleine had shown an astonishing resilience and courage; but she had been suffering since the event. The repercussion of the mental shock seemed to have struck her physically, and her stomach could no longer tolerate any aliment. Monsieur Cartaux, summoned to see the young woman, had not been unduly worried. Anyway, Aline could provide fresh news, since she had been to see her cousin that morning, in company with a chambermaid.

"Isn't that right, Aline?" asked Madame Romé.

But Aline was not attending to the conversation. Staring into space, lost in the mirages of her reflections, she was kneading a piece of bread in the tips of her slender fingers. Her brown hair, her pale and delicate complexion, her vaguely-arched eyebrows surmounting the bistre of her eyelids went marvelously with mourning-dress, harmonizing with her somber costume.

"Isn't that right, Aline?" her father repeated, surprised by such inattention.

She did not reply, content to inline her head in a melancholy fashion.

"Come on, child, what's the matter with you?" Monsieur Romé went on. "You're not speaking, you're not listening and you've scarcely touched your plate. What's wrong my dear?"

With the rebelliousness of a spoiled child, to whom everything is permitted, she replied: "You know very well what's wrong, but you don't want to admit it. I'm suffering from a liver complaint. Do you think it's for pleasure that I leave my food—I can't swallow it. I assure you that I can't. I've got a stabbing pain here"—she pointed at the right side of her waist—and I can scarcely tolerate my corset. Yes, there..."

As she plunged further into her explanation, she felt a blush invading her cheeks. Was she lying? No, not absolutely. But why was she obstinate in that fiction? Why was that young woman, healthy in body, born of sturdy stock, and thus far well-balanced herself, in spite of certain social frequentations that might have been harmful to her if she had not been protected by her education, so persistent in that absurd desire to be, and above all to appear to be, ill, without wanting to reflect on all the anxiety and sadness that the comedy might provoke among those surrounding her?

Since the day when she had seen Armand Caresco for the first time, at Madame Bise's country property at Les Bolois, she had never ceased to dream about him. The obstinately nasty rumors that had run around regarding the man's morals, and even Madeleine's appreciation, had not raised any obstacle to her thoughts. She attributed to the surgeon's glory the faults that others found in him. Armand Caresco had mistresses? What man didn't? His gaze was fugitive, his handshake limp? Timidity. He was a Jew? No, he had converted, and with what austere piety! He was avid for money? But was it not necessary to make the rich pay, for the sake of all the poor who could not pay anything?

And then, what masculine beauty! How intelligent and serious his forehead was, dominated by the undulating forest of his brown hair, expressive of active will, the pride of triumph! And his teeth...how white and superb they were, how they quested for kisses—entire and profound kisses, such as, instinctively, she knew that the amorous must give them! Finally, how glorious he man was, in spite of his youth! How much some admired him, how bitterly others discussed him—that being another form of admiration! Yes, he was the Unique; it was him that she wanted, that she would have, to whom she would get close in spite of all the obstacles.

However, she had never seen him again during the three months that had almost gone by. She had used her authority as a spoiled child to persuade her parents to abandon their country retreat sooner than in previous years. Back in Paris, in her visits, in the excursions in which she was entrusted to the guard of a chambermaid, at times when the surgeon ought to be in his consulting room, she had directed her walks along the Avenue Hoche.

Seized by a sudden passion for trinkets, she had undertaken long stations in the shop of a local antiquary. From there, quivering, she had watched the coaching entrance of the sanitarium. Private carriages paused outside; a few people came in or out, who made her shiver.

Then, when she could no longer decently prolong her conversation with the antiquary, when she perceived that the merchant was weary of making sales talk, showing her things whose value he talked up but which she subsequently rejected, she swiftly decided on a item that she bought with her savings—savings that were dwindling rapidly in that game—and left, carrying a parcel.

She went past the house slowly, darting her gaze at the windows with all her will-power, endeavoring to see him through the curtains, clinging to the hope that he might draw them momentarily in order to give her the intoxication of an appearance. But hearts cannot speak through walls, and even aspirations as violent as hers could not pass through stone to awaken the attention of the desired individual. The façade always remained cold and banal, the curtains obstinately closed, the main door mute.

One evening, after dinner, while her parents were in the small drawing room, yielding to the soporific joys of a game of piquet by the soft light of a muted lamp set on the green baize of the card-table, she, in the aggravation of the idle evening and her ever-discontented dream, had gone into the next room to run her fingers over the keyboard of the piano, seeking a release from her enervation in the sad languor of the vague sonorities of Grieg. As she rummaged through the piles of musical scores abandoned on the piano, an article in the *Gaulois* caught her eye.

Under the rubric *Académie de Médecine*, the newspaper related a presentation by Armand Caresco relative to the surgery of the liver. The history of the diseases of that organ and their symptoms was recounted there at length. She read and reread every line, impregnating her brain with them, and, by searching hard, found in herself the elements of one of the maladies described there, under the label of cirrhosis. She experienced the phenomenon common to all those who put their noses into a medical textbook for the first time, and who, by a deception of which they are the sole promoters, feel the symptoms of the malady about which they are reading.

In her, the discovery of her illness was aided by the desire to conserve the illusion. Was it not the only means of getting close to the surgeon? Why had she never thought of it before?

That evening, she complained of internal pains to her parents. In the following days, the suffering grew worse; she lost her appetite, felt her strength ebbing away, became disgusted with everything. Dr. Cartaux, summoned by Monsieur Romé, had found nothing precise, and, attributing the troubles to a nervous state, had prescribed cold showers and a bromide to help her sleep. No improvement was produced, however. The young woman submitted to the cold water, but in the evening she threw the spoonful of potion into her chamber pot.

Her nights were ardent, her dreams voluptuous, in which the image of Caresco imposed itself on the overexcitement of her nerves, leaving her tired in the morning, her limbs numb, her eyes sticky. And the pains of which she complained, imaginary thus far, she really began to feel, by virtue of a kind of auto-suggestion. A temporary jaundice even gave her skin a saffron tint.

Then her parents became alarmed. Dr. Carhaux, who possessed an absolute authority over them, returned to see the young woman, examined her again from head to toe, tapped her and ausculated her, searched conscientiously, and persisted in his original diagnosis. In her prescription, valerian replaced the bromide that was not having any effect—for good reason.

Before quitting Monsieur and Madame Romé, the doctor took them to one side, enquired as to Aline's frequentations, asked whether the patient had not experienced any moral disturbance, any contradiction. No, nothing, the parents replied. He departed almost convinced that Aline had a secret that she did not want to reveal, and into which he, although something of a psychologist, did not dare to enquire.

Days passed thus; the symptoms were accentuated; Aline, such a sweet-natured girl hitherto, became bad-tempered; her approach was impregnated with acrimony, she no longer responded to her mother's kisses and tenderly interrogative glances.

She was about to get up from the table to hide the sobs she was stifling when her father retained her with a gesture.

"Come on, dear, stay with us for a little while longer. Are you suffering a great deal?"

His voice was so paternal, so anxious, and so touching in its emotional affection, that Aline could not hold back the overflow of her bitterness. She buried her face in her handkerchief and wept, and wept. Madame Romé was infected by those tears, and began to blow her nose noisily. It was the first time that a genuine dolor had disunited the three enchained souls.

Aline emptied her bile in a flood of words. "Yes, yes, I'm ill, very ill, and I feel that if I don't receive better care I won't be long delayed n disappearing into a tomb. Do you believe that I can continue to live on what I eat? I'm getting thinner, in a frightful fashion, and I always have these frightful pains, which rack me. Monsieur Cartaux doesn't understand my malady; he's old school. He'll let me die without even soothing me. You love me, though, and you're going to let me fade away like this? Oh, I'm truly unfortunate!"

Madame Romé could not longer contain her grief. The father, equally distressed, but braver, put his napkin down on the table and tried to reason with her.

"Come on, dear, you're exaggerating the situation somewhat. I can see that you're suffering but, after all, Monsieur Cartaux has reassured us as to your condition. You don't have confidence in our old friend? Would you like us to ask him to bring another physician for a second opinion? Gladly, my child."

"No," said Aline. "I no longer want Monsieur Cartaux, who treats my illness too lightly. I want to go see Monsieur Armand Caresco, who knows these matters admirably, since he's operated on all these diseases of the liver. Aunt Bise told me so."

Monsieur Romé was astonished by the insistence with which his daughter put Armand Caresco's name on the table. He saw the advisory influence of Madame Bise therein—and saw nothing else.

"But my dear child," he went on, "you know very well that it's not appropriate to go and see another physician without being accompanied by the family physician…it would be a breach of manners with regard to Monsieur Cartaux—a serious breach—and we ought not to do that to him."

Aline was seized by a further crisis of despair. Madame Romé dried her red eyes, and then, desirous of not prolonging her daughter's pain implored: "Come on, we're not obliged to tell Monsieur Cartaux."

"No, I don't want to do things that way," her father insisted. "It lacks dignity."

At that moment, a footman announced Madame Bise. She came in like a cyclone, bubbling with all the impetuosity of her southern blood, out of breath from having climbed the stairs. Without paying any heed to the parents, she immediately went to the young woman.

"Well, darling, how are you? What, you're crying! Oh dear, something's wrong!"

She interrogated the dignified and calm attitude of Madame Romé, who, fearful of her sister's exuberance, had repressed her tears when she arrived.

"What! You're letting her cry…!"

"It's nothing," said Monsieur Romé, dryly. "Childishness."

"In that case," proclaimed Madame Bise, "since your parents are causing you strife, I'll take you away. We'll go for a ride in a closed carriage. A little air will do you good."

A quarter of an hour later, Madame Bise's coupé stopped in front of Armand Caresco's house. Aline got down, profoundly emotional, upright, svelte and light on her feet, having forgotten her illness, entirely occupied with the adjustment of her skirt, heartbroken to be appearing before the desire man in mourning-dress.

Finally, Madame Bise was taking her over the threshold at which she had gazed so many times in anguish. What was she going to tell the surgeon? What was he going to do? She did not even ask herself that, utterly given over to the joy and distress of seeing him again, of feeling the caress of his brown eyes again. She was no longer thinking about the comedy she had been playing for a month, the fault she was committing in going, with the sole and inconsequential support of Aunt Bise, into a house to which her access had not been authorized by her parents.

The surgeon was expecting them. The valet immediately introduced them into the doctor's study. The luxurious austerity of the place, and Armand's gravity, chilled the young woman's dreams to begin with. Then too, she was so petrified that she was disturbed; her cheeks turned pink and white in succession; the ground seemed to be vacillating under her feet. Armand, however, looked at her profoundly; she drank in the man's domineering gaze.

"Here's the child," said Madame Bise. "Save her."

Obsequiously, he offered them seats, took his place at his desk, and asked questions, to which Madame Bise responded most of the time, for Aline, who was hypnotized, in a contemplation akin to ecstasy, could only stammer incoherently. Madame Bise, however, took great care to specify that only the liver was afflicted.

"We shall see," said Armand. "Will you please take your clothes off, Mademoiselle."

Take her clothes off! Aline had never thought about that eventuality. She blushed scarlet, but was nevertheless desirous, and madly desirous, of contact. Behind a screen she unfastened her bodice. Her trembling fingers fumbled with the cords, no longer following the directions of her will, becoming disorientated among the knots.

The skirt fell away.

"The corset, Mademoiselle. It's necessary to take off the corset so that I can examine you completely."

There was a further labor. Finally, the thin batiste chemise floated free...she had such pretty silk chemises...if she had only known! But she had not expected to be thus laid bare.

She lay down on the low bed upholstered with an Oriental tapestry, and abandoned herself to palpation, her hands over her face, confused and trembling.

Through the thin fabric he felt, taped, interrogated the sonorities of the thorax and the hypochondrium.

"Don't stiffen your abdomen, Mademoiselle, Relax. I won't do you any harm."

He resumed his examination, with a lighter, subtler, more profound palpation. For the young woman it was an exquisite caress, which brought her to the confines of sensuality.

"Yes," said Caresco, "the liver is overflowing slightly, but there's nothing very evident. It requires observation. In any case, surgically, there's nothing to be done for the moment."

He withdrew the hand evocative of sensations from Aline's abdomen. Only then, as he looked at her, did he have an intuition of the voluptuous effect that he had just produced. The young woman's eyes were shining with a strange gleam, her attitude, simultaneously abandoned and tremulous, revealed the expectation of supreme spasms, reminding him of hysterics observed at the Salpêtrière, at the moment of crises of erotic overexcitement. If they had been alone, he would have been able to graze the fodder of amour, she offering herself with a violent contentment, exasperated by three months of troubled dreams, three months of obscure aspiration toward the blossoming of an instinct. And as the virgin still had an incomparable lust in her eyes, the surgeon could help submitting to their alluring radiation and could not look away.

Aunt Bise marched in her southern fashion straight into the midst of that intimate drama, infinitely satisfied with Caresco's opinion, which consisted precisely in having none.

"That's it," she said. "At least, with you, one always knows where one stands. The little one will come to see you again soon. You understand that we can't let her perish like this. Anyway, I'll take all the responsibility."

"What responsibility can be in question?" asked Caresco.

"Her family," replied Aunt Bise, "only wants to hear mention of Dr. Cartaux..."

Armand interrupted her. "One doesn't go to consult Cartaux! He's behind the times!"

"So, he can't tell from what my niece is suffering. He says it's her nerves...everything's put down to nerves nowadays. In my day, it was the blood. So I said to myself, my dear friend is the only one who can clear this up, and I brought her. Anyway, it's quite simple—if her parents don't like it, I'll disinherit her."

During this chatter, Aline got dressed behind the screen, still overwhelmed. While veiling the brown splendor of her flesh she remained under the influence of the emotions of a little while before, aggravated by an unaccomplished act, enervated by a lack of satiation.

Her ignorance, of a well-brought up girl, was not unmitigated by certain vague notions regarding the practices of amour, an imprecise knowledge extracted from conversations with friends, and the dangerous flirtations in which young people already old, initiators, delight in letting themselves divine things that they cannot explain, in sowing the seeds of a profligacy whose benefits they might reap later, after marriage. So she was surprised by the sensations she had experienced, desirous of pushing further on, convinced that the contact ought to go beyond a simple pressure on the abdomen, to lead to other satisfactions, and almost annoyed that the circumstances, the presence of Madame Bise, and the surgeon's reserve had not permitted a more complete information.

Armand Caresco returned to take his place at his desk. He scribbled a prescription. What was the matter with the young woman? He did not know. Perhaps it really was a particular nervous state, as Monsieur Cartaux had said. At any rate, it was nothing to worry about.

While he wrote, his mind reverted to problems other than questions of pathology. He wondered by what enchainment of ideas, by what latent work of nature, Aline had just offered herself to him thus—for his superior intelligence had not been duped by the pretext. In her, there was no ancestral flaw; her parents were healthy and well-equilibrated. She had always been astonished by her own fortitude, her easy childhood, even sheltered from the usual minor injuries of childhood. Why, then, had she received such a violent cut of the whip, such a forceful impulsion to bring her to black malady? Would a similar adventure have happened to Aline with another man than him? Was he physically the first, as he was intellectually? Was he The Man, as he judged himself to be The Surgeon?

As he rose from his seat to hand Madame Bise the piece of paper that he had just covered with his handwriting, a mirror sent back his portrait, and he contemplated it momentarily, studied the harmony of its lines, and found it strong and handsome.

CHAPTER XII

The Louis XV clock was slowly chiming nine, with a bright and cheerful ring, when Armand Caresco woke up in his mistress' large soft bed. Weighed down at first by a leaden sleep due to fatigue and the ardent work of the preceding days, he had some difficulty in extracting his thoughts from the beneficent chaos in which they had been stranded, and, with a slack lassitude in his back and legs, he had an urge to prolong his repose—but the last strokes of the chime were like an appeal to the need for agitation that never slept within him, and the dominant idea of work and conflict tore through the mists of his mind, brutally completing the work of bringing him out of his blissful uncertainty.

He moved, turning toward Mathilde, who with her right arm slid under her doll-like head, continued sleeping, filling half the bed with the abundance of her flesh. He took pleasure, in the obscure daylight that was filtering through the large curtains, in watching her sleep, following the regular oscillations that her regular breathing imparted to the covers, and as she did not wake up, he granted himself another quarter of an hour of inaction, which he employed in organizing his ideas in accordance with his daily method.

To begin with, the burning memory of Israel and the enormous debt that he had to settle at the end of the month persecuted him. It was the twentieth of November, and of the hundred and ten thousand francs that he had to pay, he only possessed fifty thousand. That money came in part from old debts that he had finally been able to collect by putting pressure on his debtors, threatening them with the bailiff—which had brought thirty thousand francs into his wallet. The other twenty thousand came from the particularly fortunate activity of his operating theater at the beginning of the month, and the fortnightly accounts that had been settled with Soeur Cunégonde, which had brought him four thousand francs.

General de Rion, having undergone an operation for the "resection of the *vas deferens*," and very happy with a temporary amelioration—due as much to the forced rest as to the operation itself—had paid out ten thousand francs without blinking. The farmer's wife brought by the Vicomtesse de Mesma had increased the sum by four thousand, and the other two thousand francs, completing the fifty thousand, had come from numerous interventions accomplished on petty individuals, poor wretches, more useful to his propaganda and his erudition than to the augmentation of his profits.

The result was that, by making every effort, he had gathered almost half the sum that he owed Israel—but that was not sufficient, and he wondered anxiously how he was going to confront the rest of his debt, and satisfy the demands of the baleful banker, who had formally declared that he would not renew the debt again, being pressed himself with imperious demands for money.

The clinic, following the last batch of operations, was empty for the moment, and he did not anticipate being able to fill it up before the end of the month. There would only remain clients of an inferior order, necessitating frequent dressings, and Mademoiselle Romé, newly admitted, for whom there was no question of surgical treatment. At the most, he might have some stroke of luck, some accident of fate bringing invalids to the Avenue Hoche on which operations had to be carried out urgently—but those cases were very rare, and often, the families and the family physicians hesitated to decide immediately on extreme methods, preferring to temporize.

So, which way could he turn? He had no friends to whom he could reach out, and he wanted to maintain the susceptibility of Madame Bise, one having recourse to her as a last resort. Money-lenders, shady usurers and other dubious businessmen that he had felt out had imposed conditions so draconian that he preferred not to have recourse to them, even to avoid being ruined by Israel. Allowing them to get their teeth into him would only increase the depth of his fall, and another month, by reason of the engagements undertaken, would have seen the edifice that was shaking now, and which a few stones might consolidate, collapse completely. But where could he find the materials to sustain the work, and to what architect ought he to commit himself?

Again, Armand looked at the calm face of the mistress whose rapacity caused him such anguish. Mathilde continued her slumber, a stranger to the torments that were racking her lover. Under the more exasperated impulsion that a dream imparted to her respiration, her cheeks inflated repeatedly, to relax afterwards with a noise like a bellows emitted between her parted lips. Armand experienced a momentary resentment against that comfortable insouciance, but it was only a flash, and he quickly began to reflect on the multiple joys that he obtained from her, the satined contact of her majestic body, the intoxication of savant caresses, independent of her sex, with the professional expertise of which she was able to satisfy his monstrous appetites without too much fatigue on her part.

Nothing sentimental traversed the vibrations of his recollection; it was the carnal gratitude of a hearty eater confronted with a dish with which he has regaled himself and for which he still has an appetite. And a bitterness took hold of him, emanating from the present circumstances, his shortage of money, the supreme struggle he was about to attempt, at the idea that if he were vanquished, he would lose the satiation provided by that woman, that he would be without his habitual outlet for the gross satisfactions of lust.

Even more than the swallowing of his cash, that perspective tormented him; he must really have been possessed by the power of that flesh to have reached the point of relegating the atavistic joys of money to second place.

He moved closer to Mathilde, put his arm around her waist and woke her up.

"It's you, my wolf! How sleepy I was...can you imagine what I was dreaming?"

She narrated the banality of the dream. He scarcely listened, dominated by her proximity, by her flesh—but the ringing of the telephone placed in the dressing room next to the bedroom brought him back to reality.

"Again!" he groaned. "How tiresome. Go and see who is it, my dear. It's preferable that they don't recognize me voice. If it's nothing serious, you'll put them off, won't you? Tell them I'm not here...that I have an urgent operation to do."

Mathilde hastened to obey. She thought that the telephone call might be for her, and she did not always like to take her lover into her confidence. She leapt out of bed, put on some light slippers and a pink flannel peignoir, and in the coolness of the morning air, no longer combated by the dead ashes in the fireplace, she went into the dressing room.

The bell fell silent; Armand listened, trying to make out the conversation, but Mathilde's voice was muffled by the thick door-curtain. However, from the repeated appeals of "Hello, Sister!" he understood that the call was coming from the Avenue Hoche.

Indeed when Mathilde returned, she said: "Remember this address, my cabbage: 18 Rue Breda, Monsieur Savoie. You have to go there this morning for a consultation. They'll send for the family physician as soon as you arrive. He's expecting you. It was Soeur Cunégonde who telephoned me."

Soeur Cunégonde often communicated with Mathilde in that fashion. Her investigative science had apprised her of Armand's irregular situation, having no private apartment and living with his mistress, but she preferred to ignore that irregularity, pretending to believe that she was telephoning a domestic. Was it not necessary to accord a few petty sacrifices to the wicked ways of the world, for the greater good of the patients and the service of the good Lord?

"I'm going back to bed," Mathilde said. "I need sleep. That dream has upset me. Poor cat! Going to work for his Tithilde while she's asleep! Oh, if I could only do something for you!"

She climbed back into bed, heavily. At the same time, Caresco's carriage, which came at nine o'clock every morning to stop outside the door of the house, troubled the aristocratic silence of the street. Armand embraced his mistress one last time, then abandoned the soft warmth of the sheets, put on his trousers and went into the next room to finish dressing.

While preparing his ablutions, perfuming his water, he consulted his diary of visits. Numerous addresses already covered today's page—meetings arranged some time before with colleagues and instrument-manufacturers—and he wondered how he would find time to fit in a further appointment. He decided to sacrifice his morning session at the sanitarium; Bordier could fill in for him.

Freshly dressed, his hair lustrous, ready for the fray, he rapidly drank a cup of tea, and left.

In an elegant first-floor apartment in the Rue Breda, Monsieur and Madame Savoie formed a happy and peaceful household. An eight-year old child, a sweet cherub previously healthy, completed the harmony of the family. Life for the trio had been limpid. The days had scattered a beneficent manna, and nothing had presaged a catastrophe when, a month ago, the child had begun to get thinner, had lost his customary gaiety and begun to complain of vague abdominal pains. At the same time, the abdomen had swollen, taking on unaccustomed proportions, like the belly of a batrachian—and all of that formed an ensemble of symptoms so alarming that the family physician, Dr. Varon, an honorable and experienced practitioner, who had diagnosed a tubercular peritonitis, had, in order to disengage his responsibility, even though the malady was getting no worse, suggested soliciting the advice of a colleague. Immediately, Madame Savoie had mentioned Dr. Caresco, who had operated on and cured one of her close friends.

"Monsieur Caresco," Dr. Varon had replied, "is not exactly the consultant we need. Your child's case requires medical treatment, not surgery. Monsieur Caresco is only a surgeon. However, if you insist, I shall be happy to make his acquaintance, for he is an authority."

When Armand Caresco went into the drawing room, to which a footman introduced him in a grand manner, he found Dr. Varon and Monsieur and Madame Savoie waiting for him. The mother was weeping, anxious about the imminent verdict. The father was inoffensive in appearance. The aged colleague was grave, sincere, under no illusion regarding the scope of the encounter. Once the initial politenesses had been exchanged, Caresco was immediately taken to the patient's bedroom.

In bed, the poor stricken boy was waiting for the doctors' visit. When his old friend Varon appeared he extended a fleshless hand toward him, fearfully, seeking an encouragement in his parents' eyes, instinctively frightened by the cold and incisive gaze of the other physician. He had, however, been formally promised that no harm would come to him, that Monsieur Caresco was only going to examine him, in order to take away the nasty pain he had in his tummy…and he had been promised toys and candy after the consultation if he were good and did not cry. Even so, an anxiety racked the little soul, also afflicted by the malady, the unreasoned suspicion of the weak in the face of the unknown.

He lent himself meekly to the examination, and replied politely with "Yes, Monsieur" or "No, Monsieur," to Caresco's interrogations. The latter, by reason of the luxurious appearance of the people who had asked for him, modified the brutality of his questions, striving to put a caress into his voice. The child even allowed his belly to be palpated, and heroically suppressed his tears when the surgeon, seeking to disturb the fluid that the walls of the abdomen contained, provoked a veritable stab of pain. Behind Caresco's bent back, the mother blew her son reassuring kisses, and he received them with a pale smile, swollen by the desire to weep.

The physicians conversed in technical terminology while measuring the extent of the malady. Strange words struck the child's ears: ascites, meteorism, peritonitis and hypogastrium. At any rate, the diagnosis was manifest and they were completely in agreement. There was only the treatment to discuss, and to do that they went into another room, which had been reserved for them. An inkstand and paper had been set on a table for the drafting of the prescription.

When they were seated, Armand Caresco looked at his colleague. The old man had a noble and grave attitude. Honesty radiated from his white-haired head, his benevolent eyes and his clean-shaven face, framed to the side by short side-whiskers that he pushed back toward his ears with a familiar gesture. His black frock-coat, open over an immaculate shirt-front surmounted by a stiff collar, his lighter trousers and his manicured hands, of which the right bore a gold alloy ring, also testified to a noble and correct soul, and a line of conduct that went bravely on to the end without any base detours. Caresco therefore judged it prudent to maintain a certain reserve from the start, and to engage prudently in the bargain that he was about to propose.

His own opinion was already conclusive; it was necessary to operate on the tubercular peritonitis, open the child's abdomen, get rid of the filth it contained and clean it out. It was a procedure that the young school of surgery was beginning to employ, which offered every chance of success. But would his opinion be admitted by his colleague? Would he not run into the conviction that maladies of this sort could be cured without the intervention of the knife, with prolonged treatment? Was Dr.

Varon up to date with the progress of the science, would he admit the necessity of the operation, and, if he did admit it, might he not have a surgeon to propose to the family, some old comrade of his studies who had achieved a high official position?

Caresco tormented himself with those problems while weighing up his colleague. He was determined not to let go, to press his resolution all the way and to impose it as soon as possible—for, behind the operation, he glimpsed the saving emoluments, the large sum that might be extracted from the purse of people surrounded by comfortable luxury, taxable at discretion. His resolution was accompanied by a joyous clink of coins, the rustling song of banknotes, to add to those already put in reserve for Israel.

Mentally, he settled on a figure: ten thousand. But first, he judged it as well to envelop the old man, to make him a partner.

"My dear colleague," he said, "I thank you for having thought of me on this occasion. I know that the papers I've published on intervention in the course of tubercular infections of the abdomen must have attracted your attention, but after all, you could have asked someone else..."

"Pardon me, my dear colleague," Dr. Varon replied, surprised by a language to which he was not accustomed, "but it wasn't me who asked for you. I would have preferred to seek the advice of a physician. It's the family who wanted to see you." To soften his words, however, he added: "I was delighted by the decision, which has permitted me to make the acquaintance of a young master."

Armand inclined his head, pleased by the eulogy. That battle, however, seemed to have started badly on his side. He resolved to launch a frontal attack.

"Well," he said, "I think we're in absolute agreement. We're dealing, as you've said, with a tubercular peritonitis, which has spread, without considerable inflammatory reaction, immediately chronic. You've searched for the tuberculosis in other organs without finding it; there are no antecedents in the family except an aunt and uncle who died of tuberculosis; the direct parents seem healthy; the general condition of the child is not too bad. I believe that it's an appropriate case for a laparotomy. My statistics include thirty-three similar cases, and I've had twenty-five successes."

"What do you call twenty-five successes?" asked Dr. Varon. "Do you mean that twenty-five of your patients out of thirty-three survived the operation, or that they were completely cured?"

"You know how difficult it is to follow patients," Caresco replied. "I lose sight of many, and I've often operated on people who, once out of my hands, neglect to come to see me again subsequently. I can't, therefore, answer in an absolute fashion, with figures, for the consequences of the operations. What I can affirm, however, is that I operate quickly enough to be the man who exposes the lives of his patients to the least risk..."

"Yes, I know, I know," said the old man, in a slightly weary tone.

Certainly, he knew that Armand Caresco operated brilliantly. The newspapers had publicized that sufficiently, and it had always been a subject of indignation for him to see publicity so easily accorded to questions of a purely professional order. Why inflate the organs of Renown to proclaim to the four corners of the world dis-

221

coveries that were often recognized subsequently to be errors, and bring the ignorant masses up to date with scientific questions that they could not understand, and would judge with their irremediable stupidity?

No, reputations thus acquired were unreliable, and science itself ought to remain mute, working humbly for the good of society, not causing either individuals or theories to burst forth in an apotheosis of glory, but only absolute verities, such as are discovered perhaps once a century. How many of these sensational discoveries touted by the drums of the press the old practitioner had seen! Now, he greeted them with a skeptical smile, contenting himself with doing his beneficent work honestly and simply, sickened by shameful publicity and feeling a sincere pity when he saw, among his clients, the incurable abandon him to run head first into the traps set for their ignorant credulity by unscrupulous colleagues.

To be sure, those desperate individuals obtained a small benefit from their imbecility; the glimmer of hope that sustained them momentarily reacted on their nervous system, and even rendered them for a time, by virtue of the stimulus given to their nerves, an appearance of health—but afterwards, when disillusionment followed, when they perceived that the new treatments had no more effect than the old, and that, in spite of everything, *disease* was continuing its irrevocable work of destruction, that the cancer was still gnawing away, that the gangrene had not surrendered an inch of ground, that the tumors were continuing to grow, the ulcers to bleed and that nothing could stem the inexorable work of decay, what a dire repercussion there was, what a frightful reaction! How often he had seen those unfortunates come back weeping, extending their thin hands toward him, demanding his science and his humanity, with furious appraisals of the methods of the supposedly new medicine!

"Yes," Dr. Varon went on, after a hesitation, "I know that you operate remarkably, but I don't believe that in the present case, a surgical intervention is appropriate, at least for the moment. I think that the general condition of the patient is too poor for the child to be submitted to such an ordeal. Would he survive an operation? I don't think so. And then, I ought to tell you that he's better at this moment than he was a week ago. It's impossible for you to appreciate that change, my dear colleague; you haven't followed the patient, but I can assure you of the regression of the illness. Now, if you have cured similar cases with your scalpel, I have seen many, in my practice, get better by themselves, and I hope that it will be the same for that child."

Armand Caresco was amazed by Dr. Varon's opinion. He had never heard a controversy expressed so clearly. Generally, colleagues who did not share his enthusiasm for an operation in similar consultations seemed at first to endorse his opinion and then, as soon as his back was turned, proceeded to demolish his theory piece by piece, and to demand another, wiser consultation; they never imposed their appreciation so brutally. He therefore sought the reason for that resistance, and thought that he had found it in self-interest. Was Dr. Varon not opposed to the operation out of fear of losing a lucrative client? The surgeon's mercantile soul lowered the soul of the old man to its own level, and he resolved to strike a bargain, skillfully to prepare a division, a sharing of the honorarium.

"I confess, my dear colleague, that I'm slightly surprised to find you so hostile to the idea of a laparotomy. Independently of my statistics, there are also the statistics of other surgeons, less good in reality, because they do not operate as well as me, but all favorable to this kind of intervention.

"But I'm not denying the beneficial effects of laparotomy," Dr. Varon interjected. "I'm only claiming that the child is not in a condition to support one. Later, perhaps, there might be grounds to have recourse to one, if the child improves without being definitively cured."

"One is often wrong to want to wait," Caresco said. "How to do you know that the regression you have observed will continue, and that you won't regret one day not having taken a more rapid decision? Yes, I know, one hesitates before the disturbance and anxiety it will cause, and often before the sum of money that the family must expend..."

Dr. Varon made a gesture of protest, which Caresco pretended not to see. Determined to make his proposal, he continued: "For one thing, I have no interest at stake. The honoraria I'm offered are indifferent to me, and I always leave to the family physician the care of setting them. Then again, I ought to tell you that I consider it a duty to thank the practitioner who calls me in for his aid. I deem that physicians are not sufficiently well paid for their work and inconvenience, and I generally offer them a percentage of my emoluments. That's how things should be done within the great medical family."

How cleverly he had launched that proposal, the man who knew that nothing can resist the great motor of money! Money, with which one can buy everything, the consciences of politicians and the favors of women: the metallic stream that stuffs the belly, delights the eyes, leads to all enjoyments and all sensory satisfactions, even those of the heart! And as he spoke, his atavistic face lit up, with the avid expression of his mercantile ancestors, with its insinuating smile, the profile of his nose straying toward the thick-lipped mouth, and his think curly hair.

But he had run into a noble soul, and this time, the old man rebelled.

"Pardon me, Monsieur, but I don't take commissions. Thank God, I have no need of that to live. You could have found other arguments to invite me to have recourse to your talents."

That was said dryly. Caresco understood that he had adopted the wrong strategy, that the battle was lost. He adopted an emollient tone.

"I beg your pardon, Monsieur, if I've offended your sentiments. I made that proposal not to force your hand on the subject of an operation that I consider, on reflection, not to be absolutely urgent, but because I know that there many of our unfortunate colleagues to whom the offer of an equitable remuneration often gives pleasure. So, we shall say no more about it, and draft, if you wish, a medical prescription that will not change the treatment that you have instituted in any way, while making the reservation that an operation might become indispensable at some future time."

Already, he had sat down at the table, had taken up the pen, and, contrary to custom, which dictates that it is the treating physician who writes the prescription, prepared to draft it—but Dr. Varon stopped him with a gesture.

"There's no need, Monsieur, since you don't consider any change in the treatment to be necessary. It will be sufficient to explain it to the parents."

"If you wish."

They returned to the child's bedside. The parents were waiting anxiously. The mother was caressing her son's hair with a trembling hand, lovingly protective. Caresco was cold and reserved, saying very little, administering the final blow to the hopes of Monsieur and Madame Savoie.

At the moment of departure, the young woman went to take an envelope from the mantelpiece containing a hundred-franc bill, and while Dr. Varon was delayed, taking to her husband, she followed the surgeon into the antechamber.

"Doctor," she said, "permit me to thank you for your visit." She held out the envelope which Caresco pocketed, and continued: "I have the greatest confidence in you. You saved one of my friends, who was believed to be a lost cause. So, I beg you to reply to me frankly. Is my child doomed? Is there nothing to be done?"

Her eyes were full of tears. The surgeon darted a suspicious glance toward the drawing-room door, and as his colleague did not appear, he resolved to make a reply that was perfidious with regard to the aged physician, abominable for the mother drowning in grief.

"My God, Madame, it's very difficult for me to reply to you. I'm not absolutely in agreement with the physician caring for your child that it's necessary to let things take their course. Personally, I consider there might be a chance of salvation."

"Speak, Doctor, speak!"

"I believe that an operation attempted immediately—not in a week, you understand, but immediately—might still save your child. The explanation is quite simple: there is a nucleus of disease in his abdomen that is secreting a liquid that makes it swell. If that disease is not alleviated, the abdomen will continue to swell and your child will die."

The mother was no longer weeping. Every word fell upon her head like a stunning hammer-blow. A difficulty in breathing caused her contracted throat to gasp. Caresco had succeeded; he held her in the claws of his will, encircling her with terror.

"Yes, I said all that to Dr. Varon, but he knows little about these matters, which are very specialized. He's very much of the old school—very conscientious, but very old school! And before that force of inertia, I confess that I'm impotent. I regret having to speak to you so brutally, but I believe it to be my duty."

Distressed, Madame Savoie had seized his hand.

"Thank you, Doctor, thank you. You'll save my child. I admire you. I'll come to you today, bringing you my cherub. You can do as you wish with him. I give him to you."

"No," said Caresco, "it's necessary to protect the susceptibility of your physician, who is also your friend."

An ironic exclamation escaped the mother. "Oh, Dr. Varon! My child first! Your consultation day is today? I'll be with you in an hour."

"So be it—in an hour."

Dr. Varon came back with Monsieur Savoie. At his approach, the young woman became marble, chilling him with an icy glance.

He had a sudden intuition of the surgeon's underhand stratagem. The shot that had wounded he mother struck him by ricochet. He refused to shake Caresco's hand and went his own way.

No matter! thought Armand Caresco, sinking into the back of his coupé and turning up the soft collar of his fur coat. *I'm the stronger, anyway. The circumstances of life are trying to get the better of me, but I'm warding off the evil blows...yes, I'm the stronger.*

That evening, the operation was decided between the mother and the surgeon. Monsieur Savoie, overcome by his wife's panic, in a moral depression that prevented him from reacting, let her have her way, apologizing weakly to Dr. Varon, who demanded another consultation in vain, on the authority of his friendship and devotion.

The child was transported to the Avenue Hoche.

CHAPTER XIII

That evening, after having wished Madame Bise—
with whom she had been living since the disruption of
her bereavement—good night, Madeleine retired to the
bedroom that had been set aside for her. Georges
Ponviane, retained later than usual at the factor by virtue
of the absence of his father—who had gone to Lyon in
order to make some wholesale purchases—had not spent
the evening with his fiancée, and she felt a kind of distress at that temporary abandonment, the slow conclusion of the dragging in the company of a relative who
was a stranger to her heart.

Aunt Bise, whose absurd chatter had been solicited
by libations during dinner, aggravated her to an extreme
degree. She regretted all the more bitterly the two cherished images, one distanced by professional exigencies,
the other disappeared forever, borne away in the arms of
the ineluctable. Her initial nervousness seemed to have
been reawakened by the shock she had experienced. She
lived in a perpetual existential tension and wondered,
anxiously, whether she was going to be gripped once
again by the strange illness that had spoiled her childhood, once again falling victim to the crises that had
overwhelmed her before.

She found in her present condition the symptoms of
the sufferings of old: the vapors that, without any appreciable cause, invaded her face; the nauseas; the distaste
for food; and, above all, the horrible sensation of a ball
departing from the epigastrium, rising through her gut,
and clenching her gullet as if to stifle her. Other, equal-
ly-incomprehensible malaises were now manifest: her

loins seemed heavier, crumpled, as she had been punched repeatedly, and her abdomen, in particular, was heavy, becoming a veritable burden to her. It also seemed that it was increasing in volume, and as her monthly warnings had not appeared, she concluded that some inimical deposit of blood was forming within her, causing her health to deteriorate.

To tell the truth, she was not overly frightened, for during the tormented blossoming of her puberty, the wound that ought to have been regularly manifest had often failed to appear, and Dr. Cartaux, interrogated by her alarmed mother, had not seemed to be worried by it, attributing it to the general state of her health. She therefore believed that it would reappear one day, when she was better, and refrained, in her modest reserve, from confiding those intimate details to Madame Bise, whose exuberant solicitude she feared. However, she had a kind of unconscious fear of what was about to happen, and of what had happened in Armand Caresco's house—when, during a recent visit to her cousin Aline, now installed in the Avenue Hoche, the sight of the bloodstained apron the surgeon was wearing had caused her to faint.

She went upstairs heavily, therefore. She had only just reached the top step when an imperious shock in the lower abdomen nailed her, astonished and in pain, to the landing she had attained. It was like a dull blow, a muffled explosion originating in her bowels. Her face became pale with anguish; in order not to fall, she had to lean on the balustrade, holding on to the rail.

What affliction was within her, then, for her to find herself endlessly the target of repeated attacks of that tenebrous disease, which had not let her go for several months, seemingly intent on overwhelming her with incessantly-renewed assaults? What wrong had she done to nature for it to show itself so inclement in her regard, seemingly wanting to crush her beneath the burden of this strange malady?

She asked herself that, fearfully. For long minutes she remained there, immobile, waiting for a further shock that did not come.

In the meantime, Madame Bise climbed the stairs to go to her bedroom. On perceiving her niece, whom she thought was getting ready for bed, she could not suppress her astonishment.

"Why, what's wrong? What are you doing here?"

"Nothing, Aunt," Madeleine replied. "I'm a little out of breath..."

"There's something else, darling, which you don't want to tell me. Tomorrow, we'll have to send for the doctor."

"Oh, no, Aunt, it's not worth the trouble."

"Go on! You're quite pale. Go to bed, and tomorrow, I'll ask Monsieur Caresco to come to see you."

"Aunt, I'd prefer Monsieur Cartaux."

"Monsieur Cartaux's an old doctor, who's behind the times. Anyway, he's ill. Go in, child, and I'll send up some orange-blossom water. Tomorrow, the doctor will come."

The aggressive tone did not admit any protest, so Madeleine went to her room, and idled for a while, opening the mirror-fronted cupboard, which saluted her with the gift of a whiff of discreet perfume, mingled with the odor of clean linen. She took out a night-dress with a delicate collerette and laid it out on the bed. Then she went to stir the logs on the fire, which were almost consumed, opened the wood-box, and, with the aid of gilded tongs, took out more logs, which she piled on top of those that were burning. What life there was in those golden sparks! What a contrast with the mourning-dress of her heart!

She lingered for a moment to fix her memory on the lightly-framed portraits that ornamented the mantelpiece: her father, the handsome face of a *bon viveur*, who was almost unknown to her; her mother, still adored, bearing in her expression a generous pensive melancholy; and Georges Ponviane, the handsome and healthy fellow of noble stature, with all the attractiveness of his virile youth and the ardent profundity of his eyes. The past and the present. But why did the future seem to be symbolized by a fourth portrait placed there be Madame Bise? How did Armand Caresco come to be in the company of that dear trio?

He too was handsome, though, with his high and intelligent forehead surmounted by his forceful hair, and the velvet of his dark eyes. But even in the portrait, the gaze was ungraspable, seeming to flee as it did in reality. Obsessed, Madeleine turned the image to the wall, but as it was still imposing, reflected by the mirror, she laid it flat upon he marble.

Finally, as the bed was tempting her with a soft and warm promise, she decided to get undressed, and took off her garments unhurriedly, freeing her figure from the embrace of the corset, and then letting her chemise fall. She was naked. Before covering herself chastely with the fine batiste, in the anxiety of the malady that might be germinating in her abdomen, she considered the lily-white splendor of her flesh.

She had not submitted herself to such an examination for a long time. Thus, it was with a genuine amazement that she observed the transformations that her body had undergone.

The line of her neck was still the same, infinitely graceful, losing itself in the cascade of her gilded hair. But her breasts, augmented in volume, almost doubled, were proudly pointed and had taken on a brown coloration around the areola that contrasted violently with the milky whiteness of the skin under which the blue streaks of veins ran. Lower down, the abdomen bulged abnormally, sufficiently developed to hide from the young woman's eyes the gilded tuft, the veil of mysterious regions. The hips, marbled by the pink imprints of an overly tight corset, had thickened toward the immeasurably enlarged waist.

Madeleine stood there looking at herself for a long time, seeking in vain for an explanation of the illness that was disrupting the harmony of forms that she had once taken pleasure in admiring, knowing that its lines were beautiful, and having an instinctive notion of the purity of its contours. A host of bleak ideas passed through her mind, a gallop of bitterness and poignant suppositions.

Toward what abyss was she being led by that abdomen, swelling to the point of forcing her to let her corset out by another notch every day? And Georges, her Georges, so tender and sweet—would he still want a deformed wife, dragging with her the misery of all those frightful maladies of the abdomen of which she had vaguely heard mention, which had caused so many ravages around her, which had even killed a few ladies of her acquaintance, like Baronne Spirs?

Not for a single instant did the idea cross her mind that a glorious maternity had invaded her loins, and that she was the victim of an abominable crime accomplished during a cataleptic sleep. How could she have suspected it?—she whose candor did not suspect that the approach

233

of a man could go much further than the brush of a kiss and the union of lips.

Dolorously, she veiled her radiant affliction with the light fabric of hr night-dress, and went to sleep, anxious, with a wrinkle of sadness on her forehead, in the gilded scatter of her hair.

The next morning, Madeleine had a calm awakening. Her ideas seemed to have been subject to an unconscious labor during sleep, to have been filed away, and she envisaged her situation with more tranquility.

Her resolution was made; she would talk to Georges Ponviane about her condition. In whom could she have more confidence than him? Was he not the only one who really loved her, and whose well-balanced mind was capable of making a sane decision?

But she had counted without Madame Bise. In fact, she was still in bed when the latter presented herself, already dressed to go out.

To begin with, she surrounded her niece with affectionate caresses and puerile attentions. She brought chocolate croquettes, which Madeleine, in order not to displease her, tried to swallow. Then, thinking that she had seduced her with that naïve prelude, she suddenly brought up the idea that was haunting her.

"I'm going, out, you know, darling. I'm going to pay a visit on your behalf."

"On my behalf, Aunt?"

"Yes, for you, alas. I'm going to ask Dr. Caresco to come here. I love you too much to bear this. He'll cure you, as he's cured your cousin Aline."

"Oh, Aunt, I beg you…not Monsieur Caresco!"

"Who, then?" demanded Madame Bise, her voice inflated by anger. "I only have confidence in him. Monsieur Cartaux is nothing but a donkey, and a sick donkey too."

"Don't do anything without having talked to Georges," Madeleine begged, in a tearful voice.

"Monsieur Ponviane's advice is of no account at present, alas. It's me who has the responsibility"—and, content with the terms she had employed, she repeated it—"yes, the responsibility for your health, and no one will make my change my idea. Come on, little silly, you know full well that I'm afraid for your welfare, don't you? Poor darling!"

She covered the insensible Madeleine with kisses. Then, with her usual versatility, she started talking about a meeting of the Feminist Association at the home of her great friend Miss Pisword, for the redemption of the oppressed sex. Then she returned to Madeleine's malady, and went away, saying that she would not be long in coming back in the company of her favorite physician, and that Madeleine had only to stay in bed and wait for them.

As she arrived at the house in the Avenue Hoche, she saw Monsieur and Madame Romé whose were in discussion with Armand Caresco in the partly-open porch. Their attitude permitted the divination of grave preoccupations. The surgeon's gestures were emphatic and persuasive.

Madame Bise went up to them, eternally thoughtless, without noticing the drama that was darkening the expressions of the parents. For a veritable fear was drowning their hearts in distress; their daughter Aline, an inmate of the house for a week, after having been admirably well during her sojourn at the clinic, when the color had blossomed in her cheeks again and her sufferings have vanished as if by enchantment, on the very day when her parents had manifested the intention of taking her way from the surgeon's house, had been suddenly stricken by a new crisis of the liver of unprecedented violence.

Bordier, who had been making his afternoon rounds at the time, summoned in haste, given the exasperation of the pain, had authorized an injection of morphine, which had knocked the young woman out. But the following morning she had woken up jaundiced from head to toe. That persistence of the crises and renewal of the pain—by which the surgeon had not been duped—had nevertheless led him to propose to the parents an exploratory operation in order to search for gallstones that might be blocking the bile duct.

That was what he had just declared to Monsieur and Madame Romé, frightening them with the suddenness of the decision to be made, for here was no time to lose before the threat of the retention of bile, which might produce abscesses and fatal peritonitis. Discreetly, with retinues of words, he displayed for them the alarming list of accidents to be feared, bathing them in terror, enveloping hem with is persuasive speech, pushing them toward the determination to have recourse to his saving scalpel.

The artifice, and the overstatement of the perfection of his method, passed unperceived even by the investigative gaze of Monsieur Romé, so much warm conviction was there in his language, of real effort toward the good. What was the operation, anyway? Very little, in reality: a simple incision in the right flank, and one would fall directly upon the liver. He would avoid any considerable disturbance of the intestines and damage to the peritoneum, and he could, by removing those troublesome gallstones, save a life under threat.

Besides which, did he not make similar interventions every day, without any of his patients ever succumbing to the after-effects of the operation? Yes, when one had waited too long, when suppuration had already set in, abscesses had formed, peritonitis was in progress, it was a veritable crime not to have acted sooner. As for him, he believed that he was doing his duty as an honest man by raising the alarm.

"Let's see, Doctor," aid Monsieur Romé, "if the operation isn't attempted, will the accidents that you fear certainly occur?"

"Certainly? Damn it, I'm not inside her abdomen. No, not certainly, as two and two make four, but probably—very probably. And then, think for a moment, what reproaches would one make in the case of a fatal outcome?"

The sensitive soul of Madame Bise was impressed by that speech. She began to weep, and Madame Romé, sadder than her but until then more courageous, infected by her sister's tears, could not retain the expression of her grief. Already, idlers were stopping to look at them. Caresco closed the door, and all four of them stood there uncertainly, variously troubled, between the cold walls of the passage, on the threshold of the factory of death, as if the door, in closing, had plunged them into mourning.

"You can't stay there, in the cold draught," said the surgeon, pushing them toward the vestibule. Come in for a moment. Since there's a decision to make, you can discuss it, all the more so as Madame Bise, who has a say in the matter, is with you."

He was glad to add the trump card of the fortuitous presence of his protectress to his hand. He knew that she would press for the desired objective.

Monsieur Romé refused to come in, however. "Thank you, Doctor, but I have a meeting, and then, I prefer not to see my daughter again this morning. You understand that sentiment, don't you? One more thing: I have absolute confidence in you, in your talent, but will you permit me to bring in a medical consultant?"

"Please do," said Caresco, secretly distressed by that hitch.

"Dr. Cartaux, for instance," added Monsieur Romé.

"If you wish."

"Eh? Monsieur Cartaux is till indisposed," Madame Bise put in. "He's not leaving his room. I sent for news of him yesterday. Why so much dickering, though? Who else can see the matter more clearly than Monsieur Caresco, who has made a specialty of diseases of the liver? One either has or hasn't confidence in him. If you have, let him go ahead. That's what I think, in a nutshell."

Confronted by that brutal dilemma, Monsieur Romé felt his resistance fading, and came to an abrupt decision. Madame Romé, accustomed to passive obedience, also acquiesced.

The operation was arranged for the following morning.

Again, Armand Caresco, triumphant over destiny, prepared for a fruitful harvest. The Savoie child and Aline Romé were about to contribute to filling the hole excavated by Mathilde's necklace. Both would undergo operations the following morning; they would be cured or dead before the end of the month and the honoraria would be paid before the due date.

Armand Caresco, who was superstitious—as are the majority of disequilibrated brains, in which genius brushes dementia—had noticed that operations never came singly, one always leading to another. Would this be the commencement of a new series? The veil obscuring his horizon seemed to be tearing in the wind of chance.

Monsieur Romé left for his meeting. Madame Romé stayed to accompany the surgeon during his visit to Aline and to support the proposal that he was about to put to the young woman. As for Madame Bise, in spite of the gravity of events, she had not given up on her plan to take Caresco to Madeleine's bedside. So, while Aline's mother climbed the stairs, she took the surgeon to one side.

"By the way," she said, "I believe that won't be all. My other niece, Madeleine de Jancy, is unwell. I want you to come to see her this morning."

"Yes, I know, I know..."

"How do you know?"

"The other day, when Mademoiselle de Jancy fainted, I was able to take account of her condition, which isn't very reassuring."

"Well, then?" trumpeted the aunt. "What's wrong with her?"

"My God, Madame, you know that I'm bound by professional secrecy. But in sum, as you represent her family, I can't conceal from you that here's an abnormal growth in her abdomen, which I can't easily explain."

That was news that the stupid woman had not expected. She was flabbergasted. Her face, as wrinkled as an old apple, was hollowed out by even more wrinkles. Her mobile eyes fluttered more actively. She did not even think about voicing her suspicion, so great was her surprise."

"What! A growth! Are you sure?"

"I'm absolutely sure."

"Another operation, then! Too much! What a calamity for the family!"

"An operation?" said Armand, unable to hide a smile. "Oh no! Not now, anyway."

"When, then?"

"I don't know."

And he gave her a little lecture, explaining that the growth that was hindering the young woman's digestive functions, occasioning reflexes, was the cause of her fainting fits. He toyed with the old woman's emotions, taking pleasure in making a fool of her with misleading explanations, and she listened with approving nods of the head, drinking in the fantastic science that the doctor was imparting, accumulating incomprehensions, aliments for her expansive faculties, which would permit her, later, to give explanations of it in her turn, to make herself look good in the eyes of her entourage, and to influence a decision.

When he stopped speaking, she said, with a comical gravity: "I think it's necessary to operate too. The child can't get married with that, alas. Oh, you'll have saved the entire family!"

Armand Caresco made a gesture of negation, protesting strongly. No, no, the growth wasn't to be removed. He was convinced that it would disappear of its own accord. But Madame Bise grabbed his hand and compressed it violently, with forceful emotion.

"No! You'll have saved us all! You must come and see her today, the child—she's staying in bed, waiting for you."

"Today, my dear Madame, is impossible. Tomorrow morning I'm operating on Mademoiselle Romé. Perhaps tomorrow afternoon..."

They were climbing the stairs. Madame Bise was breathing heavily with emphysema and emotion. Armand Caresco was wondering how he ought to propose the operation to Mademoiselle Romé.

Very observant of the psychological state of his patients, always on the lookout for sentiments that their frequentation allowed him to perceive, and modifying his attitude in accordance with the nature of those sentiments, he was slightly at a loss in the present case. He was aware of the enormous role that the mental state of subjects plays in the evolution, and even the cure, of maladies, and what suggestion the practitioner is always called upon to exercise on the morale that is subject to the repercussion of physical effects. How many times, moreover, had he not taken advantage of that debility of the soul, that atony of passion, to obtain consent for an operation that had been refused the day before?

However, he had never had to deal with a fictitious malady—but a malady nevertheless, since the contrariety experienced by Aline had sufficed to contract the ducts of her liver and afflict her with biliary resorption. She had come, out of love for him, to offer herself to his care, but how far would that self-abandonment go? Might not the shock offered to the young woman's dementia be violent enough to cause her finally to open her eyes and revolt against the scalpel?

Certainly, antiquity offered even more surprising examples of immolation, and the long list of martyrs, expiring voluntarily for their religion, was proof of the unfathomable aberration of souls led astray by faith, whether that faith was the love of a God or the love of a man. But those sacrifices had occurred in tormented times, when hearts had been subject to the traction of wild predications and promises of future felicity; it could not be the same in this skeptical *fin-de-siècle*, and Caresco, as he opened the door of the room, was convinced that he would encounter resistance.

Aline Romé was still in bed, her ideas misted by morphine. The jaundice, an intense saffron hue, denatured the somber pallor of her complexion, and the blue transparency of her cornea. The icteric tint was accentuated in the eyelids, which, violently circled, were almost black.

Beside the bed, Madame Romé, her heart drowned by the tears that she was repressing with great difficulty, was holding her daughter's hand knotted in her own. In a corner, Soeur Cunégonde, who had scented the importance of the event, was displaying the indifference of her acne-scarred face. And all around the invalid, in the luxurious room, was the same spectacle of things, the rectitude of the great floral curtains, the neatness of the tables covered in pharmaceutical bottles, the regular tock-tock of the clock, the muffled footsteps on the soft Oriental carpet.

When Armand Caresco came in, followed by Madame Bise, Aline's face became radiant, with a violent afflux of blood beneath her ochreous skin. It was the second time that morning that the surgeon had come to see her; she understood that something decisive was about to happen, and she was quivering all over as she listened to the words emerging from the surgeon's lips.

"Mademoiselle, you had a new crisis yesterday, more serious than the preceding ones, and that has given your family, and me, pause for reflection. We don't want to prolong this poor state of health—which is occasioned, as I've told you, by gallstones that had formed in your liver and are interrupting the normal flow of the bile, causing it to spread through your bloodstream instead of passing into the intestines. If these accidents are reproduced, there's no doubt that it could result in serious consequences. That's why, with the agreement of your parents and Madame Bise, I've come to propose to you a radical remedy, which consists of removing the little stones. The operation is not dangerous, and of short duration. In any case, you won't feel anything under the artificial sleep, and it will only leave an insignificant scar. What do you think?"

He had spoken modestly, correctly, without difficult terminology, his gaze turned away, with his nacreous smile. Aline received the shock without flinching. It seemed to her that the proposal that had just been made had had to arrive, quite naturally, when the time came—and the time had come.

Around her, the people present expected a revolt, some cry of alarm, an explosion of revulsion, or a manifestation of terror before the danger toward which she was being pushed, but there was nothing. At the most, Madame Romé, who would have liked to be able to pass on her life and health through the clutch of her hand, felt a slight tremor.

Aline turned toward the man she loved the lamentation of her eyes, soiled by jaundice, and her gesture was a confession, an abandonment of herself, like that of a virgin surrendering to the first dolorous approach of the man she adores, like that of a woman of sacred legend immolating herself for Christ, like that of Jeanne d'Arc mounting the pyre. Her gesture was made of glory, of devotion, and of love.

Her gesture said: "Take me; I sacrifice myself. Do with me what you will. Deflower my beauty with your knife, cut my flesh, take my blood; I am yours, I give myself with joy. The operation is unnecessary and my malady the result of a comedy? What does it matter, since you want me in that fashion? I will lie down on the sacrificial table without recrimination, devotedly, passively, and I will belong to you thus, for I am your object, your thing, and you will do with me what you will, all that you will!"

As Armand Caresco was astonished not to receive any response, uncertain of the success of his attempt, he repeated: "Well, what do you think?"

She replied, softly: "I believe it will be the only means of curing me."

Among the women, that simple consent, of which they could not divine the psychology and which they attributed to reason, provoked an emotional flood of words. Madame Romé seized Aline in her arms and covered her with kisses veiled by sobs. Madame Bise abandoned herself to the impetuous evacuation of southern epithets and hosannas of gratitude toward the surgeon. As for Soeur Cunégonde, who tasted the triumph of a work of traction to which she had submitted the young woman since she had arrived in the house, she did not neglect either to offer her felicitations for the consent given, albeit in a more restrained fashion.

"Mademoiselle is so reasonable! You'll see, my dear, how we shall all look after you."

And there was almost a celebration in their hearts. It seemed that the operation was already accomplished, that the great act had been consummated; they no longer felt the anguish behind that false urgency. The gray light falling from the large windows impregnated them with a kind of lukewarm gaiety, illuminating contented faces.

The surgeon took advantage of the moment to announce that the operation would be carried out the next day and then left, satisfied, followed by the thankful gaze of the young woman, while Soeur Cunégonde stayed in the room, to continue to warm imaginations by recounting the daily miracles that her young master performed, while attenuating, by the obsession with success and the promise of the prayers of her entire community, the horror of the blood that was about to flow.

Madame Bise, utterly joyful, was no longer thinking, for the moment, about Madeleine, her other niece, who was in bed, dolorously waiting for the surgeon's visit.

In the room where General de Rion was, who had undergone his operation a week before, Armand Caresco encountered Bordier, who was changing the dressing. The consequences of the operation had been admirably straightforward, with no fever and no pain, and the old man admitted that if it were not for the reaction of the chloroform and the ennui of being confined to bed, he would willingly be butchered again. He was experiencing real amelioration, which caused him to believe in a complete success, exciting the hope of a return to activity and a long and vigorous old age, exempt from the cacochymy and procrastinations resulting from his hypertrophied prostate. He was deluding himself with images of a gilded old age, of rides through the Bois de Boulogne, and even a courtesan, once a month. When his benefactor entered, he glorified him.

Bordier removed from the groin region the small bandages that were hiding the collodion-soaked cotton wool.

"Pardon me, General, if I hurt you."

"Get on with it, damn it," grumbled the deep voice. "I've commanded in Africa, I know what's what. Then again, here, I have nothing to say. I'm a conscript; I obey. Aah!"

Bordier has just unstuck the last morsel of cotton wool, uncovered the precise neatness of the cut. One after the other, he extracted the horsehair stitches that were sealing the wound. He lifted the stitches with forceps and then cut them with a precise snip of the scissors.

"You're cured, General," Caresco said.

The old man howled with joy, and wanted to get up immediately. It was necessary to threaten him with a relapse to keep him in bed.

Armand Caresco took Bordier out on to the landing.

"The Romé girl is scheduled for tomorrow," he told him.

"Mademoiselle Romé? What are you going to do, then?"

"I don't know exactly—an exploration. I wouldn't be astonished if there were a calculus obstructing the bile duct or the cystic duct. By reason of the persistence of the symptoms, I think it useful, in order to avoid complications that are always to be feared, to go in and see..."

Bordier searched for the truth in Caresco's gaze, but the eyes fled. The frightful suspicion that had already tortured him several times recurred; what Savre had said returned to obsess his judgment; he glimpsed an atrocity. At first he tried to resist, attempting to convince Caresco that they could wait, that no serious symptoms demanded an operation, and that they might be dealing with a simple inflammation of the bile duct that would disappear of its own accord, as had been observed many a time.

"But she had a violent hepatic colic yesterday!" said Caresco.

"A hepatic colic?" Bordier repeated. "Are you sure?"

"Soeur Cunégonde affirms it, and I judged it appropriate to give her an injection of morphine, but how do we know that our judgment is sufficiently sound?"

They continued the discussion in technical terms. The surgeon was irritated that his lead was not being followed by his collaborator, by running into the objections of pure reason. His voice inflated with a hiss of anger, and a veritable conflict, almost hateful, compounded out of a determination to triumph on one side and a convinced resistance on the other, was engaged in a corner of the landing. But Madame Savoie, who emerged from her son's room, came to put an end to the argument. She was pale and pretty, clad in a blue morning-dress, and her appearance brought something akin to a ray of sunshine into the tempest.

Caresco went to meet her and took her by the hand. "Well, Madame, how is your boy? Did he have a good night?"

With delicate sad gestures, fatigued by sleepless nights, the mother replied that the scamp had not sleep well, constantly shaken by dreams, prey to a painful agitation since he had quit his own bedroom to take possession of the room in the sanitarium. It distressed the mother to see her child, ordinarily so placid and mild, suddenly become anxious and nervous. Was it necessary to operate in those conditions, and would he have the strength to support the frightful shock?

"Certainly, certainly!" Caresco replied, fearing an offensive return by Dr. Varon, the family doctor. "It would even be dangerous to wait longer than tomorrow. Anyway, I'll come in with you."

They disappeared into the child's room. Abandoned on the landing, Bordier was not tempted to follow Caresco. A nausea was rising within him at the constant comedy, the path toward wrongdoing along which he felt unwillingly led.

In the six months that he had been collaborating with the surgeon, he admitted, he had lost the concern for human life that had griped him before, that had made of him, during his time as a local physician, a heroic fighter against disease. A kind of indifference to events was beginning to numb him; unsuccessful interventions did not disturb him as much; he was relaxing into an indolence, a macabre apathy, and felt that he was clad in a straitjacket of egotism that paralyzed his intentions of revolt.

Was he going to participate tomorrow, again, in actions that he thought blameworthy, lending his aid to two operations he judged unnecessary? The change of tack caused him anguish, held him, bitter and uncertain, in the place where Armand Caresco had just abandoned him, in the lukewarm and dolorous solitude of the sumptuous stairway.

Finally, his work being concluded, he went down the stairs, thoughtfully, giving himself until the end of the day to make up his mind and decide to send the surgeon his resignation. He would resume the beneficent and glorious work of the most obscure physician, return to install himself in the quarter he had abandoned, where clients were still waiting for him. His daily bread would be more difficult to earn, but he would eat it with a better heart, with less tormenting regret.

His bicycle was waiting for him in the entrance courtyard. Anticipating an hour of liberty, he had brought it on that cold, crisp morning, in order to go for a ride in the Bois before lunch. He sat astride it, almost content, relieved of a burden of anxiety.

All along the Avenue Hoche, to the Barrière de l'Étoile, and further still, as far as the Porte Dauphine, on the open road, whipped by the morning chill, he yielded to a pedaling full of forgetfulness and hope, and finally, having reached the pathways of the Bois, in the white profundity of the frost-covered trees, he flew, gripped by the intoxication of space, on the dear steel bird.

Blessed little machine! How, thanks to her, he was able calm his nerves, chase away the clouds of frightful sadness that afflicted his heart, in the enjoyment of his favorite exercise, forgetting all the miseries and abominations that rolled in bitter waves behind him, over the roads of the giant city!

CHAPTER XIV

Armand Caresco had not failed to detect a nascent hostility in Bordier. He suspected that his assistant's retreat was guided by scruples that he judged, in his own implacable heart, to be of an inferior order. Infusorial delicacies, he thought; those who wanted to be the kings of the day, to triumph in this *fin-de-siècle* corrupted by money, dissociated by egotism, lucre and enjoyment, ought not to succumb to such weaknesses of character.

Would he, the young master, have achieved such renown, such surgical authority, if he had stopped to listen to the echo of miserable murmurs of conscience, if he had allowed himself to be vanquished by remorse, if he had not gone on, coldly self-composed, continuing his tragic route, indifferent to the groans of the dying, the sobbing of families, the muttered prayers before rigid corpses by the tremulous light of two candles?

No; Bordier was a weakling, a humble individual, destined to mark time, inadequate to the kind of collaboration that was required of him. When would he find what he had never encountered, another self, as ferociously audacious, endowed with as violent an initiative, not recoiling before the means necessary to arrive at an envisaged goal? How far, in the company of such an aide, might he be able to take the surgical science to which he had already contributed so much, by means of his young and glorious talent, taking it out of the beaten track in which it was marching on the spot?

No corner of the human body would then remain inaccessible to his scalpel; all those maladies, supposedly incurable because no one had dared go to do battle with them on location, would become susceptible to cure thanks to his innovations. Was not the human machine comparable to certain industrial machines that one dismantled in order to find the defective components, to change and improve them?

In his dreams of devouring ambition, of apotheosis, he calculated the results of his scientific conquests: fortune, first of all, the millions brought into his coffers solely by dint of his talent and intelligence, without recourse to the dishonoring power of capital—for his entire edifice was built with his ideas and his fingers. What would the fabulous sum be of those masses of gold extracted from the inexhaustible mine that was his brain?

To begin with, he would abandon his present house in the Avenue Hoche, which would become insufficient in the near future. On land that he would buy outside Paris, bathed in healthy woodland air near one of the outlying railway stations, he would commission the building, in accordance with his own plans and incorporating all the genius of his modifications, an immense sanitarium, a veritable model hospital for the rich, with several operating theaters, laboratories, spacious rooms, a park, all the perfections of a rich and luxurious organization.

There, he would be able to suppress the undesirable proximity of the rich and the poor, and operate upon everyone according to their fortune. He did not even refuse himself the idea of also building a house for the unfortunate, whom he would treat gratuitously, or in return for very feeble remunerations—not with a humanitarian objective, but in order to possess another field of experimentation and demonstration, which would permit him to continue to invite foreign colleagues to witness astonishing manifestations of his surgical genius. There, he would form pupils: an entire innovative surgical school surging from his example would spread the publicity of his doctrines and his skill throughout the world.

And who could tell whether, one day, the government, distressed not to be seconding such an active authority, might not seek to sanction the Force that threatened to take the pupils away from the hospitals, by consecrating it officially, by creating a special chair for the surgeon, like the one already created during the Empire for another scientist, also an Israelite?[15] Then along with wealth, the manna of honors would fall, and he would only have to pick it up to satisfy his glory and gorge his ambition.

And what bankruptcy for his enemies, the officials—what a muddy puddle in which he would enjoy seeing them flounder, as one sees inferior organisms battling in a miserable and repulsive conflict in a drop of dirty water through the objective lens of a microscope!

Those ferocious ambitious ideas had always haunted his soul. He sometimes extended them to the worst limits, in moments of unhealthy excitement, after periods of hard work in which he had racked the fibers of his brain. It seemed then that he no longer had an accurate appreciation of the regions that he might attain, and his dreams bordered on delusions of grandeur. Some of the people who approached him at those moments were amazed by the flight of his ambition, and, like Dr. Savre,

---

[15] This reference is slightly puzzling; it probably refers to Claude Bernard, for whom Louis-Napoléon created a special chair during the Second Empire, but Bernard was not Jewish. Caresco might be taking the wrong inference from his surname; Couvreur was probably acquainted with the writer and velodrome manager Tristan Bernard, who was Jewish.

had the anxious suspicion of a mental unbalance. But Caresco recovered quickly, dominated even so by the sense of practicality, and it had required his strong and stupid passion for Mathilde de Guinac to drag him into the disastrous consequences of a debt of a hundred thousand francs.

Now, resolved not to succumb to wretched financial embarrassments, he allowed a monstrous project to germinate within him. In fact, for the sum of sixty thousand francs that he still lacked, was he going to see the edifice that he had built with so much somber effort and shady endeavor crumble? Was a man of his stripe going to be defeated by something so trivial and fall back into the mud?

No, he would fight, he would emerge victorious, by whatever means, in order to resume thereafter his surge toward the road of triumph.

But before arriving at the worst solutions, he would make a supreme effort by the regular means that were even more pleasing to his character, stamped with a hereditary prudence.

So, that day, he decided to go and see a few of his most faithful suppliers of operations, to ask them to hasten the execution of those that they had in suspense. Warmly wrapped up in his fur cloak, beneficent in the dry and frosty weather that covered the roofs, balconies and trees on the boulevards with a white glacis, in the caress of the air warmed by a hot-water bottle, he sank into a corner of his coupé and began his round of visits, like the representative of a large industrial concern visiting his clients in quest of business.

He crossed disreputable thresholds, climbed dark stairways to penetrate into insanitary rooms in which "midwives," matrons with dirty fingernails, were exploiting dolor and misery, correcting by somber practices the amorous imprudences of whom to whom social tyranny, shame or cowardice forbade a radiant maternity.

Often, these abortive maneuvers resulted in further infirmity, an unfortunate whose organs of conception were no longer anything but a suppurating wound through which life and joy ebbed away in pus. It was Caresco who then magnified his role as benefactor by rendering them to health or eternity by an operation. And he approached those frightful matrons without disgust or repugnance, with the insouciant humor of a courtier touting for business, conscious that his work is honest and sure. Was it him who provoked the abortion, him who occasioned the horrible maladies? No, he was the savior, the skillful artisan who repaired the damage done by others.

Generally, the harvest of these kinds of measures was not very fruitful, but it had sometimes brought wealthy women to his sanitarium who, after refusals met in the consulting rooms of physicians, had also had recourse to these birds of prey, into whose claws, terrified by the threat of a scandal, they had hurled themselves. It was in the hope of a similar windfall that Caresco pursued his visits tenaciously, welcomed by smiles of complicity, dirty handshakes in which there was an infamous understanding, criminal compromise and, in some cases, gratitude.

At other times, his carriage stopped outside houses of a more bourgeois appearance. A marble plaque on the wall indicated a doctor's residence, with days and hours of consultation. There, too, he found the slavish welcome of base collaborators, poor fellows uprooted from their native soil who had come to plant themselves in the Parisian mud, retained in the soil of the great city by mirages of luxury, hopes of a quick fortune, or even by habit, passion or vice that only the agglomeration and swarming of masses could allow them to dissimulate.

He knew that these pariahs of medicine were reduced to the worst expedients, and that, in order to live, deprived of the subsidies necessary to await a clientele, they would accept his propositions. How many among these sons of ambitious peasants would have done better to remain in their fields pushing ploughs in order to fecundate he nurturing earth, breathing the healthy air of the woods, raising a happy and strong family instead of coming in displaced legions to swell the muddy tides of great cities, to attempt a frightful struggle, to waste in sterile efforts the purest radiations of their vigor and energy?

Those reflections inundated Caresco's mind while he climbed the staircases of those unfortunates, while he waited, before the empty seats of miserable reception rooms, for the appearance of men in black frock-coats with haggard features and unkempt hair, in whose faces he read the disappointment of having to deal with a colleague and not a client. But he, with his fine assurance, warmed them up regardless with a fire of hope and promises, insinuations of fruitful collaboration, enveloping them in his strange persuasion.

All of them, conquered in advance by his renown, by the honor of his approach, promised to come and visit his operating theater, to witness his brilliant sessions. Unfortunately, for the moment, they had nothing to offer him; work was scarce, the struggle difficult. The free hospitals were draining the greater part of the clientele; the mutual societies were absorbing the rest. And from those bitter mouths and weary throats emerged plaints of injustice and discouraged explosions, with which

Caresco mingled his own, exposing his ideas of resistance and renovation, ironic paradoxes, and also anger against the great usurpers of medicine, the official parvenus who gave no thought to the humble, losing, as soon as they emerged from the beaten track, any idea of confraternity, any sentiment of union and commiseration.

Certainly, he was not moved by such an implacable egotism, and he understood the needs and sufferings of the disinherited. They could, therefore, confide their surgical interventions to him without fear; he would know how to show his gratitude effectively.

He concluded the tour of his visits under an impression of lamentation and ruin. The sadness of all those wretches had made its mark on him, and his soul oscillated momentarily toward distress. But there was only a minute of discouragement, and his arrogant temperament hoisted him up again toward triumph. Even supposing that things were going badly, did he not still have ten days before the due date of his settlement with Israel? In ten days, he would find the fifty thousand francs that he lacked. The next day, he would operate on the Savoie child and Aline Romé; those two operations alone, counting ten thousand francs each, would reduce the deficit to thirty thousand.

And afterwards?

Afterwards, he heard again, with an intense verity of sound, the voice of Madame Bise, who had said to him not long ago: "You'll have saved us all," when he had affirmed that an operation was unnecessary in Madeleine's case. The old woman would reappear, pressing his hand, moved by an intense desire to see her other niece also fall into his clutches—and that desire would respond to a shameful project that he had already secretly caressed.

What explanation was conceivable of the psychology of that confidence, the abandon—which was not critical, because it was absurd—that was driving the aunt to bring him, bound hand and foot, another victim for immolation? What mental breakdown was impelling her? But history is full of such instances of alienation: the holocausts of which the Bible speaks, the sacrifices of religions, the legendary abnegations of the neurotics of Faith are proof of that.

Madame Bise's Faith was in her surgeon; no salvation was possible without him, without the intervention of his genius, and she was about to push her niece toward an abomination, as she would have offered herself to it if Caresco had only made her suppose that she ought to submit herself to his healing practices.

And he allowed himself to be invaded by the possibility of an iniquitous realization. Why not, after all, operate on Madeleine? All the considerations exciting his deceptive soul led him to that conclusion.

In the first place, he thought about his personal security. Independently of the considerable sum he could solicit, which would almost full the gap in the hundred thousand francs, might someone not, one day, by counting the months that had elapsed, establish the exact date of the crime, and remember that he had been the only one to go near the girl during the abominable moments when catalepsy had rendered her defenseless, unconscious, like a blind object?

Evidently, absolute certainty would be impossible, but powerful presumptions would impose themselves, and then, of what resentment, of what hatred, would he be the object, on the part of Georges Ponviane, when the latter realized his fiancée's condition, and when he divined, after maddening explanations, that only Caresco had been in the conditions favorable to the perpetration of such a crime?

Then again, humanely, would it not be an act of charity and pity to suppress the cause that might lead to such a disaster in two hearts, and determine the ruination of two young people, equally handsome and equally radiant with life and love? Could one tell to what extremes those excited brains might go? Might they not conceive the idea of terminating an existence that had become impossible, now that a monstrous barrier had arisen amid their intoxication, by a common death? Other examples had been seen, in instances less abominable than the problem of fear and misery that was seething in the surgeon's brain.

The more he thought about it, the more imperative the solution became, seeming sure, natural, logical and beneficent. For it is necessary not to forget the scorn in which Caresco held human life. Would he, who, in order to satisfy his cupidity or vainglory, or is need for science and research, did not hesitate to subject organized beings, unities of life, to the risks of operation and anesthesia, hesitate to suppress an embryo, a scarcely-fecundated seed—and it might cost him so much, that seed!—when it was a question of safeguarding his own future, effacing a with a thrust of the scalpel a crime, an absurdity, which he had committed in a moment of recklessness, and also, of sparing from the distress and agony of a separation two hearts that adored one another?

Then again, his triumph before everything: the abomination of the means to be employed foundered before the result. He had always envisaged himself as a general determined to win a battle, who engages in conflict ferociously and implacably, and will not recoil before any consideration or any sacrifice.

Already, he was interpreting the nature of the operation that he would attempt, the method of choice, that famous abdominal hysterectomy, so fortunate and so brilliant between his fingers. Already, while his trotter, driven by the coachman, was bringing him rapidly back to Mathilde's house through the arteries hardened by frost, through the crowds wrapped up against the cold, hastening in all directions to their pleasures or their struggles, amid the comings and goings of carriages that enabled him to perceive, in brief flashes, grave anxious faces or the muffled profiles of pretty women, he was evoking the vision of Madeleine extended on his operating table, her face pale, her abdomen open.

Before him, bare-armed, his torso covered in a white apron stained with blood, there was an aide who was not Bordier—for Bordier must be kept away from it at all costs. He would recruit to assist him, for the occasion, one of those young students or inexperienced doctors by whom he was always surrounded, and under whose eyes he could disguise the operation, passing off the gravid uterus as one of those fibrous tumors that were so frequent.

At the most, by reason of the inexperience of that occasional aide, the operation would take a few minutes longer. Was it not his custom to operate almost alone? And what a triumph, finally, what security for the future, when, the anatomical specimen having been dissimulated and destroyed, he could return that young woman to her family, to her fiancée, cured, healthy once again, and lull them all with the hope of an impossible fecundity, the hope of a strong and beautiful lineage emanating from two beings so pure and amorous!

Then again, in the tragic procession, he would find once again a temporary altar for his pride, at which to breathe in the incense of adulation, and depart thereafter buoyed up, reconciled with fortune, toward further adventures.

But Bordier had to disappear.

A letter that he found in his mail on re-entering his mistress' residence furnished him with the pretext for sending him away. The letter had been sent by a lady living in Bordeaux. A few months earlier, she had traveled to Paris for the express purpose of having him remove gallstones from the bile duct. The skillfully-executed operation seemed to have succeeded at first, and the lady had gone home blessing the surgeon, and proclaiming the victory so loudly that two of her friends had also had recourse to Caresco's talents, for different reasons. Some time ago, however, the malady had recurred and the phenomena of biliary resorption, fever, and an entire cortege of alarming symptoms had frightened the lady, who was begging the surgeon to come to see her in order to attempt a further intervention.

As he read the missive, Caresco once again felt brushed by the wings of fortune, which, of its own accord, without his solicitation, was flattening the obstacles in his path.

Immediately, he wrote a note to Bordier asking him to leave for Bordeaux without delay, to follow the rich client, to spend a week with her and to summon him be telegram if a new operation were really necessary. He added that, by reason of the shortage of patients, Bordier's collaboration was not indispensable to him for the moment, and that if would have recourse to a temporary aide if the need arose, Nor did he neglect to add that the case was particularly interesting and that he was counting on the friendship and devotion of his collaborator to accord the client who was requesting his aid not merely the solicitation of a physician but also that of a scientist. And he sealed the letter with an ironic smile.

He often decorated his maleficent actions in that fashion with a hint of icy humor, which was characteristic of his soul, afflicted by a perversion akin to insanity, in the same way that a lunatic in a madhouse might caress with a rictus the imaginary dagger with which he intends to stab his guardian.

When Bordier received Caresco's note he was at table, finishing his dinner. With a newspaper before his eyes, he was consuming the frugal meal, which the domestic had arranged around him, within arm's reach, without thinking about it. Reading whiled away his solitude, filling the void at the table, preventing him from thinking about the bitterness of a life without a wife and children. He picked up the letter that was held out to him distractedly, his brain still impregnated with the lines that he had just scanned—but when, after having glanced at the envelope, he recognized Caresco's handwriting, his attention awoke.

As soon as he read the first words, he felt a kind of relief at being sent away from Paris, far from the house of stress—an unconscious surge of egotism that made him rejoice in not having to take part in the operation on Aline Romé, which he deemed to be wrong. His mind, exempt from dishonesty, as limpid as his blue eyes, could not conceive of the surgeon's strategy. He took pleasure in the project of going to see Bordeaux, of according himself a respite in his resolution to separate from the surgeon, to resume his former way of life, of serious and honest labor.

He gave the maidservant a few instructions with regard to his departure, consulted a timetable, decided to leave early the next morning, wrote a few words of consent to Caresco, and then finished his meal with a better appetite, his heart freed from the heavy burden of indetermination. A conflict was still racking him, though. He wondered whether he had the right to abandon Mademoiselle Romé at the moment when the influence—modest, in verity—that he had over Caresco might yet persuade him to renounce an endeavor that was not justified by the young woman's condition.

Was not his duty to remain faithfully at his post, like a soldier, like a guardian of honor and life, and to put all his means of action in the service of his conviction? Was not his duty to go to find Aline's parents, and Madame Bise, and cry out to them: "Don't allow this to happen; wait for the healing that will happen on its own! Can't you see that the demon of money is agitating Caresco's soul, that the slightest of his gestures, his smiles and his actions is the reflection of vile self-interest, and that his crime is worse than any other because it carries no sanction?"

But what echo would his voice find in the consciousness of the people that the ardent seducer had already enveloped with a persuasive magnetism? Would anyone even listen to him? Would he not see irritated face turn toward him, menacing eyes furious at being distracted from a conviction equal to his own?

For the human mind is constructed in such a way that, as soon as it is entrenched in a persuasion, contrary arguments, the means employed by adverse faith, only serve to root it more deeply in conviction. And in the present case Bordier felt that he would collide with the opinion of the relatives, especially of Madame Bise, that odious little woman whose stupidity irritated him, and, even more probably, of Aline Romé herself.

Given his impotence, therefore, and under the influence of his timorous character, which liked to let things go, convinced that he would be preaching to blocked ears, he decided to maintain a silence to which he was, in any case, obliged by a kind of professional secrecy.

As he finished his cup of coffee, the doorbell rang, pulling him back from the regions where his thoughts were floating. Georges Ponviane came in, without waiting to be introduced—but as Bordier got up joyfully to take his hands, he stopped, surprised by the other's fearful expression.

"Georges! What's the matter?"

"Nothing very bad—at least, I hope so. But Madeleine has been gripped by a kind of indigestion, and when I arrived at Madame Bise's house a little while ago, where's she's been living since her bereavement, I found her in considerable pain. So I came to look for you, so that you might calm her down, and I'm very, very glad to have found you, my dear Jean." Already reassured by the idea that his friend would come to care for his fiancée, and remove her from peril, if any existed, he added: "Oh, I'm sure that it's nothing…perhaps another of the nervous accidents similar to those I've already mentioned to you…but you'll understand that I'd rather be reassured, and you're the only one in whom I have absolute confidence."

Bordier had already put on his overcoat. In the fiacre that was waiting for them at the door, Georges expressed his anxieties about Madeleine, and his astonishment at seeing the alarming symptoms recur in spite of Dr. Cartaux's expectations.

Bordier reassured him. Was it so astonishing that Madeleine was suffering after the frightful mental shock that she had experienced in the sudden death of her mother? No, no, Georges ought not to worry; all that would gradually fade way and disappear completely with the happy calm of marriage.

"When is it, your marriage?" Bordier added.

They chatted about their projects. The great desire of Georges and his father was not to delay too long the moment when Madeleine would be removed from the deplorable guardianship of Madame Bise. They were anticipating the minimum delay, while observing the proprieties—a few months at the most—and the marriage would be simple, without any pomp or a large gathering.

With a radiant contentment that dissipated the mists of anxiety, Georges again expressed to Bordier his desire to have him as a witness. Was it not to him, his truest, his only friend, the brother of his heart, that the prerogative belonged of placing the foundations of his happiness? His union with the ideal young woman would be imprinted with expansion and joy, presented under such auspices, supported by such camaraderie! Jean Bordier would then marry in his turn, would chose a companion as healthy and beautiful as Madeleine, and an intense affection would continue to unite the two households as it had sealed the hearts of the two friends.

What foursomes they would have then, what common voyages, what intimate celebrations, full of harmony and tranquility, in two families that would form one, nursed by the same joys, suffering the same difficulties, united by bonds more indissoluble than those of vulgar blood relationship! Children would be born who would love one another in their turn—and Georges, in an overflow of hope and joy, was already declaring that Bordier would be the godfather of his firstborn.

Bordier smiled at the slightly puerile expansions of his excited friend, gained by the contagion of his contentment, and shook his friend's hand warmly, promising all that he was asked, and also quivering at the comforting hope of the radiance of the dawn that was about to break.

Alas! Extinct dreams! Frightful collapse of all those ideal caresses! What did he think, the poor physician, when, after having examined Madeleine, lying in the warm softness of white sheets, her head lost in the golden waves of her hair, shaken by vomiting, her breasts swollen, with the areolas of maternity, and that abdomen already bulging under the covers? What did he think, when he was struck by that awful discovery?

In a bleak retreat, his confidence and his joy fled.

What, Madeleine! Madeleine, the young woman of such pure and calm appearance that she seemed to symbolize virginity; Madeleine, who had appeared to him on the first evening he saw her as a radiant blossoming of a lily of modest love; Madeleine, whose eyes bathed in candid repose, whose lips were so chastely pink that it seemed that a material word might bruise them in passing…Madeleine was pregnant!

The young man was astounded. Suppositions collided in his mind. Pregnant! By whom? What man had been infamous enough to tarnish that pure soul?

What man? For he did not suppose for a single instant that it was Georges. He knew the noble honesty of his friend's character too well. Then again, even supposing a fault, excusable in sum between two young people exasperated by a violent amorous impulse, even supposing such a fault had been committed, would Georges not have confided it to him, the other half of his heart, the depository of his slightest actions, his most trivial thoughts? Would not Georges have been on the lookout for these symptoms of pregnancy, so evident for alerted minds, which were now becoming so even to those that were not? And as soon as the first alarm, would he have failed to make him party to it, to seek information from him regarding the probabilities, and even the measures that might be taken to avoid a scandal?

No, Georges was not the author of the sin. An ardent conviction revolted Bordier against the mere supposition. Was it, then, Madeleine who had betrayed him, who, in a moment of recklessness, under an unconscious pressure, solicited by the ardent words of a cavalier, perhaps after the intoxication of a ball, had weakened in another's arms? No, that was not possible either. Madeleine seemed to him to be as sure, as loyal, as Georges, as respectful of the supreme grandeur of their love.

Something mysterious and abominable must have happened, which he could not imagine. And already, exceeding reality, he thought of hypnotism. But who? What wretch…?

And before the calm face, the young woman's eyes, filled with a tranquil mirage, now that the crisis was over, he thought that he might be mistaken. He posed the same questions again, repeated them with a precision that his role as a physician authorized—and he obtained the same replies, made in the same candid, almost innocent fashion.

"Oh yes, my dear Monsieur Bordier," Madeleine said to him, "examine me carefully and tell me exactly what villainous illness I have in my abdomen. Isn't it bizarre that I've swollen up in this fashion? I'm obliged to lace myself up very tightly to get into my corset, and I can foresee the moment when I shall have to let out my dresses. I believe that I have a tumor. Oh, poor Georges! Poor Georges! How he will suffer from all this!"

She was weeping now, and Bordier felt that lamentation infecting him. Could he doubt a virtue that was exhaled in such a loving plaint? How sublimely beautiful she was thus, vanquished by her body and her heart, annihilated by dolor and fear under the irredeemable menace suspended over her head! How ardently desirable she was, with her head, so fine and so aristocratic, overwhelmed by the envelope of her blonde hair, and how he could have understood how Georges, without seeking to, without wanting to dig deeply into all that was frightful and incomprehensible in his misdeed, might have accepted thus to transport her, joyful and adored, toward the summit of felicity!

But he was judging as someone who is not in love, who appreciates a situation in human terms, who does not envisage all there might be of sovereign folly in a passion so exalted.

And what about Georges? What would become of him in the presence of the fact that had fallen brutally upon his love? Would he be crushed by it, or heroic enough to resist it, to cast it off with a shrug of his shoulders?

"Alas," said Madeleine, "I can tell by your expression that it's grave. Poor Georges!"

"No, it's not grave," Bordier replied, "surely not grave; I give you my word of honor on that."

"Oh, tell Georges that!" she said, swiftly. "Reassure him, I beg you. For what does health, or even life, matter to me? But it's for him, whom I love so much!"

At these words, Bordier remained deeply sad. In the shock of the discovery, he had not had time to think of what conduct he ought to adopt with regard to his friend. A frightful problem filled him with doubt and anguish. What was he going to say to the fiancé who was out there, in the drawing room, waiting feverishly, who must be expecting precise information, a diagnosis?

Madame Bise was absent this evening, kept away from home by a conference on Feminism at which she was even to speak, increasing carried away by that new enthusiasm. The two friends could, therefore, speak in total liberty—and it was that prospect which frightened the young physician.

And Bordier, who abominated the aunt, wished, at that critical moment, for her presence, swollen with self-importance, for the whirlwind of her vain words, and even her categorical opinions. For the dear aunt would not have neglected to impose the authority of her opinions and announce the diagnosis...of a reflux of blood, or bile on the heart. But he...what was he going to say to his Georges, so confident a friend?

Dare he deceive him? Or ought he, by means of skillful questions of which he could not yet glimpse the strategy, obtain revelations, discover whether a fault might have been committed, whether Georges, going momentarily astray, might have seduced his fiancée...and then reveal the result?

But how could he pose those questions? How could he lead the conversation on to that terrain strewn with thorns? He did not feel that he had the strength of mind, or the cunning for such delicate diplomacy. Then again, he had the absolute conviction that it was not the case. Why, then, by a maladroit investigation, excite suspicions, tear a portion of the veil that he would have liked to continue to obscure his friend's sight?

But what a frightful moment it would be when Georges would finally be enlightened, when someone else, or even he, told him the abominable truth? What a collapse of gilded dreams, what an abyss, what sobs, what despair!

Was it not better, then, that he should bring him this very evening to the reality of the circumstance, gently, cradling him with affectionate and consoling words, imprinted with a philosophy broad enough to excuse anything?

And Bordier struggled in the tempest of his thoughts, tossed by surges of contrary ideas, seeking in vain for a saving plank to which he might cling, in order not to allow himself to be swallowed up by a bitter sea.

For a moment, he was dominated by the idea of flight, of the staircase that he could run swiftly down, in order to escape into the street and avoid further explanation. That was the idea most pleasing to his imprecise character, but he judged that it would be cowardly, unworthy of his amity.

Then, a subterfuge came quite naturally to take form in his mind, which satisfied both his dread and his conscience. The secret that he had just discovered was, in sum, a medical secret—a professional secret, discovered in the exercise of his art, while he was performing his function as a physician. What right did he have to reveal it, even to Georges? Although his friendship ordered him to speak, was he not, on the other hand, obliged to remain silent by the absolute rules of his profession?

That was a subtlety that would permit him to wait, to reflect during the few days ht he was about to spend in Bordeaux, to take inspiration from the advice of his masters if necessary. Another might have resolved the problem *ex abrupto*, leaving himself to the impulse of the moment, but Bordier accorded himself that half-measure.

And as he saw Madeleine, before his mutism, dissolve into tears again, he thought once again of the cheerful projects to which Georges had made him party a little while ago in the carriage, of the tender and sweet dreams so close to their realization, of united households, of children. "You'll be the godfather of my firstborn," he had said to him. And he was here, that firstborn, before time, brought by a mystery, conceived in a crime, already tormenting his mother's organs before breaking her heart.

"You're not saying anything," said the pale, tearful woman. "So it's very grave!"

"No, I affirm again that it's not grave. Believe me, for you're the person most dear to my dearest friend. But your case requires reflection, perhaps another examination more expert than mine..."

"Not Monsieur Caresco—I don't want that!" Madeleine hastened to say.

Caresco! The name fell into the conversation like a shell that blasts apart a wall in a dark house, and, letting the daylight in, expels the shadows. Caresco! Instinctively, stupidly, Bordier associated the name with the crime, and wanted to seek, to know."

"Caresco?" he said. "You know him, then?"

"I've only seen him twice. The first time it was at my Aunt Bise's house at Les Bolois, the day when I had a prolonged fainting fit and he cared for me. Then I saw him again the other day, in the Avenue Hoche, when I went to visit Aline. Bizarrely enough, I fell ill again. Oh, how I dislike him!"

"You had a fainting fit," said Bordier, whose voice was trembling. "What happened? Where? What did he do to care for you?"

And Madeleine recounted the adventure, explaining how, alarmed by the storm, in one of those crises of nervous excitement to which she had been subject since childhood, she had fallen unconscious during the visit to Château Gaillard, and had been picked up by the surgeon, who had taken refuge beside her, alone, to shelter from the storm.

"Alone?" Bordier insisted.

"Yes, alone. Why?"

"And for how long?" he asked.

"About five minutes. It was toward the end of July."

Five months! The date coincided with the development of the pregnancy. A frightful suspicion invaded Bordier, suddenly: a suspicion founded on probabilities, on a plausibility, on the vileness of the man, the baseness of his soul, on everything that he had seen, and which now tormented him like a bitter whirlpool, on everything that Dr. Savre had said to him.

With a horrible tenacity, that suspicion took hold of him, became a certainty, and was elevated to the level of reality, with the flap of a wing that chased away doubt.

Yes, such an infamous thing could only have been done by that ferocious dominator, devoid of faith or law, always so seconded by circumstances that one was led to doubt in an immanent Justice and Truth.

"Oh, what did he do? What did he do?" the physician let out, his throat constricted by anguish.

Madeleine did not understand that exclamation. Surprised by the panic that was brightening Bordier's eyes, she replies: "What did he do? I don't know. He probably sprinkled water on me."

The hazard of the words aggravated the irony. The lamentation appealed to laughter. Both of them had mournful faces, and they were producing vaudeville dialogue. Was it that, the absurd shock of it, which pulled Bordier out of the frightful situation?

He stood up, and took Madeleine's hand.

"Don't worry, Mademoiselle—and whatever happens, remember that you have a great love, Georges' love, and a great friendship, mine."

He went out.

Down below, another struggle was about to begin, and he shivered as he went down the stairway and took hold of the door-handle of the drawing room where Georges as waiting. A shrill voice came through the door to strike his ear. Madame Bise had returned, and Bordier blessed the fact, feeling an immense relief at being able to avoid being alone with his friend.

Madame Bise was crying out. She was reproaching Georges for having left the young woman in the sole company of Bordier; her feminism was emboldening her suppositions. In vain, Georges was protesting that Bordier was a doctor, and that his quality as a physician authorized him to go to any bedside. The old fool did not want to hear it. She had come back in a state of excitement impossible to describe. The meeting had been inflammatory, and it had ended with a cat-fight.

"They behaved like men, no less!" she said to Bordier, when the latter, judging that the reproaches had concluded, had come into the room to listen to the account of the battle.

She had scarcely finished that declaration than Miss Pisword came in. The Englishwoman was in a lamentable state, her garments torn, her right eye surrounded by a black bruise. One of her front teeth—the one that stuck out furthest, like an elephant's tusk—having been broken, had disappeared in the brawl. It was while wanting to defend her seat on the committee that a kind of concierge had attacked her, manifesting her chauvinism by giving the daughter of Albion a thrashing. She concluded therefrom that men had paid women to fight, and aggressively indicated to the two young men the horror of her demolished mouth. The scene was too funny for words, and would have delighted Ponviane and Bordier had disaster not been in their hearts.

The physician, however, judged the moment propitious to beat a retreat, and took his leave of Madame Bise, who did not even think of asking about Madeleine.

Georges accompanied him to the door and offered him his hand fraternally.

"Well, what do you think?" he said.

"Nothing, for the moment," Bordier replied. "It's necessary to wait. There are curious accidents. Another opinion than mine might be indispensable. In any case, we can wait. I'll be back in a week. Don't attempt anything without my advice. Do you hear me, Georges? Nothing at all."

"But you can assure me," the other said, "that you're not anxious, that there's no danger for the future?"

"No—from the point of view of health, there's no danger for the future."

He had a second impulse toward a confidence that would terminate the affair, but the surroundings—the cold vestibule, the excited voices of the two women, who were continuing their lamentations in the drawing room—scarcely lent themselves to it. Then again, he had

273

to go away, would not be there to sustain his friend's dolor during the few days that were to follow, to attenuate the worst resolutions, to assist him with the acceptance of a sage philosophy.

He shook Georges' hand more vigorously and added: "No don't do anything for a week. *Bonsoir*, old man."

"*Bonsoir*, Jean."

When the door closed he went along the façade of the house. At the windows of the drawing room, the shadows of Madame Bise and Miss Pisword were coming and going, agitating like the marionettes of a magic lantern.

Were they not a thousand times justified, those two mad old crones, to abominate man, the monster, capable of profiting from the unconsciousness of a creature to abuse her, and to extend by that abomination the icy veil of anguish and misfortune over other simple and loving hearts?

CHAPTER XV

For a few minutes, in the common room of the luxurious restaurant in which he had reserved a table for
two, Dr. Savre had been waiting for a guest—a young
student, one of his friends, who was on the point of pre-
senting his doctoral thesis in medicine. He had invited
him to dinner in order to ask him to substitute for him in
his practice during a fortnight's absence, which he intended to employ in traveling. The young man had not
yet arrived.

He asked for the menu and selected a few dishes,
while the clean-shaven *maître d'hôtel*, discreet and ceremonious, standing next to the table, his torso slightly
inclined, noted down his client's choices. Then it was
the turn of the sommelier, who came to take his order.

"Beer, Chablis and a bottle of Corton," Savre ordered.

Then, rid of the cares of selection, he abandoned the
menu, ornamented with an engraving, and sat back in the
velvet-upholstered banquette, interesting himself in the
luxury of the room, the golden flames dancing in the
wood-paneling and the mirrors, the comings and goings
of busy waiters, and the faces of the diners, the individuals and couples coming in, warmly wrapped up, and subsequently blossoming in the warmth of the air, perfumed
by the odor of sauces and truffles.

The women, some dressed up and bejeweled for the
theater, in an amusing flutter of bright and shiny fabrics,
took off their gloves with precious and supple gestures.
The men, mostly in evening suits with flowers in the
buttonholes, shiny in their immaculate shirt-fronts with

lustrous hair sat down with a stretch of sleeves and waistcoats, or rectified the symmetry of a triumphant moustache with a slight torsion.

Savre, with a slightly hard gaze and angular features, followed the various movements and efforts of decorum made by the futile puppets with a certain irony. The women were costly objects of luxury for which he had a profound scorn, on account of a perversion and a prostitution to which he had several times fallen victim. In every face, by ferocious analysis, he tried to discover a vice, a passion, a habit. In accordance with theories of physiognomy, by the facial tics, the form of the nose and the expression in the eyes, he reconstituted a race and a profession.

The people, sensing that they were being studied, discomfited by the persistence of his gaze, turned their heads away, fleeing the investigation, starting conversations that soon concluded, killed by the ceremonial of the restaurant, the urgency of the waiters, the brief orders discreetly whispered and rapidly executed.

The young student came in. His name was Berger, and he had a very mild, blonde head, brightened by admirable brown eyes. A little surprised at first, embarrassed by the sight of the high-class restaurant, whose like he was not accustomed to frequent, he circled the room with his gaze, searching for Savre, his complexion reddened by the awareness of being noticed. Then, when he had perceived his friend, he recovered his self-assurance and headed rapidly toward him.

"You're late, my friend," said Savre, with a forgiving smile.

"Oh, if you knew where I've come from!" said Berger. And he recounted that he had been invited the day before by Armand Caresco to assist him in his operations, replacing Bordier.

"What!" said Savre. "Bordier is no longer with Caresco?"

"Yes, still, but he's gone to the Midi to see a patient, with whom he's staying for a few days. I'm filling in. I began my service his morning. What a man, that Caresco! What a Surgeon!"

"What a dentist," Savre added.

Berger uttered an exclamation of disapproval and astonishment. "What do you mean, what a dentist? Caresco, the foremost surgeon in the world, you call a dentist! But you've worked with him, you've seen him at work. This very morning, he was admirable!"

"Come on, my lad," Savre put in. "You'll get over it."

"I tell you," the young man went on, energetically, "that he was admirable, and I don't understand, Savre, why you call him a dentist, you who are generally so just!"

He rummaged in his fob-pocket and brought out a kind of little stone, brown in color and faceted, about the size of a hazelnut, which he deposited on the tablecloth with a triumphant expression.

"Here—do you know what that is?"

"That," said Savre, picking up the object, "is a calculus, most probably a gallstone."

"It is, indeed, a gallstone, which I saw Caresco remove this morning."

"Which you saw him remove this morning?" Savre repeated, stressing the words.

"When I saw that I saw it," the young man went on, "no, I didn't see it. He goes so quickly, that devil of a man, that in the space of a minute, which I was washing my hands on his instruction, he removed six similar calculi, and only showed them to me at the end of the operation, when he showed them to the parents of the young woman on whom he was operating, a Mademoiselle Romé. But what rapidity, what sureness of hand! How, with a single stroke of the scalpel, he arrives exactly at the fault! I'm still amazed! And if you had seen the joy of the family, especially an aunt, who was waiting in a nearby room! Truly, it's marvelous!"

With increasing astonishment, Savre examined the calculus, turning it over in his fingers. He looked at Berger with pitying sadness—for he understood the entire deception himself, at the sight of the old foreign body, which had not been extracted recently, but which the naïve young man, as well as the relatives, had accepted as a fresh calculus. And he reconstituted the fraud: the unnecessary operation, justified by the presentation on old calculi.

In spite of everything, until then, he had not believed Caresco capable of such baseness. To be sure, he recalled the legendary words of a celebrated surgeon who said: "When one attempts to remove a bullet, it's necessary to take two vital precautions before beginning the operation: firstly, to enquire about the weapon that fired the shot; and secondly, not to neglect to have a bullet in one's pocket that one can show to the family—and try to make sure that it's the right caliber!" That anecdote ran around guardrooms and the student amphitheaters, justified by the necessity of reassuring the patient and the entourage as to the consequences of an operation that might have been useful, honestly and sincerely attempted. Alas, in the present case, with regard to the man's banditry, he understood the full infamy of the procedure.

To support his conviction, he asked: "Were there many people present?"

"No," Berger replied. "Because of the social situation of the patient, Caresco didn't want spectators. There were only the sisters and the two of us."

That was that. Colleagues kept out, the sisters accomplices, the attention of the assistant deflected.

Savre, revolted was about to explain everything to the young man, to take the scales from his eyes, when the latter continued, increasing inflamed by his enthusiasm. "That damned Caresco! If you had seen him rebuke an old physician, Dr. Varon, who wanted to watch a following operation, a laparotomy for peritonitis, on a young boy—his client, it appears! Dr. Varon had opposed to the operation with all his might, and had the audacity to present himself in order to watch it! I can assure you that Caresco didn't mince his words! He sent him away, called him an old cretin! The poor man left, furious. It was a consummate comedy, and Caresco was still laughing at it when he opened his patient's belly."

And Berger laughed at the incident too, with the pitilessness of youth. But Savre became serious, and with a soft sadness in his voice, he said: "Dr. Varon was right, my friend, and you're wrong to mock the old man, who wanted to do his duty until the end."

The student, surprised, interrogated Savre's face, searching for a sign that he was joking—but the latter remained serious, with a calmness that denied humor. The waiter had deposited eggs scrambled with truffles on the table; the delicate aroma rose toward their mucus membranes, incensing their appetite—and in the first satisfaction of their hunger, they did not talk for a few minutes, eating the first-rate food.

"By the way," Savre said, "don't be astonished to be eating scrambled eggs at dinner. I chose what I liked. If it doesn't suit you, change it. I've ordered Ostend oysters to follow, and a good slice of English roast beef. Is that to your liking, my boy?"

"Is it to my liking? If you knew how I eat in my local soup-kitchen!"

Having finished the eggs they went on to the oysters. Savre washed them down with an amiable Chablis, complacently refilling Berger's glass. The latter, his complexion pink and his eyes gleaming under the contentment of the expertly-prepared dishes, the generous wine and the warm and caressant luxury of the ambience, was in a mood for chat, disposed to part with and receive confidences.

"My dear Savre," he said, "you seem to be holding a grudge against Caresco? Didn't you spend a year in his employ? I thought you'd separated on good terms. What do you have against him?"

Savre paused momentarily, his oyster-fork in mid-air, just as he was about to engulf a mollusk. "My dear Berger," he said, "If you don't mind, let's not talk about Caresco this evening. If you knew how full my head is of the deeds and actions of my former collaborator, how much he haunts me! I can't take a step in the street, go to a restaurant, go into theater or even visit a brothel without hearing someone say to me: 'Oh, you've been with Caresco? What an interesting individual! Tell me about him!' I'm so weary, so sick of that repetition, to which I always reply with formulae so invariable that I know them by heart—and if I go home and, in order to get away from the obsession, I pick up a political newspaper, I find the name I abominate on the first page! A scientific textbook will also talk to me about him. I'm finally driven, completely mad, to reread my old Classical and Roman texts, and I'm still not sure that I won't find the word Caresco at the end of a verse or at the climax of a dramatic situation.[16] No, enough, Berger, enough!"

He swallowed the oyster.

Amused, Berger smiled at Savre's wit. There was, however, an acrimony in the fluency and the grave tone of voice that surprised him. Perhaps, after all, he had had his difficulties with the surgeon. He judged it wiser and more prudent to let the subject drop. By way of conclusion, however, he added: "Yes, it's said that he does a great deal of advertising."

That last word, however, had the effect of causing Savre to remount his favorite hobby-horse. He abandoned his plate, moistened his lips with the pale wine, and then, with his elbows on the table, in a sudden rush, without searching for words, he let fly with the ideas that often haunted his mind.

"Advertising, my friend, is already something bad in itself, in the sense that it is one of the manifestations of the power of capital, that it kills the efforts of the small. One can, however, understand its employment in commerce, in industry, for it aids the development of labor and can, by virtue of that, be considered as a force useful to the general good—but where it's a truly abominable thing is in our profession.

"I'm not talking about the particular case of Caresco, who redeems by a real value the guilty aspect of the method. Besides, since you'll be called upon sooner or later to join his staff, you'll be able to judge the case for yourself; I prefer to say nothing about it. But

---

[16] As, indeed, he might, the Latin word in question meaning to want—or, more precisely, to be without.

281

look at the infamy to which medical advertising leads in the lower classes of society, where it's all the more effective because it's more stupid, and hence within the range of general intelligence.

"How many poor devils attained by a malady that a reasonable medication could alleviate, if not cure, throw themselves head first into the traps set by the host of bandits who lay out their bait on the back pages of newspapers? And what bait! Imagine the most inferior, the most ludicrous things. It seems that the more ridiculous it is, the more readily people will be taken in.

"I know one man—and he's founding a school!—who claims to cure cancer with brewer's yeast. I've seen him sell bottles of that yeast to unfortunate domestics, for twenty francs—half their monthly pay—which can be bought from a brewer for six sous. He assures them that ten bottles will cure them. Some buy two or three; then, weary, and not seeing any improvement, finally understand the fraud; others go on to the end, and their last gasp of life is extinguished in their final bottle of yeast!

"I know another, a son of Israel, who, without any special training, imagined that he could set up a surgical clinic. Do you think that he carries out abortions there? Not at all. He's too clever. He only does major surgery. His advertisements in the newspapers bring clients in, and he does a great many operations—a great many."

"How does he do it, then?" asked Berger.

"How does he do it? It's quite simple. If, for instance, he's dealing with one of those fibrous tumors that our Caresco removes so brilliantly, he has the patient come to his establishment, puts her to sleep and makes an incision in her abdomen. Then he sews up the incision. A week later, the patient is cured, and he collects a big fee."

"But after all, the lady might well perceive that she still has her tumor."

"Naturally. Then he declares that it was inoperable, that removing it would have posed a risk to her life. And as a last resort, he sends the patient to be treated electrically by an accomplice, who shared the payments he receives with him."

"But that's frightful!" exclaimed Berger, revolted. "And he finds aides for these simulated operations?"

"Yes, he has one. And then, there's also his father, a manufacturer of lorgnettes, decorated as such with a fine rosette of the Légion d'honneur, who takes the pulse during the operation, and who is remunerated as an eminent colleague."

"Oh, that's abominable!" said Berger, again.

"You find that revolting, my lad, and I'm not surprised. But be prepared to see many others during your career. I'm talking about gross things—so gross that they seem farcical—but you'll surprise many other ignominies, and you'll sometimes experience yourself the temptation of certain base actions. You'll resist them because you're honest, and because you have a certain fortune..."

"Even without that," affirmed the young man.

"Yes, even without that," Savre continued, "and you'd be all the more virtuous because, for the crimes we can commit, there's no sanction. A physician is above the law. Sell someone two sous' worth of bread of poor quality, and you won't be long in seeing a policeman put his hand on your collar. Promise him, thanks to improbable medicines, an impossible cure, make a fool of him, suck him dry of his last penny for that cure without result, and no one will have the right to get in your way. That's the way things are, and it's truly painful to think that our profession, as noble and as beneficent as it might be, is, at the same time, thanks to the faults of a few black sheep, susceptible to so much scorn and shame!"

The waiter had put two succulent slices of roast beef on the table, surrounded by boiled potatoes and a dusty bottle of Corton lying in a wicker basket. Around them, people were still coming in, filling the tables, sitting down, eating and drinking, with polite manners and drawing-room reserve. A few bursts of laughter were already rising, however, less discreetly than in the beginning, under the influence of good cheer and sparkling champagne. Savre and Berger, deep in their conversation, did not take part in that blossoming of *bon viveurs* and girls with price tags, who come to display a corner of Parisian prostitution in restaurants. The question they were discussing seemed much more grave than the study of the pleasurable flesh set out along the banquettes with a joyful flutter of bright fabrics and gemstones.

Savre refilled the student's plate.

"But how do you expect anything to change?" said the latter. "Doesn't the diploma give us the right to practice as we wish? It's up to the public to distinguish between the good and the bad."

"No," said Savre, "it's not up to the public, who don't know anything. Society needs to protect itself from bad physicians, just at it puts ramparts on the banks of the Seine to prevent people from falling in the water."

"But how? It's not possible, as you know full well."

"Yes, my boy, it's quite possible. Imagine an Order of physicians, a sort of Bar, not only recruited from among the high lamas of the professional you understand, but from among all the members and all the steps of the medical ladder. For a start, that order would be obligatory. Everyone, to obtain the right to practice, would be obliged to swear an oath before it. It would also be disciplinary—which is to say that it would strike with penalties varying from simple warnings to complete expulsion those who commit offences against the principles of honor and ethical duty. I promise you that that would suppress, at a stroke, the base advertising that ornaments public urinals and the shameful angling practiced by way of the newspapers."

"It's a utopia," said the young man.

"No," said Savre, "it's not a utopia.[17] Obviously, the organization of the system would be surrounded by real difficulties at first, but it would succeed, my friend. And then, what glory and was radiance for our profession, and how much more our elite, by virtue of their integrity, will enter into the development of contemporary philosophy and morality. For our role in life is very fine, my boy, and I don't know of any more noble. By the very reason of that importance, it requires men capable of a kind of apostolate, free of egotism and self-aggrandizement. Yes, medicine is relevant to all the

---

[17] Although the existence in France of localized Facultés de Médecine did not provide the measure of protection proved even then in England by the General Medical Council, established in 1858, the fact that medical practitioners already swore oaths—although the modern version of the so-called Hippocratic Oath did not come into use until 1948—surely makes it odd that the idea of such an Order should seem "utopian" even to Berger. Subsequent history has, however, demonstrated very clearly that Savre's optimism regarding the results to be obtained from such a system is not entirely justified.

great social problems, it touches on all the arts, all virtues and all charity. The practice of medicine requires saints!"

Savre stopped for a moment to ask the waiter for cigars. Boiling mocha filled their cups; bottles of various liqueurs were distributed on the white tablecloth, which had been changed at dessert. From a box of Havanas, Savre chose a sufficiently crepitant cigar for the student, and lit one himself. The blue-tinted incense rose in perfumed spirals toward the gilded ceiling.

At that moment, a decorated gentleman came in, young in appearance and clean-shaven, with a black-rimmed lorgnon, escorting a rather pretty brunette wrapped in a red velvet pelisse trimmed with sable fur. He helped her to take off the garment, and then both of them sat down at a table with five settings reserved for them. When they were installed, facing one another, the lady noticed Savre, nodded to him, and then whispered a few words in the ear of her escort, who also turned round and greeted him. Savre responded with a rather cold nod of the head.

"Who's that?" Berger asked.

"It's one of my former comrades, when I was an intern," Savre replied. "A Rumanian."

"Decorated?"

"Yes, decorated—no one knows why. Because he's Rumanian and Jewish. O noble and generous France! O Revolution! There's another of your creations, the flashy foreigner to whom you accord your privileges and your medals for bravery. That individual, my dear Berger, arrived in France nineteen years ago, having made summary studies in his native country. He wanted to practice medicine, but as he couldn't be registered with the Faculté, having no baccalaureate, he was hastily accorded equivalence. He therefore obtained his inscription, and, not being subject to the obligation of military service, since he was not French, had plenty of time to prepare for his internship, to which he was admitted. He therefore already enjoyed, at that time, prerogatives, a title, a salary and study facilities only attributable to French citizens who had accomplished their obligations and duties. I believe that, as he was not rich, he was even given a bursary.

"So he passed his examinations and was accepted as a doctor. Then, as he was a foreigner, he was decorated. Why? Because his government, with whom he had influence, had demanded a medal for him, in the name of foreign entitlement. You can now see the shrewdness of the man. Once a doctor, and decorated, he was naturalized as a Frenchman, and as he had passed the age of active military service, he was appointed as a physician with the rank of major in the reserves. Thus, he's a French officer. Well, my dear Berger, I say that we're great imbeciles. What do you think?"

"I share that opinion," Berger replied. "But the law has been modified and such things are no longer possible now."

"Better late than never," Savre concluded. "But that's a good example of our national stupidity. We have in the depths of our French hearts a kind of need for abnegation, a folly of altruism that causes great prejudice to the flight of our national energy. And that dimwittedness is not peculiar to the medical profession; it's rife throughout all the branches of society, eating away at the heritage that our ancestors acquired at the price of so much hard labor and blood."

Savre breathed out the smoke of his cigar and aromatized his coffee with a drop of fine champagne. Fac-

ing them, the lady accompanying the decorated colleague never took her eyes off them, perhaps attracted by
the student's pleasant physiognomy. The latter, embarrassed by the persistence of the observation, said to
Savre: "And the lady who's with him, who greeted you.
Who's she?"

"I'm surprised to see them together," Savre replied.
"The parsimony of the one ought not to be in accord
with the prodigality of the other. There must be some
commerce behind it. The lady is a courtesan who no
longer has any ovaries. She's keeping up with fashion
because, in a certain society, to employ a facile and oft-
repeated joke, ovaries no longer bear fruit. She pro-
claims it loudly enough from the rooftops for me not to
be betraying professional secrecy in revealing to you that
she's incomplete. It's thanks to her that I left Caresco."

"How's that?" asked Berger, interested.

"For the simple reason that Caresco, in occupying
himself with her, carried out an operation whose utility I
could not see. That happens to him more often than
might be expected. I don't say that, my friend, to turn
you against the surgeon…no. Go to his house and you'll
see admirable things there. But he operates too readily.
When you've seen that for yourself you'll leave him of
your own accord.

"So, one day, we were in the consulting room in the
Avenue Hoche when we see that demi-mondaine come
in with one of her lovers, a kind of prodigal imbecile, an
inadequate man to boot, of whom she said to me afterwards—listen to this, it will amuse you—that he had
neither a head nor a tail. Caresco interrogates her, exam-
ines her, and asks me to examine her. She complains of a
few vague pains in the vicinity of the right ovary, but the
examination reveals nothing very positive—nothing, at

288

any rate, necessitating an operation. Afterwards, Caresco proposes the removal of the ovary. She accepts, begging him to take out both of them; that's what she's come for. The inadequate man supports her request, and the double removal is decided. Then, not wanting to be involved in that speculation, I handed in my resignation to Caresco, under some pretext or other."

"You did the right thing," said Berger, "and I won't go to work for Monsieur Caresco."

That was said with a lofty assurance that charmed Savre, and persuaded him of the rectitude of his young friend. He made a gesture of vague insouciance, however, and said: "Wait—judge for yourself. It's possible that I'm mistaken. But during my collaboration with the surgeon, I was surprised by the truly incredible quantity of women who had him suppress their reproductive organs. Many of them were certainly suffering, carrying disease in their loins and its entire cortege of dolors and annoyances—but how many of them, with sage treatment, would have been able to avoid the horrible subtraction of their viscera!

"I noticed that it was precisely those who, by virtue of their situation, their fortune and the ease of their existence, were best able to wait for a return to health who were the most impatient for such a risky cure. Are they so given to vice, so avid for the enjoyment of the life they prefer, that, instead of dragging things out as eternal casualties, they cast the dice of the operation on to the green baize of their life? Or is it that the surgeon that they seek out possesses, like our Caresco, such persuasive powers of speech, so convincing and enveloping, that he makes them envisage his intervention as a simple matter, facile, benign and necessary? Both, I think.

"It's obvious, however, that in this *fin-de-siècle*, the psychology of society is being subject to an evolution, and that science, the effects of which ought to lead hearts to such a radiant peace, has very disappointing results! That progress had led to this: that amour is becoming a science of methodical sensuality, calculated to the point that its excesses, which set aside still-susceptible consequences, in these incredulous times, put a brake on the breakdowns and follies of neurosis.

"Once, in heroic times, that neurosis, avid for satiation, led to mysticism, to the ideal; now it leads to materialism, to sensation. It's the eternal struggle of the ideal and the material, of faith and skepticism. Yes, skepticism has triumphed, and it is in that direction that the holocaust tends!"

He stopped momentarily, selecting a bottle. "A glass of chartreuse, my boy?" he said. "You can see that the infertile have their uses, all the same, since the Charterhouses manufacture this exquisite liqueur for us. You might, however, reply that they could do it just as well while perpetuating the race..." He smiled as he filled Berger's glass and his own. Then, having moistened his lips with the gilded liqueur, he went on, more seriously.

"All that leads to depopulation. You see, my dear chap. I have depths of chauvinism that certain intellectuals would qualify as absurd, but which make me regret seeing the population diminish so much in our France, when everywhere else, especially in the East, it is increasing in considerable proportions.

"You're smiling, Berger, and I believe that I comprehend your smile. It says to me: 'Set an example.' You're right, and it's wrong of me to remain a bachelor—but I'm afraid of marriage, my friend! Then again, I'm only thirty-three; all is not lost—and if I take a wife,

I promise you that I shall have a fine family, with a host of children twittering around me and making my head ache with their screams. In that alone rests the happiness of the household.

"But for that depopulation, menacing for the interests, and for the very life, of our nation, it's not only necessary to seek an explanation in the general egotism that recoils before the responsibilities of a family, or even in the destructive effects of the maladies that are corroding our race, like syphilis and tuberculosis...no, it's also necessary to seek the reason in the enthusiasm of our surgeons to operate, who, in the hospitals as in the city, for various reasons of interest—whether pecuniary interest or scientific interest—remove so many wombs and ovaries, rendering the loins of so many women sterile.[18]

"That is one of the principal causes, and I'm frightened, my dear friend, of the profound scorn in which the majority of the virtuosos of the scalpel hold human life, both present life and future life consequent on reproduction. A little while ago, you cried utopia when I spoke about the idea of an order of physicians. I'll go much further now, with regard to the particular case of operations on the female genital organs. I'd like a surgeon not

---

[18] Savre surely cannot really believe that the *fin-de-siècle* fashionability of hysterectomies in the Parisian demi-monde (mostly carried out on women who would have been rendered infertile by venereal diseases anyway) had a significant effect on the national birth-rate—at least, by comparison with the factor he does not mention at all, in spite of having seen the golden clyster-pump on Mathilde's mantelpiece. It testifies to the strength of the taboo in question that that a text so willingly to be deliberately shocking in other ways refuses to mention birth control, even when it is a salient point of argument.

to be able to perform an ablation without a special authorization accorded by four inspectors—two physicians and two surgeons—chosen from a kind of jury of special supervision, also recruited from all levels of the medical profession."

"But that's impossible, my dear Savre!" exclaimed Berger, laughing. "No law authorizes such a manner of conduct."

"A law would be made," Savre replied, climbing more enthusiastically the slope of his dream. "A law would be made. We have legislators for that! It would offend susceptibilities, you tell me? It would kill all personal initiative, entrench surgery in practices presently known? First of all, I believe that from the viewpoint of surgery, there isn't a great deal left to learn: innovation is complete; nothing further can be produced but modifications of procedures—and then, it would be free for anyone to operate as he pleases once authorization is granted.

"As for offending the susceptibilities of the few, to what extent can that be taken into account, when it's a matter of the general interest, the vitality of a race? Would the regulation not have the result of reviving our crumbling prestige, which would be a good thing in itself?

"Yes, once people laughed at physicians; Molière ran the gamut of facile jokes. Now, people no longer laugh at them; they fear them, consider them to be executioners, and the syringe that once appeared to be comical has been transformed into a menacing instrument of torture. And look at the repercussion on our profession: once, medical practice served as a stepping-stone for individuals of modest origin to rise into a superior class; at present, it seems to be the other way around."

Savre became excited as he spoke; his rude physiognomy was filled with an even greater rudeness, and Berger understood that he was unveiling his soul, the suffering of whose wound he was hiding beneath an amiable irony.

As he finished speaking, he saw a pretty young woman come in, with an anxious and careworn face, who came to sit with the couple he had noticed a little while before.

"Look," Savre remarked. "That's Stella, the singer from the Opéra-Comique who's just come in. Stella...the star. A star who's fading, for she seems very weary, poor thing. Partying to excess, or illness? Illness, probably, since she has no lover with her and is coming to sit down at a physician's table."

The newcomer while responding to the smiles and attentions of her companions and smoothing the unruly curls of her hair, scanned the restaurant with her eyes, darting toward those unknown faces than recognized her the loveliness of her blue eyes, emphasized by dark circles, and her features, jaundiced by an intimate defect.

"Look, my boy," said Savre. "Fix the physiognomy of that Stella in your mind. She has uterine facies. That's a woman suffering in her abdomen, I'm convinced of it."

And, to confirm his diagnosis, Mathilde de Guinac, the beautiful Tripe-merchant, came in, followed by Caresco, filling the room with her carnal presence. The couple distributed handshakes and nods of the head to the right and left, then came to complete the table with five place-settings at which Stella was seated.

"And she must indeed have an abdominal disease," Savre continued, in a low voice, "for the operation is in prospect, and will be decided by the end of the meal. You'll be collaborating in it, my young friend. Be glad, for you'll see falling between your feet a womb that's famous from more than one point of view."

"I'll preserve it in alcohol," replied the student joker, "to remind me of the vanity of the pleasures of the flesh."

CHAPTER XVI

There was the busy disorder of the conclusion of an operation. Berger, the student, who had been replacing Bordier for a week, was finishing the application of cotton wool and a large bandage to the thin body of Stella, the pretty singer, while the sisters hastened to take advantage of the patient's unconsciousness to remove the chemise stained with blood and antiseptic fluid and slip on another that was immaculate.

With a sigh of satisfaction, Armand Caresco, his arms bare and his face covered in sweat, abandoned the dangling subject to his aides; she was as limp as a rag, and her head, intoxicated by chloroform, was bobbing at the whim of the movements imparted to it by the torso. He bent down and picked up a lamentable fragment of flesh from among the cotton and linen that lay of the mosaic floor—the sacred viscera that he had just abstracted from the singer's abdomen with his prestigious skill.

Around him stood a few colleagues, and a novelist in search of a scene for his book. He deposited the dead, slippery, exsanguinated flesh, from which a few drops of yellow pus were still oozing, on a table and, taking a knife, made a series of deep cuts from which pus spurted. Then, in response to the seemingly-hostile expression of one of his colleagues, he felt a need to justify his operation.

"You see, Messieurs, that it really was endometritis with double salpingitis. That patient has passed through all the hands of the Faculté. They would simply have allowed her to die. And people say that I don't operate appropriately!"

He turned toward the novelist, who had stepped aside, nauseated. "Isn't it true, my dear Master, that all of this isn't very pretty to see, and that it takes away the inclination to address sonnets to a woman?"

The pale man of letters with the thick shock of hair smiled discreetly, like a superior individual who would prefer a nice rhyme to that display of butchery, exciting as it was. Then, before the threat of fainting, he thought it best to run away.

The other spectators withdrew in their turn, disappointed at only having witnessed a single operation, which had only lasted ten minutes, instead of one of the legendary series that brought all Paris running.

Soeur Cunégonde came over to Caresco. "Doctor," she murmured in is ear, "Monsieur and Madame Savoie are in the reception room."

"Did you tell them that I was here?" the surgeon groaned.

"I couldn't do otherwise, Doctor—but Abbé Marnier is with them."

The presence of the red-faced abbé, who was like a faithful dog, calmed anger that was ready to burst forth. Abbé Marnier was a friend of the house. Once operated on by Caresco for a grave malady, he had avowed a gratitude to his savior that was in accordance with the religious milieu of the establishment and the infantile practices of the sister. Every time a decease terrified a family, he came running, soothing and obliging, to pour out the good word, attenuating the shock of resentment and attributing to the account of the divinity a denouement that as imputable to the excessive temerity and recklessness of the surgeon. He was a good man otherwise, obscure and pious. Many priests had been brought to the house by him, had undergone operations gratuitously, and left blessing the lover of life and preaching holy advertisements.

After washing his hands, Caresco put on a jacket and went to the reception room. He found the parents there in mourning-dress, the mother with a plaintive despair in her red eyes, the father somber and grave, holding an envelope in his hand. And when Madame Savoie saw the destroyer appear, who had so wretchedly promised the health of his son, now pale and icy, she burst into dolorous sobs, which, shaking her entire body, resounded with an ironic contrast in the large luxurious room, as if hurling a violently bitter reproach at all the wealth and gaudiness.

Already, Abbé Marnier was forcing her to sit down, resuming the litany of his consolations, invoking the divine name, and the tenebrous power of superior designs—but those murmured washed over the dolor of the disillusioned mother; there was no emission in her frightful desolation. Timid and meek, however, she let the rebellion of her heart escape in a comment that wounded the surgeon more deeply than any other.

"Oh, I should have listened to Dr. Varon!"

Less expressive, but just as dejected, Monsieur Savoie advanced toward Caresco and, with a curt gesture, handed him the envelope he was holding.

"There, Monsieur," he said. "Ten thousand francs: the agreed fee."

There as such criticism in that brutal fashion of regulating the murder that the surgeon's comprehension was aroused of the enemies he had just made. He sensed all the danger of it, and, like the heroic fighter he was, tried to modify opinion.

"Alas, Monsieur," he said, pocketing the money, "We have not been fortunate with your poor child. I truly believed, however, that he could be returned to you."

There was the ring of truth in his voice, but deceit and treason in his fugitive gaze, which turned away, attaching itself to the arabesques in the Oriental carpet. Monsieur Savoie did not reply, sealed like a wine-cellar, immured in his dolor.

"But the thing is," the surgeon continued, "that he came to us too late, and the intervention that would have been so benign at the outset became very perilous in the end. You can't imagine how much filth I found in your child's abdomen! I don't want to put Dr. Varon on trial, whose only sin was ignorance, but it's evident that if the decision had been made a fortnight or a month earlier, your child would still be alive."

In order to deflect blame from himself, not only was the wretch reopening the wound before the parents, displaying it in all its horror, but attributing the fault to an honest and decent absent colleague.

"Look," he said, "At the same time as your son, I operated on Mademoiselle Romé, whose condition was at least equally serious, but she was reached in time; she's doing very well, and in a week she'll be cured, as your son would have been if..."

"Enough, Monsieur, enough!" said Monsieur Savoie, finally. "Respect my wife's grief, I beg you. You can see that she can take no more!"

In fact, Madame Savoie had been gripped once again by a terrible fit of tears. The chimes of the clock sounded eleven times in the icy silence of the drawing room; it was like the plaintive toll of a death-knell. It was the time at which the funeral directors were to take away the body.

Soeur Cunégonde had asked in vain for the removal to take place at daybreak in order not to throw discredit on the house, attracting the attention of passers-by and the residents of the little street on to which the back gate of the house opened—a street too often troubled by sinister convoys. Monsieur Savoie, who had to arrange for the coffin to be taken to a distant location, had not wanted to yield to those interested reasons—and the time for the lugubrious departure had arrived.

Soeur Cunégonde came in, with a pitying glance at Caresco. She understood his embarrassment. She went to Monsieur Savoie and said, discreetly, as if for a religious confidence: "The undertakers are here, Monsieur."

"Yes, let's go, let's go," he replied, in a weary and defeated fashion, glad to flee the abomination of that house.

He took his wife's arm with the delicacy of a nurse, and led her to the door. Abbé Marnier sustained her other arm. She allowed herself to be guided, unseeing, almost uncomprehending, dazed by an extraordinary despair.

Caresco remained alone in the vast reception room, understanding the futility of his efforts to attract the sympathy of the unhappy household to himself, and not having the courage to pursue, by means of an attitude of participation, the movement he had commenced toward his own rehabilitation.

But if he was cursed down below he knew that he was blessed up above. So, while the dolorous cortege headed toward the funerary chamber, he hastened to climb the stairs that led to joyful effusions, to the triumph of hope. And as he climbed, his face was transformed, filling with happy serenity.

Indeed, as soon as he had gone into Aline's room, the sight of the friendly group around the patient's bed, the beaming faces, the seeming good health of the person who had undergone the operation, and the exuberance of Madame Bise, welcomed him favorably. Laughter filled the bright and cheerful room.

Madame Bise, the sister serving as a nurse, and even Madeleine, were enormously amused by the declaration that Aline had just made that she did not want ever to leave the house, and always to be ill.

"You have only to marry him," Madame Bise had replied, voicing a secret wish—and when Aline went pale, that response had awakened general gaiety. They laughed without knowing why, in the infantile contentment of seeing the patient make such a rapid post-operative recovery, her appearance now being radiant.

Caresco came in at this junction.

"Here's the Word!" proclaimed Madame Bise.

"The Word?" the surgeon interrogated, unfamiliar with Catholic terminology. "Why the Word?"

"The savior, of course!" replied Madame Bise.

Aline considered him ardently. The Master's eye became positive and cold. He sensed the necessity of cutting short the enthusiasm, because another serious game was about to begin.

"Let's see, you're doing well now?" he said, going to wash his hands at the wheeled basin in a corner of the room.

He came back to Aline, unfastened the pins of the dressing, uncovered the wound in the side that had closed completely, admirably healthy, without a drop of pus. The young woman shivered from head to toe, seeking the caress of the hand that brushed her flesh.

"Don't move, Mademoiselle, don't move!"

With a pad of cotton wool steeped in a solution of sublimate, he gently dabbed the points of the suture.

Madeleine gazed at the cut, which as neither large not ugly, with all the force of her vision—for the question had been raised the day before of her also undergoing a minor operation to cure her rapidly, like her cousin.

It was Madame Bise who had submitted that proposal to her, invoking reason, and the delay that such a state of health might cause to her marriage. She had not replied either by a refusal or an acceptance, wanting to talk to Georges first. But truly, her cousin's operation, about which so much fuss has been made, seemed to have been accomplished in a very benign fashion; the wound did not have the frightening appearance that she had imagined, and scarcely any trace of it would remain in time.

"Isn't it admirable," exclaimed Madame Bise, speaking for Madeleine's benefit, "to see such serious maladies cured so swiftly!"

"But Madame," said Caresco, turning to Madeleine, "the results would be just as sure and as prompt for Mademoiselle de Jancy."

"Oh yes," said Aline, supportively. "Consign yourself to the devotion and skill of the doctor. It's so good to be cured! I'm so content!"

Madeleine remained nonplussed, surprised by that extension of will toward her. She was beginning to submit to the influence of the environment, the seduction of the example. Her antipathy for Caresco was blurred by the desire for a rapid cure, and the desire to be united sooner with the man she adored.

Oh, certainly, if the operation could deliver her from that inexplicable and frightful illness, she would submit to it wholeheartedly—for she understood that it was time to act, to do something to liberate herself from the astonishing tumor that as growing in her belly without emission, with dull pulsations that made it manifest that an intimate, horrible and mysterious process was being accomplished in her loins.

She did not like Caresco; a kind of physical repulsion caused her to recoil from him; but in spite of that, in spite of the perverse rumors that were going around concerning the surgeon, which Aline herself had passed on to her—she had certainly changed her mind since!—and in spite of the repugnance that his avid and base gaze caused her, it was necessary to recognize that the doctor was a skillful scientist who had just extracted her cousin from a bad situation. Could he not do the same for her? Had Madame Bise not told her that the surgeon, having had plenty of time to examine her on the day when she had fainted in front of him, had affirmed that her cure was certain, offering an even greater probability than Aline's?

Her disorientated mind not daring, by reason of the base materiality of the subject, to confide in the good sense of her fiancé, without a reflective guide since her mother's death, by virtue of a sort of deviation resulting from her unhealthy and nervous weakness, now accorded a powerful credit to the opinion of Madame Bise. She was like the frightened bird that directs its flight toward the hunter's rifle. The possibility of a cure by Caresco became imposing, deflecting her resolution, precipitating her toward his practices.

And once born, the idea was not about to stop; it was about to come to the boil in the pressure-cooker of the sanitarium, where the environment, the example and the encouragements were lending such powerful aid to its fermentation.

The surgeon had finished the dressing, and went to wash his hands again. Aline, pink and fresh, took Madeleine's hand.

"You see, eh? You see how simple it is? One despairs, on seeing death arrive, one becomes sad, one weeps—but it only requires a minute of resolution and an hour of courage. Oh, I'm very content."

"Can you at least make a decision?" demanded Madame Bise.

"Personally, I'd like nothing better," Madeleine replied, "if Georges consents..."

A flame of triumph lit up in Armand Caresco's heart. Although seemingly occupied with his ablutions, he was lending all the might of his auditory faculties to the whispered murmurs at the foot of the bed.

So, still—as ever—formidable chance was taking his side, holding on to him like a mysterious hand, sweeping away the dangers suspended over his head.

That operation was the annihilation of his crime, the reparative effacement, the salutary destruction; it was fortune entering yet again through the wide-open door: the debt settled; the banker Israel impotent to harm him; the bailiffs put off; prosperity uncompromised; the glory of the house made illustrious by his talent and audacity, having tottered momentarily, taking flight again, also cured and fortified. It was also Mathilde, his passion, his addiction, retained to him, still possessed, still his.

Before the insistences of the family, before Madeleine's decision, surely, Georges Ponviane would not raise any objection, would also be resolved. The sole obstacle to overcome would be Bordier: honest Bordier, perspicacious and knowledgeable; Bordier, who might smash everything if he found out. He felt threatened— but Bordier was absent, due to remain in Bordeaux for a few more days, and Caresco resolved that the operation would take place before his return.

"If George consents," Madeleine had said. And at that very moment, someone knocked on the door.

Georges Ponviane came in, preceded by his father, very pale after having seen Stella's intoxicated body being dragged out of the elevator. But the joyful radiance of the room, the contentment of the faces, quickly dissipated that painful impression. He came to Madeleine and hugged her to his bosom. Then, noticing the rings around her eyes, and her poor dear features fatigued by the toil of maternity, he interrogated her.

"You're pale this morning, Madeleine. You're not suffering?" And as she remained indecisive, with a confession on her lips, he added: "And for some time now, I've noticed that you haven't been very well. What's wrong, Madeleine?"

"I have something disquieting to tell you, my friend—but I don't have the courage. Ask Aunt Bise."

Frightened by that reticence, the young man turned to the aunt, who tried to soften the blow.

"No, no…the little darling's exaggerating her condition. It's not as grave as she implies. Ask the doctor."

And it was the surgeon who submitted to the anxious interrogation of Monsieur Ponviane and Georges. Deeply delighted to see that the battle was going his way, sure of the means of victory, he adopted a grave expression. "Indeed, Mademoiselle de Jancy offers certain symptoms about which I'll be happy to inform you, Messieurs. Would you be kind enough to come down to my study? We can talk more freely there."

They went out, Georges after a glance at Madeleine, into which he strove to put all the force of his tenderness and devotion.

When the three men had gone, an immense sadness reigned in the room, squeezing the hearts of those who remained in an expectantly emotional group around the bed. The artificial exaggeration of gaiety that had radiated a shot while before had fallen flat; a few rare and heavy words were exchanged, but remained unechoed, so keenly did they sense that a grave conversation was taking place downstairs, that a destiny as about to be decided.

What were they saying? What would Georges think? Madeleine shivered, and the minutes of frightful uncertainty were eternities.

Finally, Monsieur Ponviane and Georges reappeared; the latter had the trace of revelations in his eyes. The father, feigning indifference, came to pinch Madeleine's cheek.

"Come on, come on, my daughter-in-law," he said, "it'll be nothing. A little cut, and in a week, it will all be over."

So the operation had been decided!

The surgeon's persuasive genius had been manifest once again, and had wound itself cleverly enough around the fiancé's soul to lead to an acceptance. It had not been without tears and suffering; the young man's red eyes testified to that; the expression of affectionate commiseration with which he considered Madeleine was a further proof of it—but as he took Madeleine by the hand, astonished to find, even so, a smile upon his lips, what Bordier had said to him came back to mind.

"Don't do anything without me," his friend had said, with an unforgettable expression.

Now, Caresco, during the conversation he had just had with him, had insisted on the urgency of the determination, had declared that every day that went by

305

would make the difficulties greater, the success less certain. He had been so affirmative, so convincing, so warmly persuasive, that the father and the son, without reflecting on the gravity of the resolution, without demanding another expert opinion, had decided, under the restriction of Madeleine's willingness, that the operation would take place the day after next.

Now that he was not longer subject to the surgeon's magnetism, Georges was seized by a frightful doubt, cursing the weakness of character that had prevented him from discussing the problem before resolving it.

What could he do, now that everything was decided, now that even the number of the room destined for the young woman had been chosen? How could he take a step back, go against the current?

I'll write to Bordier immediately, Georges thought. *He'll receive the letter tomorrow morning, and will have time to telegraph his opinion. Oh, how I regret his absence!*

The appearance of Soeur Cunégonde provided a distraction. Her nose, more congested than ever, seemed all the more triumphant at the victory won by her master. She had been quickly informed of it, with the result that she had come in search of Madeleine in order to take her to her room—and the young woman, whom she had take by the waist, thought of those engravings in which a husband, after the ceremony, draws his wife amorously to the nuptial chamber.

Toward what hymen, what defloration, was she going on Soeur Cunégonde's arm? Toward what beach dolorously abandoned by the waves of dreams and joys was she being drawn?

Fortunately, in the dark immensity of her soul, a lighthouse was blazing, and that lighthouse was Georges, her handsome, her dear amour.

Alas, would the lighthouse still want to shine for her. Would George still want a scarred wife?

"My dear, it's necessary to put you to bed immediately. It's what the doctor wants."

And Soeur Cunégonde turned down the white sheets on the bed, and patted the pillows. Madeleine got undressed slowly, and again, the dolorous formation of her abdomen appeared to her, seemingly more accentuated.

When she was in bed, she said: "Sister, will you ask Monsieur Georges to come to talk to me? I'd like to be alone with him."

Soeur Cunégonde started. Leave a young man and a young woman alone! Propriety was opposed to it. But the fiancé came in, as if solicited by an interior voice, and the sister left.

"Georges," said the young woman, "come closer to the bed. Sit down here. Take my hand; I need to talk to you."

She was serious and affectionate. Georges tried to smile, but the joy died on his lips.

"Georges," Madeleine continued, "the day after to-morrow, I have to undergo an operation. It is, I believe, not very serious—but still, it's an operation, and I've heard it said that chloroform sometimes puts people to sleep...definitively."

"That's crazy!" he said, rendered crazier himself by fear, with a desire to weep that absorbed all his contention.

She shook her head, pensively, and went on, her eyes lost in the vagueness of the room: "No, not crazy.

I've already thought hard about all that. I seem timid and tranquil, but you see, Georges, I've also been seething with ideas. I've thought that my illness might not be cured by the operation, and that you might thereafter have the burden of a permanently debilitated wife to care for, instead of a happy companion, vigorously traversing life on your arm.

"I know that you're good and loyal to the extent of devotion, but I would judge myself truly wretched if I were to take advantage of that generosity and that loyalty, to the point of demanding such a sacrifice from you. That's why, Georges, for the reasons that I've said, and in order that you won't have to wear mourning for me if I die, and in order for you not to have to care for me if I continue to live as an invalid, I'm asking you— look me in the eyes, Georges, and you'll see my heart therein—to take back your promise."

Before that manifestation of superb abnegation, Georges could not hold back his tears. He pushed away the chair on which he had been sitting and knelt beside the bed. Without her resisting, he passed his arm beneath her charming head, through the blonde wave of her hair scattered on the pillow, and, slowly and melodiously, his voice flowed, enveloping the young woman with an exquisite charm.

Was she truly crazy, to have such dark thoughts? Had he not sworn her an eternal love? She did not have the right to ask him to betray such an oath, to take back his promise.

"Separate myself from you, Madeleine for such reasons! From you, who are everything of which I dream of the superior, everything for which I am ambitious, everything that I desire! But I feel that my love is made, precisely, of a need and a devotion. If you are ill, I shall bless you again for having to sustain you, to protect your weakness, to surround you with delicacies and cares. But you will be valiant after this ordeal, my beloved. Believe me, believe me!"

The fiancé's tears had dried up. Now he was playing with Madeleine's white hands, interlacing the fingers. She looked at him proudly, forgetting her chagrin, entirely given over to her adoration for the handsome youth with the beautiful soul. And in spite of, or perhaps because of, her condition, gripped by an obscure sensuality, she thought about the joy that she would have in feeling the young man's vigorous torso against her breast. As ignorant as it is possible to be of physical love, it nevertheless seemed to her that something intoxicating must emerge from the approach of heir two bodies.

But again, that thought plunged her back into her obsession.

"But what about the scar?" she said.

"The scar! I shall cover it with so many kisses that all trace of it will be effaced! Reassure yourself, my beloved. We're magnifying things at present, we're seeing things too darkly. I've talked very seriously to the doctor about this operation; he's assured me that you'll be cured, and that your health won't suffer thereafter. Of all this, he tells me, nothing will remain in a year's time but a little white line a few centimeters long. He's made me understand the nature of the operation very well. And then, what does it matter, my dear, what does it matter, since I love you...since I love you, my adored Madeleine, enough to die of it?"

The young woman squeezed Georges' hand more forcefully. But a veil still darkened her tenderness. Her eyes strayed toward infinite dreams. One question, of which she dared not let go, reddened her lips.

Georges divined her alarm.

"There's still something else?" he asked.

"Yes…what about children?" she replied, in a low voice, hesitant with all the dread of seeing her dearest aspirations cut short by a single word.

"Children, my dear love! Nothing opposes our having them. The doctor has assured me of it: pink blonde cherubs, darling tyrants that I shall adore, for they will reflect your beauty, your grace and your candor. We'll have a great many, and they'll be as many sacred forces binding me even more to you, to your ecstatic eyes, to your holy lips!"

The young man's voice had become tender and soft again, melting into an incantation of love that lulled his fiancée, outside of all materiality, offering to her dreams, to her joys, to her hopes, and even to her dolors, a blessed repository.

Rapidly, under the melody of the passionate words that he was now saying at the hazard of his heart, as rapidly as thoughts come to the lips of a lucid individual on the point of death, she remembered the delicious moments in which she had made the young man's acquaintance. The slightest scenes of their love story, the slightest tender and delicate words, and innocent details—an entire flood of dormant memories came to assail her consciousness, passing once again before her eyes.

She remembered the décor of that autumnal evening at Madame Bise's house, with the flight of tall trees charged with gold in the woods, and the blossoming of the horizon in the infinity, when Georges had taken a first kiss, and the profound emotion of the thrill that had invaded her.

How short that story was, alas—and was it now to be interrupted before the end? It seemed to her that a voice was crying out to her: "No, you shall go no further!" And that voice had the strange sonority of Caresco's voice.

Why was that man persecuting her at this moment? What fatal bond of unknown fibers incessantly brought his evil personality between the two lovers?

An anxiety darkened Madeleine's face, and George understood that she was drawing away from their dream, that she was returning to the menace of the day after tomorrow.

At the very least, he wanted to calm the anxieties of his beloved and put her dread to sleep. And while soothing her with his language, while she leaned upon his arm in the silky aureole of her hair, she was dreaming, pensively, of the approaching hour that threatened their happiness, it was the fiancé wronged by the worst of crimes who sang the praises of the surgeon...

CHAPTER XVII

Dr. Cartaux, who had been Bordier's master at the Hôpital Lariboisière, was in his bedroom, which he had not left for nearly a month. He was sitting in an armchair, his legs extended, covered by a plaid. On a table beside him, within arm's reach, were a cup of milk and a bottle of Vichy water; on the mantelpiece facing him, surmounting the crackle of logs in the hearth, was a display of labeled bottles and potions.

Falling from the window, daylight blanched by large snowflakes was illuminating the morning disorder of the room in a melancholy fashion, and the bed in which the savant had passed an atrocious night of pain and poignant thoughts. His features were drawn, his jaundiced face careworn, thinned and disillusioned by the slow conclusion of existence, but that did not prevent his dark eyes from remaining active and brilliant, as if all the life had fled the rest of his body to take refuge therein.

The clock chimed ten, and the sequence of climes made him shiver.

"It's time," he said, aloud. "Time for the cup of milk. Why? Why want to continue living? What folly, to cling on to a wretched existence, when one is doomed, when the few months that it might still last offer me nothing but the frightful spectacle of my decay. What folly!"

From the pocket of his dressing-gown he took a bottle of dark glass, bearing a red label with the words EXTERNAL USAGE ONLY printed on it in capital letters. It was a pharmaceutical euphemism meaning "poison." For three days he had been haunted by the idea of a rapid, abrupt death by means of a few drops of that liquid, a blessed death that would cut short his suffering, the bitterness of the futile struggle that his colleagues had undertaken against the irremediable illness.

He looked at the bottle without horror, handling it without a tremor in his fingers, and then put it back in his pocket, tranquilly, reassured in a way by knowing that he had it about his person, as a supreme remedy, a final drug that he would find ready for absorption at the moment when, completely resolved to end it, he took the ultimate decision.

Then he reached out with his trembling hand for the cup of milk, and drank it, disgustedly.

At that moment the valet came in and handed him a card.

"This Monsieur insists on being admitted to see Monsieur," the domestic said.

"Monsieur Bordier!" exclaimed Dr. Cartaux. "Send him in right away."

The young man came into his master's room with astonishment, surprised to find such a transformation in the valiant worker that he had seen in the breach, making his round of the hospital beds, only a month before.

"My dear Master! You're still suffering, then? Oh, it pains me to see you like this. But it won't be for long, will it—not much longer?"

"Indeed, my friend, ii won't be for much longer." He paused momentarily, let out a sigh, and then added, somberly: "I'm done for."

"What are you saying?"

"Cancer of the stomach, my boy. My friends, my physicians, are trying to delude me, employing with me the little lies that I employed with my own patients, the innocent little tricks...but I can see clearly. Anyway, look!"

He uncovered one of legs, extended on a chair, and offered it to his student's gaze, swollen, pale, taut and painful.

"*Phlegamasia alba dolens*,"[19] he said, sententiously, as if he were teaching a class using an example. "Phlebitis! That confirms my opinion. I'm dying of the same malady as my master, the great Trousseau,[20] and I've made my diagnosis in the same fashion as him. My poor friend! You're more frightened than I am. Oh, life is very little, you know. If I weren't suffering as much..." He took the young man's hand and squeezed it paternally. "My boy, your visit is doing me good. Why haven't you come before?"

"I was away, Monsieur, traveling—and I didn't know; otherwise..." He abandoned the sentence, desolate now because of the motive that had brought him to see the old man, but burning nevertheless to tell him about it. He went on: "No, I didn't know that you were suffering to this extent, and I assure you that it isn't the reason that brought me to see you."

"Do you have something to say to me, Bordier?"

---

[19] Literally "painful white oedema"—a consequence of deep vein thrombosis associated with the clotting problems consequent to some cancers. The supplementary term that Cartaux also uses, phlebitis, is nowadays used to refer to a less serious condition involving superficial veins.

[20] Armand Trousseau (1801-1867) had a long career in public health administration, supervising the hospitals of Paris, where he built a reputation as an outstanding teacher and helped to develop many new treatments; he died of pancreatic cancer, for which he had previously indentified a crucial diagnostic sign.

"Yes, Master, to ask for your advice—important advice. I've always appreciated your ability and your knowledge, but those qualities are commonplace, whereas one can't find everywhere the generosity, the justice and the loyalty that have brought me to you. Oh, what I have to tell you is so painful; it's a confidence within the jurisdiction of professional secrecy, and I'm so frightened by the consequences of what I've discovered that I believe that you alone are capable of giving me direction, of telling me what to do."

The passed his hand over his forehead as if to gather up the ideas that were upsetting him; then, at a sign from the old man, he continued: "This is it. A young woman, one of your clients, the fiancée of one of my friends, a young man who is also one of yours, has become pregnant due to the act of a stranger. Everything leads me to believe that he abused her during a crisis of hysteria, and that she is not guilty of a treason toward her fiancé, The young woman, counseled by those around her, goes to consult a surgeon, who, for a reason I dare not define, diagnoses a uterine fibroma and advises the family to permit an operation that he is about to carry out. What should I do?"

He stopped, with other words swelling his throat— word of indignation and revolt that were about to overflow in a tumultuous flood. But the old man suspended his story with a gesture, and slowly, firmly, in a voice that became firmer still as it progressed, said: "This young woman is Mademoiselle de Jancy; the young man is George Ponviane; and the surgeon is…Caresco…isn't it?"

"What!" Bordier exclaimed. "You know?"

"No," replied Dr. Cartaux, shaking his head, "I don't know—but I deduce. I can deduce it for several reasons: firstly, because they're the only engaged couple among my friends, and secondly because, now that you mention it, I remember having been asked to go to see Mademoiselle de Jancy with regard to some symptoms of illness that surprised me. As for the surgeon, I'd like to believe that only Caresco is capable of such an abomination. Oh my dear boy, my friend, my pupil! Why have you followed that wretched surgeon, why didn't you come, before going on your journey, to ask my advice?"

"That's true, Master, that's true! I should have spoken to you. Forgive me; advise me—for I'm so demoralized before the gravity of the resolution to be made. What should I do? Is it necessary to betray the confidence of my friend, or to tell him everything, at the cost of breaking is heart? I beg you, Master, enlighten me— help me! Let me rediscover in your words the good faith of old. Master, what must I do?"

He spoke in a hasty and low tone, of an individual overwhelmed by the rapidity and enormity of events, with mirages of surprise and flushes of impetuous anger in his wide naïve eyes behind his gold-rimmed spectacles. But Dr. Cartaux remained taciturn for a moment, perhaps waiting for a stabbing pain raking the hollow of his stomach to end.

"Let's see, Bordier," he said, finally. "Let's clarify the matter. The individuals are those I cited just now?"

"Alas yes."

"How did you discover this secret?—for you've been traveling, you tell me."

"Six days ago, on the eve of my departure for Bordeaux, where that wretch Caresco had sent me to care for a client, in order to get rid of me, I was asked by my friend Ponviane to go see his fiancée, who was suffering.

She was in bed; I examined her and acquired the certainty of her pregnancy. I got back from Bordeaux this morning, the client having died. My first concern was to run to the Avenue Hoche, to the sanitarium, and what do I hear? That Mademoiselle de Jancy's fibroma is to be removed tomorrow—her fibroma!"

"Why do you assume that Ponviane is not the author of the pregnancy?"

"Why? Because I'm sure of it."

"Have you questioned him?"

"No—that would have been to reveal everything. But I sounded out the young woman, in a roundabout fashion. And Georges is honesty personified. Do you believe that, seeing his fiancée in that condition, he would not have thought of the consequence if he had committed the act? Then, there are other reasons still, reasons that I dare not tell you, so much would they seem to you to emerge from an infamous machination, which make me presume, which affirm to me, that Caresco has a superior interest in the disappearance of this crime!"

"So you think that Caresco is the father?" demanded the old man coldly, as if researching the symptoms of a malady.

But at that question, which shook his fearful soul, Bordier stood up, his arms in the air, extraordinarily distressed to see the thoughts that he was hiding in the remotest corner of his heart discovered.

"Oh, no, Master," he said. "Don't ask me that! I don't know anything; I can't tell you anything; I have nothing but suppositions. For pity's sake, don't ask me that."

The distressed appearance of his pupil, and his fearful response, cemented Dr. Cartaux's convictions. How-

317

ever, he pretended to abandon that trail, to resume the conversation as a disinterested, impartial judge in search of the best solution.

"But my dear friend," he said, "are you sure of your diagnosis? Might you not be mistaken? Or might Caresco's science have been deceived? One could cite other errors just as gross. For my part, I've made several..."

"Yes," Bordier replied, "sometimes diagnosis is difficult, but that's not the case here. I affirm on my honor that Caresco should not have had a moment's hesitation...unless he's gone mad."

"Which is quite possible," the old man continued. "At any rate, in the present case, Caresco's personality and motive are indifferent to us. All the interest of the conversation pivots around the conduct you ought to adopt in regard to your friend. Well, my boy, my opinion is that you ought to say nothing, that you don't have the right to say anything."

"What!" cried Bordier, with an exasperation that could no longer be held back by the respect due to his master. "I don't have the right to say anything! A crime is about to be committed; something frightful is about to happen, on which a woman's life might depend—a woman I esteem, that I ought to love, because she is going to be the wife of my best friend—and I don't have the right to go to that man, my brother, to reveal the trap, to show him the abyss and turn him away from it? Why? What power closes my mouth? What authority shackles my arm?"

"Professional secrecy, Bordier," said the old man, firmly. "Professional secrecy. You discovered this secret in the exercise of your functions, and even if you had discovered it outside them, you wouldn't have the right to reveal anything. The rules are formal and absolute; they are laws, and you would be committing a crime against conscience by breaking them."

"Master, Master! Is it you who are speaking thus? You, who have so often given me the example of the purest and sanest justice and verity? But does not my conscience, if I listen to it, order me to violate those absurd rules, to place well above them the tribute that I owe to friendship, to my brother's confidence, and, in any case, to prevent a crime when I have the possibility of so doing? Professional secrecy!—an absurd amalgam of prejudices and customs, which is at odds with natural sentiments and which I have the right to scorn, to trample underfoot when it's a matter of unmasking a villain, paralyzing a murderer!"

"No, no, Bordier," the old man repeated, more violently, "you don't have the right. The day when you received the diploma of a doctor from your masters, you pronounced an oath that you cannot break. Go reread our great legist authors, Tardieu, Brouardel and the rest. Even if such an adventure happened to your own mother, to whomever touches you most profoundly, you would have an absolute duty to remain silent. Oh, my boy, my friend, I realize that the constraint offends your generous and proud sentiments, that there is a revolt in your heart that might lead you to a culpable action. Believe me, though, believe me, since you have submitted yourself to my good sense."

Bordier was overwhelmed, with a need for reaction that might have brought him to tears. Thus, his character, having emerged momentarily from its ordinary placid timidity, willingly took refuge in sadness. It was with a real joy that he heard Dr. Cartaux continue as follows:

"But if the law is formal and absolute, my friend, there are means of getting around it without lowering one's conscience to an infamy. In the present case, this is what you could do: go find Monsieur Ponviane, and in the name of the amity that unites you, ask him—beg him—to submit his fiancée to the examination of another physician. Perhaps he'd listen to you."

"He'd listen to me," Bordier replied. "I'm sure of it—but would the entourage, particularly that old fool Madame Bise, consent? And the operation is so imminent! Oh, I'm afraid of not succeeding, Master, of acting in vain and only awakening suspicions by taking that step. I'm desperate—desperate!"

And he looked at his interlocutor with a veritable fear in his eyes, in his gestures, in his attitude, already feeing defeated by the difficult of the task.

The old man got up dolorously from his armchair, uttered an exclamation of suffering as he moved his heavy and swollen leg, and then, after a moment of reflection, continued:

"Just now, my friend, I invoked professional secrecy, legality, the power that binds your devotion and prevents action. Let me now give you other reasons, more human and more logical, in favor of the happiness of your friends.

"Think: what will happen to that amorous young man, full of hope in the future, full of confidence in his fiancée, if you tell him, or if you have someone else tell him: *That woman, so pure and so chaste, has been soiled by another, and is bearing in her loins the product of that soiling…?*

"He will immediately cry treason, will not believe in your hypothesis of a cataleptic sleep, will search for the sin, for the ignominy…because he is a man. It will be a catastrophe, for him and for her, perhaps suicide.

"And, supposing that he accords some credit to your explanation, will his soul be generous enough to admit the innocence, to marry regardless, to attempt happiness? No, certainly not.

"I'll go even further. I'll admit that Monsieur Ponviane, being of a particularly noble essence, has understood the sublime beauty of what he is doing in taking Mademoiselle de Jancy for a wife. What will happen? An impossible existence, my dear Bordier, for the crime will always loom up between the two spouses, extinguishing their joy and their tranquility. The specter of the monstrous act will always loom up in their intoxications, their embraces. The husband, in taking his wife in his arms, will always sense another body between them, and his kisses will not efface the trace of the caresses of the other, the first, Caresco."

"Caresco!" howled Bordier. "You said Caresco. You think…"

"Did I say Caresco? Forgive me, my boy, my tongue went astray. A bizarre association of ideas made me pronounce that name."

He stopped for a moment, indecisively. But Bordier had understood that he had had the same presentiment as himself, that the words he had let escape a little while ago had struck him with the same obsession. And now, standing aside from the drama, he returned to the admiration of his master's pitiless logic, the intelligence of superior deduction that had made him such a remarkable clinician.

"That's the situation for the young couple," Dr. Cartaux continued. "But what about the child? Have you thought about the child? What will become of that innocent, repudiated by his father and mother, the product of misfortune and shame? In other cases, when a woman has consciously, amorously, made a child with a first lover, the little being still obtains kisses, tenderness and attentions from her, a cortege of affections that are like the memory, the regeneration of the love accorded to the father. But here! What will become of that defective peg, that burden of ignominy, which blind nature has accorded to the Fatality that inseminated it? Where will it grow up? In what obscure country, under what dubious care? The object of rejection and shame, will it claim the share of growth, or enjoyment—of life, in short—to which it has the right?…for it is not guilty of anything! Can you imagine all the horror, all the injustice of its existence? Can you hear its reproaches, its clamors of revolt against social infamy? What tears, what torments, what anguish!"

"Where are you taking me, Master!" Bordier interjected. "Where are you guiding me?"

"I'm guiding you to this: to the utility, the necessity, of letting that wretch Caresco go ahead."

"And if she dies?"

"She won't die. You know how simple the operation is in the hands of that man when he wants to take the trouble—and he will, for his interest and his reputation will demand it."

"But the woman will be sterile, Master, and that will hurt Georges, who loves his fiancée nobly and would like children! He said as much to me the other day, before my departure, and I sensed that he was putting into that desire for children all the aspirations, all the joy and al the reason of love! Children, he said to me, are the sweet beings in whom one lives again, in whom one is reborn when one dies: children, who make

322

your youth anxious, but who soothe and charm your old age."

Alas, Bordier had unsuspectingly struck a blow. When he looked up at Dr. Cartaux, he perceived that the savant was weeping.

The sensitive corner of his aged heart, which had not shuddered at the evocation of death, was stirred by that of children. At that moment, he judged all the desolation of his desert and celibate existence, his solitary old age, the slow and dolorous termination of his egotistical life, solely caressed by science, without the generous and consoling urgency of a family.

"Excuse me my friend," he said. "It's a moment of weakness, quite excusable in an old man whose morale is depressed by malady. You can't imagine how much the character weakens in suffering, and suddenly succumbs to the impact of age. Forgive me."

He wiped away his tears, and then murmured: "Yes, children. That would be the one reason, the only..." Then, reconquered by his desire to regulate Bordier's conduct, to impose on him the most just, and the most humane solution, he went on, firmly: "But is life itself, setting aside the egotistical desire for a pampered old age, worth the trouble of making a gift of it to children? Can one tell oneself, in creating them, that what is happening to me, for instance, will not happen to them? I've worked hard since my youth; I've consecrated to science in laboratories, to the poor in the hospitals, all the force of my intelligence and my energy. I've sometimes had the real sentiment that I was playing a useful role, that I was doing good, that I was good. I didn't marry, in order not to distract myself from my work, from the glorious goal that I wanted to attain..."

"Yes, you've been a saint," Bordier put in. "A veritable saint."

"Well, here's the result. I'm laid low by a frightful malady. Others talk to me about a future life, dangle the shiny recompense of the world beyond the grave before me yes, but I have neither that faith nor that weakness, alas. In any case, my work would have been less noble had it been done in view of some ulterior compensation. And that's why I say to you, my dear pupil, my child: what good is there is allowing life? What point is there in creating it? I search for general Harmony, Justice, the radiation of a superior organization that ought to be fine and good, but I don't find them! I invoke the Force of good, and I only encounter hazard, circumstances, the power of Evil with all its derivatives: deceit, hatred, cupidity, cowardice...which let creatures like Caresco triumph!"

He stopped again, overcome by pain. In the pocket of his dressing-gown, with a feverish hand, he felt the bottle of poison, almost forgetting Bordier's presence, so sharp was his agony.

The latter got up to take his leave, as anguished morally as his master as physically, as desperate and as defeated. "*Au revoir*, Master," he said.

"Don't say *au revoir*. Say adieu."

"Why adieu? I'll come back to see you every day, with your permission."

"Say adieu, my son," the poor man repeated, nevertheless. "I might succumb at any moment. You know, a hemorrhage...an accident can happen quickly."

"Oh no, no, my beloved Master," Bordier protested. He had taken the savant's jaundiced hands, and squeezed them in a filial manner, ready to burst into sobs.

"Embrace me, my dear boy!"

324

That was the limit of their contention. The two men hugged one another, in tears.

Where were those plaints going? Toward what distant shore were they flying? With what mountains of desolation would they collide?

It seemed to them that a frightful laceration was ripping their hearts to shreds, but that, in spite of what the old man had said, those shreds would come together again in time, reconstituting a whole in the Peace of the beyond.

And when he was alone, Dr. Cartaux resumed a calm expression, illuminated by the imminence of deliverance, took the bottle with the red label out of his pocket, and slowly, methodically, counted out the drops into his cup of milk...

Once in the street, Bordier began to wander at random, like a disabled ship, over the waves of the sidewalks. The weather was awful, but it left him indifferent. Squalls of snow were falling, which quickly melted, covering the roadways with a dirty slush that splashed the feet of the horses.

The mud made him dirty, the rain made him wet; he did not bother to get out of the way of carriages or open his umbrella. He went straight ahead, under an impression of ruination and devastation. A catastrophe erupting at his feet, a conflagration, or the collapse of a house, would have seemed to him, at that moment, a natural, logical thing, by which he would not have been at all astonished.

All the things that the despairing old man had said came back to him, in hasty impacts that hammered his thoughts, without giving him time to reflect on the circumstances that had produced them.

He admitted, at that moment, that he ought not to do anything, that it would have been a betrayal of the sacramental laws of his profession and the principles of honor to reveal the situation, to open his friend's eyes. He admitted it because his master had said it to him, by virtue of the system of obedience, a vestige of his university education.

Humble human thought, a fragile reed, how small a crease is required to break it! The weakness of understanding, always under the domination of sentiments!

He went on thus, advancing, as if into oblivion, insensible to collisions with passers-by, the jostling of the crowd whose members maneuvered around him, smiling, thinking that he was drunk.

It was almost noon. He went past a flamboyant rotisserie, and sniffed the odor of sauces without remembering that his stomach had been empty since the previous evening.

Suddenly, he found himself outside the door of the house in the Avenue Hoche, without knowing how, without having guided his footsteps there, perhaps having been driven toward the house by the same inconceivable force that leads the unknown criminal to the slabs of the Morgue or causes the lover to pass before the threshold of his vanished mistress.

For in his heart, all the life of toil accomplished under that roof, the active hours that he had spent there, the agitations of that laborious hive, the comings and goings of the patients, the urgency of the ants in white headdresses, the heroically murderous deeds of the director, and the great dilapidations of flesh, and the floods of blood, and the flash of the instruments, and his own personality, so interested in the fermentation of that vat, all seemed to him to be something dead, extinct, already distant.

Mechanically, he rang, opened the door when the bolt was drawn back, and went in.

The cold and empty vault, the view of the garden desolated by winter, the commons dirtied by the rain, complicated his sadness. He climbed the steps of the vestibule, penetrated into the gaudy luxury.

Armand Caresco was just coming out of his consultation room in the company of the student, Berger and three foreign colleagues whom he had invited to lunch at Mathilde's house. He seemed joyful and amiable, his eternal smile fixed on his lips, his gaze evasive—but the appearance of Bordier transformed his physiognomy, furrowed his brow with a crease of surprise and anger.

Bordier was the enemy returning to the charge when he thought the battle won, the obstacle surging forth unexpectedly, which might transform everything into a rout. Master of himself, however, come what may, he advanced toward him, holding out his hand, limply.

"Why, Bordier—you're back! You didn't let me know? And our patient—you've abandoned her?"

"She died yesterday evening," Bordier replied, without taking the extended hand. "She died suddenly. So I came back."

Caresco's first thought had been that his aide had been recalled by George Ponviane. Perceiving that that was not the case, he thought that the game was not lost. No, Bordier must not know anything about the plan he had made, which he was about to put into action the following day. Was it not possible, in the circumstances, to get rid of him for one day, to find some machination to take him way during the hours in which he might still be

327

dangerous? Already his inventive mind was working, scheming, imagining a pretext.

"You've arrived just in time," he said. "I'm going to need you again. It's a matter of taking the train..."

"Not before I say a few words to you," Bordier replied, with a surge of despair, understanding the new role that the surgeon wanted him to play in the drama.

Caresco excused himself from his guests with a gesture, opened the door to his study and went in first. When they were alone, he went to sit down at his desk, while Bordier remained standing, like a stranger, already frightened by the unconscious impulsion that had brought him here to protest, wondering how he was going to begin the contest—for he sensed its terrible approach, before breaking one or the other; he divined its implacability, the gaze of the bird of prey that was no longer fleeing, imposing a strange dominion over him, penetrating him to the marrow of his bones. Even Caresco's voice, that musical and humble voice, became dry and metallic, as trenchant as a scalpel.

"What have you to say to me?"

"You know," he said, in a low voice. "You know better than I do. I've been told that you're going to operate on Mademoiselle de Jancy."

"Yes, tomorrow. So what?"

"Well, it can't happen."

"It can't happen? Why? Who will prevent me?"

"Me," said Bordier, very quietly.

"You! You're insane! You want to prevent me from removing her fibroma?"

"Her fibroma! Wretch! You know very well that she's pregnant."

"Well, so what?"

Bordier shivered. He was not even trying to deny it. Accustomed as the man was to expert lies, he was not even trying to color his crime with an appearance of faith; he was displaying all the hideousness of his project, without covering it with the veil of a pretext, impudently, ferociously, as he laid bare secret wounds with the blade of his scalpel.

What bandit blood was running in his veins? What soul of terror and horror made him reveal himself, so contradictory, so possessed with harmful violence? What frightful reasons did he have for confessing his act so brutally, without excusing it? Was it money? Had he arrived at the phase of madness whose premonitory symptoms Bordier had observed several times, in which he became unconsciously criminal, accomplishing evil for the joy of evil?

Evocations of the Salpêtrière, of howling and grimacing lunatics, tragic masks with wild eyes, twisted bodies, panting against the grilles, parading in frightful sarabands, passed through Bordier's mind. He looked at the surgeon. Did not the features, screwed up by implacable fury, offer the contractions of mental imbalance? Did not the decomposed mouth, raised in the corners by two hateful creases, the almost-fused eyebrows, the forehead streaked by two violent lines, and the eyes, most of all, the eyes with metallic glints, declare that reason had fled that head?

Yes, he was mad—mad! And it was necessary to talk to him like a man gone astray who could still be returned to the right path, who was not yet insensible to the manifestations of the light.

So Bordier pushed his anger back into the utmost depths of his being, and prepared arguments franked with common sense.

"Come on," he said, "think about what you're doing. You're not denying Mademoiselle de Jancy's condition; you're not retrenching behind a diagnosis that
might have been an error; but you're proposing, deliberately and consciously, to perform an operation that, if it
were divulged, would bring you directly to the Court of
Assizes? But consider what a fall that would be for you,
how you would lose in a quarter of an hour the fruit of
ten years hard work! Even supposing that you pleaded
error before a jury, and were acquitted, could you still
resume your profession? Think of the blow that you're
about to inflict on yourself, which is all the more idiotic
because you have no need of the operation, either for
your reputation or your fortune. For those, I think, are
the only two motives that could make you do it, aren't
they? The only possible motives?"

He was about to continue his reasoning in that extinct tone, without persuasion and without embellish-
ment, when Caresco suddenly relaxed his expression,
and said, with a smile imprinted with disdainful irony:
"Come on, my poor Bordier, you've been babbling for
ten minutes about impossible circumstances. Who do
you think is going to denounce my…error, if it were
admitted that I'm making an error?"

"Me!" exclaimed Bordier. "Me!"

"You! Get away—you're bound by professional secrecy."

"And what if I prove that your error is a crime?"
said the young man, advancing toward him, menacing
him with his tall stature, while the other remained bent
over his desk, without raising his eyes.

"A crime? What do you mean?"

"What if I prove," Bordier continued, increasingly
excited, "that you're about to operate on that young

woman to obliterate the traces of an abominable crime accomplished by you while she was unconscious!"

This time, Caresco looked up, his eyes full of surprise. His surprise came from knowing that he had been discovered, and yet the expression in his eyes interrupted his adversary's momentum.

Bordier stopped dead. What was he going to say? Was he not about to accuse the surgeon on the basis of deductions that derived, in sum, from mere suppositions? Had he been there when Caresco had acted? Had he heard evidence from a witness to the scene? No, he was making the accusation on the basis of a personal impression, perhaps influenced by hatred of the man and the brutality of the action—but he had no conclusive proof.

And his entire strategy crumbled and collapsed, in the absolute impossibility of continuing to make allegations without foundations.

Was he about to implore now, to attempt to find a fiber of emotion to set in vibration? No, everything slid over that ferociously walled heart, without any fissure to let sentiment through.

In any case, to conclude the conversation, Caresco stood up in his turn, cold and determined.

"My fried," he said, "I don't have time to listen to you. I have people waiting for me. You've been traveling all night; I expect that your mind is as fatigued as your body. Go get some rest. Tomorrow, you'll have thought about the error of your diagnosis and you'll come of your own accord to offer me your collaboration. Then again, remember that I'm cut out for the game, that I have all the trumps in my hand and that when someone gets in my way, I make arrangements to get rid of them."

That was said casually and unhurriedly, with a resolute air that impressed Bordier more than any rhetorical posturing. What atrocious will buoyed up that man!

As he went through the open door behind him, Bordier had a furious desire to lay the man dead at his feet—and yet, he felt dominated nevertheless.

In the vestibule, the foreign colleagues and Berger were still waiting. The student said to Caresco: "Tomorrow, then, for the fibroma?"

"No need to put yourself out, my friend," the surgeon replied. "Monsieur Bordier, whom I introduce to you, has returned from his journey and has agreed to resume his service with me tomorrow."

CHAPTER XVIII

In front of the Pavillon de Madrid, where the rendezvous for the encounter had been arranged, the landau that brought Jean Bordier came to a halt with the sound of hooves striking the frost-hardened ground. Georges Ponviane got out first, holding a pistol-case under his arm. Then, with sighs of liberation, came the other witnesses, Monsieur des Trieux, a friend of both Bordier and Ponviane, a renowned fencer who made a specialty of direction affairs of honor and Dr. Piliat, a former student comrade, who had accepted the ingrate role of assisting Bordier medically, and finally, Bordier himself, apparently very calm and confident, only revealing his emotion by a more pronounced blinking of the eyelids behind the lenses of his spectacles.

The weather was fine and dry; a pale sun emerging from the morning mists was brightening the distant road, launching the effort of its rays through the inextricable thicket of bare trees, whose branches and twigs were clearly outlined in black steaks against the blue-tinted atmosphere. The melting of snow, due to the milder temperature of the preceding days, had accumulated pools of water in places, which the return of the chill had frozen; on the edge of the ditches, incompletely-dissolved snow formed long ermine stripes that extended like a winter wrap along the deserted road.

Georges Ponviane took out his watch.

"Nine o'clock precisely. We've arrived first."

"Punctuality is the politeness of duelists," said Monsieur des Trieux, parodying a famous saying. He relieved his fellow witness of the pistol-box, took the guns out of the case and checked the triggers. Dr. Piliat had taken Bordier to one side and as plying him with questions.

"Come on, old chap, what's happened? Why this quarrel with Caresco? What do you have against him?"

"Don't interrogate me, my dear Piliat. It's a secret that I haven't even told my witnesses."

"A woman, eh?"

"Perhaps."

The previous day's scene, after Mademoiselle de Jancy's operation, at which he had assisted, passed before his eyes again. He saw himself issuing the slap, with a reasoned self-composure, in front of witnesses, when, Madeleine, having been carried back to her bed had woken up from her terrible operation, he had gone back down to the surgeon's study, where several people were present. He recalled Caresco's sudden pallor, the flash of hatred that had traversed his face, and the marvelous force of contention that had enabled him to control himself, and not to respond to the insult with violence.

He also recalled the stupefaction of Georges Ponviane, who was there, enquiring about the probable consequences of the operation, and who had seized him by the arm, saying: "What are you doing? Are you mad?"

"No, no, I'm not mad," he had replied. "Monsieur Caresco knows perfectly well why I slapped him."

Then, there had been the fastidious consequences of the gesture, the visit of the seconds to the physician, the negotiations, rendered more difficult by his refusal to give a reason or the insult. Was it to Georges—for whom, in sum, he was fighting—that he was going to explain that the sole means of getting out of the moral dilemma in which he was caught was to kill or be killed?

Could he tell him why he had decided that moment of redemption? Could he tell him that he had waited, before provoking Caresco, for the outcome of the operation carried out on Madeleine, because he was able until that moment to be useful to his friend, by keeping watch with an extreme zeal over the success of the abominable crime?

He could have refused to assist in the crime, letting Caresco work with his temporary aide, young Berger, but would not his friend's fiancée have been running greater risks in the inexperienced hands of the student? Since the action was inevitable, because he was gagged by the secrecy of his profession, by friendship, by the logic of the situation and by his own conscience, which screamed at him to remain silent, he had wanted to carry through his alleviating task to the end, doing what he could to ensure the maximum chance of success by offering to assist in the operation.

But with what anguish he had applied the chloroform compress to the young woman's mouth! How he had quivered, with halting respiration, at the outset. How he had trembled as the knife cleaved the flesh, as the blood spurted forth, as Caresco had withdrawn the parcel of formless meat, the gravid uterus, the lamentable debris of the rape, with a regal mastery!

The monstrous virtuoso had not felt the chill of the murder pass, had been no more stirred than in the arduous minutes of other procedures. How Bordier had admired that calmness, and how he had hated it!

And now, before the magnificent perspective of the Bois, where, in a moment the pistol would be aimed at him by that same ferocious and sure hand, what would become of him?

Death, probably, emerging from the barrel, laying him out on the cold ground.

He knew that Caresco was an excellent shot. He had only had practiced extensively with the épée, but the quality of the insulted party and the choice of weapons belonged to his adversary. He had, therefore, in all consciousness, fully informed as to the consequences of his action, decided this minute of reparation, of expiation, during which he would again play the role of the weaker party, manifesting once again the self-renunciation, the obscure disinterest with which destiny seemed to have stigmatized him since birth.

But what a pity to be obliged to go like this, in the annihilation of his dreams, paying the reparative debt for another, without having drawn from life what it might contain of the restful, the consoling, without having savored amour, a family, going like a rudderless boat to run on to a reef within sight of port!

Fatality! Fatality and ridiculous abnegation, which he almost cursed now, before the Bois, which would, in a few weeks' time, at the first caresses of spring, become so seductive again by virtue of the glorious manifestations of the life of plants and people! There, flowers would grow; there, the green carpet of the grass would extend, the trees would cover themselves with the ardent life of buds and leaves; there, the steam would sing its slow plaint again, and along the path, the cyclists would glide in graceful flight.

His soul was recharged by bucolic emotions, and he wept over everything that he was about to lose. But now a revolt set in, a determination to hurt the man who wanted to harm him. His arm would be steady and sure; he would strike, for Honor, for Right, for his friend, for himself.

"Here they are!" exclaimed Monsieur des Trieux.

Indeed, at the bend in the road, a landau appeared.

Georges went to Bordier. "Jean, here's you adversary...isn't there a means of settling things? There's still time."

"You know that's impossible."

"You still don't want to tell me anything?"

"Nothing."

"Finally, if misfortune befalls you—for it's necessary to be prepared for anything—don't you have some last recommendation, some confidence to transmit?"

"I can see," said Bordier, with a melancholy smile, "that you think, as the others do, that I'm fighting because of some matter of a woman. I know that my obstinate silence regarding the motive for my insult must aid that supposition, and I'm not astonished that you, my best friend, my brother, have come to offer yourself as a supreme messenger—but make no mistake; the person for whom I'm fighting will never suspect it if I remain alive; all the more reason why she should not suspect it if I die."

"Jean, my dear Jean," Ponviane replied, extraordinarily distressed by that simple declaration, "you'll always be the same, devoted and good to the point of folly. I don't know what's causing you to act; I can't imagine the reason for your gesture of violence toward Caresco. Well, in spite of the signal service that the man has rendered me in saving the life of my fiancée, I sense that justice and right are on your side, and I'm with you, with all my heart."

"Thank you," said Bordier. "Your words will console me as I die."

"Die!" Georges exclaimed. "Why talk about dying? Go on...with two bullets at thirty paces..."

"It's absolutely necessary, however that one of us dies!"

Bordier had spoken with a somber fire that struck his friend. Nevertheless, he did not have the leisure to continue the conversation, for the adverse party had arrived. For his seconds, Caresco had Dr. Savre, his former assistant, and Berger, the student, very proud of the role that he was playing, divining that he was about to take Bordier's place after the affair.

As soon as he set foot on the ground, Savre came straight to Ponviane and shook his hand vigorously. "You know," he said, "that I could not do other than assist Caresco, but I hope that all goes well for Bordier. Tell him that."

The surgeon had got down from the landau, well rested after an excellent night of ten hours' sleep. As a physician he had chosen an inoffensive colleague, saying to his witnesses, with a broad laugh: "Bah! If I'm wounded, I'll operate on myself!"

Thus, he always seemed to accompany the gravest concerns with a jovial irony, as if, being endowed with a doubling of his personality, one Caresco was always mocking the other.

Savre, who had studied him for a long time, and tried to separate out, from the tangle of his actions, the threads of reasons and those of unconsciousness, had not baulked at agreeing to be his second. It was one more thread or his dossier, the attitude of the man during that grave quarter of an hour. And he judged him extraordinarily confident in his destiny, going to meet danger with an insouciance akin to unconsciousness.

Was it that the Harmony of things wanted to cover the man, useful to its obscure designs, with a kind of latent immunity, protecting him with its somber wing?

Savre's philosophy accommodated the theory of the evil necessary to good, the vice necessary to virtue. A new proof was manifest in this encounter, and he awaited the result with a keen interest.

As soon as Caresco saw Ponviane he went to him. "I've just come from seeing Mademoiselle de Jancy," he said. "She's doing very well. Pulse normal, no fever. I'm sure that she'll heal rapidly and that it won't be long before you're a fortunate spouse...a fortunate father."

Ponviane, who had quivered with joy and gratitude at the beginning of that declaration, suddenly felt his enthusiasm vanish at the last word pronounced by Caresco. What irony, what evasion, what malevolent expression he divined in the intonation of the voice! It was an obscure intuition that put him on his guard against that incomprehensible man and now, with all the force of his soul, he wished that the fate of arms would turn against him.

Monsieur des Trieux drew the groups into side-path, and, after a conference with the witnesses, tossed a coin in the air to decide the positions.

"Heads!" called Georges Ponviane.

The witnesses bent down. The coin showed tails. Bordier would have the sun in his eyes. Ill-luck was pursuing him to the end.

Dr. Savre counted out the paces.

At that moment, when a new contest was about to be engaged for him, in which he could ask himself whether Fortune was still on his side, whether he projectile that emerged from his adversary's weapon might either kill him, or ruin him by putting him in a state of incapacity for work for the rest of his life in consequence of the loss of a limb, a hand, or even one of the ten fingers of which he had so much need for his daily endeavors, Armand Caresco was truly admirable in his audacious tranquility.

Was it courage? No. Courage would have consisted of having, like Bordier, a anguished soul, a heart downing in bitterness, sadness and lassitude, but nevertheless remaining, in spite of the fear, upright and proud in confrontation with the danger, with the probability of a fatal outcome. Courage also consists of being like good King Henri IV, who, seized by an atrocious fear before the enemy, dung the steel of his spurs into the flanks of his mount, in order to charge.

He, the surgeon, was not shaken by any sentiment of dread. He came to the encounter with confidence in his star, with the conviction that the skill, precision and rapidity of his fire would permit him to lay his adversary on the ground before Bordier even had time to press the trigger of his pistol. He knew that his gesture would have the rigorous, mathematical precision of the days when he held the scalpel, when he avoided one artery in order to cut another.

He was coming to an operation—and it was that marvelous composure; that self-confidence; that will to succeed; and also that carelessness of a danger he did not perceive, and did not admit, acting like a tightrope-walker who is sure of his goal as long as he does not look down; that sovereign scorn for consequences, the result of an unhealthy cerebral organization which had modified common sense; and finally, that ardent will to achieve the end without lingering over the choice of means—everything that had aided him thus far to succeed in life—which haloed him with superb indifference at that critical moment.

And while Bordier came and went, moved by the supreme contemplation of nature, but the flood of memories, by an intimate revolt, experiencing a real suffering in having to master his nerves, he, immobile granite, wrapped in his fur cloak, with his hands in his pockets in order not to be taken by surprise by a shiver due to the morning chill, considered his adversary with a hard face and a dominating eye, searching for the spot that he would strike. For he had decided not to kill, because of the annoyances that might attract to him, the tedious and harmful publicity that such an event would not fail to produce. He was sure now of Bordier's silence; his conduct had proved that to him.

Monsieur des Trieux was busy. He placed the adversaries, handed them the loaded weapons. On contact, without looking, Caresco recognized that fate had also allotted him the weapon of his choice. He was accustomed to it, handling it daily, fingering it habitually. Chance was marching with him, implacably. He posed himself, his upper body leaning slightly backwards, sideways on, the left hand behind his back.

At that moment, he felt Bordier's gaze fixed upon him. He turned his own way, fleeing before the bitterness and the reproach.

In the distance, a military band struck up an allegro.

"Are you ready?" shouted Monsieur des Trieux.

Bordier squeezed his pistol, his eyes blinking in the sunlight. He felt Ponviane's frightened heart reaching out to him.

The solemnity of the occasion gripped the witnesses and the physicians, frozen in sculptural poses. Monsieur des Trieux's voice rose again, grave and slow.

"Take aim! One…two..."

He had no time to cry three. A detonation had resounded.

From the pistol that Caresco held, a spiral of smoke escaped.

Bordier raised his arms in the air, half-turned, tried to struggle against the fall, then crumpled on to the dry ground, dropping his useless weapon.

For a second, he remained kneeling on the ground, his hand clenched, reaching for the pistol. At the end of his tether, however, very pale, with a roar that brought blood to his lips, he finally fell.

With him, faith, justice and right also collapsed.

Thirty paces away, in the person of the surgeon, Evil remaining standing, dominating and terrible.

There was panic. Already Ponviane was kneeling beside his friend, covering his forehead with fraternal kisses, striving to pass a breath of life through the warmth of his embrace into the dying body.

"He's dying!" he cried. "Help! Jean...Jean! Help!"

With a cry of fright, he renewed his desperate appeal—and in the disarray of his dolor and his mercy, it was toward the man still standing that his invocation went again.

"You! You!" he cried to Caresco. "Come see, for pity's sake. Save my friend, my friend...my only friend.

And something magnificent and horrible happened.

Caresco came to his stricken adversary, had him undressed, examined the hole made by the bullet, near the right shoulder, at the precise spot where he had intended to strike.

A flame of triumph and energy illuminated his eyes. He looked up at Savre.

"It's the sub-clavial artery that's bleeding," he said. "We can get him out of it by making the ligature. I'm going to cut through the clavicle. Bring my instruments—they're I the carriage."

And while the surgeon prepared his tools for that new manifestation of his audacious skill, Savre, confronted by the hard and skeptical mask, admired without reserve the power of genius that was about to save a life, thanks to the experience acquired at the price of so much bloodshed, so many lives scorned, so many unpunished abominations.

He found it an unexpected confirmation of his concept of the necessary evil.

Afterword

Why did Couvreur entitle his book *Le Mal nécessaire*, and why did he advertize it as the first of a trilogy entitled *Les Dangers sociaux*? We cannot know for sure, but there is no harm in guessing. The answer to the second question is probably that, by the time he finished writing the novel, he already intended to write *Les Mancenilles*, and perhaps *La Source fatale* too, and that the trilogy title was invented to package them. It is unlikely that *Le Mal nécessaire* was planned in advance to illustrate a "social danger." In the same way, the implication of the last line of the novel—that the title relates to Savre's thesis that good social progress typically results from historical processes involving a good deal of evil and, at least, a little madness—is probably an afterthought, the chapter in which Savre sets out his thesis being a late improvisation.

If so, the title of the story probably referred, when first invented, not to any general necessity, but to the very specific necessity of Dr. Bordier's dilemma, when he discovers Madeleine's pregnancy and has to decide what to do about it. In that context, the necessity of the evil derives simply from the fact that it is the lesser of two. Madeleine's situation is catastrophic; the possibility of a happy outcome is long gone, and the only outcome toward which Bordier can direct his efforts is the one that does the least damage. The fact that that option requires him not merely to let evil take its course and triumph, but actively to co-operate in it, and then to offer himself up as a further lamb to its ritual slaughter, merely adds a couple of extra turns of the screw.

That is, of course, a harsh conclusion, arguably one of the most brutal ever attached to a work of fiction. Most readers tend to agree with Oscar Wilde's Miss Prism in thinking that that, in the conclusion of a story, the good should end happily and the bad unhappily, because that is, in a sense, what fiction *means*. The author of a story—a "secondary creator," in Alexander Baumgarten's terminology—is omnipotent; he is the sole determinant of what happens in his story; he merely has to write it for it to occur. Readers know that, and therefore tend to be resentful if a writer refuses to use his omnipotence to punish the evil done within his story and save the innocent from disaster. It is precisely because that does not seem to happen often in the real world that readers often feel a powerful desire for compensation and consolation in fictional worlds... and precisely because it does not seem to happen often in the real world that authors sometimes feel that, if they meekly satisfy the reader demand in question, they are committing a different kind of moral treason, by misrepresenting the world as it is.

Not all works of fiction do end happily, of course; there is an entire genre of "tragedy," which attempts to make hearers and readers feel sad about the horrid state of the real world, in which the innocent routinely suffer the consequences of dire fate and human evil. The sense of tragedy is, however, predicated on the feeling of the hearer/reader that it shouldn't really be that way, and the knowledge that, in fiction at least, it needn't be. *Le Mal nécessaire* is, not, however, a tragedy. It belongs to a different literary counter-tradition, particularly strong in France, in which the writer's purpose is not so much to make readers feel sad as to make them feel sick. Writers of that kind of fiction attached many different labels to it; two of the earliest consistent practitioners, S. Henry Berthoud and Petrus Borel, employed the labels *contes misanthropiques* [misanthropic tales] and *contes immoraux* [immoral tales], but the one that is now most frequently cited is Villiers de l'Isle Adam's *contes cruels* [cruel tales], which has the seeming advantage of not being sarcastic, in that such stories, while not really being misanthropic or immoral, really are cruel.

Berthoud's tales were not misanthropic and Borel's were certainly not immoral; both writers shared with their readers a perfectly clear sense of what would count as a heart-warming and morale-building ending, and their refusal to provide such endings did not derive from the fact that they were misanthropic men rejoicing in the triumph of evil—quite the reverse. They were writing books of lamentations, but not the often-lachrymose and somewhat-resigned lamentations of tragedy; they were writing savage lamentations in which the cruelties of humans and nature were presented cruelly, hurled in the reader's face with an intention to startle and offend rather than laid out for somber contemplation.

The most extreme of all writers of that ilk, in France or anywhere, was the Marquis de Sade, whose works were banned because they were so very extreme in their calculated indecency and repulsiveness, encouraging the assumption on the part of unsophisticated readers that their author must, in fact, be immoral, misanthropic and cruel, or at least mad. Perhaps he did experiment with such sentiments, but the fact that Sade was sacked from the Revolutionary Tribunal for excessive leniency—in effect, for flatly refusing to behave as his characters did, even when those around him were—suggests that his extremism was a rhetorical strategy, intended not to make the intolerable seem attractive, but to emphasize its intolerability.

At its most basic, the rhetorical strategy in question is known as irony, or sarcasm: the use of a statement in such a way that the hearer is intended to take an inference opposed to the literal meaning of the words employed. It has two names because its use varies according to a spectrum of subtlety, sarcasm generally being less delicate, or more brutal, than irony. Anyone unaware of, or insensitive to, the existence of sarcasm is likely make terrible blunders, not merely in everyday social life but in reading fiction—and, for that matter philosophy. Unfortunately, readers of philosophy are often prone to that kind of misunderstanding, and there are few bigger idiots in the world than people who assume *a priori* that Plato, Decartes, Leibniz, Hume, the Marquis de Sade and countless other great thinkers always meant what they said literally.

Philosophers are, of course, particularly relevant to the present argument because philosophers have frequently been obliged, by tradition and social pressure, to deal with the problem of the necessity of evil. Rationally, the problem in question probably does not exist, and the real answer can be summed up, as it often is nowadays, with the observation that "shit happens." The fact that the world is a bad place where the innocent routinely suffer and evildoers routinely thrive probably has no further explanation, and the fact that people want one results from the conceptual error of thinking that the real world is like a work of fiction, that it has a creator who could make things turn out better but is, for some strange or mysterious reason, refusing to do so. That is an essentially stupid idea, so it is not at all surprising that lots of people have espoused it, or that they tend to turn exceedingly ferocious when its stupidity is pointed out—which is why philosophers, being mostly mild-mannered as well as attempting to be rational, have mostly chosen diplomatic and delicate ways of endeavoring to disabuse them of it, routinely taking advantage of the fact that irony and sarcasm offer "potential deniability." The principal salvation of atheists throughout history has been the ability to assert publicly that God exists while really meaning the opposite.

One of the most notorious attempts to deal with the philosophical "problem of evil" was made by Leibniz in his *Theodicy*, in which he pointed out that if one wants to reconcile the notion that God is good with the existence of evil, then one has to surrender the notion that God is also omnipotent, ultimately reaching the conclusion that although he was doing his best to construct a good world, he was let down by the poor quality of his materials and ended up with a ramshackle one.

Voltaire, who probably knew that Leibniz was being sarcastic and that the conclusion he actually hoped that his readers would draw is that the notion of a good God is an infantile fantasy, nevertheless took the trouble to put the boot into the argument more crudely with his own sarcastic fantasy, *Candide*, in which Dr. Pangloss struggles with futile heroism to sustain the hypothesis that the world we live in is the best of all those possible, while the horrors of the Thirty Years War unfold around him, further intensifying the routine inhumanity of man to man (and especially to woman).

The contrast between *Theodicy* and *Candide* illustrates one of the great problems of sarcasm as a rhetorical strategy: its essential and irremediable unreliability. When it is subtle, it can easily pass unnoticed, as in *Theodicy*; but even when it is too blatant to be mistaken, removing all margin of doubt, it cannot be satisfactory, because "shit happens—or, in the case of *Candide*, "we have to go work in the garden"—is not a satisfactory answer, precisely because it is no answer at all. In exactly the same way, the conclusion of *Le Mal nécessaire* is essentially and inherently unsatisfying, precisely because it argues the impossibility of providing an answer. Indeed, the final chapter, by providing two further ironic twists to the story, adds two further brutal wrenches to its inherent unsatisfactoriness.

In fact, there is a third cruel twist—arguably the cruelest of all—in the fact that the last chapter of *Le Mal nécessaire* is the last. The plot has no coda; the reader is left deliberately uninformed as to the outcomes beyond the ending, which leaves Bordier, Madeleine, Aline and many of the minor characters in essentially sticky situations, without any possibility of a fortunate result. For them, it seems, things can only go from bad to worse, and the reader is offered not the slightest crumb of reassurance that the worse in question might not be as totally terrible as seems all too likely.

André Couvreur was not merely content to say no more that he actually said at the end of *Le Mal nécessaire*, but insistent upon it. Even though he went on to write a sequel featuring the further exploits of Armand Caresco, he was careful therein not to say a single word about any of the other characters in the earlier novel, consigning them to the same cruel silence forever. Nevertheless, he did write a sequel. He felt obliged, or at least irresistibly tempted, not to let Caresco rest in peace. That was not because he wanted to add the "moral settlement" painfully lacking at the end of the first novel, but quite the reverse; he wanted to extrapolate the character's ambitions and achievements to the limit, and to address the question of the necessity of evil in a much more extravagant fashion.

Caresco surhomme is not an extended *conte cruel* but a Voltairean satire, in which Caresco becomes a kind of god intent on outcompeting the one he refers to as "the Other" by really creating the best of all possible worlds, with the aid of the better working materials provided to him by surgery and science. He is provided with a rather down-at-heel philosophical adversary in Zéphirin Choumaque who, while counting Leibniz a hero, has his own doctrine with which to account for the problem of evil. Choumaque, on behalf of the author and the reader alike, engages Caresco in a contest of ideas that does not lack interest, even though it is obvious from the very start that some drastic intervention by his secondary creator will be required if he is not to end up simply crushed like a bug.

Caresco surhomme does not end in the same fashion as *Le Mal nécessaire*, but its rounding out did not put an end to any controversy so far as the author was concerned. He went on to do other things in his novels, but he could never let the problem of evil alone for long, no matter how satisfied he might have been in his own mind that it was a problem that did not and could not have a viable solution; that only made it more interesting to him. Nor could he let Caresco alone, even though he killed him off. He killed Professor Tornada too, but in fiction, death is not terminus: a secondary creator can always work a miracle of resurrection simply by saying so, with or without an explanation or a change of name. Caresco stayed dead after *Caresco surhomme*, but only in name; in essence, he was simply absorbed into Tornada, and kept on, and on, carrying out his extravagant surgeries and making his scientific discoveries, never knowing himself whether what he was doing was reasonable or benevolent, or whether it was mere madness—or whether, in fact, there was anything in the perversely malevolent world but mere madness.

Inevitably, and appropriately, Couvreur's ideative exploration never reached a goal. He never did "solve" the problem of the necessity of evil, or find a way to settle for the philosophically-correct but psychologically-unsatisfying non-answer of "shit happens," although there is certainly a sense in which all his literary endeavor was work in the garden, with all the virtues that might imply. One of those virtues is that Couvreur's particular literary garden is unusually exotic, quite unparalleled in the history of imaginative fiction. It is by no means a neat and tidy garden, although it is far from a wilderness, nor is it a pretty garden, although it is certainly not devoid of color, but it is a garden whose cultivator was always restless, always innovative, and always—most essentially of all—devoted to the cause of sarcasm.

As everyone committed to that cause knows very well, it has its own phases of development. Once you have a reputation for sarcasm, no one to whom you speak will ever be entirely sure what you actually mean by what you say, and eventually, you will no longer be entirely sure yourself—and that is the point at which philosophy and fiction become genuinely exploratory, and even more interesting than before.

SF & FANTASY

Adolphe Alhaiza. *Cybele*
Alphonse Allais. *The Adventures of Captain Cap*
Henri Allorge. *The Great Cataclysm*
Guy d'Armen. *Doc Ardan: The City of Gold and Lepers*
G.-J. Arnaud. *The Ice Company*
Charles Asselineau. *The Double Life*
Cyprien Bérard. *The Vampire Lord Ruthwen*
S. Henry Berthoud. *Martyrs of Science*
Aloysius Bertrand. *Gaspard de la Nuit*
Richard Bessière. *The Gardens of the Apocalypse*
Albert Bleunard. *Ever Smaller*
Félix Bodin. *The Novel of the Future*
Louis Boussenard. *Monsieur Synthesis*
Alphonse Brown. *City of Glass; The Conquest of the Air*
Emile Calvet. *In a Thousand Years*
André Caroff. *The Terror of Madame Atomos; Miss Atomos; The Return of Madame Atomos; The Mistake of Madame Atomos; The Monsters of Madame Atomos; The Revenge of Madame Atomos; The Resurrection of Madame Atomos; The Mark of Madame Atomos; The Spheres of Madame Atomos*
Félicien Champsaur. *The Human Arrow; Ouha, King of the Apes; Pharaoh's Wife*
Didier de Chousy. *Ignis*
Jules Clarétie. *Obsession*
Michel Corday. *The Eternal Flame*
Captain Danrit. *Undersea Odyssey*
C. I. Defontenay. *Star (Psi Cassiopeia)*
Charles Derennes. *The People of the Pole*
Georges Dodds (anthologist). *The Missing Link*
Harry Dickson. *The Heir of Dracula*
Jules Dornay. *Lord Ruthven Begins*
Alfred Driou. *The Adventures of a Parisian Aeronaut*
Sâr Dubnotal *vs. Jack the Ripper*
Alexandre Dumas. *The Return of Lord Ruthven*
Renée Dunan. *Baal*
J.-C. Dunyach. *The Night Orchid; The Thieves of Silence*
Henri Duvernois. *The Man Who Found Himself*
Achille Eyraud. *Voyage to Venus*

Henri Falk. *The Age of Lead*

Paul Féval. *Anne of the Isles; Knightshade; Revenants; Vampire City; The Vampire Countess; The Wandering Jew's Daughter*

Paul Féval, *fils. Felifax, the Tiger-Man*

Charles de Fieux. *Lamékis*

Louis Forest. *Someone is Stealing Children in Paris*

Arnould Galopin. *Doctor Omega; Doctor Omega and the Shadowmen* (anthology)

Judith Gautier. *Isoline and the Serpent-Flower*

H. Gayar. *The Marvelous Adventures of Serge Myrandhal on Mars*

Léon Gozlan. *The Vampire of the Val-de-Grâce*

G.L. Gick. *Harry Dickson and the Werewolf of Rutherford Grange*

Edmond Haraucourt. *Illusions of Immortality*

Nathalie Henneberg. *The Green Gods*

V. Hugo, P. Foucher & P. Meurice. *The Hunchback of Notre-Dame*

Romain d'Huissier. *Hexagon: Dark Matter*

Jules Janin. *The Magnetized Corpse*

Michel Jeury. *Chronolysis*

Gustave Kahn. *The Tale of Gold and Silence*

Gérard Klein. *The Mote in Time's Eye*

Fernand Kolney. *Love in 5000 Years*

Paul Lacroix. *Danse Macabre*

Louis-Guillaume de La Follie. *The Unpretentious Philosopher*

Jean de La Hire. *Enter the Nyctalope; The Nyctalope on Mars; The Nyctalope vs. Lucifer; The Nyctalope Steps In; Night of the Nyctalope; Return of the Nyctalope; The Fiery Wheel*

Etienne-Léon de Lamothe-Langon. *The Virgin Vampire*

André Laurie. *Spiridon*

Gabriel de Lautrec. *The Vengeance of the Oval Portrait*

Alain le Drimeur. *The Future City*

Georges Le Faure & Henri de Graffigny. *The Extraordinary Adventures of a Russian Scientist Across the Solar System* (2 vols.)

Gustave Le Rouge. *The Mysterious Doctor Cornelius* (3 vols.); *The Vampires of Mars; The Dominion of the World* (w/Gustave Guitton) (4 vols.)

Jules Lermina. *Mysteryville; Panic in Paris; To-Ho and the Gold Destroyers; The Secret of Zippelius*

André Lichtenberger. *The Centaurs; The Children of the Crab*

Jean-Marc & Randy Lofficier. *Edgar Allan Poe on Mars; The Katrina Protocol; Pacifica; Robonocchio; Return of the Nyctalope;* (anthologists) *Tales of the Shadowmen 1-10*

Xavier Mauméjean. *The League of Heroes*
Joseph Méry. *The Tower of Destiny*
Hippolyte Mettais. *The Year 5865*
Louise Michel. *The Human Microbes; The New World*
Tony Moilin. *Paris in the Year 2000*
José Moselli. *Illa's End*
John-Antoine Nau. *Enemy Force*
Marie Nizet. *Captain Vampire*
C. Nodier, A. Beraud & Toussaint-Merle. *Frankenstein*
Henri de Parville. *An Inhabitant of the Planet Mars*
Gaston de Pawlowski. *Journey to the Land of the 4th Dimension*
Georges Pellerin. *The World in 2000 Years*
Ernest Pérochon. *The Frenetic People*
Pierre Pelot. *The Child Who Walked on the Sky*
J. Polidori, C. Nodier, E. Scribe. *Lord Ruthven the Vampire*
P.-A. Ponson du Terrail. *The Vampire and the Devil's Son; The Immortal Woman*
Edgar Quinet. *Ahasuerus*
Henri de Régnier. *A Surfeit of Mirrors*
Maurice Renard. *The Blue Peril; Doctor Lerne; The Doctored Man; A Man Among the Microbes; The Master of Light*
Jean Richepin. *The Wing; The Crazy Corner*
Albert Robida. *The Adventures of Saturnin Farandoul; The Clock of the Centuries; Chalet in the Sky; The Electric Life*
J.-H. Rosny Aîné. *Helgvor of the Blue River; The Givreuse Enigma; The Mysterious Force; The Navigators of Space; Vamireh; The World of the Variants; The Young Vampire*
Marcel Rouff. *Journey to the Inverted World*
Han Ryner. *The Superhumans*
Angelo de Sorr. *The Vampires of London*
Brian Stableford. *The New Faust at the Tragicomique;The Empire of the Necromancers (The Shadow of Frankenstein; Frankenstein and the Vampire Countess; Frankenstein in London); Sherlock Holmes & The Vampires of Eternity; The Stones of Camelot; The Wayward Muse.* (anthologist) *News from the Moon; The Germans on Venus; The Supreme Progress; The World Above the World; Nemoville; Investigations of the Future; The Conqueror of Death*
Jacques Spitz. *The Eye of Purgatory*
Kurt Steiner. *Ortog*
Eugène Thébault. *Radio-Terror*
C.-F. Tiphaigne de La Roche. *Amilec*

Louis Ulbach. *Prince Bonifacio*

Théo Varlet. *The Golden Rock. The Xenobiotic Invasion; The Castaways of Eros; Timeslip Troopers* (w/André Blandin); *The Martian Epic* (w/Octave Joncquel)

Paul Vibert. *The Mysterious Fluid*

Villiers de l'Isle-Adam. *The Scaffold; The Vampire Soul*

Philippe Ward. *Artahe*

Philippe Ward & Sylvie Miller. *The Song of Montségur*

MYSTERIES & THRILLERS

M. Allain & P. Souvestre. *The Daughter of Fantômas*

A. Anicet-Bourgeois, Lucien Dabril. *Rocambole*

A. Bernède. *Belphegor; Judex* (w/Louis Feuillade); *The Return of Judex* (w/Louis Feuillade); *The Shadow of Judex*

A. Bisson & G. Livet. *Nick Carter vs. Fantômas*

V. Darlay & H. de Gorsse. *Arsène Lupin vs. Sherlock Holmes: The Stage Play*

Séamas Duffy. *Sherlock Holmes in Paris*

Paul Féval. *Gentlemen of the Night; John Devil; The Black Coats ('Salem Street; The Invisible Weapon; The Parisian Jungle; The Companions of the Treasure; Heart of Steel; The Cadet Gang; The Sword-Swallower)*

Emile Gaboriau. *Monsieur Lecoq*

Goron & Emile Gautier. *Spawn of the Penitentiary*

Rick Lai. *Shadows of the Opera: Retribution in Blood; Sisters of the Shadows: The Curse of Cagliostro*

Steve Leadley. *Sherlock Holmes: The Circle of Blood*

Maurice Leblanc. *Arsène Lupin vs. Countess Cagliostro; Arsène Lupin vs. Sherlock Holmes (The Blonde Phantom; The Hollow Needle); The Many Faces of Arsène Lupin*

Gaston Leroux. *Chéri-Bibi; The Phantom of the Opera; Rouletabille & the Mystery of the Yellow Room; Rouletabille at Krupp's*

Richard Marsh. *The Complete Adventures of Judith Lee*

William Patrick Maynard. *The Terror of Fu Manchu; The Destiny of Fu Manchu*

Frank J. Morlock. *Sherlock Holmes: The Grand Horizontals; Sherlock Holmes vs Jack the Ripper*

Jean Petithuguenin. *The Adventures of Ethel King*

Antonin Reschal. *The Adventures of Miss Boston*

P. de Wattyne & Y. Walter. *Sherlock Holmes vs. Fantômas*

David White. *Fantômas in America*
Pierre Yrondy. *The Adventures of Thérèse Arnaud*

SCREENPLAYS

Mike Baron. *The Iron Triangle*
Emma Bull & Will Shetterly. *Nightspeeder; War for the Oaks*
Gerry Conway & Roy Thomas. *Doc Dynamo*
Steve Englehart. *Majorca*
James Hudnall. *The Devastator*
Jean-Marc & Randy Lofficier. *Royal Flush*
J.-M. & R. Lofficier & Marc Agapit. *Despair*
J.-M. & R. Lofficier & Joël Houssin. *City*
Andrew Paquette. *Peripheral Vision*
Robert L. Robinson, Jr. *Judex*
R. Thomas, J. Hendler & L. Sprague de Camp. *Rivers of Time*

NON-FICTION

Stephen R. Bissette. *Blur 1-5. Green Mountain Cinema 1; Teen Angels*
Win Scott Eckert. *Crossovers* (2 vols.)
Jean-Marc & Randy Lofficier. *Shadowmen* (2 vols.)
Randy Lofficier. *Over Here*

ART BOOKS

J.-M. Lofficier & D. Taylor. *Tongue*Lash*
Jean-Pierre Normand. *Science Fiction Illustrations*
Raven Okeefe. *Raven's L'il Critters; Rave's Faves*
Randy Lofficier & Raven Okeefe. *If Your Possum Go Daylight...*
Daniele Serra. *Illusions*

HEXAGON COMICS

Franco Frescura & Luciano Bernasconi. *Wampus*
Franco Frescura & Giorgio Trevisan. *CLASH*
L. Bernasconi, J.-M. Lofficier & Juan Roncagliolo Berger. *Phenix*
Claude Legrand, J.-M. Lofficier & L. Bernasconi. *Kabur*
Franco Oneta. *Zembla*

L. Buffolente, Lofficier & J.-J. Dzialowski. *Strangers: Homicron*
Danilo Grossi. *Strangers: Jaydee*
Claude Legrand & Luciano Bernasconi. *Strangers: Starlock*